THE PENFORD MANOR MURDERS

FIONA VEITCH SMITH

embla books

First published in Great Britain in 2025 by

embla books

Bonnier Books UK Limited
HYLO, 5th Floor, 103–105 Bunhill Row, London, EC1Y 8LZ
Owned by Bonnier Books
Sveavägen 56, Stockholm, Sweden

A CIP catalogue record for this book is available from the British Library.

1

ISBN: 9781471417566

This book is typeset using Atomik ePublisher.

Printed and bound in Great Britain by Clays Ltd, Elcograf S.p.A.

Embla Books is an imprint of Bonnier Books UK.
www.bonnierbooks.co.uk

FSC www.fsc.org MIX Paper | Supporting responsible forestry FSC® C018072

For Rod.

Thirty years.

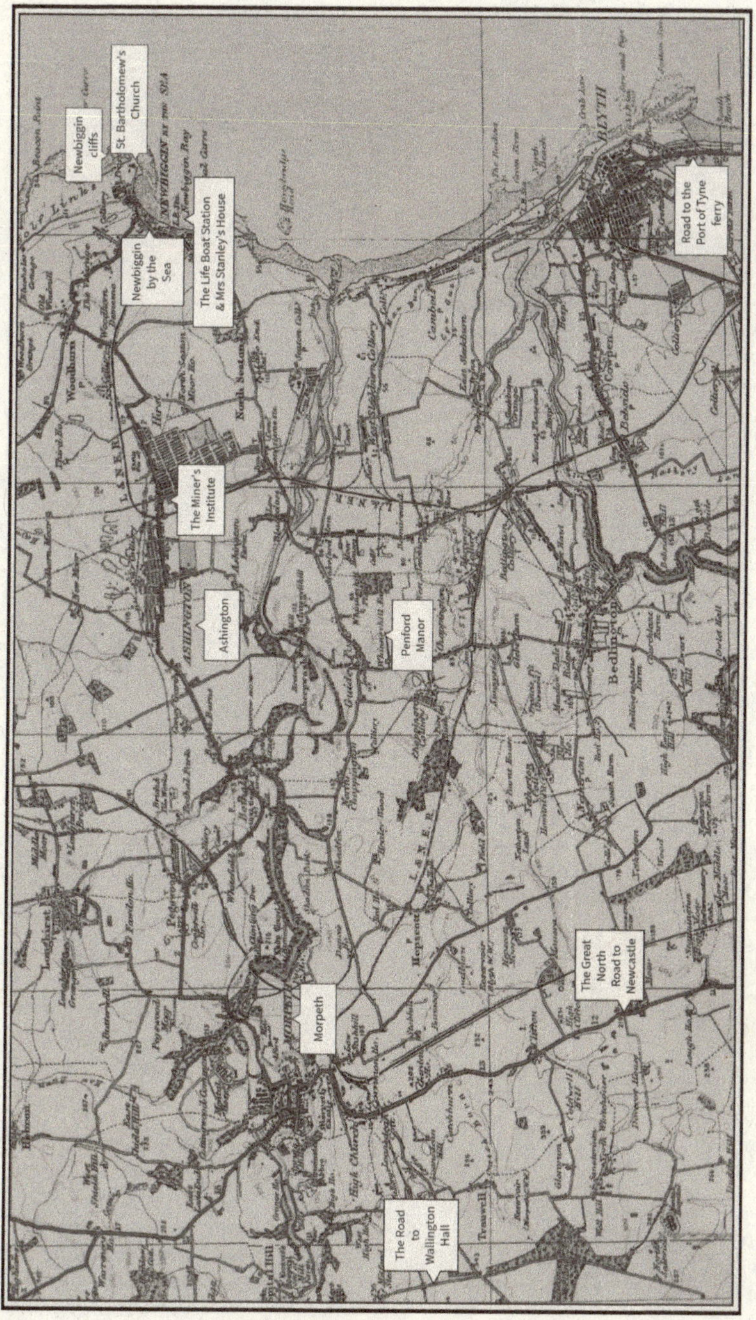

South East Northumberland, 1930
Source: Ordnance Survey Map 1925

Prologue

Tuesday 5th August 1930, Penford Manor, Northumberland

Lady Justina Penford had had a tiring day. The first of her guests for the opening of the grouse season next week – on the Glorious 12th – had already arrived, three days before their due date. The house staff had not had time to air their usual suite of rooms and the grounds staff had had to take time away from their preparations for the hunt to mow the croquet lawn and the tennis courts. Why on earth the von Schneider cousins wanted to play almost as soon as they had arrived, Lady Penford had no idea.

It had annoyed her, but not surprised her. *That* branch of the family – her late husband's family – had always taken liberties with her hospitality. And if it weren't for her grown children's fondness for the cousins from Germany, and the guilt she still carried about the loss of their father, she would have spoken about it years ago. But there were certain things one did not speak of if one wanted to keep the peace. Certain secrets that must, at all costs, remain unspoken.

With a wave of her hand Lady Penford dismissed her maid, Parker.

'Should I close the curtains before I leave, your ladyship?' asked the maid, knowing her mistress often took a nap in the afternoon.

'No, I'll do it myself.'

Parker curtsied and left her mistress alone.

Lady Penford walked to the window and looked out over her vast ancestral estate. Beyond the magnificent house, the gravel drive, the manicured lawns and the ancient woodland, which had been planted in the days of Henry Tudor, were moorland and farmland, stretching all the way to the North Sea coast. And it was there that the true Penford wealth lay. Deep under the ground in coal seams that for the past two centuries had made the family one of the richest in the region – and the Penford name one to be proud of.

Lady Penford picked up a gilt-framed photograph on her dressing table. It was of her four children in happier times, before the war. The children were playing at a family picnic. The two older boys who would be taken from her a few years later, and the younger two: her only daughter, and her very last boy. Sweet, sweet Teddy. The last chance to keep the Penford name alive. Poor Teddy. Why was life such a struggle for him?

She stroked the photograph with her finger and placed it back on the table, then kicked off her satin-heeled shoes and stretched out on top of her bed. A short nap would rejuvenate her. She needed to be on her best form to entertain her guests this evening – and to ensure that Teddy would not embarrass her.

She had just started to nod off when there was a light knock at the door. It was enough to wake her. She sighed. Could the household not survive without her for just one hour?

'Who is it?' she called.

There was no answer, but an envelope was slipped under the door.

Lady Penford thought of leaving it until after her nap, but curiosity got the better of her. She swung her long legs in their satin house pyjamas off the bed and padded over to the door. The envelope was addressed to: 'Lady Penford, Penford Manor'. It had been typed.

She took the envelope to her writing bureau and slit it open with a mother-of-pearl letter opener. There was a single, folded page encasing a dried, pressed cornflower. Lady Penford's heart quickened. *Surely, it can't be . . .*

She held the flower between thumb and forefinger as she read the note. Then the flower fell from her grasp as the words sank in. *Dear God, no . . .*

Lady Penford's hand clutched at her throat. Someone knew her secret.

She flung open the door and looked left and right. The corridor was empty. Whoever had delivered the note was gone. Lady Penford's eyes narrowed. *But I'll find them. On my children's graves, I'll find them.*

Chapter 1

Friday 8th August 1930, Newcastle upon Tyne

Miss Clara Vale was annoyed to see that someone was squatting in her usual parking spot. She glowered at the chauffeur in his ridiculous hat as he sat, eyes fixed forward, in his employer's spanking new silver Rolls-Royce Phantom II. Clara, who had recently bought a more modest motor, knew exactly how much the Phantom was going for: *more money than sense*, she thought as she drove past and found an alternative spot further along Percy Street.

Clara locked her own car – a wine-red Lagonda – put on her straw sunhat and smoked-lens sunglasses, then walked back up the street to her office.

She approached the Rolls on the kerbside beside Levine's Costumes, and was tempted to knock on the window and ask him to move. But Clara knew she didn't have a leg to stand on. She did not own the parking spot, but she was used to owning the *only* motor car on the block, and the spot outside the shop, above which was her office, always being available to her. She pursed her lips as she passed the vehicle, reminding herself that she was only five minutes' walk from home and she could have left her car there instead.

The chauffeur was now reading a newspaper. *Not about to move, I see.* Clara huffed to herself, wondering who the owner of the vehicle was and what he was doing on the busy Newcastle shopping street, where trams brought ordinary shoppers to the town. She doubted a gentleman of that standing would be doing his own shopping and knew that the banks and solicitors' offices where he might have an appointment were in a different part of town. Still, she was not expecting, when she pushed open the door of Vale Investigations, to see the owner of the Rolls seated in her office. Nor to find that the owner was a woman. And particularly not to find that she knew who she was.

'Lady Penford!'

Lady Justina Penford was, after the Duke and Duchess of Northumberland, possibly the most famous aristocrat in the county. She and her second husband – a wealthy coal magnate who had worked his way up from more modest means – were friends of Clara's parents.

And here was the lady sitting in the office of Vale Investigations with a foot-long cigarette holder pincered between two fingers.

'Miss Vale,' observed Lady Penford, looking her up and down and not attempting to get up, 'I did not expect to wait this long.'

'I'm sorry, Lady Penford,' said Clara, hanging her summer frock coat and sun hat next to Lady Penford's cream cashmere swagger coat and matching Garbo hat, 'but I wasn't aware we had an appointment.' She flashed a look at her assistant, Bella Cuddy, who was hovering at the entrance to the office's small kitchenette. 'Miss Cuddy, did you fail to tell me Lady Penford had called?'

Bella shook her head, her eyes wide with alarm. 'No, Miss Vale. No appointment was made.'

'Nonsense, girl! I instructed my secretary to do so.'

Bella was just about to reply when Clara held up her hand. 'There's obviously been a misunderstanding. But not to worry, we're both here now.' She then offered her hand. 'How do you do? And how may I help you, Lady Penford?'

Lady Penford pursed her lips then after a reluctant, settling breath took Clara's hand. Her grasp was firm and brief.

'I am here to engage your professional services, Miss Vale.'

Clara was surprised but pleased. Business – which had been quiet over the summer – was picking up! 'Ah, well in that case, Lady Penford, shall we have a cup of tea while you tell me all about it. Miss Cuddy, if you'll put the kettle on . . .'

Five minutes later and Clara was pouring Lady Penford a cup of tea. The lady visibly noted the mismatched cup and saucer – inherited from Clara's Uncle Bob, the previous owner of the agency – but fortunately declined to comment.

She's making an effort to put us on an amiable footing, thought Clara, who knew exactly what her mother would have said when confronted with the horrors of a mismatched tea set.

'Well,' said Clara, returning to her side of the desk, shooing the office cat from her chair, and opening a notebook, 'tell me why you need the services of a private detective.'

Lady Penford wafted her cigarette holder from side to side in a tick-tock motion. 'Ashtray?'

'Bella?' prompted Clara.

Bella, who was an occasional smoker herself, moved an ashtray from her desk to in front of the visiting aristocrat. The lady removed her cigarette from the holder and stubbed it out without a word of thanks. Bella stood behind her and rolled her eyes. Clara gave a warning frown then turned her attention back to Lady Penford as Bella retreated to the kitchenette, followed by the black cat.

'Right. Shall we get down to business?'

Lady Penford gave a terse nod and opened her handbag. She removed an envelope and slid it across the desk. Clara examined it, careful to only touch the corner in case she needed to take fingerprints. It was a plain envelope, cheaply available at any stationer's. It was addressed simply to: 'Lady Penford, Penford Manor' and had been typed. There was no stamp. She opened the envelope and removed a single folded piece of paper, again careful to hold it at the edge. She opened the sheet to reveal a short note and a pressed flower. She allowed the flower to fall to her desk as she read the typed note:

Cornflowers, you say, just cornflowers,
gemming the golden grain;
Ah no! You can't deceive me.
£50 or your secret will be out.
Put in silver tea caddy (you know which one).

Find under lobster pot.
Newbiggin lifeboat hut.
By midnight 12th August.
Don't grouse about.

Clara looked across the desk at her potential new client. She was met by eyes as blue as cornflowers. 'You are being blackmailed?'

'That's what I think, yes.' Lady Penford returned a stray silver-blonde hair to its place behind her ear.

Clara picked up the pressed flower and twirled the stem between thumb and forefinger. 'A cornflower,' she said. 'And this: "Cornflowers you say, just cornflowers . . ." Do you understand the meaning of that?'

'I do not,' said Lady Penford.

'Does it mean anything to you? Any of it? Tell me what you do understand.' Clara leaned forward.

Lady Penford pursed her lips like a drawstring bag. 'I understand that I am being blackmailed by someone. That if I do not pay fifty pounds by next Tuesday they will besmirch my family name.'

'They will tell your secret,' observed Clara. 'Which is?'

'Which is none of your business, Miss Vale.'

'But there is one?'

'Everyone has secrets.'

'Yes they do, but not all of them are worth paying fifty pounds to keep.' Clara raised an interrogative eyebrow.

'I agree entirely. Which is why I want you to catch the blackmailer before I am forced to pay them.'

Clara sighed and leaned back. 'I'm afraid I will need more information if I am to help you.'

'Fine,' said the lady brusquely, 'but you will not be knowing this alleged secret. The entire point of hiring you is so that nothing more will be said of that. I can, however, give you a few points to get you started.'

Clara nodded. 'Go on.'

Lady Penford pursed her lips then continued. 'Well, firstly, the tea caddy. They are right when they say I know the one. It was a gift from my late husband, Baron von Richner. It was embossed with an enamel cornflower relief on sterling silver.'

Clara cocked her head. 'The cornflower again. That's now three references. What is the significance?'

Lady Penford inhaled then exhaled slowly. 'It is my favourite flower. My first husband would pick them for me.'

Clara nodded. 'So this has something to do with your late husband . . .'

Lady Penford shrugged. 'It might. However, you do not need to know what the message means to find the blackmailer. The reason I mention the tea caddy is because it is now missing. As soon as I got this letter I checked to see if it was still there. It wasn't. Which, along with the hand-delivered letter, means only one thing: the blackmailer has access to my house. And as perfect strangers do not wander around within its walls, that means the blackmailer is known to me. I know too that on Tuesday morning the caddy was still there. I saw it. But by the time I received this letter on Tuesday afternoon it was gone. So that means the person took it between Tuesday morning and Tuesday afternoon. Which again narrows it down to who was in the house then. Now that makes it easier for you, wouldn't you say?'

Clara nodded, impressed with Lady Penford's logical thought process. 'It certainly does. And as you have already pointed out, the letter was hand-delivered.'

The lady raised a finger. 'Not necessarily delivered. It did not arrive with the other post which my butler brings to me each morning and afternoon. No, this was slipped under my bedroom door. During my afternoon nap on Tuesday. I questioned all the staff and family and no one admitted knowing anything about it. But of course, one of them is lying, and I need you to find out who. Do you accept the challenge?'

Clara thought for a moment and then nodded her agreement. 'Yes, I do,' she said, pen poised to make notes. 'If you could give me a list of everyone in the house – staff and family – and set up interviews for me, I can get started.'

Lady Penford raised her finely manicured finger again. 'I'm afraid it won't be that simple, Miss Vale. Firstly, it is not just staff and family in the house. I have visitors too, who have come up for the opening of the grouse season next week.' She smiled, wryly. 'Hence the reference in the note to not grousing around. Two of them arrived early on Tuesday, so technically they are suspects too – along with their servants. Although I can't imagine why they would be as silly as to stick a blackmail note under my door the very day they arrive, drawing obvious suspicion upon themselves. But whether they're involved or not, I cannot have you interrogating my guests, not overtly anyway. And more guests will be arriving today and over the weekend. So, it is imperative that any investigation you do should be conducted with the utmost discretion. I do not want it to get out that there is any whiff of scandal. It could ruin my family name. Do you understand?'

Clara did. She had lived in and around Lady Penford's social circle for long enough to understand the woman's fear. She also had an inkling of the best way to conduct the investigation. 'I understand you fully,' she said. 'However, I will still need to speak to your guests and staff – even if they don't know why I am speaking to them. So, I propose the best way forward is—'

'To go undercover,' finished Lady Penford. 'And that, Miss Vale, is why I have approached you rather than the other private detectives in the area. You may be the least experienced, but you will blend in better than any of them.'

Clara cleared her throat. She did not like to be referred to as 'inexperienced'. It was true, she had only been operating as a private detective for a year, but in that time she had solved a number of murders, at home and abroad, as well as a crop of lesser crimes. However, this would be her first blackmail case. And the first where she was to go undercover. Which might pose some problems . . . 'Do you not think your guests might ask why I am there? I may not have been long in the job, but my cases have made it into the local, national and international papers. It may be known that I am a detective.'

Lady Penford nodded. 'Yes, it may be. That is how I myself came to know of your surprising new profession. However, surely even a private detective has to have a break sometime. And it is the summer.'

She suddenly gave a disarming smile, her face softening into an endearing beauty. 'How about a little rest and recreation, Clara?'

Clara tapped her pen against her notebook and considered the contents of the blackmail note. It was certainly an intriguing case . . .

'All right,' she said, returning Lady Penford's smile. 'I could do with a little holiday.'

Chapter 2

Saturday 9th August 1930

'I really don't think this is a good idea, Miss Vale,' grumbled Bella as they drove up the Great North Road on the way to Penford Manor. 'I don't know how to be a lady's maid.'

Clara looked across at her assistant, slumped in the passenger seat of the Lagonda as they passed fields flecked with sheep under a summer-blue sky.

'Oh Bella,' she said, with genuine sympathy, 'I'm sorry but I don't think there's any other way. I'm supposed to be blending in with the landed gentry. The gentry travel with servants, not assistants. I think it may be known that I don't normally have a maid, but the toffs will at least expect me to temporarily employ one for an event like this. Besides, it will be really useful for us if you have access to the servants' quarters at the manor. I can investigate upstairs and you downstairs. And I promise,' she said, with a playful wink, 'you won't have to empty my chamber pot.'

'I should bloody well hope not!' said Bella.

Clara laughed. 'And that must be the end of your coarse language, Cuddy!'

Bella scowled. 'Will you really be calling me Cuddy?'

Clara sighed. 'I'm afraid I will. Ladies refer to their personal maid by their surnames. Oddly, it's a mark of higher station. A chambermaid – who *will* be emptying my pot – or a scullery maid would just be referred to by their first name. Secretaries and governesses would get "Miss". However, a servant would not refer to someone of their station or above as just the surname. So you would be Miss Cuddy to other servants. The men are just as complicated. But—' she smiled '—I'm sure you'll pick it up quickly. Listen and learn, Bella.'

'And if I make a mistake?'

'Don't worry about that. Let's just be honest and say you're new to the job. Tell them you normally work as my office assistant. I don't see why we can't be open about that.'

Bella bit her lip. 'All right. I'll try. If you really think it's the only way.'

'It's the only way you can come with me, Bella. And I need you. Not as a maid. But as an investigator. This is going to be a tricky case. Have you got that list Lady Penford made for us to hand? Let's go through it to see who the suspects are.'

Bella reached into Clara's satchel in the footwell and extracted the list.

'Well, according to this list,' said Bella, 'these were the people in the house from Tuesday morning, when the tea caddy was last seen, to Tuesday afternoon, when the letter was pushed under Lady Penford's door. Top of the list is Lady Justina Penford herself.'

'Who else?'

'Parker. Her lady's maid.'

'Any notes on her?'

'Nothing.'

'Then that's who you will start with,' said Clara. 'Try to befriend her. Ask advice on how to do the job from a professional. Flatter her as much as you need to.'

'Lawd . . .'

'Bella . . .'

'Sorry, miss. Right, next there's Sir William Fowler, her husband. Second husband, I assume. Hang on, why isn't he Lord Penford? He got all her estate when he married her, didn't he?'

Clara shook her head. 'Ah, no. It's complex when the petty bourgeois marry into the even pettier world of inherited titles. Don't know if I fully understand it myself – my mother despaired of ever drumming it into me – but this is what I think happens. Sir William Fowler – a mine owner and friend of my father – is a commoner. He, like my father, was granted what's called a discretionary knighthood.

Neither of them were born into it. Lady Justina inherited the title Lady because she is the daughter of an earl. In this case, the Earl of Penford. When he died, she was his only heir. No boys. The peerage went into abeyance – put on hold until there was a suitable male heir – and she became custodian. She continued to call herself Lady Penford. She then married a German baron, von Richner, and so was able to take on his title too. So she was, technically, Baroness von Richner, but also kept her English title because they were from two different countries, and she was still custodian of the Penford estates. Besides, an earl is a higher rank than a baron. However . . .' Clara glanced at Bella. 'Still with me?'

'Barely,' said Bella, rolling her eyes. Then she grinned. 'Yes, I'm following. Carry on.'

Clara took a deep breath. 'Well, this is where it gets even more complicated. Her son Edward, they call him Teddy, he should be on that list . . . well, Teddy is actually the Earl of Penford but is known as Lord Penford, shorter than the full Lord Edward Richner, Earl of Penford. As the last remaining male heir – his older brothers died in the war – he inherited the title. However, as far as I know, he is Earl in name only. His mother and stepfather still run things. And I expect Sir Bill will keep a tight fist on the purse strings.'

'Bill?' asked Bella, running her finger down the list. 'I don't see a Bill.'

Clara sighed. 'Sorry, that's Lady Penford's second husband. Sir William. My father always referred to him as Bill. So Sir Bill, I think, is the custodian of the Penford estate. He's certainly the one who keeps it afloat financially. Everyone was surprised when Lady P. married a commoner – she's a notorious snob – but apparently she was left in dire straits after her first husband died and desperately needed the money.'

'Hang on,' said Bella, 'wouldn't Lady Penford's name have changed when she married again?'

Clara nodded. 'Yes, it would, and it did. She is now, officially, Lady Justina Fowler. But she still refers to herself as Lady Penford. And as there is no other Lady Penford around, everyone just humours her.'

'I expect a lot of people humour her,' said Bella. 'She's a tough old nut.'

'She is that!'

'You say that there's no other Lady Penford around. But what if the son – this Teddy – married? Wouldn't his wife become Lady Penford?'

Clara laughed. 'Actually, she'd be Countess Penford! The wife of an earl is a countess – even though we have no counts in this country!'

Bella rolled her eyes.

Clara chuckled. 'I told you it's complicated. But while Teddy is – as far as I know – still a bachelor, we won't have to worry about that for this case. His sister, though, is a Lady. Lady Richner – from her father, minus the von. I forget her first name . . .'

Bella ran her finger down the list. 'Kate, is it? We've got a "Kate – daughter" here.'

'That's it,' said Clara. 'Kate. Lady Katherine Richner. She'll be known as Lady Katherine. She was a couple of years behind me at Oxford. Studied English Literature, I think. I met her once at a dinner my parents hosted. Sweet, quiet girl if I recall. Don't think she's married either. If she were, she would take on the title of her husband. But this is getting ridiculous. Let's get back to who was in the house. And let's stick with the first names, rather than titles, or we'll have ourselves in knots. So there was Justina, Bill, Teddy and Kate. The family. And did they all have either maids or valets attached to them?'

Bella nodded. 'Looks like it. I won't bother you with their names. Beyond the family we have two guests – with a valet and maid attached.'

'And who are the bigwigs?'

'Oh lawdy,' said Bella, squinting at the list. 'Something foreign. Von S – c – h – n – e – i – d – e – r. Baron and Baroness.'

'Von Schneider,' said Clara. 'German. Might be the first husband's family. I'll find out.'

Clara turned off the Great North Road and onto a meandering country lane, hemmed in on both sides by hawthorn hedgerow in full summer bloom. 'Just another couple of miles,' she said. 'So, apart from the family, the guests and their attendants, has she given us a staff list?'

Bella gave an exaggerated sigh. 'She has. There's a couple of dozen of them. Housekeeper, butler, chauffeur, cook, chambermaids times four, scullery maids times two, footmen times four, head gardener, three under-gardeners, a groundsman, stable and hunt master, and then a number of "lads" – no names or job descriptions given. Oh, and finally, right at the bottom, a Miss Fowler, secretary.'

'Fowler? Related to Bill, I wonder? Can't be his daughter, I'd heard he was childless. Might be wrong though . . . we'll find out.'

They drove through a small village then past a farmyard before reaching an impressive wrought-iron gate. Atop each gatepost was a carved eagle, and on the gate the heraldic crest of the Penfords: a wolf's head with a crown, set against a wheel. A man wearing a flat cap and wellington boots emerged from a gatehouse with a spaniel at his heels and approached the car. Clara wound down the window and announced that she was here for the weekend at the invitation of Lady Penford. The man tipped his cap and said, 'Of course, Miss Vale, Lady Penford said to expect you. Go straight up the drive and someone will meet you. Mr Rogers will park your motor in the garage.'

'I wonder who he is,' said Bella, consulting her list as they drove away. 'Too old to be one of the lads . . .'

'He might be the groundsman.'

'Righto. The groundsman . . . that's Foster. A suspect?'

Clara laughed. 'Everyone's a suspect, Miss Marple! For now though, I think it's more likely someone who has easy access to the house. I doubt he'd be clomping through the manor and pilfering silver tea caddies unnoticed. But you never know . . .'

They drove through a copse of silver birch and beech trees, shimmering golden in the summer sun. Then past a row of stone cottages, and then stables and kennels. It was feeding time for the dogs and even through her closed window Clara could hear them baying with excitement. A horse munched lazily over its half-door, watching them curiously as they drove by. The gravel drive circled around an expansive manicured lawn where a middle-aged couple played croquet. The gentleman raised his mallet to them. Clara smiled and waved.

Beyond the croquet lawn was a tennis court and then further gardens and then the manor itself came into view. It had a central fortified tower, built in the thirteenth century, with the wings to left and right contributing later seventeenth-century additions in Palladian style.

'Bleedin' heck, Miss Vale, all of this for just one family? And not a very big one at that. Me next-door neighbour has seven bairns in a two-up, two-down. It must cost a fortune to keep this going. How do they manage?'

'Many of them don't,' said Clara, thinking of her own family who were having to sell off some of their property as the worldwide financial depression tightened its grip and the government hiked land and inheritance tax.

Clara came to a stop on the gravel drive, directly adjacent to the front door. A second had barely passed when the door opened and a butler followed by a footman descended the granite steps. The butler strode to the car and opened the door for Clara, with the footman hovering close behind.

'Good afternoon, Miss Vale,' the butler intoned, his voice as melodious as a church bell. 'We have been expecting you.' He reached his gloved hand towards her. She took it and he helped her out. Clara noted a twitch of the head towards Bella and the footman rushed around and opened the passenger door of the Lagonda. Clara doubted they were used to ladies driving without a chauffeur. It would not be in the etiquette manual.

A moment later, Lady Penford appeared, silhouetted in the doorway. She was wearing a tweed riding jacket and breeches with a lavish white silk cravat cascading down her chest.

'Ah, Miss Vale!' she declared, tapping a riding crop against her thigh. 'You're earlier than expected. I was just going for a ride. But not to worry, I'll cancel.'

'Don't change your plans on my behalf,' said Clara, as the footman took hers and Bella's suitcases from the car boot.

'Nonsense! I couldn't possibly leave my guests to flounder on their own. Spencer,' she addressed the butler, 'Miss Vale will be in the Rothbury Room. Then send Parker up to show her maid where to go after that.'

'Yes, Lady Penford.' The butler bowed.

Lady Penford nodded her approval. 'I'll speak to the groom to rearrange my ride. And get the chauffeur to put your motor in the garage. Leave your keys there, that's a good girl.'

Clara did not appreciate being called a 'girl' but she expected she'd have to just put up with it for the next few days. She fixed a smile on her face. 'Righto. I'll put the door key on the seat. Ignition is a button on the floor.'

Lady Penford wafted her riding crop as she descended the steps. 'I'm sure he'll find it. I'll see you in the drawing room in half an hour. Bring some tea, Spencer, and ask Sir William to join us at four o'clock.'

'Yes, madam,' intoned the butler and bowed again.

Chapter 3

The grand entrance hall of Penford Manor was quite a surprise to Clara. She had expected the standard country house decor with stags' heads, dark panelled wood and gloomy oil paintings, but instead, she and Bella were greeted by an extravaganza of art deco interior design.

The floor was an intricate geometric pattern of black and white marble lit from above by a domed skylight three floors up, from which hung an ornate chandelier. In the centre of the floor was a large, round, glass-topped table set on two semicircles of bronze. In the middle of the table was a cut-glass vase of lilies, their scent filling the atrium. The staircase, a continuation of the white marble, had two wings, curving upwards to meet on a mezzanine landing, backed by a seventeenth-century stained-glass window featuring the Penford family crest. The old wooden banister had been replaced by a black wrought-iron creation, topped with a bronze handrail. The wrought iron continued the repeating geometric pattern of the floor all the way up to the mezzanine.

'Golly!' said Clara, remembering seeing something similar in one of her sister's magazines. 'This is all very modern.'

'Indeed,' said Spencer. 'Lady Penford insisted on having it all redone after she returned from Paris last year.' Was that a twinge of disapproval Clara detected?

'And what did Sir Bill think?' she asked, remembering him to be of a more traditional bent.

'Sir *William* is happy when Lady Penford is happy,' observed Spencer.

'I expect he is,' said Clara, raising an eyebrow at Bella. Neither of them would want to be around Lady Penford when she was *un*happy.

Spencer led the ladies up the left wing of the sweeping staircase, followed by the footman carrying both suitcases. But once they got beyond the mezzanine and progressed up to the second floor, the design aesthetic reverted to a more traditional country house.

'I see Lady Penford's new design hasn't got as far as this,' Clara whispered to Bella.

'She might have run out of money,' whispered Bella in return.

A slight twitch of the butler's spine suggested he'd heard. And as they rounded a bend, Clara noticed a fleeting smile on the footman's face.

The Rothbury Room was a comfortably sized suite with a small sitting area and a four-poster bed. The drapes around the bed were embroidered with sprigs of purple and green heather with a lilac quilt on the bed. The cushions on the two armchairs had the same embroidered motif. The tall sash window overlooked the wooded area of Penford Manor estate, to the rear of the building, and below was the stable yard as well as the garages. Clara could just see the nose of the Lagonda.

Inside the room there was a white-painted washstand with basin but no en-suite bathroom – or lavatory. *This isn't a hotel*, Clara reminded herself.

'Is the bathroom nearby?' she asked Spencer.

'Lady Penford's maid, Miss Parker, will be along shortly to show you.' He gave a curt bow. 'We shall see you for tea in half an hour, Miss Vale.'

'Thank you, Spencer,' said Clara and waited for him to retreat and close the door. The moment he did she threw herself down on the bed, arms and legs spread. 'Thank heavens he's gone. Like having Death's Apprentice in the room.'

Bella chuckled. 'Aye, miss. He's got a rod up the old rear.'

Clara rolled her eyes. 'There'll be a lot of that for the next few days. Everything I have been trying to get away from. My mother would adore it all!'

'My mam would say we're working for Lady Muck!'

'Oh, Lady Penford's not that bad,' said Clara. 'There are far, far worse than she. And as you say, we are working for her, and she is paying. After that case in Egypt when the museum refused to pay my bill, there's been a bit of a hole in the agency's coffers. We need this job, Bella. So we'll just have to put up with it all.'

'Aye, miss,' said Bella, gesturing to the well-appointed bedroom. 'And at least one of us will be doing it in comfort.'

Clara chuckled. 'I'm sure they will put you in decent accommodation, Bella. You're a lady's maid, not a scullery maid. Speaking of which, you should probably put on the uniform Juju gave you.'

Bella pursed her lips but refrained from rolling her eyes again. *Progress*, thought Clara.

Bella opened her suitcase and withdrew the black dress with white collar and white cuffs. There was no white apron and hat – which Bella had initially feared – as a lady's maid did not dress the same as a parlour maid.

'We're lucky to have a costumier downstairs from our office!' said Clara, who wasn't sure where else they could have got something for Bella at such short notice.

Bella sighed and slipped out of her yellow and white summer dress and into the black frock.

'Not a bad fit,' said Clara, then passed Bella a pair of black lace-up shoes and stockings. As Bella finished dressing Clara arranged with her to meet back in the room half an hour before dinner. 'You're supposed to help me dress. But we can use that as an excuse to compare notes. Not sure what we can find out in a few hours, but let's see.'

'Aye, miss. I'll keep me eyes and ears peeled.'

Bella had just finished tidying her ginger hair when there was a knock at the door. She opened it to reveal a middle-aged woman in a plain grey skirt and blouse, her light brown hair tightly drawn back into a bun, accentuating the sharpness of her nose and chin.

'Good afternoon,' she said, her voice marked with a north Northumbrian brogue, tinged with borderland Scots. 'I am Parker, Lady Penford's maid.'

'And I'm – er – Cuddy,' said Bella in her broad Geordie. 'Miss Vale's – er – maid.'

'Ah, Parker. Just the woman I wanted to see,' said Clara. 'First things first. Where's the bathroom? I *really* need to use the lavatory. Spencer did not seem to appreciate the urgency when I asked him.'

'Right this way, miss,' said Parker with a little curtsy.

After using the facilities then bidding farewell to Bella, who accompanied Parker like a lamb to the slaughter, Clara unpacked. Parker had said she would wait while Bella did it, but Clara assured her she could manage on her own. Parker raised an eyebrow but didn't comment and the two women left Clara alone.

Clara had made sure to pack her best and most fashionable clothes. She had acquired some French couture gowns for her cruise to Egypt earlier in the year and her very gifted seamstress friend Juju had made her a Chanel-inspired gown for her thirty-first birthday in June. Clara unfolded it from the suitcase and held it against her, checking out her reflection in the mirror. It was made of teal crepe georgette, with a sleek bias-cut silhouette, which skimmed her hips and billowed out at the bottom into a flounced hem. A cape-style collar echoed the hemline and tied at the sternum. Now comfortably in her thirties, to mirror the new decade, Clara was relieved that the more playful flapper frocks were going out of fashion. The sleeker lines, using the new technique of cutting the fabric on the bias, suited her figure far better than the boxier shapes of the last few years.

She hung the dress on a hanger in the wardrobe along with her other two gowns (a Worth and a Patou), two summer frocks and two sets of trousers and blouses. The Chanel tweed knickerbockers had served her well on her adventure in Egypt and she expected she'd be able to wear them again for the shooting party next week. The other trousers - again Chanel - were dressier but might be considered too manly for conservative tastes. She would test the social temperature before wearing something so scandalous. However, if Lady Penford's riding breeches and art deco interior style were anything to go by, she might be able to get away with it.

Clara finished unpacking and prepared to head down to meet Lady Penford for tea. She decided to stay in her sky-blue summer dress for now. Changing twice in one day was just too much fuss, but she did take the time to brush her ebony bob until not a hair was out of place. Just as she was about to leave, she heard a commotion in the stable yard below.

She went to the window and saw a young man straddling a motorcycle, emerging from the garage. The engine had not yet been started. Two men were striding towards the motorcyclist, angrily gesticulating. Clara could not hear what was being said and worried that opening the window might alert the men below that someone was eavesdropping. However, it was clear that an argument was afoot. Clara watched. The older, gesticulating man in the tweed suit was Sir Bill Fowler. She had met him a number of times at her parents' houses in London and Oxfordshire. He had put on a fair bit of weight since she'd last seen him. He was accompanied by a powerfully built man in a black serge suit and bowler hat. He was possibly Sir Bill's valet. She had never seen the young motorcyclist before, but wondered if under the leather jacket, leather helmet and goggles was Teddy Richner.

The argument continued. From the body language – a jutting chin, a cock of the head – Teddy (if it was him) was not backing down easily. But as Sir Bill and the large valet drew closer, their demeanour grew more menacing, and Teddy's chin dropped to his chest. His shoulders hunched as he got off the motorcycle. He didn't kick out the stand but let it fall to the ground. Sir Bill bellowed something. Teddy stalked back to the house. Clara caught a glimpse of his face. He looked humiliated.

Poor Teddy.

Clara had heard stories about Teddy Richner. Stories about how he'd spent much of his youth in and out of facilities that were politely called convalescent homes but were really just lunatic asylums for the well-heeled. She wondered about the letter Lady Penford had received. It had sounded a little unhinged: might Teddy have penned it? It was far too early to tell. But she would certainly file the little tête-à-tête she had just witnessed away for further consideration.

There was a knock on the door. She opened it to see a bobbing chambermaid. 'Lady Penford said I must show you downstairs for tea, miss.'

Clara smiled at the girl. 'Thank you. I could do with a nice cuppa.'

Chapter 4

Bella followed Parker along the landing, lined with austere portraits of Penford ancestors, and down a back staircase. She memorised the route from Miss Vale's room so she would know how to return later. The staircase was worn stone with a threadbare carpet runner down the middle that looked like it had been there for at least a century.

Two floors down and Parker pointed to a doorway. 'That's where you go to get to the ground floor.' She passed the door and carried on descending.

Bella had expected a bit more chatter. She wasn't going to get far with her investigations if no one would talk to her. So, she probed. 'You been with Lady Penford long, Miss Parker?'

'Twenty-seven years.' There was no reciprocating question. This was not going well.

'But who's counting, eh?' chirped Bella. 'I've been with Miss Vale less than a year.'

'So I've heard,' said Parker, continuing the descent. She pointed to a door. 'The kitchen, scullery and service rooms are through there. Come up for tea when you're finished unpacking.' She continued down yet another flight of stairs.

'Righto,' said Bella. Then, after a beat: 'What've you heard? About me and Miss Vale?' Bella endeavoured to keep her tone friendly rather than defensive.

Parker cast her a quick glance. 'Just that a lady's maid is not your usual job. That Miss Vale doesn't have a *real* maid.'

Bella noted a disapproving edge. 'Well,' she said, grinning, 'I'm real enough. Flesh 'n' blood, I am. And there's nowt mysterious about it. Lady Penford asked Miss Vale for the weekend, for a bit of relaxation, but Miss Vale didn't want to come unaccompanied. So, she asked me to be her maid for the weekend. As I'm already her assistant, this isn't much different. I get paid either way.'

Parker gave a delicate snort. 'Oh, you'll find it's quite different, *Miss* Cuddy. It takes years of experience to be a *professional* maid to someone of Lady Penford's standing. Someone with *generations* of aristocratic blood. There are certain standards that need to be maintained.'

'Oh, I don't doubt it. I'm sure you know far more than most.' But before Bella could probe further, Parker reached a door and opened it.

'And here are the servants' bedrooms. Just for your bearings – they're one floor down from the kitchen, and two from the ground floor.'

'So we're underground then.'

'In the basement, yes. The serving floor is actually on ground level, but the house is built on a slope. The kitchen has an outside door at the back, into the stable yard. But yes, the sleeping quarters are below that. And here is where you will sleep.'

They had been walking along a corridor with panelled wood walls and no further adornment. Parker stopped at a door and knocked. There was no answer. She pushed it open to reveal a small room with twin beds and a washstand between them. Bella was relieved to see there was a slat window at the top of the wall, letting in a sliver of daylight. *So not entirely below ground . . .*

One of the beds had a suitcase sticking out from under it.

'You'll be sharing with the von Schneider maid. Her name's Klopp. German. But she speaks a bit of English.' Parker looked at her watch. 'I expect she'll be in the kitchen for tea now. I'll leave you to get settled in. Come up when you're finished.'

And then she gave a surprising little smile. 'Oh, and if you're anything like your mistress, you'll be needing to use the lavatory. Third door down on the left.'

Bella smiled back. Not too brightly so as not to alarm the woman. 'Thank you, Miss Parker. I'm looking forward to the weekend.'

Parker's lips pursed again. 'Hmmm. Well, I hope you'll cope, Miss Cuddy.'

Bella grinned. 'Don't worry about me. I'm a quick learner.'

'Hmmm,' said Parker again, and left the room.

Bella could hear the tinkle of teacups and murmur of conversation as she approached the kitchen door. It had been easy enough to find. And if she'd forgotten where to go, the smell of freshly baked confectionery lured her in the right direction. She was just about to open the door when she heard a female voice call out, 'You're just in time, Mr Seymour, the tea's freshly brewed and Cook has made some jam tarts too. What was that commotion with the young earl?'

The reply came in a gruff baritone. 'He was wanting to go to Newcastle. He said he was having dinner with friends and would be staying over. Sir William told him her ladyship was expecting him to stay for dinner as we have guests. And that he was to stay home until after the shooting party on Tuesday. Young Master Teddy was not pleased.'

Another female voice replied: 'Well he's not a lad anymore, Mr Seymour. You'd think at twenty-eight they'd let him make his own decisions.'

'Aye,' came the gruff reply. 'But we all know what happened the last time they did that, don't we, Mrs Rogers?'

'I suppose you're right,' replied Mrs Rogers, with a regretful sigh.

'Are you looking for the kitchen?' A soft voice with a foreign accent startled Bella.

She whipped around to see a tall, slim blonde woman of around thirty, dressed in what Bella was coming to recognise as lady's maid attire.

'Aye, I am,' said Bella, hoping the woman would not think she'd been eavesdropping. Which of course she had been. 'I'm Bella Cuddy. Just here for a few days with . . .' she paused a moment, wondering how to refer to her boss . . . and decided that, even though it stuck in her craw, she might as well jump in, boots and all, '. . . with me mistress, Miss Vale. And you are?'

'Gretchen Klopp. I am here with my mistress too. Baroness von Schneider and her husband.'

Bella grinned at the woman. 'Then we're room-mates! Pleased to meet you.' She stuck out her hand.

Gretchen looked slightly taken aback, but not offended. She took the hand and gripped it firmly. 'Let us go in.' The German woman pushed the door open and Bella followed her into the kitchen.

Seated around a large oak table, set for tea, were two older women, one with the mop hat and apron of a cook and the other with a large bunch of keys on her belt – Bella suspected she was the housekeeper. A tall middle-aged man in a serge suit was seated beside her, eating a jam tart. Beside him was a man in a black chauffeur's uniform. In addition, there was a young woman dressed as a lady's maid seated beside Parker.

'Ah, Miss Klopp and Miss Cuddy. This is Miss Cuddy,' Parker announced to the rest of the staff, 'Miss Vale's . . .' she paused allowing the slightest twitch of the lips '. . . maid. And of course, you've already met Miss Klopp. Miss Cuddy, Mrs Barnes here is the housekeeper. She runs everything and her word is law.'

Mrs Barnes, a dignified woman with battleship grey hair, appraised the newcomers. 'Thank you, Miss Parker. I've already spoken to Miss Klopp, but for Miss Cuddy's benefit, I'll repeat it. We run a traditional house here, so I expect traditional manners. I understand they might do things differently where you're from, so if there's something you don't understand or can't find, just ask. Your mistresses' needs will be accommodated as best we can. If you have concerns about your mistresses' accommodation – ablution facilities, bedlinen, towels and so on – speak to me. Miss Parker here is best placed to advise on any other ladies' matters, and if she is not available, you may speak to Miss Wren, who is Lady Katherine's maid.' The younger woman – with strawberry blonde hair and wearing spectacles – nodded shyly.

'Now,' continued Mrs Barnes, 'may I introduce Mr Seymour, Sir William's valet, and Mr Rogers, the family chauffeur.' The gentlemen both stood to greet the ladies.

'And finally,' said Mrs Barnes, with a touch of warmth, 'Mrs Rogers here is our splendid cook – and this is her domain. If there are any concerns with your mistresses' meals, do let her know.'

Mrs Rogers beamed at the two guest maids. 'Welcome to you both. Have a seat. Jenny, pour some tea for the ladies.' A young scullery maid emerged from a corner of the kitchen and picked up the teapot as Bella and Gretchen took their seats.

As tea was served and the plate of jam tarts passed around, Mrs Barnes continued, 'There are other staff who are about their duties. You'll meet them around the house and grounds. Mr Spencer, the butler, you will have already met, he's upstairs now overseeing the afternoon tea for the family and their guests. Try not to bother him with any questions. He is a very busy man. Now, enjoy your tea and then I expect you'll be back to your duties.'

Both Gretchen and Bella nodded. Bella was trying to memorise who was who and wondering where on earth she'd start in her investigation. She noticed that there was a hierarchy to the staff – which might account for who called whom 'miss'. Young Jenny, for instance, hadn't even been introduced. And Mrs Barnes had said there were others too. How would she manage to speak to them all? However, she had already been given permission to speak to Parker and the young Miss Wren – or was it just Wren? She glanced at the bespectacled woman quietly sipping her tea. *Yes*, thought Bella, *she's probably the best place to start.* For now though, she would enjoy the delicious jam tarts.

Chapter 5

'Ah, Miss Vale! Do come in and have a seat. Thank you, Emily, that will be all.'

The maid bobbed a curtsy and withdrew, leaving Clara standing in the doorway. They were in a sunny drawing room, which had also recently benefited from an art deco-style makeover. The wallpaper was cream, accentuated with concentric rectangles in bronze. The cream and bronze were picked up in the circular carpet, with concentric circles lined with black. The black was then extended to the Macassar ebony-veneered furniture with cream and bronze cushions, and in the midst of it all, with her long legs draped in cream silk pyjama-style trousers and a cream silk blouse with black trim on the mandarin cuffs and collar, was Lady Penford, poised with a black cigarette holder pincered between two fingers.

Clara noted the trousers with approval. Lady Penford certainly had a youthful style for a woman of her years. But her voice carried all the authority of her generation and social position.

'Tea for Miss Vale,' she instructed the hovering butler, 'then please leave us. But do let me know when Sir William arrives.'

Spencer bowed. He directed Clara to a Macassar-framed armchair and then poured some tea. The tea set, unsurprisingly, was art deco too. The sharp, angular lines and orange geometric patterns suggested Clarice Cliff, if Clara was not mistaken.

'May I compliment you on your style, Lady Penford,' said Clara, as Spencer withdrew. She gestured around her. 'It's refreshingly . . .' She paused, searching for the word.

'Modern?' asked Lady Penford. She cocked her head to the side. 'And why would that surprise you, Miss Vale?'

Clara thought for a moment, then decided that honesty was the best policy. 'Because most people I have met of your generation and class have more conservative tastes. But you obviously are a woman of distinctive character.' She smiled. 'And I respect that.'

Lady Penford exhaled a long plume of smoke as she looked out of the window, across the manicured lawns of her ancestral home. Then she turned to Clara, her blue eyes challenging but not combative. 'Well, I think that is a compliment, Miss Vale, so I shall take it as such. But do not think my libertine tastes mean I am a liberal. I am certainly not. But enough of politics.' She exhaled the last of the smoke through her nostrils then stubbed out her cigarette. 'Come, let us get down to business.'

Clara added milk to her tea, stirred, and picked up the cup. 'Agreed. I have a few questions before I can proceed with the investigation.'

'Then ask them. We don't have long before the others arrive.'

Clara took a sip of tea then reached into her bag and withdrew her notebook. 'All right, let's start with fingerprints. I took the letter and envelope to my laboratory after you left on Friday and dusted them for fingerprints. There were some clear prints on the envelope. I suspect some of them are yours. I will need to take your fingerprints in order to confirm that.'

Lady Penford looked down her nose at Clara. 'Now?'

Clara shook her head. 'Not now, no. I don't have my kit in my little handbag. I'm supposed to be here for leisure, so I thought it best not to carry a fingerprinting kit around with me! But perhaps we can arrange a time for you to come to my room and we can do it discreetly.'

Lady Penford nodded. 'Good idea, Miss Vale. You said *some* prints. Are there others that might not be mine?'

'Yes. I think – but am not yet sure – that there are prints from at least two people. Possibly three. But first I need to eliminate yours. You said the note was pushed under your door during your afternoon nap on Tuesday. And that you questioned staff and family but no one knew anything about it.'

'That is correct.'

'And the von Schneiders? Your guests? Did you question them too?'

Lady Penford nodded. 'I did. They said neither they nor their servants knew anything about it. They said they were playing tennis at the time it was delivered.'

'I see,' said Clara. 'Thank you. And did anyone else touch the letter after you received it? Parker for instance?'

'No. Parker didn't touch it. But I asked her about it. If she'd seen anyone. She said she had not.'

'Did you share the contents of the letter with her?'

Lady Penford shook her head. 'No. She does not know what is in the letter. No one does – apart from you.'

'But people know that you received an anonymous letter. And that it upset you.'

Lady Penford gave the slightest of shrugs. 'It is now widely known that there was a letter, yes, and that I made enquiries about who delivered it to the house. But I doubt anyone knows that it has upset me. I am – how shall I put it – not effusive with my emotions. And I didn't tell anyone that it was unsigned. As far as anyone is aware, I know exactly who it was from, just not who delivered it.'

'But you called a private detective after receiving it. Or at least asked your secretary to. A . . .' Clara consulted her notes. 'A Miss Fowler?'

'That is correct. Margaret Fowler. Margaret – or Maggie – is my husband's niece. She is his secretary around the house and estate – he has another secretary at the mine. I sometimes use Maggie's services myself.'

'You asked her to put on an appointment with me?'

Lady Penford pursed her lips. 'On reflection that was perhaps not the wisest thing to do.'

'No,' said Clara, trying not to sound sarcastic, 'perhaps not. Not if you wanted to pretend that I was only here for leisure purposes. It won't take much for people to connect the mysterious letter with my sudden invitation.'

Lady Penford lit another cigarette and inserted it into her long holder. She struggled with the lighter a few times before succeeding. Clara expected a servant was usually at hand to light it.

'Well, I'm not entirely a fool, Miss Vale,' said Lady Penford after mastering the lighter.

'I never suggested you were.'

The older woman gave a tight smile. 'In this case though, you would have good reason to think so. It was not the wisest thing, I admit. I should have telephoned you myself. I was thinking about that on the drive home from Newcastle. That we needed a more plausible reason for you to be here this weekend.'

'And do you have one?'

'I do. I have invited some people you know. They shall be arriving tomorrow. On the train from London.'

Clara's heart sank. 'My parents?'

'Yes. I'm sorry, I should have told you, but I only thought about it after I'd left your office. I wasn't sure if they would come at such short notice. But they are. Turns out your father and my husband have some business to discuss anyway. And your mother . . . well . . . she rarely turns down an invitation, does she?'

'No,' said Clara, wryly, thinking how delighted her mother would be to receive an invitation from the aristocratic Justina Penford. *Was that a twinkle in Lady Penford's eye?*

'So,' said Lady Penford, tapping ash into an onyx ash tray, 'if anyone questions you – or me – I have asked you so you can see your dearest mama and papa. And you were delighted to take up the invitation.'

Clara must have winced visibly because Lady Penford quickly added: 'Do try to look vaguely delighted, Miss Vale.'

Clara sighed. 'I shall try. You say they are arriving tomorrow?'

'Late afternoon. My chauffeur will pick them up from Morpeth station. They should be here in time for dinner.'

Clara nodded. 'All right. So that gives me twenty-four hours to focus on work before they arrive. Let's get on with it then.' She consulted her notebook again. 'Righty-ho, so I'll need to take your prints – can you come up to my room before you dress for dinner?'

Lady Penford nodded.

'Good. Ideally, I'd like to take everyone else's too, after I've excluded you, but that might be difficult to do without disclosing the real reason I'm here.'

'Quite,' said Lady Penford. 'I don't think we can do that. Have you any other ideas?'

Clara tapped the notebook with her pen. 'I have a few. I'd like to know where the tea caddy is usually kept and who has access to that room. I could take fingerprints there and see if any match the ones on the letter – the ones that don't belong to you.'

Lady Penford brightened a little. 'Now that's a good idea. It is normally kept in a sideboard in the breakfast room. I shall show you after we've had tea here.' She checked her watch and at that moment the clock on the mantlepiece struck four.

With impeccable timing, the door opened and Spencer, the butler, announced Sir William and Lady Katherine's arrival.

Lady Katherine – Kate – was a younger, paler version of her mother. Not paler in colouring – they were equally fair-skinned and fair-haired – but she shone less brightly. There was a quiet, unassuming aura around the younger woman, which would not draw all eyes in a room to her, as invariably happened with her mother. Kate was around thirty and wore a pretty but conventional pink summer frock. Clara stood to meet her. 'Lady Katherine.' She reached out her hand.

The younger woman took it and bestowed on Clara a gentle, friendly smile.

'Please, Miss Vale, we attended the same college. You must call me Kate.'

Clara inclined her head. 'Indeed we did, Kate. Then you must call me Clara.' Their eyes met and both smiled as they recognised the bond of sorority between them. Very few women were granted degrees from one of the country's most prestigious universities. And it was rare for a young woman even to aspire to do so. Clara wondered what Kate was doing with her English Literature degree.

But before she could ask, the tall, dark-haired, and broad-framed Sir William Fowler stepped into the room.

'Miss Vale,' he said in a gravelly voice, revealing his lower-class roots. 'Welcome to Penford Manor. It's been a few years since I last saw you.' He gave a brief bow and shook her extended hand. Then he bent to kiss his wife's cheek. 'Hello, my dear.'

His wife smiled up at him with more warmth than Clara had expected. It was always said that Justina Penford had married William Fowler simply to secure his money to save the Penford Manor estate. But Clara remembered that the times she had seen them together at her parents' estate, Running Brook, they had been comfortable in one another's company. It was not for her to say that they married for love, but she wouldn't discount the notion that there was now love between them.

At Lady Penford's insistence everyone sat down, then Spencer poured tea and placed a plate of jam tarts on the table.

'I asked Spencer to bring up some of Mrs Rogers' little tarts, my dear. I know how much you like them. But,' said Lady Penford, with a playful note of reproach, 'I asked him not to bring up anything else. We have a five-course dinner to get through this evening!'

Sir Bill patted his substantial belly and declared, 'Oh, I think I'll manage.'

His wife gave a little wag of her finger, then looked to the door. 'Is Teddy not coming?'

A look passed between Kate and her stepfather.

'I think he has a headache, Mother.'

'Yes,' agreed Sir Bill, 'I don't think he'll be joining us.'

Lady Penford appraised her husband shrewdly. 'I hope you and he have not been having words again.'

'No, no, nothing like that. I've hardly spoken to him all day.' Then Sir Bill helped himself to a second jam tart.

Clara, remembering the exchange she'd overheard in the stable yard, sipped her tea thoughtfully.

With Teddy apparently forgotten, Sir Bill turned his attention to Clara and asked after her family's health. 'You'll be glad to see them tomorrow night, I expect. I must say, my wife took me by surprise when she told me she'd invited them and you. We already have quite a full house, as you'll see at dinner this evening. But,' he added quickly, after receiving a 'look' from Lady Penford, 'you are of course most welcome.'

'Kate,' said Lady Penford after everyone finished their tea, 'why don't you take Clara for a walk around the gardens. I need to discuss table arrangements for this evening with your stepfather and Spencer. But Clara,' she added, with a little wiggle of her fingertips, 'I shall see you later.'

Chapter 6

It was a gloriously warm August day so neither Kate nor Clara felt the need to wear a cardigan. They walked side by side in their pink and blue cotton frocks across the lavish green lawn. The croquet set lay abandoned and from the satisfying sound of ball on racquet, the players had now progressed to tennis. Kate led Clara along a winding path between topiary shrubs, mimicking animals. Beyond a giant squirrel were two tennis courts, one of them occupied by the middle-aged couple Clara had seen playing croquet on her drive in.

They were both tall, blond and athletic. The woman raised her racquet and smiled. 'Cousin Kate!' she called out.

Kate waved. 'Hello! Are you winning?'

'She always wins!' laughed the man. 'And who is this?'

'This is Miss Clara Vale. Miss Vale, these are my cousins – Baron Klaus von Schneider and Baroness Adeline. We call her Ada. Mama will no doubt introduce you properly at dinner.'

'How do you do?' said Clara, then smiled. 'And may the best woman win!'

Ada laughed. 'Oh I will! We look forward to meeting you later, Miss Vale.'

Kate led Clara away as the game resumed and Ada cracked an ace serve.

'Cousins from your father's side?' asked Clara.

'Yes, the German side. I'm sure you already know that my name, Richner, is really von Richner. But we had to drop the "von" during the war. At least we didn't have to change it completely!'

'Like the Saxe-Coburg-Gothas?' asked Clara.

Kate grimaced. 'Well, it was quite a mouthful, wasn't it? Windsor is so much easier. As is Richner. And we now pronounce it Rickner, so far less foreign.'

The women were now walking through the cool of the beech wood, the golden light catching the highlights in Kate's blonde hair.

'Your stepfather said you have a full house. Could you tell me who else is here?'

'Didn't Mama tell you?'

'Oh, just in passing. But I've forgotten . . .' She paused, wondering if Kate might be suspicious if she started asking probing questions, but the young woman appeared to be in a talkative mood, so she pressed on. 'And I'm not sure *why* everyone is here.'

Kate gave Clara a curious look, but then shrugged and said: 'Well, Sir Bill is right, it is a houseful. They host a shooting party for the opening of the grouse season every year – on the twelfth of course – but this year they have extended the time and the guest list.'

'Why is that?' asked Clara.

'Well, no one really tells me anything, but I think it's because they're thinking of charging in future years. This is a test run, to see if the household and staff can cope.'

'*Charging?*'

Kate gave an embarrassed shrug. 'To stay at a grand country estate and enjoy the life of the landed gentry for a while. Everyone's doing it now, according to my stepfather. We have to find a way to run the estate.' She gestured around her. 'It costs a fortune to keep this all up, Clara. And since they hiked death and land duties to pay for the war, even the oldest families in England are finding it hard to stay afloat. Despite all the mining money my stepfather has poured into it, it's still not enough.' She sighed. 'I've probably said more than I should already. But . . .' and she paused to push open an ancient gate in an even more ancient stone wall '. . . you and I are modern women, Clara. Seeing you here has reminded me of my ambitions when I first went up to Oxford. Education and work are the way forward, not inherited titles and money. The time of the great families is over. But don't tell Mama I've said this, she already thinks I'm a socialist!'

Clara's surprise at Kate's extraordinary statement was replaced for a moment by a gasp of delight. Through the doorway was an exquisite walled garden with stone terraces, curving stairways, lawns, hedges, ponds and rockeries, with border after border of herbaceous shrubs, perennials and blousy annuals, in a palette to delight any watercolourist. Down one wall was a lean-to glass house overflowing with tropical exuberance, while at the bottom of the garden, the gravel paths all led to a miniature Greek revival temple of shimmering white marble, sparkling in the August sun.

'Goodness me, this is beautiful!'

'It is rather,' said Kate. 'The bones of it were designed by Capability Brown, no less, and it had a more recent planting makeover by Gertrude Jekyll. But it requires three full-time gardeners to keep it in order. Which, of course, adds to the cost. I've suggested to Mama she gives the whole place to the National Trust, but she won't hear a word of it. She'll contemplate charging the right sort of guests to spend a week here, but she won't have the great unwashed traipsing all over the place for the price of a few shillings.'

Clara chuckled. 'So that's why she thinks you're a socialist?'

Kate gave her an endearingly wistful smile. 'Well, that, and also because I try to help the families of my stepfather's workers. I teach English at a school in Ashington that caters for mine children, and I also help run adult education classes for the miners.'

'Well,' said Clara, 'I'm very glad you're putting your degree to good use.' She smiled. 'And I think you'd be a very good teacher, Kate. You have a gentleness and intelligence about you. And a desire to help people.'

Kate stopped and looked earnestly at her fellow Oxford alumna.

'Thank you for saying that, Clara. I didn't think you'd really noticed me before. Not many people do.'

Clara shrugged. 'Well, that's the impression you give me. I never knew you well at Oxford, but I can tell that you are the type of person who *would* do well at teaching, while I was not, as I found out when I gave it a go myself.'

Kate gave Clara a grateful smile and indicated they should continue walking. So they meandered companionably along a gravel path, hemmed by sprays of English lavender in full bloom.

'And then you became a detective,' said Kate as she trailed her fingertips over the lavender, disturbing the bees buzzing around the feast of nectar.

Clara was taken aback by Kate's matter-of-fact statement. *Is she saying she knows why I am really here?* Well, it was a tissue-thin alibi that Lady Penford had concocted.

But Clara was being paid to maintain the charade, so she needed to be very careful. She thought for a moment and then said: 'Well, not at first. I started teaching science, but as I say, I wasn't a good teacher. Then I tried applying for laboratory work. But no one would hire a woman. So as a stopgap I took a job in a library. And that was when my uncle, Bob Wallace, left me his detection business in Newcastle. Just last summer.'

'And the science?' asked Kate. 'Have you left that behind now?'

'Not at all! I have a basement laboratory at home. And I use scientific methods in my work. It's called criminalist science or forensics. Not that I'm working this weekend, of course . . .'

'Of course not,' said Kate with a little twinkle in her eye.

Clara met her gaze, and the two women shared an unspoken truth.

'So, who else is going to be here this evening?' asked Clara eventually as they continued their walk, skirting a lily pond splashed with yellow irises.

'The Labour MP for Newcastle and his wife.'

'Sir Charles Trevelyan?' asked Clara.

'Indeed,' said Kate.

Clara knew something of the rogue aristocrat, although she had not actually met him. He was from one of the most prestigious families in Northumberland and was the lord of the nearby Wallington Hall. He had stood as a member of the Labour Party in the 1929 election which brought the socialists to power. He was considered a traitor to his class, and it was a shock people like Kate and Clara's parents had still not got over. However, things were not going well for the socialists, and it looked like they might soon fall from power. The financial crash in New York just a few months after the election had sent shock waves around the world, and the Labour government was struggling to cope. The bold plans they had to extend workers' rights and social security programmes had to be mothballed. Unemployment had soared to nearly two and a half million while exports had halved by fifty per cent. Mines – like those of Bill Fowler's – were drastically cutting production and laying off workers. It was becoming clear that socialism, despite its admirable goals, had no quick fixes for such an immediate crisis.

'Goodness,' said Clara, 'that *is* a surprise.'

Kate shrugged. 'Despite his politics – and my mother's fears that he's a bad influence on me – he is an old family friend. And my stepfather needs to keep the local MP onside – for business reasons, if you know what I mean.'

Clara knew exactly what she meant. And she expected her own father's invitation – as a prominent London banker – would be for 'business reasons' too.

'And will your brother be there? After all, this is now all legally his, isn't it?'

They had reached the mock Greek temple which Clara saw was a typical Georgian garden folly. Kate stopped and plucked some dead heads from a glorious pink climbing rose which wound its way around one of the Doric pillars. She allowed the browned petals to fall from her fingers onto the white marble steps. 'Shall we sit?' she asked, indicating a bench in the portico. From the new vantage point Clara could see that the flower beds around the white marble folly were given over to cottage garden-style planting, with an abundance of buttercups, daisies, poppies and Lady Penford's favourite blue cornflowers.

When settled, Kate straightened her pink skirt and turned to Clara. 'Well, Clara, to be frank, this is why Mama asked me to take you on this walk. They need time to deal with Teddy – with you out of the house – and my mother hopes I will diplomatically fill you in on what to expect from him over the next few days. So it's not too much of a shock. The von Schneiders are playing tennis and our other house guests are on a day trip to the seaside. Some of Sir Bill's family who will be coming tonight are already in the know, while your parents and the Trevelyans haven't yet arrived. So, it's only you.'

Kate continued her smoothing. Whatever she had to say was obviously going to be difficult.

'Don't worry,' said Clara, kindly, 'I also have a – how should I put it – *difficult* brother.'

Kate's eyes narrowed. 'With all due respect, Clara, I've met Tony, and while he's a bit of a gadabout, the situation with Teddy is quite different.'

Clara lowered her eyes, chastened. 'Yes, I'm sorry, it is. Do go on.'

'No, I'm sorry,' said Kate. 'I'm sorry I snapped. I didn't mean to. But when it comes to Teddy . . . well . . . let's just say my feelings are complicated. He's only two years younger than me and now, at twenty-eight, he's a grown man. But I've never been able to treat him as anything more than a child. None of us have. And he resents that. But . . . what else can we do? I'm not sure how much of this you've heard – I know there's been plenty of gossip – so forgive me if I tell you anything you know already, but here goes . . .'

She stopped smoothing her skirt, took a deep breath, and then continued. 'Well, we had two older brothers – Michael and Rupert – but both died during the war. First Michael, then Rupert. Rupert was the biggest shock as we thought we were getting him back. He was on a troop carrier on the way home after armistice in 1918 when it hit a German mine. The war was over, but he was killed anyway. Can you believe it?'

Clara shook her head in sympathy.

'Well, Teddy really couldn't. It was on his sixteenth birthday. He went to his room and cried for days. And then – without wallowing in too much detail – we got the news that our father had killed himself when he heard about Rupert's death. Papa had fled to Germany when the war started to avoid internment in one of those camps. He was classified as an "enemy alien" because he was born in Germany. We children were not included in that as we were born here, but poor Mama had to endure all sorts of gossip suggesting she was spying for the Germans and feeding information to her husband in Berlin. It nearly broke her – being thought of as a traitor and people believing she had sullied the noble Penford name. She still hasn't got over it. But I digress . . .

'We were all hoping Papa could come home at the end of the war – but of course, he never did. That pushed Teddy over the edge and for the next ten years he has been in and out of rest homes and, at his worst, mental hospitals and lunatic asylums. He's been home now for the last two years, and is better than he was, but he still has what you might call fits of mania. He occasionally runs around naked. He hasn't done it for well over a year now, so we aren't expecting him to do so this weekend, but forewarned is forearmed, eh, Clara?'

She gave a sad smile. Clara reached out and squeezed her hand.

'I don't think Mama would have wanted me to tell you about his nudity, just a more general "he could possibly get a little upset", but there you go. You might as well know. And he has also, sometimes, been violent. His valets take an occasional beating. In fact, he's currently between valets as we struggle to get anyone to take on the job. I honestly don't think Teddy means it, but if someone is trying to restrain him, for his own protection, he lashes out.'

Clara remembered what she'd seen in the stable yard. She decided to ask Kate about it. 'So, what I don't understand is, if Teddy can be erratic, why would Sir Bill and your mother want to keep him here while there are guests. Surely it would have been better if he was allowed to leave for a few days.'

Kate sighed. 'Well, yes. I would have thought so too. However . . .' she bit her lip '. . . this is where it gets complicated. And please, don't tell Mama I've told you, but you see, she thinks he's well enough now to be released from the jurisdiction of the Lunacy Office, and that he might be able to get married. And if he gets married and produces an heir, then the succession to the Penford title is secured. And that means more to Mama than anything.'

'The Lunacy Office? What's that?'

Kate raised a brow. 'Ah, sorry, I forget that not everyone knows the ins and outs of the legalities around the mentally ill. You see, since Teddy is the Earl of Penford, all this—' she gestured around her '—belongs to him. But, due to his . . . well, his fragile condition . . . he was not able to take control of it when he turned twenty-one. The

Lunacy Office is an office of the courts that looks after the financial and legal affairs of the mentally ill. It appoints a trustee – or trustees – to manage the patient's affairs. In Teddy's case it is Sir Bill. He applied for the role with the support of my mother after they were married. But the trusteeship is renewed every couple of years. A renewal hearing is due again this autumn. Mama and Teddy hope that he'll be well enough to be released from the trusteeship. Sir Bill doesn't think he will be.'

'And you?' asked Clara.

Kate shrugged. 'Sometimes I do, and sometimes I don't. But I'm not sure pushing him into marriage will help.'

Clara frowned. 'Yes, you mentioned something about marriage. Is he engaged?'

'Not that I'm aware! But with Teddy, you never know. He can be very charming with the ladies when he wants to be. And—' she shook her head despairingly '—Mama thinks that if he is to be married, it will be in his favour at the Lunacy Office hearing. That a potential fiancée will be a good witness. She thinks a match may be made this weekend.'

'Good Lord! That's not the real reason I've been invited, is it?'

Kate laughed out loud. 'Oh Clara! Good gracious no. Don't worry about that. There are another two candidates . . .'

But before Kate could divulge who the fortunate – or unfortunate – women were, a maid approached the portico and gave a little curtsy. 'I'm sorry to disturb you, Lady Katherine, but Lady Penford has requested Miss Vale be called back to the house and shown to the breakfast room. She said she'll meet Miss Vale there.'

'The breakfast room?' asked Kate. 'Whyever there?'

'I have no idea, Lady Katherine.'

But Clara certainly did.

Chapter 7

Clara was on her hands and knees in front of the sideboard in the breakfast room. Lady Penford sat on a nearby dining chair watching her while cleaning ink from her fingers with a napkin. The door was shut and the staff had been told not to come in. *This is not the way to do an undercover investigation*, thought Clara. Lady Penford seemed to think that just ordering people not to look would do the trick. If it had been left to Clara, she would have found a quiet time when everyone was busy and slipped into the breakfast room unnoticed. But it was too late now, Lady Penford had taken control of the 'crime scene'.

'Tell me how this works,' said the lady of the house.

'Well,' said Clara, after she had dusted the door of the sideboard with aluminium powder to reveal some fingerprints, 'this powder adheres to the fatty residue left by fingertips. Our fingertips have very fine ridges and troughs in a patterned swirl. Those are our unique fingerprints. No two are alike. Your fingerprints, Lady Penford, are different from every other person's on earth. It's really quite remarkable when you think about it. Now, look at this . . .'

She took out the photographs of the letter and envelope she had developed back in Newcastle. 'It is not very easy to get fingerprints from ordinary paper. Normally the shinier and smoother the surface the better. So, things like glass, highly polished wood – like this dresser – or brushed metal surfaces are the easiest to find prints on. But it's not impossible on paper. There is a new method called iodine fuming. I won't bore you too much with the details, but instead of using aluminium powder like one does on more sympathetic surfaces, iodine gas is used which temporarily reveals the print in a brown stain. I then fix the print with a dusting of carbonyl iron powder and then I can photograph it. So that's what I did back in my laboratory.'

Lady Penford looked more closely at the photographs. 'So these are the fingerprints you found on the envelope?'

'Yes.' Clara nodded. 'I then photographed and enlarged the image so you can see the patterns clearly.' She pointed to two fingerprints, one on the front of the envelope and one on the back. Then at another two prints on the letter. She then placed the card with Lady Penford's inky prints next to it. She pointed with a red wax crayon. 'These are your prints here and here. The thumb and forefinger of your left hand. So this proves you touched the letter and envelope. Which we already knew you did. There are no other prints that I could find on the letter. But there were on the envelope. These are not yours, which suggests they belong to the person who delivered the letter to you.' She then pointed to the dusted sideboard door. 'I'm hoping the same print will be found here. I hope to find a match that suggests two points of contact with the blackmailing: the delivery of the letter and the location of the stolen tea caddy. It will not be conclusive proof, of course, and it might be the case that a separate person to the one who delivered it wrote the letter and put it in the envelope without leaving their prints, but it will still help us narrow down the suspects.'

She then took out her magnifying glass and examined the prints on the door, comparing them to the photographs. 'Hmmm,' she said.

'What?' asked Lady Penford, leaning forward, her voice tinged with excitement. 'Have you found something?'

Clara nodded. 'Yes, I think I have.' She pointed to one of the prints on the door and then at the odd one out on the photograph. 'I think we have a match. I'll have to photograph this and look at it properly when it's magnified, but I think we might be on to something here . . .'

'Well, that is just marvellous! Bravo, Miss Vale! When will we have the guilty party in custody?'

Clara leaned back on her heels. 'Oh, I'm sorry, Lady Penford, it could take quite a while. Firstly, I don't have a photographic dark room here, I'll have to go back to Newcastle. Then I'll have to fingerprint everyone in the house. And that, if you want to keep the investigation quiet, will not be an easy thing to do.'

Lady Penford pursed her lips. 'I see. Well, what if I just order everyone to let you take their prints?'

'Well, I'm sure you could . . .' said Clara. 'But don't you think they'll want to know why?'

Lady Penford let out an exasperated sigh. 'Oh bother! They might *want* to know, but I simply can't – and won't – tell them.'

'You mean about the blackmail?'

'Of course! What else would I not want them to know?'

Well, that is the question . . . thought Clara. She felt like she was working on this investigation with one arm tied behind her back. And then she had an idea. She rose from her knees and took a seat next to Lady Penford.

'What if you tell them that you are investigating theft? Which is actually true. The theft of the tea caddy. You could tell them that we're trying to find who stole that. There will undoubtedly be a bit of a hullaballoo and it might very well alert your blackmailer that you're onto them, but that's not such a bad thing. If someone declines to have their prints taken that will be a red flag against them.'

'Hmmm,' said Lady Penford. 'That is a possibility. But I don't want to put everyone on tenterhooks just yet. We need to get through this evening's dinner party first. At the very least. Can this wait?'

Clara nodded. 'It can. I will need to go through to Newcastle tomorrow anyway and can't really do much more until I have developed the photographs. So, let's talk about it again after that.'

'All right,' said Lady Penford. 'And thank you, Miss Vale, for your discretion.'

'Not at all, Lady Penford. I'm just doing my job.'

The dressing gong had sounded and Clara was waiting for Bella to arrive. She hoped someone would tell Bella that that's what the first of the two pre-dinner gongs meant. Clara did not *need* Bella to dress her, but she did want to discuss the case with her, and she wanted to task her with making enquiries about something.

Clara was frustrated by Lady Penford's recalcitrance in sharing information about the possible motives of the blackmailer, what secret they might be privy to and what the cryptic blackmail note might actually mean. Clara was not very confident that fingerprint analysis alone – assuming she could in fact get a match for the rogue print – was enough to solve this case. So she looked again at the only other physical evidence she had: the note and the dried, pressed cornflower. She laid the flower aside and spread the note flat on her dressing table.

Cornflowers, you say, just cornflowers,
gemming the golden grain;
Ah no! You can't deceive me.
£50 or your secret will be out.
Put in silver tea caddy (you know which one).
Find under lobster pot.
Newbiggin lifeboat hut.
By midnight 12th August.
Don't grouse about.

What is it about cornflowers? she wondered. The opening line of the note was phrased very peculiarly. 'You say'. Who is you? Lady Penford? When did 'you' say that to the writer of the note? And what did she mean by it? And why did the writer think that Lady Penford was trying to deceive with whatever she had said about cornflowers. And what on earth does 'gemming the golden grain' mean? Literal grain? Was this to do with a corn or wheat field? Or was that a metaphor for something? The line did sound quite poetic.

There were, of course, cornflowers growing on the estate. But they were a common flower. What might their significance be, other than that they were Lady Penford's favourite; and that her late husband had picked them for her. She had not denied that the 'secret' might have something to do with her late husband. Perhaps that was an angle Clara could pursue. The von Schneiders had seemed friendly enough. She would try to sound them out about the late Baron von Richner.

Lady Penford had already explained the tea caddy – again, an association with her late husband. *Hmmm . . .* thought Clara. But this was all speculation about meaning and motive. That was of course important, but so too were means and opportunity. Who had the means to type this letter? Who had access to a typewriter? And this was something Clara wanted to ask Bella to investigate. Was there a typewriter in the house? Miss Fowler, the secretary, was a likely candidate. Did she have one? And did anyone else have access to it? That was something the servants might know.

Clara, with her magnifying glass in hand, examined the note again. She caught her breath. With a flutter of excitement she observed there was a little chip out of the bottom curve of the 'e'. Every single 'e' had a little bit missing. Clara smiled to herself. Now that was a very useful clue.

There was a knock on the door and Bella entered. 'I'm supposed to get you dressed,' she announced with a roll of her eyes.

Clara chuckled. 'Oh, don't worry about that. I'll dress myself. But while I do, I'll tell you what I've found out.'

So Bella positioned herself on the bed while Clara undressed, washed herself down at the basin, and then slipped into her teal Chanel-inspired gown. All the time she talked, filling Bella in on what she'd heard from Kate on their garden walk and the fingerprinting she'd done in the breakfast room.

In return Bella told her what she'd heard about Teddy in the kitchen, which seemed to dovetail with what Clara had heard from Kate.

'So what's your plan now?' asked Clara.

Bella shrugged. 'I don't really have one other than watching and listening. I'll try to make friends with the maids but not sure what I can ask them about the case yet. I could also try to find out who the two marriage candidates are. Apparently, there is a family that arrived on Thursday with two unmarried girls. I didn't get their names. They've been away for the day, but they should be back now.'

'Yes,' said Clara, 'Kate mentioned that too. I expect I'll see who they are this evening. I'm just glad it's not me!'

Bella laughed.

Clara zipped up her dress then turned her attention to her hair and makeup. As she did, she asked Bella to look at the note and the chip out of the 'e'.

'Crikey, Miss Vale, you're right! So, if we find this typewriter with the damaged letter, we find the blackmailer?'

Clara sat at her dressing table and lined her dark brown eyes with a black kohl pencil. 'Well, we at least find out where the letter was typed. Then if we can find out who has access to the typewriter that will narrow it down. It is also typed with no mistakes, so that suggests someone familiar with typing and good spelling and punctuation.' She chuckled. 'It's not everyone who knows how to use a semi-colon!'

'So, a well-educated person then?' asked Bella.

'Very possibly. See what you can find out, Bella. Who has a typewriter in this house? Start with Miss Fowler, but don't restrict yourself to that. There might be another one. Or more than one person could use the one Miss Fowler has.'

Clara outlined and then filled her lips with a dark red paste. 'What do you think?' she asked, pouting and turning to Bella.

'I think it's a good idea. I'll see what I can find.'

Clara grinned. 'Not the typewriter, me!'

Bella chuckled. 'Well, you look the cat's whiskers, Miss Vale. That colour really suits you. And Juju has done a grand job with the dress.' Then she gave a sly smile. 'Are you sure you're not out to catch a husband?'

'I certainly am not!'

Chapter 8

Clara, carrying the flounce of her skirt in one hand, did her best to glide regally down the marble staircase towards the main hall. Under the sparkling chandelier, the central glass table held pre-dinner drinks and canapés, while footmen fluttered around like black and white moths, holding silver trays aloft. A gramophone played in the corner and Clara wondered if the absence of live musicians was a cost-cutting exercise or a statement of modernity. She stopped for a moment on the mezzanine floor, in front of the stained-glass window, to observe the other guests before she joined them. She needed to be as strategic as possible in her conversations this evening, surreptitiously interviewing the 'upstairs' suspects in the blackmailing case. Bella, she knew, was doing the same with the downstairs suspects. Although, so far, with the literary evidence of the note, the culprit was more likely to be of a higher class.

Sir Bill was standing, drink in hand, near a full-sized suit of armour, which had somehow managed to survive the art deco makeover. With him was Baron Klaus von Schneider, his athletic middle-aged frame looking just as comfortable in a tuxedo as it had in his tennis togs. They were joined by a tall, distinguished gentleman of around sixty. Clara knew him immediately as Sir Charles Philip Trevelyan, 3rd Baronet of Wallington, and the Labour Member of Parliament for Newcastle Central.

Their respective partners – Lady Justina Penford, Baroness Ada von Schneider and a woman Clara had never met, but had seen in press photographs: Lady Molly Trevelyan, wife of Sir Charles, and sister of the celebrated lady explorer, Gertrude Bell – stood in a separate group, sipping champagne and apparently enjoying one another's company.

Of those guests, Clara noted, only the von Schneiders were present the day the blackmail note was delivered. *Although . . .* she thought, with a start, *so was Sir Bill. Golly, could he possibly have had a hand in it?* It would be very strange if he had, but this was a very strange case. No, she would not be crossing Sir Bill off her suspect list until she had firm evidence to do so.

In the corner, near the gramophone, was a dark-haired couple in their mid-thirties. They looked so much alike that they had to be brother and sister. The man, particularly, bore a strong resemblance to Sir Bill. Could the woman be Maggie Fowler, Sir Bill's niece? If so, the man must be his nephew.

The next group of guests was being hosted by Lady Katherine Richner, standing on the opposite side of the hall. Kate, Clara thought warmly, looked beautiful in a floor-length gold gown. But all warm thoughts fled when she saw who her new friend was talking to. Two women in their early thirties tittered together in response to a comment from the only man in the group: the forty-something Archie Fitzgilbert, who, on the recent death of his father, had become the Right Honourable Viscount Fitzgilbert. Clara, who had only a few months earlier been the object of Archie's unwelcome romantic attention, knew that he was unmarried, but from the way he was looking at Kate Richner, she expected he was hoping to remedy that very soon. *Poor Kate . . .*

The two tittering women were his cousins, the equally odious Lily and Elsie Fitzgilbert. They, she assumed, must be the two candidates for the hand of Teddy Richner. *Poor Teddy . . .*

There were two people missing from the Fitzgilbert party, but Clara, with a sinking heart, spotted one of them joining the group of older ladies, hosted by Lady Justina. Lady Gertrude Fitzgilbert, Archie's mother and Lily and Elsie's aunt by marriage, was an acquaintance of Clara's mother from London. Clara had recently met her and her family in Cairo and, after a disastrous day picnicking at the pyramids, had hoped never to see them again. Only the very elderly gentleman known as The Major, a great-uncle of Archie's, was unaccounted for now. Perhaps they had not brought him with them on this excursion, thought Clara. Or perhaps he'd finally popped his clogs . . .

'Hello. Miss Vale, is it?'

Startled, Clara turned to see that someone had joined her on the mezzanine. It was Teddy Richner. Up close, he looked more mature than she expected, and was rather handsome in his tuxedo. His hair was as blond as his sister's and his eyes as blue as his mother's. He had a soft smile on his face and looked perfectly calm. Clara caught herself wondering what a mentally deranged person would look like. But that wasn't fair. Teddy had periods of illness, yes, but why should he be defined by his worst days? She remembered what Kate had told her about him being 'quite well' for the last two years.

She smiled in return. 'It is. I'm Clara Vale. I assume you are Teddy Richner – or should I say, Lord Penford.'

His smile broadened. 'Guilty as charged. And please, it's just Teddy.' His eyes twinkled teasingly, as if he knew what she'd been thinking. 'And don't worry, there won't be any drama tonight.'

Embarrassed, Clara looked down at the gathered guests. 'No, they don't look like the dramatic type, do they?'

Teddy grinned. 'Definitely not. I'm afraid it will be a dull evening. So,' he added, after a moment, 'are you surveying your suspect list?'

Clara took a step back. 'Suspects? Whatever do you mean?'

'Come, come,' said Teddy. 'No offence, Miss Vale, but it is laughable to think you are fooling anyone with your presence. You are number fifteen, the unmatched one.'

Clara furrowed her brow. 'Number fifteen? What are you talking about?'

Teddy gestured to the guests below. 'Count them.'

Clara did. 'There are thirteen of them.'

'That is correct. Then I am number fourteen and you are fifteen. Very unlucky for some.'

'I thought it was thirteen that was unlucky,' observed Clara.

'Only for the predictably mundane, Miss Vale. No, fifteen is the unlucky number tonight. But if they'd let me go this afternoon as I wanted to, we wouldn't have this problem.'

'And what problem is that?'

'Fifteen people at the dinner table, of course!'

'Well, it's a little odd, but surely it's not a disaster,' offered Clara, wondering if this was one of Teddy's peculiarities. She knew people who could not abide odd numbers. She liked balance herself, but this wasn't anything to get distressed about, was it? She looked anxiously at Teddy. But his demeanour remained calm. Even ironic and playful. Was he just toying with her? Knowing she was curious about his erratic mental state?

'Well, I'm sorry for being the odd one out,' she said eventually, not knowing what else to say.

'Oh, it's not your fault,' he said, brushing her apology away. 'It's my mother's entirely. She's not superstitious. So she forgets that other people are. However, you being number fifteen is not the real problem. The real problem – for you – is that everyone knows why you're really here.'

'Everyone?' asked Clara.

Teddy quirked an eyebrow. 'Well, everyone who was here when the wicked note was delivered. I don't think the Fitzgilberts or the Trevelyans know about it, but everyone else does.'

She turned to him, leaning one elbow on the balustrade. 'Why do you say "wicked"? Do you know what the note said?'

He shook his head, slowly. 'No, I do not. That much my mother has managed to keep secret. But it has clearly shaken her. Enough to hire a private detective. Do you know what's in the note?'

'I do, but I shan't be sharing,' said Clara, brusquely.

He laughed. 'A proud, professional woman. I like that. Shall we?' He crooked his arm.

Clara bit back a retort. There was nothing to be gained from getting into a spat with one of the suspects. She relaxed and slotted her hand through his elbow. 'Yes, let's.'

Teddy and Clara descended the stairs and Clara very much enjoyed seeing the misses Fitzgilbert staring daggers at her. No, she was not out to attract a husband, but it wouldn't do any harm to let them believe for a while that she was. After the snooty way they had treated her and Bella in Egypt, it was the least they deserved.

'Would you mind introducing me to that dark-haired couple over there,' she whispered to Teddy. 'They're the only two I don't know.'

'My pleasure,' said Teddy, and pointedly swept past the Fitzgilberts and his sister to join the couple standing beside the gramophone. A recording of a chirpy Mozart minuet was playing, but not loudly enough to drown out conversation.

'Miss Vale,' said Teddy. 'May I introduce my stepfather's nephew and niece, Mr and Miss Fowler. Mr Fowler – Matt – is the manager of my stepfather's mines, now that he spends most of his time running the estate. And his sister Maggie is Sir Bill's secretary. This beautiful lady is Miss Clara Vale. Number fifteen. Guest of my mother. I believe Miss Vale's parents will be arriving tomorrow, is that correct?'

'Yes it is,' said Clara, nodding a greeting to the siblings.

Teddy shook his head. 'Well, that will only make seventeen. It's still not right.'

Miss Fowler narrowed her eyes. 'Are you all right, Lord Penford? Did you not have a rest this afternoon?'

A flash of anger animated Teddy's face then just as quickly subsided. 'I did not know you had taken on duties as a nursemaid, too, Maggie.'

'So,' said Clara, interjecting before anything escalated. 'How are the mines coping with this dreadful recession?'

Matt Fowler, with a look of relief, leaped at the change of subject. 'We're managing, Miss Vale. Although there's no denying these are difficult times.'

Clara nodded in sympathy. 'I've heard production is being cut. Have you had to close any pits?'

Matt shook his head. 'Not close, fortunately, but we've had to reduce shifts and are only active four days a week now.'

They were suddenly joined by Kate Richner who had managed to escape the Fitzgilberts. 'I really don't see why you've had to lay off so many men, though, Matt,' she said.

Matt's lips tightened. 'I can't pay them out of thin air, Kate.'

'But we have a moral responsibility to look after these men and their families . . .'

And so the conversation continued and by the sound of it, it was a well-worn routine.

Teddy rolled his eyes. 'My sister the socialist. I blame her Oxford education.'

Before Clara could respond he winked at her. 'Only jesting, Miss Vale.'

Kate and Matt had now stepped away from the group to continue their disagreement. Clara turned instead to Miss Maggie Fowler. 'Miss Fowler,' she said, 'I'm very glad to meet you. I believe you tried to make an appointment with me for Lady Penford on Thursday.'

Maggie Fowler lowered her eyes then raised them again. She looked boldly at Clara. 'I did. Apparently your assistant didn't tell you.'

Clara returned the gaze but kept her voice polite. 'My assistant said no such call was received. And with all due respect, Miss Fowler, I believe her. So can you tell me what really happened?'

Teddy chuckled. 'You've been rumbled, Maggie.'

Maggie flashed daggers at her step-cousin then her eyes flitted first to Lady Penford, then her uncle on the other side of the room.

'Well, Miss Vale, the truth is, Sir Bill found out that his wife was going to hire a detective and he asked me to delay contacting you. He was hoping to talk her out of it as – no offence – he did not want a hired private investigator poking around on such an important weekend, for what he considered just a trivial matter. But unfortunately he was unable to change her mind. She left for Newcastle before I could tell her that I had not in fact made an appointment.'

Clara's eyes narrowed. 'So you thought it better to try to lay the blame on Miss Cuddy.'

'I thought it better to follow my employer's instructions,' Maggie snapped back. But then her face softened. 'However, I apologise. I did not intend to get anyone into trouble. Please pass on my apologies to Miss Cuddy. You need to understand, though, that I was put in a difficult position . . .'

Clara did understand. And she appreciated that Maggie had confessed. She would not get very far in this investigation if she made an enemy on the first day.

She smiled indulgently. 'I do understand, Miss Fowler. And thank you for telling me what really happened. Such honesty is refreshing.' She reached out her hand as a peace offering. Maggie appraised it for a moment, then took it and shook it warmly.

'Thank you, Miss Vale.'

'Drat it all,' said Teddy, playfully. 'This is rather rum. I was hoping for more of a catfight.'

'Sorry to disappoint you,' said Maggie, tersely.

No love lost between these two, thought Clara, and filed the information away for future consideration.

An awkward silence fell between the three of them, and before Clara could decide how to get out of it, the dinner gong sounded.

'Saved by the gong!' laughed Teddy, then gestured in the direction of the dining room. 'After you, ladies.'

Chapter 9

The large banqueting table was set for fifteen: seven on either side and Sir Bill at the head, with the place at the foot of the table unset. To Sir Bill's right was Lady Penford and to his left, Lady Gertrude Fitzgilbert. Next to Lady Gertrude was Teddy and then Elsie Fitzgilbert, with Matt Fowler then Lily Fitzgilbert next to them. Lily's lips were pressed into a tight pout, making no bones about showing her displeasure that her sister was sitting next to the eligible Lord Edward Richner, Earl of Penford, and she was not. Clara could not help but think of the two ugly sisters from *Cinderella* vying for the attention of Prince Charming. Although Elsie and Lily were certainly not ugly – at least not on the outside. Who in this scenario was Cinderella, Clara wondered. Then noted with alarm an admiring look from Teddy in her direction. *Good grief no . . .*

The last two places on that side of the table were taken by Maggie Fowler and Lady Molly Trevelyan. Opposite Lady Molly was Baron Klaus von Schneider, who had slipped into an easy conversation with the Member of Parliament's wife as the soup course was served. Clara was next to Klaus, with his wife Ada to her left. Clara was pleased at her positioning as the von Schneiders were the two people she wanted to speak to next. She caught Lady Penford's eye and the meaning was clear: *be discreet.* To Ada's left was Sir Charles Trevelyan who was conversing enthusiastically with Kate, on his left, about various socialist causes. On Kate's far side was Viscount Archie Fitzgilbert who tried, unsuccessfully, to lure Kate's interest away from the Labour MP. Finally, next to Archie, was Lady Penford, who did her best to make up for her daughter's lack of interest in the wealthy, unmarried aristocrat. *Well*, thought Clara, *if you wanted to keep Kate away from political chatter you should have seated her elsewhere! Unless she had been, and Kate had deliberately ignored the seating plan?*

Well, whatever the case, Clara was glad that Kate had an alternative distraction to Archie's seedy romantic overtures.

Clara was just about to turn her attention to a subtle interrogation of Ada von Schneider when Lady Gertrude Fitzgilbert hailed her from across the table. So far, Clara had managed to avoid contact with the older woman, but she was now pinned with an imperious stare. 'So, Miss Vale, have you recovered from your trip to Egypt yet? I must say, our entire holiday was ruined. I'm trying to get our money back from Thomas Cook.'

'How was it ruined?' chirped Teddy, sitting next to her.

Elsie, beside him, gave a very unladylike snort.

Lady Gertrude turned to Teddy. 'Thanks to Miss Vale's efforts at amateur sleuthing, we were forced to stay in our hotel for three days while the police interviewed everyone. It totally ruined the holiday. We had to cancel our cruise up the Nile to Luxor!'

'Utterly ruined it,' said Elsie, scowling at Clara.

Clara cleared her throat, ready to reply, when Teddy said: 'I assume that was the mass murderer and international artefact-smuggling ring Miss Vale exposed. I read all about it in the papers. Jolly good job you did there, Miss Vale. I'm sure the families of the victims will be grateful for your efforts even if a few British tourists were inconvenienced for a day or two.'

'It was three whole days!' snapped Lady Gertrude, quivering with indignation.

'Well, it's hardly Miss Vale's fault, is it?'

Before Lady Gertrude could retort, Lady Penford interjected: 'Well we won't have to worry about any of that now. Miss Vale is not here tracking down international smuggling rings or mass murderers. She's having a well-deserved rest. Isn't that right, Miss Vale?'

'Yes,' said Clara, demurely, 'that's exactly what I'm doing. Rest and relaxation. Thank you for inviting me, Lady Penford. You have a delightful home.'

Teddy started to laugh but a withering look from his mother and a scowl from his stepfather quenched it.

Ada von Schneider smiled sympathetically, first at Teddy, then at Clara. 'So, Miss Vale, I believe you are originally from London . . .'

'That's correct,' said Clara, grateful for the distraction. 'My mother hails from these parts but I never visited here until August last year. I inherited my uncle's estate and relocated up north.' She smiled and gestured around her. 'And by "estate" I don't mean anything as grand as this, just a nice town house in Newcastle and a small business.'

'A detection business?'

'Indeed,' said Clara. 'But as Lady Penford has said, I'm not here on business.'

'I understand,' said Ada. 'Still, it's an unusual job for a woman.'

'It is,' said Clara. 'But it suits me very well.'

'Well, I'm very glad to hear that. I admire you young working women, you know. Let's be frank, any job for a woman of a certain social standing is unusual, isn't it? Take my cousin Kate for instance. She doesn't *have* to work – not for money – but she wants to. However, she also tells me that if she gets married she will have to give up her job as a teacher. That that is the law in your country. Is that why you are unmarried too?'

Clara was taken aback by Ada's blunt question. But the woman's grey eyes were curious, not confrontational.

Clara decided to not take offence and answered simply: 'Not at all. I own my own business. No one can tell me to resign. I am single simply because I choose to be.' She decided not to mention that someone had proposed to her earlier in the year – someone she was attracted to and very fond of – and that she had turned him down.

Ada smiled. 'A new breed of woman. A bachelorette, I believe you are now called. Better than a spinster!'

'Quite,' agreed Clara.

'But,' said Ada, lowering her voice so only she and Clara could hear, 'you have more freedom to make these decisions than Kate. She is second in line to all this. If anything happens to Teddy before he can produce an heir . . .'

Clara leaned forward. 'What do you mean? What might happen to Teddy?'

'Well,' said Ada, casting a sympathetic glance towards her young cousin. 'I'm sure you've heard of his difficulties.'

'I have,' said Clara.

Ada shook her head, sadly. 'Then you'll be aware too that there have been a couple of attempts to take his own life.'

Clara had not been aware of that, but she just nodded, encouraging Ada to go on.

The German woman continued speaking, her voice still conspiratorially low, muffled by the hubbub of general dinner conversation to left and right. 'I have asked Justina more than once to let him come live with us in Germany. We have doctors there. Doctors of the mind. Who, if you don't mind me saying so, Miss Vale, are far more advanced in their techniques than your doctors here.'

Clara understood what she was saying. German psychiatry was renowned throughout the world.

'Have you asked Teddy if he would like to go?'

Ada lowered her eyes then raised them again. 'I'm afraid Teddy's wishes are rarely taken into consideration. It frustrates me immensely, and I know his father would treat him very differently if he were alive.'

Clara scanned the table, ensuring that no one was listening, then asked, 'How well did you know his father?'

'Oh, very well indeed. We grew up together. Our fathers were brothers. Otto was my elder cousin. So Teddy and Kate are actually my second cousins.' She bestowed a maternal glance on Teddy who was gamely trying to look interested in whatever Elsie Fitzgilbert was telling him. Then Ada turned back to Clara and sighed. 'I see a lot of Otto in Teddy. For good and for ill.'

'What do you mean?'

Ada shrugged. 'Let's just say some of Teddy's difficulties are in the blood, if you catch my meaning. I don't know if you know this, but Teddy is also heir to his father's titles in Germany. He could move there and be Baron Edward von Richner. He could, with help from the doctors I know, live a healthy and happy life. If only his mother would let him go.'

'Why doesn't she?'

Ada paused for a moment as a footman took her soup plate away, then resumed. 'Because for Justina, carrying on the Penford name, not the von Richner name, is the most important thing in the world.'

Clara waited for her own soup plate to be removed and took a sip of white wine. What Ada was telling her was all very interesting, but it was not getting her any closer to finding out who sent the blackmail note to Lady Penford. So as the fish dish arrived, Clara decided to risk the wrath of her client and ask Ada a direct question. If Teddy was to be believed – and why shouldn't he be on this point? – the family, including the von Schneiders, all knew about the note and why she, Clara, was really there. She considered how to phrase her question and then said: 'Do you have any idea of who might want to upset Lady Penford? Who might want to do it anonymously?'

Ada's eyes narrowed. 'You're talking about the note.'

'I'm not at liberty to say . . .'

Ada tutted. 'Oh for heaven's sake, Miss Vale, this is a silly game. But I understand you are in a predicament. So, to answer your question: yes, I can think of quite a few people who might want to upset Justina. And most of them are at this table.'

Clara sighed, inwardly, and took another sip of wine. Well, that didn't narrow things down much. She thought of asking about the typewriter but felt that would be a bit too overt. Instead, her eye caught the floral display on the sideboard. It was a medley of summer flowers, and among them were cornflowers.

Clara waited until her fish was nearly finished and then asked, as casually as she could: 'Do you know why cornflowers are so important to Lady Penford?'

Ada's eyes widened. Her hands shook slightly as she put down her fish knife. 'Why do you ask about cornflowers, Miss Vale? Does this have something to do with the note?'

'It does,' said Clara. 'But unfortunately I cannot tell you more than that. Other than that Lady Penford told me they were her favourite flower and that her husband – the late Baron von Richner – used to pick them for her.'

'So she told you they symbolised Otto's love for her.'

Clara shrugged. 'I suppose that was the implication.'

Ada sniffed. 'Well, Miss Vale, all I can say is that you should not take that at face value.'

'Meaning?'

'Meaning,' said Ada, casting a glance at Lady Penford to ensure she was not listening, 'that during the war, when Otto was in exile in Germany, desperate to come home, he sent Justina dried cornflowers – as a reminder of their love. And also, after the death of their first son, as a reminder of their mutual loss. I don't know if you're aware, Miss Vale, but in Germany the cornflower is symbolic of loss in war just like the poppy is here in England. But Otto's sensitivity was lost on Justina. Her letters to him in reply were cold and terse. As the years passed, Otto feared her love for him was waning. His despair deepened. Until, well, the death of his second son was the final straw . . .' She smiled sadly and picked up her fish knife again. 'And that, Miss Vale, is all I am at liberty to say.'

Chapter 10

Sunday 10th August 1930

It had been a hot, humid night and Bella and Gretchen had kept the window to their small bedroom open to cool the air. Bella, who didn't sleep well in new surroundings, had finally fallen asleep well after midnight, only to be awakened at dawn by urgent voices from the stable yard.

'Fetch the master!' said a male voice. 'There's a dead body in the beech wood.'

Bella sat bolt upright. After assuring herself she wasn't dreaming, she checked her watch and saw it was five o'clock. The German maid was sleeping soundly in the next bed, so as quietly as possible Bella clambered up onto her own bed and stood on tiptoes, trying to see out of the window. In the dim dawn light she was able to discern a collection of boots, slippers and the paws of a dog on the cobbles of the stable yard.

'Should I call the doctor?' asked another voice in reply.

'Too late for that. The fellow's dead. Though I suppose we'll need a doctor for confirmation. But let's see what the master says first. He might not want anyone to know. Jump to it, man. Wake him up!'

Bella leaped out of bed and pulled on her clothes. If there was a dead body to be found, Miss Vale would want to know!

Bella made her way up the back staircase to Miss Vale's room. As she stepped onto the landing she saw a man rushing up the main staircase to the third floor which, she assumed, housed Sir Bill's bedroom. If she could rouse Miss Vale quickly, they might just have the jump on him!

Fortunately, Miss Vale was a light sleeper, and it didn't take much to rouse her. After a few seconds of confusion where Bella had to repeat her news that there was a dead body in the beech wood, Miss Vale was wide awake and pulling on her clothes. Then she and Bella peeked out the window and saw the groundsman who had met them at the gate yesterday anxiously pacing in the stable yard while a springer spaniel circled around him. The fellow was carrying a shotgun and Bella wondered if he had shot the person in the wood. A trespasser, perhaps? A poacher? Hopefully they would soon find out.

As the two women left the room, Miss Vale grabbed her camera satchel. 'I might be able to get some snaps.'

Let's hope we don't get shot in the process, thought Bella, and considered for a moment if they were doing the right thing. But what was the alternative? Pretend she hadn't heard what she'd heard? Wait for the news to be announced to the household? Assuming it even would be . . . what had the man in the stable yard said? *He might not want anyone to know . . .*

'Let's hurry, Miss Vale. Before they try to hide what's happened.'

Clara and Bella reached the kitchen only to hear that someone was inside. Perhaps the cook or scullery maid lighting the fires. There was no way they could go through without alerting attention. And besides, the groundsman was still waiting at the kitchen door. They heard male voices at the end of the corridor – Sir Bill and someone else.

'Quick, this way!' said Bella and led Clara away from the kitchen. They slipped out of the corridor and into what looked like a serving room.

'In there!' directed Bella, pointing to a dumb waiter. 'This will take us up to the breakfast room. I had a little nose around last night.'

Clara's eyes lit up. 'Yes! There's a French window there. Good idea, Bella.'

Clara went first, cramming herself into the small lift, and Bella pressed the button. Fortunately, the system was electrified and Bella didn't have to physically winch Clara up. A few minutes later Bella too unfolded herself from the dumb waiter and the two women were out the French window and onto the terrace. Clara then took over directions. Kate's tour of the grounds yesterday had helped her find her bearings and she led Bella towards the beech wood, using the topiary and shrubbery of the gardens for cover. As they rounded the tennis courts, they saw Sir Bill and two other men – the groundsman and Sir Bill's valet, Seymour – entering the beech wood with the springer spaniel running alongside.

'Let's follow but keep our distance,' whispered Clara, and the two women ran across the open stretch of lawn, wet with morning dew. By the time they reached the edge of the wood they could not see the men but could hear them. The overweight Sir Bill was huffing and puffing loudly. Clara and Bella quietly followed as the first rays of sun bathed the wood, accompanied by the joyful song of the morning chorus.

What a place to die, thought Clara, wondering who the unfortunate victim might be.

Voices carried through the wood.

'Good God!' said Sir Bill. 'What the hell happened to him?'

Clara and Bella reached the edge of a clearing, crouched down and watched, unobserved.

The three men gathered round the splayed body of a man, while the spaniel circled, sniffing and whimpering.

'I don't know, sir,' said the groundsman. 'This is how I found him when I was doing my morning rounds. Sammy here sniffed him out.'

The men were blocking Clara's view, but she could just make out that the corpse was dressed in what might be described as a working man's suit. He was lying on his back, his arms flung wide.

'He's taken a beating,' muttered Sir Bill's valet.

'To death?' asked Sir Bill.

'Hard to tell. We'll need to get the doctor to look at him.'

'Bloody bad timing,' said Sir Bill. 'What with the guests here.' He thrust his thumbs into his jacket pockets and looked around. 'Let's move him,' he said eventually. 'Get the motor, Seymour. If he's not found on the estate then we won't have to be bothered with it. He looks like he might just have been passing through anyway.'

The valet and the groundsman both looked startled. 'We can't do that, sir . . .' started the groundsman.

'We bloody well can if I say so! Get the car, man. Then get him off my land.'

Clara and Bella looked at each other in shock. Clara wondered whether she should step forward and stop the removal of the body. She had dealt with enough suspicious deaths to know that the police would need to investigate the area around the corpse to find clues. But before she could do anything, the springer spaniel started growling and ran towards them, barking.

The groundsman followed, his shotgun raised. 'Who's there? Show yourself.'

Clara and Bella rose and stepped forward, arms in the air.

'Don't shoot!' said Bella.

'Shut that bloody dog up!' shouted Sir Bill. 'What the deuce are you two doing here?'

The groundsman stepped forward and grabbed the dog by the collar. 'Hush, boy.'

Clara and Bella lowered their arms, Bella keeping a close eye on the shotgun. But the groundsman did not appear intent on using it.

Clara, realising they were in a pickle, decided deceit was the better part of valour and gasped. 'Good heavens, is that man dead?' She stepped towards the body.

Sir Bill blocked her path. 'I asked, Miss Vale, what you are doing here?'

Clara tensed, then relaxed as an alibi came to mind. 'We're taking in the morning air. I always rise early to exercise.' This was partially true. Clara did exercise in the mornings but never quite this early. 'What on earth has happened to the poor man?'

Sir Bill's eyes narrowed. Clara suspected he was wondering if she had heard his plan to move the body. She felt it best to pretend she had not. She did not want to antagonise him. 'Has anyone checked if he's alive?'

Sir Bill's valet – the large man Clara had seen in the stable yard confronting Teddy – snorted. 'He's as dead as a doornail, miss.'

Clara peered down at the dead man. His eyes stared lifelessly upwards, beyond the canopy of leaves. His face was bruised and scraped but not beaten to a pulp. He did not appear to have visible assault wounds – such as those caused by a gun or a knife – on his person. But he was lying on his back. If they turned him over, a wound might become visible.

'Yes, poor man,' said Clara eventually. 'Dead as a doornail. I expect you've called the doctor – and the police.'

Sir Bill cleared his throat. 'We've just found him, Miss Vale. I was about to head off to ring the authorities when you arrived.'

'Then let me not stop you,' said Clara, holding his gaze.

'Good God! The lad was right! There is a dead body in the woods!'

Clara and Sir Bill turned in unison to see Sir Charles Trevelyan and Baron Klaus von Schneider with their respective valets striding towards them.

'It's like Piccadilly bleedin' Circus!' muttered Bella as the four new men swelled the ranks of the crowd gathering around the corpse.

'Please! Gentlemen!' said Clara, her forensic instincts rising. 'Please stay back. We need to keep the area around the corpse as undisturbed as possible.'

Sir Bill growled. 'I would appreciate you not interfering here, Miss Vale.'

'Nonsense!' said Sir Charles. 'Miss Vale is the only one among us qualified to do so. Do as the lady says, Fowler – and you men there too – step back.'

The Penford Manor staff looked to Sir Bill for direction. Clara could see the blood rising in his neck. Sir Bill did not take well to his authority being questioned. But if there was one person here with the authority to do so it was the Member of Parliament for Newcastle.

Sir Bill, barely holding his temper, nodded brusquely. 'Miss Vale is right. Step back everyone. Foster, guard the perimeter of the woods, don't let anyone else in. Everyone else back to the house. I'll be calling the police.'

'Actually,' said Clara, chancing her luck, 'Bella and I will stay here. I have my camera and will take some photographs of the scene. The earlier we do this the better. For forensic purposes. I will then hand them over to the police.'

'You have a camera with you?' snorted Sir Bill. 'Do you always carry a camera when you are taking in the air for your morning exercise?'

Clara smiled benignly. 'Only when I'm in a place as beautiful as Penford Manor.'

Bella stifled a laugh.

'Good Lord!' said Sir Charles, peering at the body. 'That's Harry Stanley!'

'Do you know him?' asked Clara.

'I do! And so does Sir Bill. Isn't that right, Fowler?'

Clara turned to the landowner. 'You didn't say you knew who he was, Sir Bill.'

Sir Bill's eyes narrowed. 'I didn't say because I didn't know, Miss Vale. His face is all bashed up. Damned shame if it is Stanley though. Right everyone, back to the house. I'm calling the police.'

Chapter 11

By the time Clara and Bella finished photographing the body and the area around it, the sun was well and truly up. Clara, although tempted, did not touch the body, so was not able to examine it in any detail. There did not appear to be any blood on the ground around the body, so it was unlikely that the fellow had any stab or gunshot wounds in his back, but that would only be properly determined when he was turned over – and he could only be turned over once the police and the medical examiner arrived. However, on remote examination, it appeared to Clara that the man had been dead for at least half an hour before his body had been found. The blood on the welts on his face was already coagulating and drying. She knew that in a test tube, blood would coagulate at thirty minutes and thereafter start to dry out. The blood on the victim's face was very much dried. But the body had not yet started rigor mortis, which normally set in three hours after death. So, her rough estimate was that the man had died between three and half past four, with his body being discovered by the dog sometime before five. Assuming of course that what the groundsman said was true – that the man actually was dead when he found him.

The area around the body was well trampled by the seven men, two women and one dog that had surrounded the corpse, as was the route through the wood from the direction of the house. From what direction had the man come? It wasn't immediately obvious. Sir Bill had suggested he was just 'passing through'. But from where? And to where? Had he been coming to the house? And why was it that Sir Bill had not said he had recognised him? The face was not battered enough to be unrecognisable. And Sir Charles had easily identified him as someone he – and Sir Bill – both knew as Harry Stanley. Why would Sir Bill pretend he didn't know him? Clara had yet to find out who Harry Stanley was. All she could tell was that he was a man of around thirty-five who – apart from the obvious fact that he was dead – appeared in good physical condition, with a well-toned torso.

Clara was just packing away her camera when Bella called out: 'Miss Vale! Look here!'

Clara hurried over to where Bella was pointing. About ten feet from the body – on the side furthest from the house – was an expensive-looking silver cigarette lighter. It was not tarnished from the elements or covered in debris or dirt. It – like the body – appeared to have recently arrived there.

'Good work, Bella! Let me photograph that too. We'll have to leave it there, of course, but that looks like a very good clue to pass on to the police.'

Bella frowned. 'Aye, the police. They're not likely to let us join in the investigation, are they?'

Clara smiled at her assistant. 'Oh, they might. If they want me to hand over these photographs, they'll have to be very nice to us.'

'Or – like they did last year in York – threaten to throw you in gaol if you don't,' grumbled Bella.

Clara laughed. 'That's a possibility too.'

The Penford Manor family and guests were eating breakfast by the time Clara and Bella returned to the house. Bella would eat in the kitchen with the other servants. They both committed to finding out what they could about who knew what and comparing notes later. Clara entered the breakfast room with her camera satchel still slung over her shoulder. 'Hope you don't mind me coming straight in to eat,' said Clara to Lady Penford, 'but I'm famished.'

'Detection is hungry work!' quipped Teddy, his cheeks flushed with excitement. 'So what have you discovered, Miss Vale?' he asked as the butler pulled out a chair for Clara to sit.

'Oh, nothing much,' said Clara vaguely. 'I just took the opportunity to take some photographs while the scene was still fresh. It will save the police time. Scrambled eggs, bacon and toast please,' she instructed a footman hovering at her side.

Lady Gertrude Fitzgilbert scowled at Clara. 'I see you've done it again, Miss Vale. Spoiling everyone's holiday with one of your murders.'

Clara spluttered the orange juice she was attempting to sip. 'I beg your pardon, Lady Gertrude, but none of these are "my" murders. It is pure coincidence that this poor man was found dead while I am here. And besides, there is no evidence yet that it was murder. So far, all it is is an unexplained death.'

'Quite so,' said Sir Bill. 'Pure coincidence that he was on this estate too. He may simply have been passing through and then collapsed of a heart attack. Isn't that right, Miss Vale?'

'Well, that is certainly one possibility, Sir Bill,' said Clara, carefully, wondering again why he was so keen to jump to this conclusion and to obfuscate that he knew the man. 'We'll have to wait to see what the police and the medical examiner say. Are they coming?'

Sir Bill nodded. 'Yes, I called them as soon as I got back to the house. That was nearly an hour ago now. So they should be here within the next hour, at the latest.'

Everyone (who had them) looked at their watches.

Lady Penford gave a calm, assertive nod. 'Excellent. So, once they've spoken to everyone, I'm sure we can carry on our day as usual. There's an opportunity for riding or that mini tennis tournament Klaus and Ada have been planning. Don't worry, Lady Gertrude, this won't be a repeat of your Cairo ordeal. It's just an unfortunate incident, that's all.'

'Quite unfortunate for the dead man,' said Baron von Schneider.

Teddy sniggered.

Clara found Teddy's humour crass. Was it purely down to his quirky nature, or might there be something else going on? Why did he find this man's brutal death so amusing?

The baron frowned at Teddy then turned to the MP for Newcastle. 'Sir Charles, you seemed to know who he was.'

'Well, I can't say for sure,' said Sir Charles, 'I didn't get that close to him, but it very much looked like the trade unionist Harry Stanley. He's a Labour Party member and works on Sir Bill's mine near Newbiggin, I believe.' He addressed this first to Sir Bill and then Matt Fowler.

Matt paled. 'Harry Stanley? Oh my word! I hope you're wrong.'

'Newbiggin?' asked Clara, noting that it was the same place the blackmailer had mentioned in the note to Lady Penford. 'Might Mr Stanley have had reason to visit you here at the manor, Mr Fowler?'

Matt shook his head. 'Not at all. It's Sunday. He could very easily have come to my office on Monday if it was mine business.'

'And if it wasn't mine business?'

'Miss Vale,' said Lady Penford, coolly. 'I thought you said you were *not* investigating this case. Can we leave all of that to the police please and just get on with enjoying our weekend?'

Teddy started laughing. Then Kate stood suddenly, threw down her napkin and shouted: 'Stop it, Teddy! Stop it! None of this is funny at all. There is a dead man in our woods! Can't you act normally for once?' Then she burst into tears and ran out of the room.

Everyone sat in stunned silence until Maggie Fowler stood up and said quietly: 'Excuse me, I'll go and see to her.'

'Thank you, Maggie,' said Lady Penford. And when the secretary had left the room, she turned to the butler and said: 'More coffee, please, Spencer. And make it a strong cup.'

There was a knock on Clara's bedroom door. She opened it to find a maid, bobbing a curtsy. 'The police are here, Miss Vale. They want everyone to come to the drawing room please.' Clara, who had had a chance to bathe and change into her Chanel knickerbocker suit, felt refreshed and ready to share what she'd discovered – and photographed – with the officers. But when she arrived downstairs she was not prepared for who was waiting for her.

'Miss Vale! Now why am I not surprised you are here?'

Inspector Sandy Hawkes from Newcastle City Police stood beside a uniformed policeman who was introduced as Sergeant Wilcox from Ashington.

'Sergeant Wilcox thought he needed someone more experienced in murder cases,' said Inspector Hawkes, 'so he asked me to drive up.'

'But we don't know it's murder yet,' said Clara, sweetly, while trying to decide if she was annoyed or pleased at the sudden appearance of the Newcastle police detective. She liked the man personally, but professionally . . . well, he could be quite controlling and territorial.

Inspector Hawkes chuckled. 'Quite right, Miss Vale. We don't know yet if it's murder. But just in case it is, the sergeant thought he'd need some help.'

'Fortunately, we don't have many murders in these parts,' agreed Wilcox. 'And Inspector Hawkes here is very experienced. You'll be in good hands with him, ma'am.'

Inspector Hawkes' eyes twinkled. 'Miss Vale knows what good hands she's in.'

A snigger came from the direction of Teddy Richner.

Clara interjected, before the double entendre could be taken any further. 'What the inspector means is that we have worked together before on a murder case.'

'Ah yes!' said Sir Charles, raising a finger like Sherlock Holmes. 'The case of the murdered pantomime fairy godmothers. I read all about it in the *Chronicle*.'

'But this may very well *not* be a murder case,' stressed Clara, casting a conciliatory look towards Lady Penford and her husband.

'Quite, quite,' agreed Sir Bill.

'Well,' said Inspector Hawkes, 'we'll see what Dr Malone has to say about that. He's with the body now.'

'Dr Malone is here too?'

'Of course,' said Hawkes. 'He's the best man for the job, don't you think, Miss Vale?'

At last Clara smiled. 'Oh yes. I couldn't think of anyone better.'

Chapter 12

Clara was chuffed to be invited to return to the wood under the official sanction of Inspector Hawkes and Sergeant Wilcox. A far less chuffed Sir Bill Fowler was asked to remain in the house. 'Miss Vale knows what she's doing around a crime scene,' explained the inspector. 'We need as few people traipsing over potential evidence as possible.'

Sir Bill glowered, lit a pipe and sank into a leather armchair. 'Then I'll expect a full report when you return.'

'And I shall expect your full cooperation when I question you,' countered the inspector.

'I hope that won't take long, Inspector,' said Lady Penford, hovering in the doorway. 'We have other things to do, you know.'

'It will take as long as it takes,' retorted Hawkes.

Lady Penford gave Clara a pointed look. Clara sighed, inwardly. She could not be quite as dismissive with her client.

On the way across the lawn Clara explained to Hawkes what she and Bella had observed when they first found the body and how they'd managed to photograph the area. 'I'll need to get back to Newcastle to develop the prints today.' She didn't add that she had other photographs she needed to develop too. She realised that it might come back to bite her later, but she did not feel at liberty to tell Hawkes about the other case she was working on. Not until she knew there was a connection between it and the body in the wood. Was there a connection? Was the fact that Harry Stanley was from Newbiggin pertinent? She needed to find out.

Clara led the way to the clearing where the body lay. Kneeling beside it, wearing a pair of rubber gloves, was the auburn-haired Dr Charlie Malone, her late uncle's closest friend. Charlie had put on weight since Clara had last seen him – a bit of middle-aged spread – but the twinkling hazel eyes above his neat moustache were exactly the same.

He knelt back on his heels as he saw the four people approaching. 'Clara! Miss Cuddy! What are you doing here?'

'Charlie! Hello! A bit of a coincidence, really. Lady Penford invited me for the weekend and the opening of the grouse shooting next week. Mother and Father will be joining us later too.'

Charlie raised an eyebrow but didn't comment further. He knew that Clara wasn't close to her family. And that she didn't enjoy grouse shooting.

'Well, just your luck there's a dead body to keep you occupied. What ho? Is that a camera?'

Clara indicated her satchel. 'It is. I took some snaps of the body and the scene already.'

'Excellent.' Charlie smiled. 'That'll save us some time.'

'What have you found out?' Hawkes asked the pathologist.

Charlie nodded to the body. 'Thirty-five-year-old male, or thereabouts. Rigor mortis has set in to the limbs, so he died over three hours ago.'

Clara told the men that rigor mortis had *not* set in when she saw the body at around half past five. It was now eight o'clock. 'So working back from then, I estimate that he died around three o'clock.'

Charlie pursed his lips. 'Yes, that sounds plausible. Although rigor mortis can start in the face at two hours before spreading to the rest of the body by three hours. So, it's possible time of death could have been as late as four o'clock. I'll have to wait for the rigor to wear off and then open him up to find out more. But what I can tell you – on first glance – is that he didn't die on this spot. I believe he was moved here.'

'On what evidence?' asked Hawkes.

'Look here.' Charlie indicated that Hawkes and Clara should kneel beside him, then he gave Clara a torch and a magnifying glass. 'Check his nostrils.'

Clara did as she was told and examined the dead man's nose. After a few moments she pulled back. 'Well, if I'm not mistaken there appears to be the residue of dried mucosal foam.'

'And what colour is it?' asked Charlie.

'Pinkish.'

'Good. Now look around his lips and chin. We can't open his mouth yet – due to rigor – but there is some external evidence.'

Clara did, then nodded. She could see what Charlie was getting at. 'Haemolysis.'

'I think so,' said Charlie. 'And now look down his neck a bit and onto his collar.'

Clara, with Hawkes and Wilcox looking over her shoulder, did so. 'It's dry pink mucus,' she confirmed.

'Meaning?' asked Hawkes.

'Meaning,' said Clara, 'that this man may have drowned. Haemolysis is what happens when blood vessels rupture. In drowning victims water mixes with mucus and forms a foam. If the victim has been submerged for fifteen minutes or more, then haemolysis will turn the foam pink. If for less than fifteen minutes, it is more likely to be white.'

Charlie smiled like a proud parent. 'I see you've been reading those pathology textbooks I gave you for your birthday.'

Clara nodded her affirmation.

'Well I'll be,' said Hawkes. He touched the man's legs, then his ankles, socks and shoes. 'But he's not wet. Could he have dried out by now? Assuming, from the rigor, and Miss Vale's observations earlier, that the time of death is in fact between three and four.'

Charlie shook his head. 'I'm not sure if he could have dried out completely. There's no sun or breeze here. He's been lying in the shadow of the woods. This is a heavy felt suit. You're more of an expert on fabrics than I am, Clara. You identified and dated the fabric used to wrap the body in your last case. Do you know anything about the drying time of felt?'

Clara bit her lip as she considered the question. 'Well,' she replied, 'in perfect drying conditions, a piece of felt could dry within a few hours. But, as you've pointed out, these are not perfect conditions. And this suit fabric looks like it's made up of at least two layers of felt, plus the lining. It could take up to twelve hours to dry through properly. Possibly longer. I would think if he had been submerged in water for any time, let's say at least fifteen minutes, considering the haemolysis, then the fabric would still be quite damp.'

'Just what I thought,' said Charlie, and felt around the collar and shoulders. 'You say the legs are dry, Inspector, but you haven't felt up here. It's still damp. Quite damp.'

Both Clara and Hawkes felt the damp shoulders.

'You're right!' said Hawkes. 'Which means?'

'Only his head and shoulders were under the water,' answered Clara.

'Exactly,' said Charlie. 'So that suggests this man did not fall into a body of water. If he had, he would be wet all over. That means someone else was involved. Someone who might have held his head under.'

'Murder?' asked Wilcox, with a tremor of excitement.

'Very possibly,' said Hawkes. 'Is there a pond or lake near here, Sergeant?'

Wilcox nodded. 'There's a duck pond about half a mile that way.'

'And there's a small pond in the walled garden,' added Clara. 'Much closer. Just beyond the wood.'

Hawkes grunted. 'Good. That'll give us somewhere to start. Wilcox, start searching those two locations. I'll head back to the house.'

'Oh,' said Clara, 'before you go, Bella found something that might be a very useful clue. Just over there.' She got to her feet and walked to where they had found the silver lighter. But it wasn't there. Instead, there were other items scattered around. A wallet, some loose change, a set of keys, a handkerchief.

Startled, she turned to Hawkes who had followed her. 'Inspector, these items were *not* here earlier. And the thing that was – a silver cigarette lighter – is gone.'

'Are you sure?'

'Certain. I took a photograph of it.'

'What does that mean?' asked Wilcox.

'It means, Sergeant, that someone was here after my assistant and I left. What time did you arrive on the scene, Dr Malone?'

'Around seven thirty. The groundsman showed me where to come.'

'And these items were scattered like this?'

Charlie nodded. 'Just like this. They look like they are the belongings of the dead man. I left them here for Hawkes to inspect. I just focused on the body.'

'Well,' said Clara, 'that means that between me leaving here around six o'clock, and half past seven when you arrived, someone has been through this man's pockets. And removed something from the crime scene.'

Hawkes growled. 'I think we're going to need more officers on this case.' He turned to Clara. 'Can you take some photographs of these items before I move them?'

'I can,' said Clara, and set to work.

Clara and Inspector Hawkes waited for Charlie Malone to drive off in his van – with the body in the back – before heading back to the manor. Clara would meet Charlie later at the mortuary in Newcastle after she'd developed her photographs. It was just over a half-hour's drive from Penford Manor to the city, so she would easily get there and back before her family arrived this evening.

'So, Miss Vale,' said Hawkes, as they walked back across the lawn, still damp with morning dew, 'who do you think might have interfered with the crime scene? Do you have an idea of who was where between you leaving the wood and Dr Malone arriving?'

Clara nodded. 'The most likely suspect is the groundsman. He was the one left to guard the wood and make sure no one got through. Either he didn't do a good job, or he's your man. I think his name's Foster.'

'I've already spoken to him once. He's the one who found the body.'

'That's right. His dog sniffed it out.'

'Righto,' said Hawkes. 'He'll be first on my list. Who else?'

Clara considered the quite extensive suspect list. 'Well, Baron von Schneider and his valet were there, and could have seen the lighter and come back to remove it. And also Sir Charles Trevelyan and his valet. Trevelyan was the one who identified the victim as Harry Stanley, the trade unionist.'

'Which the union card in his wallet confirms.'

'Oddly though, Sir Bill claimed he didn't recognise him,' said Clara. 'You might want to probe that a bit.'

'Did Sir Bill have a valet with him?'

'He did. A man called Seymour. There were seven men there. But all of them left while Bella and I were photographing the scene.'

'But any one of them could have returned.'

'Yes, but I'm not sure when. I went straight to breakfast when I got back and all the family members and guests were present.'

'And the staff?'

'Only the butler and two footmen. So it's possible that one of the valets – von Schneider's, Trevelyan's or Fowler's – could have gone to the wood while their masters were at breakfast. Or, one of the masters – or someone else – could have gone there after breakfast, before you arrived. I went to my room then had a bath, so there is at least half an hour or forty-five minutes before you arrived in which I didn't see who went where.'

'So it could have been anyone then.'

'Yes, it could have been,' agreed Clara. 'Including Teddy Richner.'

'Oh? Why do you say that?'

Clara shrugged. 'I don't know. I have nothing to link him to the scene, but his behaviour at breakfast was odd – he seemed to be amused by the man's death; he actually laughed! And, I've been told, he has a history of violence.'

Hawkes nodded. 'Yes, that's true. Charges have been laid against Lord Penford before. Assault charges. But they were dropped.'

'Conveniently,' observed Clara.

'But not surprisingly, considering his station and social connections.' Hawkes slowed their pace. They were approaching the house. 'Let's do a circuit around. There's more I want to ask before we go in.'

Clara agreed and the policeman and the private detective found a companionable pace as they joined a gravel path that circled the house. Clara was surprised at how relaxed she felt in Hawkes' presence. Despite what she'd feared when he first arrived – due to her previous experience of working with him – this time he appeared to *want* her to be involved. A professional respect had grown between them, and, she thought, pleasantly aware of his physical presence beside her, the suggestion of something else . . .

But before she could indulge this line of thinking, Hawkes cut in. 'Tell me how you heard there was a body in the wood?'

Clara told him the truth about Bella overhearing the groundsman in the stable yard.

'And Trevelyan and von Schneider?'

Clara shrugged. 'I'm not entirely sure. Sir Charles said something like "the lad was right". I suspect a kitchen lad or stable lad overheard the initial conversation and spread the word. But, here's the thing, I'm not sure the baron found out the same way. He and his valet were properly dressed when they arrived at the wood. Whereas Sir Charles and his valet looked like they'd just pulled something on over their pyjamas.'

'Suggesting?'

'Oh, it might suggest nothing at all. But I did note it. I wondered if it meant that Baron von Schneider had already been up and about.'

'It's not unusual for someone to be awake at five in the morning.'

'No,' said Clara, 'not if someone's got work to do. But the baron, as far as I know, is here on holiday. And if he did just want to have an early morning walk, why compel his valet to go with him?'

Hawkes chuckled. 'You have a suspicious mind, Miss Vale.'

Clara gave a brief smile. 'I expect you do too.'

'Indeed I do,' said Hawkes, pushing his black Homburg hat away from his forehead to reveal a fringe of strawberry-blond hair. 'So, tell me again why you are at Penford Manor?'

'Why, have you forgotten already?' Clara tried to keep her voice playful.

Hawkes stopped and turned to her. His handsome face was suddenly serious. 'My suspicious mind, Miss Vale, tells me you have not divulged the real reason you are here. Are you working on a case? Might it be connected in any way to the body in the wood?'

Clara sighed. It would be hard to deny this. But she had to protect her client's confidence. So she replied: 'Yes, I am working on a case. But I am not at liberty to tell you what it is. However, so far as I know it has nothing to do with the body in the wood. I promise you this, Inspector Hawkes, if I *do* discover a connection, I shall tell you. Fair enough?'

Hawkes furrowed his brow. 'If your case can shed light on my case I really need to know, Miss Vale.'

'And I shall tell you! But only if and when I see evidence they are connected. You can trust me on this.'

'Can I?' asked Hawkes, his blue eyes boring into hers. 'Can I really?'

Clara did not lower her eyes. 'Yes, you can. Dr Malone does.'

Hawkes pursed his lips. 'Yes, he does. And it's thanks to Malone's trust in you that I'm giving you the leeway I am.'

'Nothing to do with how I helped you catch a double murderer last Christmas?' asked Clara.

'Well, and that,' said Hawkes. His face and voice softened. 'But please, Miss Vale, don't make me regret trusting you. I'm going out on a limb here. My superiors would not approve of me allowing a civilian access to a murder investigation. It could cost me my job.'

'I understand,' she said. 'And I'll help you if I can. And so will Bella. She's staying downstairs with the servants. I'll let her know to tell you anything she might hear that could help with your case. And of course, you will soon have all my photographs . . .'

The French doors to the breakfast room were suddenly flung open. Lady Penford stood on the threshold, her face like thunder. 'Miss Vale. I would like a word please.'

'Ah, Lady Penford,' said Hawkes, uncowed by her domineering presence. 'Could you point me to your husband please? I'd also like a word.'

Lady Penford at least had the decency to offer her a cup of tea before giving her a dressing down.

'I would just like to remind you, Miss Vale, that you are here at my invitation and on my payroll. If that is going to be a problem, I suggest you finish your cup and leave immediately thereafter.'

Clara's hand held steady as she sipped her Earl Grey. 'It won't be a problem, Lady Penford. I can assure you that I have kept your confidence and Inspector Hawkes does not know anything of the nature of my work for you.'

Lady Penford took a moment to light a cigarette. Clara noted that it was *not* with the silver lighter she had seen that morning in the wood.

'Are you sure he knows nothing?'

'He knows I am working on a case, but I have not – and will not – divulge any details of that to him unless I am legally compelled to do so.'

Lady Penford exhaled and peered at Clara through the haze of smoke. 'And might you be legally compelled to do so?'

Clara put down her teacup carefully. She needed to manage her client's expectations. 'I may be, yes, if it is shown that the blackmailing case has some bearing on the murder case. But so far no connection has emerged.'

'*Murder?*' Lady Penford's eyes grew wide.

'Yes, I'm afraid there is evidence on the body to suggest that the man – who we think is called Harry Stanley – was murdered. Did you know Mr Stanley?'

'I did not. From what I heard at breakfast this morning he is a miner. I don't have anything to do with my husband's mines. Why are you questioning me about this?' She stabbed the cigarette in Clara's direction. 'This is my concern. Not just that you might divulge the detail of our arrangement to the police, but that you become distracted by a more exciting case and focus on that rather than the job you have been paid to do. So, Miss Vale, I need your assurance that you will continue investigating my case and identify the culprit before the Tuesday deadline. Are you able to give me that assurance?'

'I can assure you I will continue investigating your case, and I shall do my best to identify the culprit, but cannot guarantee it.'

Lady Penford pursed her lips. 'Well, I suppose that'll have to do. For now. What progress have you made?'

Not much, thought Clara, acknowledging to herself that the more exciting murder case *had* distracted her. But instead, she replied: 'I will be travelling through to Newcastle this morning to develop the photographs of the fingerprints. After that I may have more to tell you. I shall be leaving my assistant, Miss Cuddy, here, with instructions to continue the investigation in my absence. She is following up on a potential clue. If something comes of it, I shall tell you about it this evening.' She put down her cup. 'Thank you for the tea.'

Chapter 13

After all the ructions of the morning, the Penford Manor servants were finally sitting down to a late breakfast.

'They say the victim is Harry Stanley,' said Mrs Rogers, the cook, ladling some scrambled egg onto her plate. 'I knew him when he was a lad! Dreadful business. What do you think he was doing here, Mr Seymour?'

Sir Bill's valet put down his fork. 'I have no idea, Mrs Rogers. The master didn't recognise him at first. It was Sir Charles Trevelyan who put a name to him. I suppose he knows him from Labour Party circles.'

'Speaking of Sir Charles, is it true he and Lady Molly have left for Wallington?' asked Mrs Barnes, the housekeeper.

'I believe so,' said Mr Seymour. 'The inspector interviewed Sir Charles and his man then said they could go.'

'Good,' said Mrs Rogers. 'That's four less to feed.'

'They'll be replaced by another four this evening, remember,' said Mrs Barnes. 'Miss Vale's family. I expect Sir Randolph and Lady Vale will have *proper* servants?' This last was addressed to Bella.

'I have no idea,' replied Bella. 'I've never met them. Miss Clara Vale is my employer, not the London lot.'

Mrs Barnes smiled tightly. 'And will Miss Vale be returning this evening?'

'Aye, she will,' said Bella. 'She's just popped down to Newcastle for summit.'

'And that "summit" is?' asked Mrs Barnes, mimicking Bella's Geordie accent.

Bella's eyes narrowed. 'That's Miss Vale's business. No one else's.'

'Well, Miss Vale seems to have no problem making other people's business her own,' observed Mr Seymour, while buttering a slice of toast.

'Meaning?' snapped Bella.

'Meaning, she's got herself involved in the murder investigation despite both the master and mistress asking her not to.'

Bella glared at him and was just about to retort when a quiet voice asked: 'Is it true that Miss Vale is a private detective?' Everyone at the table turned in surprise to Miss Wren, Lady Katherine's maid, who had not spoken since Bella had arrived yesterday.

'It is,' said Bella, tempering her anger. 'But she didn't come to Penford Manor to do any detecting.'

Mrs Barnes raised a cynical eyebrow but didn't comment.

'But she is investigating the murder,' pressed Miss Wren.

'She just took some photographs, that's all,' said Bella. But not wanting to shut the conversation down entirely, she added: 'Tell me – Miss Wren, is it?'

'That's correct. Kitty Wren.'

Bella nodded. 'Well, Miss Wren, can you tell me if Lady Katherine's all right? I heard she became quite upset at breakfast.'

Miss Wren lowered her eyes behind her spectacles. 'Yes, she did,' she said quietly. 'And so am I. Someone has died and people were making jokes. The death of a man is nothing to joke about.'

'Quite right,' agreed Mrs Rogers. 'May God rest his soul. As I said, I knew Harry when he was a lad. His family will be heartbroken.'

'He has family?' asked Bella.

'No wife or bairns, fortunately, but he's got a couple of brothers – both miners – and his mam is still alive.'

'Do they live around here?'

'Newbiggin way. Not far. I expect Sergeant Wilcox will be telling them. Good man, that sergeant. He'll do it gently.'

Everyone at the table agreed.

Bella wondered for a moment if it was significant that Harry was from Newbiggin. Newbiggin had been mentioned in the blackmail note. However, she knew too that lots of people in the area were from 'Newbiggin way' – it was not unusual enough to link Harry to the blackmail, but it didn't un-link him either. She and Miss Vale would have to look deeper.

Suddenly there was a knock at the kitchen door. 'See who that is, please, Jenny,' ordered Mrs Rogers.

The kitchen maid did as she was bid and stepped aside to reveal the large frame of the groundsman, with his spaniel at his heels.

His face was fraught with worry. He took off his cap and clutched it to his chest. 'Sorry to bother you folk, but I need someone to look after the dog. And for one of the maids to be sent to me lodge.'

'Whatever's the matter, Mr Foster?' asked Mrs Rogers. 'You look like you've seen a ghost. Come in, man, and have a cup of tea.'

'That's very kind of you, Mrs Rogers, but I can't. The police are waiting for me. I need to go to the station with them.'

'What for?' asked Mr Seymour.

Foster shook his head in despair. 'They think I might be able to tell them something about the dead fella. But I know nowt. I swear. I'd better go with them, though.'

'They're arresting you?'

'No, Mr Seymour,' just questioning me. They've searched the cottage too. Looking for something. Turned the place upside down they have. Which is why I need a maid to tidy up when I'm gone. Can you send someone down, Mrs Barnes?'

'Of course, Mr Foster. I'll send a girl,' answered the housekeeper.

'And we'll look after the dog,' said Mrs Rogers, kindly.

'Thank you. In you go, lad.' The spaniel looked up at his master, awaiting instructions. 'In,' said Foster firmly. The dog came in and the groundsman shut the door behind him.

Everyone sat silently at the table while the dog whimpered at the door.

'Eeee, do you think he did it?' squeaked Jenny.

Mr Seymour scraped back his chair. 'I'd better go see the master.'

Bella left the Penford Manor staff to speculate on the guilt of the groundsman. She did not know the man and had nothing to add. But she did have some investigating to do. The house was quiet. The staff that were not in the kitchen were quietly going about their jobs, while the guests and the family all seemed to have retired to their rooms to recover from the early morning exertions and the subsequent questioning by the police. Bella quietly slipped up the back stairs and onto the first floor. Remembering her reconnaissance of the previous evening, she located Sir Bill's study. Making sure the coast was clear, she opened the door, relieved it wasn't locked.

She entered the wood-panelled room lined with shelves weighed down with ornaments carved from coal, polished Davey lamps and encyclopaedias of geology and industrial law. There was no typewriter on the desk. But a door to her left revealed a second, smaller room, with filing cabinets and a desk on which sat a bulky black cast-iron L. C. Smith typewriter. *Bingo!*

She slipped into what she assumed was the secretary's office, leaving the door between the two rooms slightly ajar. She approached the typewriter and examined the keys. She could not tell if there was a chip out of the 'e'. She took a sheet of paper from a neat pile and slotted it into the machine. Bella had attended a short secretarial course when she first joined Vale Investigations and had learned the basics of typing, so she knew how to wind the paper around the roller and position the carriage to start typing. Summoning up all her concentration and with her tongue firmly in the corner of her mouth she typed: `e e e my name is Bella e e e`. But just as she was about to wind the roller to check the line of type she heard male voices in the next room.

'Come in, Klaus. You too, Seymour, and close the door behind you.' It was Sir Bill's voice.

Bella fell to the floor and crawled under the desk, folding her tall frame into as small a space as possible. It was only then she realised the sheet of paper announcing 'my name is Bella' was still in the machine. *You daft lass!* She berated herself but dared not emerge from her hiding place. She just hoped that the men would not come into Miss Fowler's office.

The voices from the next room continued their conversation but did not sound like they were coming any closer to her hiding place. Bella held her breath.

'Seymour has just informed me the police have taken my groundsman in for questioning – without informing me first! I'll be sending my solicitor to get him out and then I'll be putting in a complaint to the superintendent about the lack of respect. But for now, we've got more things to worry about.'

'Such as?' asked Baron von Schneider.

Bella heard a long sigh and then: 'Foster will be able to tell them this is not the first time Harry Stanley has been to the estate.'

'It isn't?' asked the German man.

'No,' said Sir Bill. 'He came earlier this week. He arrived at the gatehouse and asked to speak to me. Foster wouldn't let him go any further. He called me and I went to the gatehouse to speak to the fella there.'

'What about?'

'He wanted to make a deal. That I guarantee not to lay off any more miners and in return he'd not tell the Coal Board about our plan.'

'*Our* plan?' von Schneider sounded incredulous. 'How the blazes did he know about *our* plan?'

Sir Bill gave a low growl. 'I don't know. But he knows.'

'*All of it?*'

'No. Fortunately not all of it. But enough to get us into real trouble if it came out. Enough to know that domestic and possibly international laws will be broken. How the hell a barely literate miner like him knows anything about international law, God knows, but he does. Did. And now he's dead.'

There was a sudden intake of breath and then: '*Gott im Himmel!* Tell me you didn't kill him to silence him, Bill.'

'I did not!' barked Sir Bill.

'Then how did he end up dead in your wood? Someone obviously beat the man. Who? Your groundsman?'

'You know as much as I do, Klaus.'

Bella heard a little snort. 'Somehow I doubt that, Bill. You say the police were searching the groundsman's house? What for?'

'He didn't say, did he, Seymour?'

'No, sir, he did not. I'm sorry I did not think to ask him.'

'Not to worry. I'll get the solicitor to do that.'

There was silence for a few moments and Bella imagined the three men's worried faces. What were they so worried about? As if reading her mind, Baron von Schneider eventually asked: 'Are you worried that the groundsman will tell the police about our plan?'

'Of course I'm worried!'

'But did he – the groundsman – know our plan? Did he hear you talking to this Stanley about it?'

'I don't think so,' said Sir Bill. 'But I am worried that the police will ask questions about why Stanley was here earlier this week. Why I didn't tell them about it. And what the hell he was doing here.'

'But if the groundsman doesn't know . . .'

'I can't say for certain he doesn't. We were in his cottage. He withdrew from the room we were in but he could have overheard. He didn't say if he did. But I would be very surprised if he did. Foster's a loyal man. A decent man. He's not the type to eavesdrop, is he, Seymour?'

'No, sir, he is not.'

'All right,' said the baron after a few moments. 'Let's say he didn't hear. Then all you have to worry about is why you didn't mention that Stanley came here before and that you had a conversation with him. That might put suspicion on you for his death, but it doesn't reveal our plan. We could still get through all this without any of that coming out.'

'Suspicion on me for his death?' spluttered Sir Bill. 'I had nothing to do with his death!'

'Calm down, Bill, I'm not saying you did. But the police will question you further on this. You'll eventually be cleared. But in the process, you need to be careful not to reveal our plan. The future of our mutual businesses depends on it.'

'I'm not a fool, man! Of course I won't. But I am worried that Stanley might have told someone else. That it will come out in the course of the investigation. And I am also worried about who actually did kill him. And why. I don't like all these unknowns, Klaus. And speaking of which, you still haven't told me why you were up and about early this morning. I expect the police want to know that too.'

'They do, and I have told them. I was taking a walk. I always rise early. And my man – loyal as he is – always accompanies me. He was my batman in the war. We've done this for years.'

'And that's your alibi?'

'I do not need an alibi. You on the other hand . . .'

'Oh shut up, Klaus. The question still remains then – who did it and why? And as long as the police are investigating that, even if it turns out not to be connected to our business at all, they are in danger of discovering what we are doing and they could – and probably will – report us to the relevant authorities.'

'That's exactly what I'm concerned about too,' said the baron. 'And not just the police. That Miss Vale worries me.'

Bella caught her breath and cocked her head to hear better.

'Do you know why she is here, Bill? The real reason?'

'Of course I know. I'm just playing along for Justina's sake.'

'As are we all. But do you know what was in that letter that upset her so much?'

Sir Bill let out a long sigh. 'I do not.'

There was a pause as the men ruminated. And then the baron broke the silence. 'She was asking Ada about cornflowers and their significance to Otto and Justina.'

'Really?' Sir Bill's voice chilled.

Bella shivered in response.

'I think you need to take your wife in hand, Bill. We don't want Miss Vale stumbling across our business plans by accident. You need to stop her.'

Suddenly, the telephone on Miss Fowler's desk rang, jolting through Bella's body. She heard someone stride into the room and pick up the receiver. 'Penford Manor. How may I help you?'

She made herself as small as possible, desperately hoping Sir Bill would not take a seat to continue the conversation. If he sat behind the desk her hiding place would be revealed.

'Hmm, hmm, all right,' said Sir Bill, thankfully still standing. 'I'll be there as soon as I can. But, Inspector, I must warn you, I am not happy with how you are conducting yourself, and I shall be having words with the superintendent . . . hmm, hmm . . . no, my man, it is *you* who needs to be careful. I'll see you in an hour.'

Bella heard the receiver click into the cradle. Her breathing juddered as she attempted to hold it in. She prayed Sir Bill would not hear her – or sit down and see her – or notice her typed name . . .

'What is it?' asked the baron. From his voice, he too was now in Miss Fowler's office.

'The police. They want me to come to the station.'

'You're going?' asked the baron.

'I don't really have a choice,' answered Bill.

'Then be careful, be very careful.'

'Of course I'll be careful! I'm not a bloody fool! Seymour, get the car.'

And with that all three men left Miss Fowler's office and Bella finally released her breath.

Chapter 14

Clara put the Lagonda into fourth gear and enjoyed the sensation as the powerful engine surged down the Great North Road. Since mediaeval times, this had been the main road between London and Edinburgh, running through Newcastle. Parts of it – particularly in northern Northumberland – were still no better than a coaching lane. But the stretch between the market town of Morpeth and Newcastle was well maintained and Clara would be home in around half an hour. Although it was a beautiful drive through open countryside, with fields of grazing sheep to either side, Clara's mind was otherwise occupied.

What an unexpected turn of events. Surely it could not be coincidence that a body was found in the woods while a blackmail plot was afoot. But until she had firm evidence linking the two she would not voice her suspicions out loud to anyone but Bella. She wished Lady Penford was more forthright with what she knew. But the fact that she wasn't reinforced Clara's suspicion that whatever secret the lady wanted to keep buried was very serious indeed. Serious enough to kill for?

Might Lady Penford have arranged for Harry Stanley to be killed? Might he have been the blackmailer? He was from Newbiggin-by-the-Sea: the very place where Lady Penford had been instructed to leave the fifty pounds at the lifeboat hut. But perhaps that too was just coincidence. Newbiggin was not far from Penford Manor. A quarter of an hour's drive at the most. A lot of people who lived in Newbiggin worked on Sir Bill's mines. But not all of them were trade unionists whose faces were known to the Labour MP for Newcastle. Did that have significance? Did this have something to do with labour relations and mine closures? And if so, what did that have to do with Lady Penford, who denied she knew anything about any of it? Clara needed to find out more about this Harry Stanley. But she also needed to tread very carefully – Inspector Hawkes would not want her freelancing in his investigation. For now, she was in his good books – she had the photographs he needed – and she had been invited to join Dr Malone at the autopsy. That was enough to keep her busy. For now.

Clara parked the Lagonda in the garage behind her four-storey Georgian town house. She was greeted on the doorstep by a meowing cat that weaved between her legs. 'Hello, Maryam. Is Juju not feeding you?' The young cat looked up at her with plaintive green eyes and meowed again.

'Oh, I think you're fibbing, you naughty cat. But let's go and see.'

Clara went to the kitchen to check that the cat flap she'd had installed in the back door when she'd first inherited the cat was fully operational. It was. And the water and food bowls – which her friend Juju had been tasked with filling – were amply supplied.

'You just want some attention, don't you?' She picked the cat up and stroked it while she waited for the kettle to boil. Finally, with her tea brewed and cat comforted, she headed downstairs to her basement laboratory. The cat padded behind her and made itself comfortable on her desk chair while Clara unpacked her camera and prepared to develop the photographs she'd taken at Penford Manor.

'Right,' she said to the watching cat, 'let's see what these reveal.'

An hour and a half later Clara had developed all the photographs and hung them up to dry on the washing line across the photographic darkroom next to her laboratory. She opened the door to let the cat in and sat stroking it in her arms as she contemplated the images. The fingerprint photos confirmed what she'd already suspected. Lady Penford's fingerprints were on the letter but not on the door of the sideboard. But the other prints – the thumb and forefinger – that were on the letter also appeared on the sideboard door. If she could find who the prints belonged to, she would be able to solve the case. She felt more optimistic about this than she had yesterday as she now had an idea of how she would be able to get the fingerprints of everyone in the house – if she could get Inspector Hawkes to agree. In the meantime, she would get Harry's fingerprints while attending his autopsy.

She then turned to the photographs of the crime scene in the wood. Three things caught her eye. The first was that there was no sign of dragging. If the corpse had been dragged from the place of death – which for now she was assuming was near a body of water – she'd expect striations on the woodland floor. Heel marks through the soil. Troughs through the twigs and leaves. There was nothing. This suggested that the body had been carried and deposited there. Which meant the person who deposited the body was strong enough to carry it on their own. Or that there was more than one person carrying the body between them. That was something she would suggest to Inspector Hawkes – carefully, of course, so as not to let him think she was telling him how to do his job. Hopefully he would spot it himself, without her having to point it out.

The next thing that caught her eye was the lighter. It was an expensive silver device in an art deco style, suggesting it was the property of a well-to-do person. Did this belong to the man – or one of the people – who had carried the body there? And why had it disappeared? Someone had returned to collect it, suggesting it could lead to their identity. But now she had a photograph of it, it could prove an important clue. This too she would give to Inspector Hawkes.

But it was the third photograph that really intrigued her. It was the one she had taken last, of the scattered belongings from the victim's pockets. It seemed likely that whoever had returned to the wood and retrieved the lighter after she and Bella had left had also turned out the victim's pockets. What had they been looking for? Why did they not do it earlier when they first dumped the body? And then, something caught her eye. She had not noticed it when she was in the wood as she had not examined the items in detail, but . . . was that a dried and pressed cornflower lying beside the wallet? She brushed the cat off her lap and got a magnifying glass. On closer examination it was definitely a cornflower. A dried and pressed cornflower. Cornflowers were meadow flowers. They did not grow in shady woodland. A shiver of excitement tingled through her. Had she just found a connection between the blackmail case and the murder?

Dr Charlie Malone's pathology lab was in the basement of the medical school opposite the city baths and gymnasium. Clara swam regularly at the baths and both she and Bella practised jiu-jitsu in the gymnasium once a week. In fact, that is where she had first met Bella. As it was a Sunday both the baths and the medical school were closed, but Clara knew that Charlie was expecting her and had left a back door open. Clara knew the way. It was not the first time she had participated in an autopsy with Charlie.

'Ah, Clara! You've returned from the wilds of Northumberland!' Charlie was wearing a lab coat and apron, already smeared with blood. He had not waited for her to begin the autopsy.

Harry Stanley was laid out on the porcelain table with only a strip of linen to protect his modesty. That too would be removed when necessary. Clara was not a prude.

A cruciform incision had been made on his torso but Charlie had not yet splayed the rib cage to examine the heart and lungs. Clara plucked a lab coat and apron from a peg and pulled on some surgical gloves.

'Not wasting any time here, Charlie.'

Charlie shrugged. 'Sorry. But I wasn't sure what time you'd arrive. Hawkes needs these results as soon as possible.'

Clara nodded her understanding. They both knew it was a courtesy that she'd been invited at all. 'I see rigor mortis is well set.'

'Yes. It'll be at least another twelve hours before it wears off. But I can't wait until then. So I've broken the jaw to look down his throat.'

Harry Stanley's jaw was lolling to the side like a ventriloquist's dummy.

'What did you find?' asked Clara.

Charlie passed her a torch. 'Have a look for yourself.'

Clara gently pulled the jaw open and peered inside the mouth and down the throat. It was filled with pink foam. The foam that had dried in the nasal tract was far fresher in the mouth. 'Does this come up from the lungs?' she asked.

'It does. This reinforces the drowning hypothesis. And when I get into the lungs I expect to see more. Plus, other signs which I'll point out when we get there. But before I open him up, there's something else I want you to see. Have a look at the back of the head. I'll hold him up.'

Charlie pulled the corpse partially onto its side so Clara could see the back. She could now see that there were no bullet or blade wounds on his back – confirming what she suspected this morning. But what she could see was the back of the skull which was swollen and bloodied.

'If you examine that wound,' said Charlie, nodding to the head, 'you'll see there's a haematoma on the basilar occipital bone.'

'Blunt force trauma?' asked Clara after a brief examination, noting the bone was bruised but not crushed.

'Yes,' agreed Charlie. 'And it looks as if it occurred while he was still alive.'

'Hmm,' said Clara. 'When did he suffer those bruises to the face?'

'I think before the bash to the head. There are bruises on his knuckles too.'

'Suggesting a fight?'

'Yes. But not long before the bash. Which came from behind.'

'Right, so it looks like the timeline was: Harry gets into a fight, he is bashed on the head either during or soon after, and then he is drowned.'

'That's my hypothesis. I will have to open his skull to confirm but a wound like that is not likely fatal. However, entry of water into the respiratory tract and the closing of the airway, causing suffocation resulting in asphyxiation, is.'

'So he either fell into the water and drowned after being bashed on the head or he was held underwater to finish him off,' she postulated.

Charlie grunted. 'My money is on the latter, because—'

'Because,' interrupted Clara, 'there is bruising around the back of the neck, suggesting finger and thumb marks. Yes, I see that.'

'Exactly what I was going to say,' said Charlie, nodding his approval. He lowered the corpse onto its back. 'Right, let's open him up. Pass the saw please, Clara.'

Once the chest cavity was exposed Charlie turned his attention to the lungs. Apart from the predicted pink foam there were additional fluid-filled bubbles, which, when incised, oozed a black liquid.

'What's that?' asked Clara.

'The bubbles are called *oedema aquosum* – definite signs of drowning – and see there,' he said, pointing to some black patches on the lower lobes of the lungs, 'those are called Paltauf's spots, named after the Austrian pathologist who first identified them. They're caused by bleeding due to increased pressure during asphyxiation. Oh, hello, hello, what's this?' He leaned forward with his scalpel. 'Pass me a petri dish, Clara.'

She did as she was bid and Charlie scraped some green-tinged material into the dish. 'How's your botany?'

'Not bad,' she said, having done three terms of it at Oxford as part of her degree.

'Good. Have a look at that under the microscope and see if you can identify it.'

'Plant matter?' she asked, peering at the green gunk.

'Yes, I think so. Aspirated during the drowning process. It's quite common. I once had a drowning patient who had traces of seaweed in her lungs. See what this is. It could help us identify the location of his demise.'

Clara took the petri dish to the laboratory microscope while Charlie completed his examination of the corpse.

She placed some of the sludge onto a slide and slipped it under the microscope, then twirled the wheels and dials until she achieved the correct magnification.

'Interesting,' she said, after a while.

'What have you found?' he asked, coming over to her desk.

She continued to peer through the eyepiece. 'I think the green stuff is muskweed – common in any freshwater pond – but there's something else here. A bit of yellow vegetation. It looks very much like a flower petal – very possibly iris. See those topographical ridges—' she stepped back so he could view it himself '—those are quite indicative.'

Charlie looked up at his mentee, nodding his approval. 'I think you're onto something. Hold on.'

He walked to a bookshelf and took down a textbook on botany. He ran his finger down the index and then turned to the page he was looking for. 'And you're right!' he announced, pointing to a photograph of a lantern slide of a microscopic image. 'That is indeed an iris petal.'

Clara smiled. 'It is. And I think I know exactly where it came from.'

Chapter 15

After taking Harry's fingerprints, which, frustratingly, didn't match the ones on the envelope, Clara left Charlie to write up his report. She also left copies of the photographs she had developed to pass on to Inspector Hawkes. She had spoken to the inspector on the telephone, after Charlie had given him a verbal report of the autopsy, and told him about the iris and where she believed it had come from. He said he would meet her at Penford Manor tomorrow morning where they could discuss it further. This afternoon he would be bringing the victim's mother down to Newcastle to view and identify the body. Clara would have liked to have stayed for that, but she had no legitimate excuse to do so, and besides, she had promised to get back to Penford Manor in good time for dinner.

It was approaching five o'clock when she turned the Lagonda off the Great North Road and onto the country lane that led to Penford Manor. But as she rounded the first bend in second gear, a motorcycle hurtled towards her at speed – on the wrong side of the road! She slammed on the brakes and veered to the right, but it was too late and the Lagonda's front left wing clipped the cycle. Clara screamed as the machine somersaulted into the air and smashed onto the bonnet before crashing back onto the road.

The Lagonda came to a stop. Clara peered through the windscreen but could not see the rider. She leaped out of the car and rushed to where the cycle lay – on top of a man.

'Are you all right?' she asked.

The man groaned.

Thank God he's alive!

Clara fell to her knees and came face to face with Teddy Richner. 'Teddy! Are you hurt?'

Frantic eyes focused on hers. 'C-Clara?'

'Are you all right, Teddy?'

'I-I don't know . . .'

Clara assessed the situation. 'Let me get this thing off you and then we'll see what shape you're in.'

She braced herself then heaved the cycle off Teddy, dragging it a couple of feet away from him.

He started to stir.

'Don't move! I need to check if anything's broken.'

But Teddy sat up, pulling off his leather helmet and gingerly tilting his head from side to side. 'I think I'm all right. No pain. Just . . .' he breathed heavily '. . . winded.'

'Are you sure?'

'I think so. Let me get up.'

Clara reached out her hand and helped him to his feet. He stood, unsteadily, as Clara held onto his shoulder. Then he shook his arms and legs, one at a time – all seemed in good working order. 'See, right as rain.' He grinned.

'Oh, thank heavens for that!' But Clara's relief was quickly replaced by anger when she saw the large dent on her car's wing and bonnet.

'What the hell were you doing on the wrong side of the road? And what speed were you doing?'

Teddy ran his hand through his hair as he appraised the damage to the car. 'Golly, Miss Vale, I'm sorry. Of course I'll pay for the damage.'

'I damn well hope so!' Then she looked down at the mangled motorcycle.

'That's not going anywhere.'

Teddy sighed. 'No. See if the car starts.'

Clara climbed back in and started the engine. It ticked over without complaint. She stuck her head out the window. 'Seems all right.'

Teddy gave a relieved sigh. 'Glad to hear it. Can I catch a lift? I'll send some fellows back to collect the cycle.'

'All right,' said Clara, reluctantly. She was relieved that he was unscathed, but that did not diminish her fury.

'Thanks awfully,' said Teddy and then he dragged the wreck onto the verge. As he returned, he saw the look on her face.

'I-I-I can walk back. Might do me some good.'

'Oh, for goodness' sake,' said Clara, rolling her eyes. 'Just get in.'

Five minutes later and Clara and Teddy arrived at Penford Manor. Teddy was still agitated and overtly repentant. He offered to give Clara some money for the damage and pulled out his wallet from his pocket, dropping his handkerchief in the process. 'We'll sort that later,' said Clara. Teddy nodded, retrieved his handkerchief and, hands still shaking, put it and his wallet back in his pocket.

The damaged car immediately attracted the attention of various members of staff, including the chauffeur. Teddy arranged with him to send some men and a truck to pick up the motorcycle. 'And can you check over Miss Vale's motor? Fix what you can now. And then arrange for it to get to the panel beaters.'

Clara – who was still annoyed – did not appreciate the men making decisions without even consulting her. 'Excuse me, Teddy, but I'll decide when it goes to the panel beaters – and then send you the bill. But yes,' she said, turning to the chauffeur, who also appeared to be the estate mechanic, 'do fix what you can here. I can't have her off the road for long, though. I need wheels.'

'When do you need her by, miss?' asked the chauffeur.

'Tomorrow morning. Is that all right?'

'I'll try my best, miss. Let me get my tools.'

The butler, Spencer, greeted Clara at the front door. 'Good afternoon, Miss Vale. I see you have had some car trouble.'

'Actually,' said Clara, tersely, 'it was Lord Penford who had motorcycle trouble.'

'Ah, I see.' The butler's voice was as blank as his face. 'Your family has arrived, Miss Vale. They are resting after their train journey and say they shall see you at dinner.'

A stay of execution, thought Clara. *That's a relief.*

'However,' added Spencer (as if to say *don't relax too soon, missy!*), 'Lady Penford requests you pay her a visit at your earliest convenience.'

Clara smiled tightly. 'Thank you, Spencer. If you can let Lady Penford know I shall call on her in an hour. I too need to rest after my, how should I put it, my *run-in* with Lord Penford. Please send word to my maid, Cuddy, to attend to me. I require tea for two to be brought to my room. At once.'

Clara then turned on her heel and strode towards the stairs, rather impressed with her impersonation of a snooty blue blood. She would ordinarily not be so imperious towards servants – or anyone, really – but she knew that Spencer would, ironically, not respect her if she wasn't.

Fifteen minutes later, as Clara was lying on her bed with her shoes kicked off, there was a knock at the door. 'Come in,' called Clara and propped herself up against the pillows.

'I can't open the door, miss! I'm carrying a tray!' It was Bella's voice. She sounded mildly panicked.

Clara sighed then rolled off the bed and padded to the door in her stocking feet. She opened it to reveal Bella carrying a laden tea tray – including a plate of jam tarts.

'Oh, you wonderful woman!' said Clara, stepping aside to let Bella in. 'I could murder a cup of tea. Put it down there,' she said, indicating two armchairs and a small table. 'And pour yourself a cup too. I've got a lot to tell you!'

'Aye, miss,' said Bella. 'And so have I! You won't believe what I overheard this morning.'

A cup of tea and two jam tarts later, Clara and Bella finished sharing their respective news.

'Did Teddy say where he was going?' asked Bella.

'He didn't.'

'He does seem hell-bent on getting out of here, though, doesn't he, miss?'

'Yes, he does.'

'Do you think that's because he's got something to hide or is it just his normal loopy behaviour?'

Clara shrugged. 'It's hard to say without having known him before this weekend. Perhaps this *is* just normal for him – laughing at someone's death and then trying to leave the scene of a crime. But let's not forget that he tried to leave yesterday too, *before* Harry was killed. If he'd succeeded he wouldn't have been here to commit the murder. Still, if you'll pardon the pun, that doesn't put him entirely out of the woods. I wonder if he is connected with Harry Stanley in some way?'

'Aye, I wonder that too. But we *do* know that Sir Bill is connected with Harry, and that he quite likely lied when he said he didn't recognise him.'

Clara nodded enthusiastically. 'Oh yes! Excellent work, Bella. Not least for not getting caught! Did you have a chance to examine the sample type after all that?'

'Oh aye, miss, I did,' said Bella, and pulled a folded piece of paper out of her apron pocket. She smoothed it out and laid it flat on the table. 'Unfortunately,' she said, 'it looks like the "e" is intact.'

'Oh drat!'

'Aye, that's what I thought. But at least we know it wasn't typed there.'

'Have you asked the staff if there are any other typewriters around?'

'Aye, miss, I have. I told them you might want to borrow one to type some letters in your room. I was told that there's only the one in the house. So back to square one then.'

Clara smiled kindly at her assistant. 'Not at all, Bella. Thanks to your sterling work we have alternative avenues of enquiry. We now know that it's not just Lady Penford who has a secret, but Sir Bill and the baron too. And by their own admission, it's illegal. I would like to find out more about the current laws around coal production. Because that's what this all suggests. Something to do with the mine – and if the baron is involved, possibly with links to Germany too.'

Bella brushed the last of the pastry crumbs from her fingers. 'How will you do that, miss?'

Clara thought for a moment then said: 'I think a visit to Wallington Hall to speak to Sir Charles Trevelyan might prove useful. As a Labour MP he should know about these things. He also knew the victim, Harry Stanley. I think I'll take a drive over there after I've met with Inspector Hawkes in the morning.'

Bella nodded. 'Are you going to tell the inspector about the blackmail plot?'

Clara sat back in her chair and crossed her legs, her foot tick-tocking back and forth. 'I haven't decided yet. I will, eventually, but I feel that I need to be a bit further along in the investigation first. I'm fairly sure there is a link between the two, even though Harry's fingerprints weren't on the envelope. There was still that dried cornflower among his effects. Surely that's not a coincidence. Perhaps he just touched the edges of the envelope. Perhaps he wore gloves. Or perhaps he had nothing to do with the letter at all. There's still much to learn and I can't afford for Hawkes to shut our investigation down before I have more evidence to give to Lady Penford. And as you know, he could very well do that.'

'Aye, miss, he could.' Bella started to tidy the tea things on the tray. 'So what should I do now? With the investigation.'

Clara stacked the saucers on the tea plate and passed them to Bella. 'You said you were sharing a room with the von Schneider maid.'

'Aye, miss. Gretchen's her name. Seems like a canny enough lass for a foreigner.'

'How's her English?'

Bella laughed. 'Better than my German. All I know is *mein liebling*.'

Clara laughed too. She knew Bella was referring to a brief holiday romance she'd had with a German man earlier in the year. 'Well, best not call her that! But can you probe her for some information on the baron's business affairs? Subtly, of course.'

Bella grinned. 'Well, subtle's not me middle name – it's Grace – but I'll do me best, miss.'

Clara smiled. 'Your best is all I ask.'

Lady Penford's bedroom suite was a boudoir of art deco sophistication. Whereas elsewhere in the house the Egyptian influence – blended with urban modern – was dominant, in Lady Penford's private space the styling was influenced by Japanese art. Black lacquer furnishings with elliptical curves and wood lattice panels were softened by cherry blossom wallpaper. Clara was ushered beyond a silk room divider, hand-painted with scenes of idyllic Japanese life, into the lady's private sitting room. The maid, Parker, withdrew, and Clara waited for her host to emerge from the bedroom. A few moments later the black lacquer doors opened, and Lady Penford swanned through wearing an emerald-green and black kimono. Her platinum blonde hair was unpinned, hanging to her shoulders in soft waves. Clara was struck, once again, by her beauty. But it was a beauty with a very sharp edge. Clara needed to be careful.

'Ah, Miss Vale,' said Lady Penford, without sitting or suggesting her guest do the same. 'Forgive me but we need to keep this brief. I have to prepare for this evening. So tell me, was your trip to Newcastle fruitful? Have you made any progress?'

'I have,' said Clara, relieved it wasn't going to be a drawn-out interview. 'I developed the photographs of the prints and can confirm that the same prints appear on your letter and the sideboard. So if we can find out who that person is, we will have a likely suspect.'

Lady Penford nodded, coolly. 'And how do you propose to find that person?'

Clara was very relieved to tell her client that she had a plan. After explaining it, she said: 'You see, if I can get Inspector Hawkes to agree to fingerprint everyone as part of the investigation into the body in the wood – who, by the way, I have fingerprinted and he isn't a match – then that will deflect attention away from our investigation. No one – hopefully – will realise that they are actually being fingerprinted for their involvement in the blackmail plot. Also, Hawkes has the authority to compel people to comply. I don't.'

Lady Penford templed her fingers. 'I see. And do you think Inspector Hawkes will agree to this?'

'Oh yes,' said Clara, sounding far more certain than she actually was. And a few minutes later, as she closed the door to Lady Penford's suite, she wondered if she had just stepped out of the frying pan and into the fire.

Chapter 16

Clara descended the stairs for dinner, one hand on the banister to steady her descent. She was wearing a claret-coloured Charles Worth cocktail gown, from his 1927 collection, with brown velvet trim on the hem and shoulder straps, and gold embroidered gardenias running down one side. It was an old dress but one that always made her feel empowered. She had last worn it the previous summer when she had set a honey trap for a suspect in her first murder case. Naturally, she had not followed through on the seduction, but she had gone far enough for the gentleman to believe that he might be in with a chance. And then Clara snapped the trap shut, gathering the evidence she needed to clear or incriminate him.

Clara didn't expect to be doing any snapping this evening, but she hoped that the memories the dress evoked would strengthen her through what she feared would be a tortuous evening.

As she had done the previous evening, she scanned the room, noting who was talking to whom. Her eyes immediately fell on Teddy Richner in conversation with his step-cousins, Matt and Maggie Fowler. Teddy took out a cigarette and offered Matt one. Then Teddy reached into his pocket . . . not finding what he was looking for, he reached into another . . . then he said something to Matt who immediately produced a lighter.

Hello, hello? Are you looking for your lighter, Teddy? Hmmm . . .

'Clara, old girl! There you are! I was beginning to think rumours of your presence were a fiction!'

Clara was taken aback to see a rakishly dapper blond man – his hair slicked back with enough Brilliantine to tame the mane of a horse – waiting for her at the bottom of the stairs. 'Antony?' she asked, incredulously, 'what are you doing here?'

He grinned and stuck out his arm to assist her down the last step. 'Accompanying Mother and Father on their trip. Very last minute, and I had to shuffle a few appointments, but here I am! Lady Penford says she's got more than enough room for me. Game old girl, isn't she?'

Clara gave her brother a disapproving stare. 'Don't let her hear you call her that.'

Antony – who was known as Tony to his friends, but not to his sister – guffawed. 'Relax, Clara, I shan't embarrass you in front of your new friends. Although I must say I was surprised to hear you were here. You normally despise these sorts of gentrified soirées. What happened to your militant descent down the social ladder?'

Clara smiled tightly. 'Better than an undignified scramble up it. But let's not have a spat. Lady Penford invited me for some rest and relaxation. I accepted. There's nothing more to it.'

Antony gave her a teasing wink. 'So there's absolutely nothing to the rumour that you're being paid to be here.'

'Absolutely nothing. Speaking of being paid . . . how are your finances these days?'

Antony's eyes narrowed. Ordinarily he would have told his sister to mind her own business, but they both knew that since she had dug him out of a hole after the big financial crash in New York had hit his stockbroking business in London – leaving him with an inability to pay off eye-wateringly high gambling debts – she had a right to some kind of report back.

'The ship is steadying,' was his reply.

'And?' probed Clara.

'*And . . . I* won't be at your door with a begging bowl.'

'And Father?'

Antony glanced over to the dignified figure of Sir Randolph Vale, recognisable by his outdated Edwardian mutton chop sideburns, who was in earnest conversation with Sir Bill Fowler and Baron Klaus von Schneider. A fleeting look of worry came over Antony's face before he settled his features into their usual nonchalance. 'Oh, don't worry about him. He'll find a way.'

But Clara was worried. She lowered her voice. 'So, they're still in trouble then. Have they got a tenant for Running Brook?'

Antony nodded. 'They have. An American family will be taking over the estate for the next twelve months. Which is why the mater and pater are doing the rounds of these sorts of invitations for the summer. Otherwise, they'd have nowhere to holiday. But I fear . . .'

He paused, biting his lip.

'You fear what?'

'I fear they'll have to sell the entire estate – lock, stock and barrel. The house, the farmland, the grouse moors . . . *My* estate. *My* inheritance. We thought we could just sell off a portion of it for a housing development. But it looks like that, and the tenancy, won't be enough to clear all the debts. And there's also a gargantuan tax bill to pay.' He sighed and shrugged his shoulders in his impeccably cut tuxedo. 'There's not much more they can do, Clara. The house in Cornwall is already on the market . . . and, well . . . hopefully they'll still be able to hang on to the Kensington town house.'

'Oh dear . . .' Clara sighed too.

A moment of shared sadness fell between the siblings and then Antony brightened. 'However, there might be a surprising turn of fortune in the offing.'

'Oh?'

'Oh yes,' said Antony, tapping the side of his nose. 'I may have a plan.'

From past experience Clara knew her brother's plans could best be described as 'hare-brained' – while he thought of them as cunning and inspired. 'You're not going to do anything silly, are you?'

He threw back his head and laughed. 'Oh Clara, you are such a worry wart. No, it's nothing silly. But I'm not yet ready to tell you what it is. I need to see how the weekend goes first. Now, if you don't mind, would you introduce me to that charming bevy of ladies over there?'

Clara looked in the direction he was nodding and saw Lily and Elsie Fitzgilbert in conversation with Lady Kate Richner. And suddenly she had an inkling of what his plan might be.

'Oh Antony, you can't seriously be thinking . . .'

'Just introduce me,' he snapped. 'And please, keep your negativity to yourself. Not everyone is sworn to be a spinster like you for the rest of their life.'

Clara left Antony to weave his charm with the three unmarried ladies and wandered over to greet her mother, Lady Vanessa Vale, who was conversing with Lady Penford, Lady Fitzgilbert and Baroness von Schneider.

Clara greeted the ladies then gave her mother an obligatory kiss on the cheek. 'How was your journey up, Mother?'

Lady Vale sniffed. 'Not as first class as it should have been. The catering was shocking. If one pays for first class travel one expects first class service.'

Lady Penford nodded in agreement. 'Indeed one does.'

'I blame the Labour government,' contributed Lady Fitzgilbert. 'Socialism is a poison to society. Giving the lower classes airs and graces above their station.'

Baroness von Schneider looked as if she was just about to say something when Lady Vale peered at her daughter.

'Isn't that your sister's dress, my dear? The one she got from Paris?'

Clara's stomach clenched. She knew where this was going. 'It is,' she said breezily, hoping her mother would not go in for the kill. She hoped in vain.

'Oh. I see. I thought now that you are a woman of independent means you'd be able to buy your own clothes. New clothes.'

Clara opened her mouth to retort when the baroness interjected. 'And doesn't she look just divine in it, Vanessa? It's not everyone who can carry off a Charles Worth like your daughter can. And you should have seen her last night in that Chanel! She looked as if she'd just stepped off a Paris runway.'

'Chanel inspired,' clarified Clara, and gave the baroness a thankful smile.

'Well, it was certainly inspired!' The German woman smiled back.

'How is your little murder investigation going?' asked Lady Fitzgilbert, changing the subject completely, but not in a direction that was any less controversial. She frowned at Clara. 'I hope it will not get in the way of Lady Penford's splendid hospitality.'

Clara's mother gasped. '*Murder* investigation? Oh Clara! Not again!'

Lady Penford stiffened. 'We shall *not* discuss this any further. Suffice to say it has nothing to do with us, Vanessa. A local man – a *working-class* man – happened to die on our land. Sheer coincidence. Nothing more. And that is the last we are going to say about it.'

And then the dinner gong echoed through the manor.

Saved by the bell.

Bella and Gretchen Klopp were having a tot of sherry in the servants' sitting room. As guests at the manor who had no role to play in the upstairs evening's festivities beyond getting their ladies dressed, it was thought best they stay out of the way. For the rest of the servants, including the valets and lady's maids of the family, it was all hands on deck. They were rushing around, helping with food and drink, making sure Lady Penford's plans were meticulously followed from the temperature of the asparagus to the texture of the trout. The other guests' servants – the Fitzgilberts' and the Vales' – had withdrawn from the sitting room when Bella produced the decanter of sherry.

'We're not supposed to drink on duty,' admonished the Fitzgilbert maid.

'Aren't we?' said Bella. 'Who says?'

The maid looked at her as if she'd asked who says the sun rises every morning. '*Everyone* knows that!'

Bella shrugged. 'Just as well we're not on duty then.'

'We *are* on duty until our ladies and gentlemen are safely in bed tonight!'

Bella rolled her eyes.

This was the last straw for the disapproving maids and valets who promptly withdrew from the den of iniquity.

Fortunately, Gretchen did not have any such qualms – perhaps they did things differently in Germany – and she accepted a glass of sherry with thanks. By the second glass she had become quite chatty and Bella, who never lost her head to alcohol, deftly steered the conversation.

'I have heard that the baron is a very wealthy man. What exactly is his business?'

'Oh yes,' said Gretchen, leaning back and casually crossing her legs. 'They have huge wealth. But they used to be even more wealthy – going back many generations. My mother worked for the family during the war. They are aristocrats, like Lady Penford. Born to it.'

'Oh,' said Bella, her interest piqued. 'More wealthy, you say? Which means they have lost some of it?'

Gretchen shrugged. 'Some, yes. It has been difficult for all Germans since the war. The whole country is poorer. Thanks to Versailles.'

'Versailles?'

'The treaty.'

Bella gave a curious cock of the head. 'Sorry, Gretchen, I've not had much schooling. What is the treaty?'

Gretchen, lubricated by sherry, didn't take Bella's admission of ignorance as anything to be looked down upon, and helpfully explained about the treaty at the end of the Great War that saw Britain, America, France, Italy and Japan imposing severe restrictions on Germany so the losing country could not rebuild its economy and wage war again. 'So it's been very hard for us. And not fair at all.'

Bella nodded her understanding. 'That does sound very hard. So . . . the baron has been affected by this too?'

Gretchen downed the last of her sherry and gladly accepted a top-up. 'Oh yes. He owns steel factories. He used to supply steel for the military and the air force. But he's not allowed to do that now. Just – how do you say? – domestic? – yes, domestic goods. So automobile manufacturers make up most of his customers. But without the military his business has been cut in half. He and the baroness had to let some of the staff go. Fortunately—' she smiled '—the baroness values me and I am still here.'

Bella smiled at the woman. 'And I see why she would value you. She has brought you all the way to England. Do you come here often? Your English is so good.'

Gretchen flushed in appreciation. 'Thank you. I have worked very hard to improve it. We come here at least once a year.'

'At least? They must get on very well.'

Gretchen twisted her mouth in an ironic smirk. 'Not *that* well. The baroness and Lady Penford have some – how do you say? – bad blood. You will know that Lady Penford's late husband was the baroness's cousin – they were very close.'

Bella nodded. 'Yes, I had heard that. But I don't understand. If there is bad blood between the ladies why do they keep coming? Is there perhaps some other business? Between the baron and Sir Bill?'

Bella leaned forward, hoping to coax the information she needed from Gretchen. But before she could get an answer, the door to the sitting room opened and Baron von Schneider's valet entered. He quickly took in the situation, snapped something in German to Gretchen, and then gave a curt bow to Bella. 'It is time Miss Klopp left. She has duties to attend to. Come, Miss Klopp.'

Gretchen, flustered, put down her half-finished sherry and hurried out. As the door closed behind them, Bella reached over and downed the remaining liquid from the abandoned glass.

'Damn,' she said, then poured herself another tot.

Chapter 17

Monday 11th August 1930

After breakfast the next morning, Clara, dressed in her knickerbockers and boots, took a walk down to the duck pond. It was on the very edge of the Penford Manor estate and she considered the distance someone (singular or plural) might have had to walk carrying a body. It took her twenty minutes without a corpse over her shoulder. Then when she got to the pond, she knew immediately that this was not the place Harry Stanley had drowned: there was not a single yellow iris in sight. She wasted no more time, turned on her heel, and proceeded to the walled garden – her initial suspicion had been correct.

As per their arrangement, Inspector Sandy Hawkes was waiting for her at the mock Grecian temple. He sat on the bench where Clara and Kate had sat two days earlier, with his Homburg on the seat beside him and his wheat-coloured hair glinting in the sun. Clara wondered for a moment if Sandy was just a nickname or short for Alexander. She did not know the policeman well enough to ask.

'Miss Vale!' He stood as she approached him down the lavender-lined path. It was just after nine o'clock and the day was promising to be a warm one. Clara had her jacket over her shoulder but considered that she might have to change into a cool summer frock after her meeting. But the Grecian temple provided enough shade to keep her comfortable for now.

Clara, after the usual greetings, talked him through her findings from the previous day at the mortuary and explained that the duck pond did not have any yellow irises. She nodded to the lily pond in front of the temple: 'But there are plenty of irises here.'

Hawkes nodded. 'Yes, I had Sergeant Wilcox check this place – and the duck pond – yesterday morning after Dr Malone first suggested drowning. He said he couldn't see anything suspicious – drag marks or any discarded items. I looked too. But if it was here,' he said, indicating the stone pavement around the pond, 'there wouldn't be any drag marks. And it was too long after the incident for the paving to be wet.'

He got up and walked to the edge of the pond and then knelt down. He bobbed his head towards the water. 'Was there any bruising on the victim's knees?' he asked.

'No. I don't think so. But you will need to confirm that with Dr Malone.'

Hawkes lay down flat on his stomach and shuffled towards the pool. When his shoulders were over the edge he lowered his face to the water. It was clear his head would go under if he went any further.

'Perhaps we should be looking for bruising on the chest,' observed Clara.

'My thoughts exactly,' said Hawkes, clambering to his feet. 'Did you see any?'

Clara shook her head. 'His chest was already cut open when I got there.'

Hawkes grunted. 'I'll get on the blower to the good doctor. If we find that bruising, coupled with your identification of the iris petal in his lungs, I think we have a very plausible place of death.'

'Agreed.'

Hawkes brushed down his knees then indicated that they should take a seat on the bench together – they did, on opposite ends. He then picked up his briefcase and withdrew a sheaf of photographs which he placed on the bench between them. 'Thank you for these, Miss Vale. They have been most useful.' He flicked through the snaps until he came to the one of the lighter. 'This one in particular may prove to be pivotal.'

'Have you found the lighter yet?'

He shook his head. 'No. We searched the groundsman's house but it wasn't there. But it may still turn up . . . elsewhere.'

'Yes,' she said, and told Hawkes what she'd seen last night. 'Could Teddy have been looking for the missing silver lighter?'

'Hmm,' said Hawkes. 'It's possible. But if he had lost his lighter and then found it again in the wood, surely he would have had it to hand. Which suggests someone else is involved.'

Clara thought about the logic of this. 'Or he *has* got the lighter and was just giving us a show last night. He knows I'm watching him. He might have been trying to knock me off the scent.'

'Possibly,' said Hawkes, not looking entirely convinced.

'On the other hand,' continued Clara, 'you *could* be right. Perhaps I might be overly focused on linking Teddy to this because he laughed when he heard about the man's death. But as Bella pointed out, this might just be his normal behaviour.'

Hawkes agreed. 'Yes, we need to keep an open mind about this and not jump to conclusions. But neither should we discount Teddy. He could still be involved. As could any of them.'

'Very true.' Clara considered for a moment what Bella had told her of the conversation she'd overheard in the study, about what Sir Bill feared the groundsman might disclose. Should she tell Hawkes? If she did he would ask where she had heard it. She would have to tell him about Bella sneaking into the study. And he might then tell Sir Bill which in turn might result in her and Bella being turfed out of Penford Manor before they could complete the case they had been hired to solve. She decided to keep that information under her hat. For now.

Instead, she probed Hawkes further. 'Is the groundsman still under arrest?'

Hawkes straightened the pile of photographs. 'He was never under arrest. We just took him in for questioning. Sometimes the fear of being arrested causes a suspect to divulge information that could be helpful to the case. Or give us due cause to arrest him.'

'And did he?'

Hawkes gave an indulgent smile. 'You're awfully curious, Miss Vale.'

She laughed. 'And that's news to you?'

He chuckled. 'No, of course not. And you have been most helpful in this case. And I suppose it can't do any harm to tell you – without actually telling you what it is – that he *did* give us some useful information. Not to implicate himself but . . .' He trailed off.

'But to implicate someone else?' Clara leaned forward, hoping to coax Hawkes to tell her more.

'Possibly someone else. He told us something very interesting which we need to follow up. I can't say more.' He sat back and folded his arms across his chest.

'And is he still in custody?'

Hawkes shook his head. 'No. We released him this morning.'

Clara nodded, considering what to ask next. Hawkes did not appear to want to bring their conversation to a close either. She hoped for a moment that he just wanted to spend time with her, but she knew it was more than that. She wondered what information he was trying to get from her. She had worked with him before and knew he had a shrewd, transactional mind. He wouldn't be here unless he wanted something. He already had the photographs. The information about the iris petal was in Dr Malone's report. What else did he want?

Well, she wanted something from him too. Perhaps there was a deal to be made . . .

'Inspector . . .'

'Yes . . .' He matched her tone with a twinkle in his eyes.

'I have been only too happy to help you with your investigation, but it has taken some time away from my own.'

'Now,' he said, his voice slightly mocking, 'that would not be the case if the two investigations were linked . . . are they?'

Clara tilted her head to one side. 'I have not yet found any evidence to prove that they are.' That was not entirely true. The cornflower in Harry Stanley's wallet suggested there was a link. But it was still tenuous. And as Hawkes had not mentioned it – even though it was in one of the photographs on the bench between them – he did not appear to know its significance. So that too she would keep to herself. For now. 'However,' she continued 'there is something you could do to help me in my investigation. As I have helped you.'

He stretched his right arm along the back of the bench and leaned towards her. 'And what might that be?'

'You could fingerprint everyone in the house and on the estate.'

He threw back his head and laughed. 'And why should I do that? Fingerprint evidence is not part of this investigation. Whatever was used to bludgeon Harry has not been found. There are no prints at the scene of the crime or where the body was found. Wood, trees, grass, paving and water. None of these are printable. You know that, Miss Vale.'

She nodded. 'I do. But what about the lighter?'

'Which we don't yet have . . .'

'Or the wallet?'

'The wallet?' He paused and considered that a moment. 'That is a possibility. It was dropped on the ground after the body was first discovered. Someone would have touched it. Yes, that is a possibility. But it's a long shot. A very long shot.'

Clara conceded that it was. 'However,' she added, 'it is a shot. And it could be enough to justify getting everyone's prints.'

'Barely enough. Tell me, Miss Vale, why do you *really* want me to fingerprint everyone? It's not for my investigation, is it? It's for yours.'

'Yes it is,' she admitted. 'I said as much. This is to help me. I need those prints. But I cannot get them without raising suspicions. And I don't have any authority to request them. But you do.'

Hawkes leaned back and interlinked his fingers across his abdomen. 'Yes, I do. But I need something from you in return.'

Clara gave an involuntary huff. 'But I've already given you something. Quite a lot, actually.'

He turned his head to her, his body still facing forwards, his fingers still interlaced. 'You have not given me enough.'

They looked into one another's eyes, his blue, hers brown, each challenging the other.

'All right,' she said eventually. 'What do you want me to do?'

He opened his arms and spread them both along the back of the bench, his right hand now just a whisker from her shoulder. 'I would like you to accompany me to a dance next Saturday evening.'

'A *dance*?' Clara was incredulous. She had expected something to do with the case – his case or hers.

Hawkes smiled. 'Oh yes, a dance. The police summer ball, to be exact. At the Newcastle Assembly Rooms. I have no one to accompany me and I would be honoured if you would be my partner for the evening.'

'But I can't dance!'

He chuckled. 'Oh, I'm sure you'll manage a twirl or two. I'm a very good dancer. Just follow me and I'll lead you.'

'Well, I—'

His face became suddenly serious. 'I'm afraid it's the only way I'll agree to doing your fingerprints . . . Clara.' His voice softened as he spoke her name.

She caught her breath. Dare she go down this path? So soon after her last failed romance? But this was not a romance, she reminded herself. It was just a dance. Just one dance. 'Well, I *suppose* I could . . .'

'Excellent! Then it's a date.' He smiled at her again. 'And perhaps you could wear that beautiful wine-coloured dress you wore last night. The same one you wore last summer at the Royal Station Hotel.'

She blanched. 'How on *earth* do you know what I wore that night. Or last night, for that matter!'

'Oh, Miss Vale,' he whispered, 'I have eyes and ears everywhere.'

Chapter 18

'Are you really going to the dance with him?'

Bella sat in the armchair beside the window while Clara changed into a sage-green summer frock with white piping trim and a Peter Pan collar.

'I don't think I have much of a choice,' said Clara, buttoning up the broderie anglaise bodice. 'We need to get those fingerprints to wrap this case up. Unless we can do that another way, we're dependent on Inspector Hawkes' goodwill.'

Bella screwed up her nose. 'Aye, but what about when the case is finished? What will he expect from you then?'

Clara did up her final button and sat down opposite Bella. 'Well, then at least I'll be able to make a decision based on my personal rather than professional feelings. You're right, I do feel a little trapped into this, but hopefully by Saturday I'll be in a position to say yes or no to him because I want to, not because I have to.'

Bella shook her head. 'It just feels a bit . . . what's that word . . . manip–summit . . .'

'Manipulative,' clarified Clara. 'Yes, it is. And it's lost him a few points in my estimation. But still . . .'

Bella cocked her head to the side and smiled. 'So, he already had a few points then.'

Clara chuckled. 'Yes, he did.' She examined her hands then picked up a nail file to smooth out a chipped nail. 'Let's just say, Bella, that I'd be a lot more concerned if someone like Archie Fitzgilbert had asked me to a dance in return for a favour. There are worse things I could think of than an evening with Inspector Sandy Hawkes.'

Bella nodded. 'Aye, that's true. He's easy on the eye. Just make sure you do still have a choice in it.'

'Yes, Mother,' said Clara and smiled at her assistant. 'Right, we'd better get on. I'm going to pick up the car – hopefully it's all in one piece still – then head over to Wallington Hall to speak to Sir Charles Trevelyan about what you heard the baron and Sir Bill talking about yesterday. I've telephoned ahead and he's expecting me.'

'Can I come with you, miss?'

Clara gave a pitying pout. 'Sorry, Bella, but we need to double our efforts. The deadline on this blackmailing case is midnight tomorrow. We're running out of time. I need you to stay here and watch while everyone is fingerprinted. Inspector Hawkes has called in a team to do it later this morning. I want you to keep an eye on things. See if anyone is looking particularly nervous. Will anyone try to *not* have their prints taken? Staff or family. Watch and listen, please, Bella. And make sure that everyone who was here on Saturday night is accounted for. Particularly Teddy Richner. Meanwhile, I'll get Sir Charles and Lady Molly's prints when I'm there.'

Bella screwed up her nose. She clearly wasn't happy about being left behind, but she finally agreed. 'All right then. I'll do me best.'

Rogers, the chauffeur-cum-estate mechanic, handed Clara the keys to the Lagonda and pointed to the scraped paintwork on the bonnet and wing. 'Everything under there is working just fine, Miss Vale. Looks like it's just cosmetic damage. I've bashed out the metal best I can, but it'll need a proper job at the panel beaters to get it looking new again. She's a lovely girl and deserves to look her best.'

'Thank you,' said Clara. 'I'll take her in later in the week when I've got more time. For now I just need to know that she's mechanically sound.'

'Oh aye, miss, she is that.'

Clara thanked the fellow and climbed in the car, placing her satchel with her camera and fingerprinting kit in the passenger footwell. She started the vehicle, put it in reverse gear and was just about to swing out when someone waved her down. It was Lady Kate Richner. Clara wound down her window and smiled at the young woman. 'Morning, Kate! Can I help you?'

'Oh Clara, your maid told me you're heading to Wallington. I need to speak to Lady Molly about something. Do you mind if I catch a lift with you?'

Clara did mind, really – she was looking forward to getting away on her own to do a bit of thinking about the case. But she couldn't tell Kate that. 'Of course not. Hop in. Oh,' she said, suddenly. 'Have you had your prints taken yet?'

'Prints? Oh, yes! Fingerprints. Indeed, I have. I was one of the first. I can tell you though, not everyone is happy about it. Not one little bit! But that Inspector Hawkes is whipping them all into shape. He's a bit scary, isn't he?'

Clara laughed. 'He can be! But it's nothing to worry about. If no one from the house or estate was involved in the death – as your mother suggests – this is the quickest way to clear everyone, then you can all focus on the opening of the grouse season tomorrow. Just as your mother desires.'

Kate nodded. 'Yes, that's what the inspector said too. So should I hop in?'

Clara smiled. 'Of course. I'll enjoy the company.'

Wallington Hall was about a fifteen-minute drive to the west of Penford. Clara had to cross the Great North Road and then go through the suburban outskirts of Morpeth, but was soon driving through idyllic countryside and farmland, coloured by yellow gorse and white hawthorn. The single-track roads, edged with dry stone walls and avenues of Douglas fir, became hillier and each dip and valley was filled with tiny, picturesque hamlets of just a handful of stone cottages. For most of the way, Clara and Kate were stuck behind a post office van, travelling from bright red post box to bright red post box, delivering and collecting letters to and from even the most remote of homes.

Clara wondered again why the blackmailer had not just sent the letter by post. Yes, it would have located them in the vicinity of a particular post office, but if they'd sent it from, say, Ashington, they could be one of any of the thousands of people who lived in the mining town – not just three houses in a hamlet. But as it was, they had narrowed themselves down to someone who had physical access to Penford Manor – and that was a much smaller pool. In addition, it was delivered on Tuesday, before most of the expected guests had arrived. This narrowed the suspect list even further – but still not far enough. She sincerely hoped today's fingerprinting exercise would, if she could excuse the pun, point a clear finger at the culprit.

After discovering the dried cornflower in Harry Stanley's effects, she was working on the hypothesis that he was connected to the blackmailing – even if his prints weren't on the envelope. If that was the case, he couldn't have been working alone. Harry himself would not have had access to the house. Had he been liaising with his partner in crime when he was killed? Someone from the house who met him in the walled garden. Who might have been up and about at two o'clock on Sunday morning? *Hmmm*, she thought, *that's another line of enquiry for Bella. Had the staff seen or heard anyone slipping out? Which of the family members or guests were prone to middle-of-the-night walks?* She immediately considered Baron von Schneider. He had already admitted to Sir Bill that he went for very early morning walks – with his valet. Could they have met and killed Harry Stanley? It would have been easy enough for them to carry his body between them to the woods. But why would they do it? Why would they blackmail Lady Penford? And why do it on the very day they arrived? Surely that would draw undue attention to them. As Lady Penford had mentioned in her office in Newcastle, the von Schneiders would not be that silly. And what of their motive? It couldn't be money, could it? Fifty pounds would be mere pocket change for the wealthy baron. Although Bella had told her the German maid had said the family's finances and business had taken a dive during the decade after the war. But surely, they were not that desperate for cash?

No, the motive – if it was indeed the baron – must be something else. Could it simply be to instil fear in Lady Penford? To let her know that her secret – whatever it might be – was not safe? That someone had the power to humiliate and ruin her? But why would he do that? Perhaps he was doing it on behalf of someone else . . . his wife? The first evening Clara had sat next to Ada von Schneider, the German woman had made no secret of the fact that she disliked Lady Penford and was bitter about the way her cousin – the late Otto von Richner – had been treated. And the way Teddy was still being treated. Could that be the motive? Pure spite? Clara had only spent a few hours with the woman, but she did not think Ada was a spiteful character. Quite the opposite. She had been warm and kind, and supportive of Clara when her mother was critical about her dress. But appearances could be deceptive. She decided to probe Kate.

The young woman had been surprisingly quiet on the drive so far. After the cheery greeting in the stable yard, she had sunk back into the cloud of pensiveness that had hung over her since the discovery of the body in the wood. It didn't surprise Clara. From what she'd seen of Kate she was a sensitive, thoughtful woman – caring and compassionate.

'Penny for your thoughts?' asked Clara.

Kate turned her head and gave a wan smile. 'Sorry, I was just thinking about the poor fellow in the wood.'

'I thought you might be. Did you know him at all?'

Kate nodded. 'Vaguely. I've met him before. He came along to a few of my adult education classes at the mine. But I never spoke to him personally – beyond the usual greetings. He was just one of a dozen or so men who dipped in and out of the classes. In fact, that's what I want to talk to Lady Molly about. She and I take turns leading the group and we need to plan the curriculum to start again in September.'

'Do you know why he might have been in the Penford Manor wood in the early hours of the morning?'

Kate shook her head. 'No. Inspector Hawkes asked the same question. I'm afraid I have absolutely no idea. But it's a sad business for someone to die like that.' Tears welled and she turned her head away.

'Yes, it is sad,' agreed Clara. 'Should we change the subject?'

'Yes, thank you,' said Kate quietly.

Clara took a moment to shift into a lower gear to negotiate a hairpin bend. Then when the road straightened, she continued the conversation. 'You know I'm here to find out who might have sent that note to your mother?'

A faint smile drifted across Kate's face. 'You're being open about that now?'

Clara shrugged. 'The horse has already bolted. No use pretending anymore. So, if you don't mind, I wonder if you might help me with that.'

'You want me to help you with your detection work?'

'If you don't mind . . .'

'Not at all,' said Kate. 'It might take my mind off all the upset. It's all a little silly in comparison to the real crime that's taken place. A note that's got my mother in a tizz. It's hardly murder, is it?'

Clara's hands tightened on the steering wheel. She needed to be careful what she said. She didn't want to give Kate any indication that there actually might be a connection between the two crimes. 'Hardly,' she agreed, eventually. 'Righto, then. What can you tell me about Ada von Schneider and her relationship with your mother?'

Kate's head snapped towards Clara. 'You think Cousin Ada might have written the note?'

'I don't know,' said Clara honestly. 'I'm still investigating. But she hasn't hidden the fact that she feels animosity towards Justina. Saturday night at dinner she made that very clear. What can you tell me about that?'

Kate bit her lip. 'It's to do with my father. Ada and Daddy were cousins. He was ten years older than her, but they were very close. What did she say to you?'

'She said she was angry with your mother for not being more supportive of your father when he was exiled in Germany during the war. Is there anything else you can tell me about that?'

Kate sighed. 'Well, I suppose she's also told you that she thought Mother was having an affair? And that my father suspected the same. And that's one of the reasons he killed himself.'

'Good grief! No, she didn't say that!'

'Oh,' said Kate and started picking at a hangnail. 'Then I shouldn't have said.'

Clara's mind whirred. *Could this be the secret Lady Penford was so desperate to keep? But if Ada and her husband and Kate knew already then it was already an open secret. No, it has to be something else. But it's still very intriguing . . .*

'Don't worry,' said Clara, 'I'm sure I would have found out anyway. I was going to speak to Ada again. Did anyone else know? About the affair?'

'Well, it's not certain there was an affair. Just a suspicion. Then Mother and Bill waited another two years before they got married, to quash any rumours.'

Clara gasped. 'Hold on, Bill? Bill Fowler? They had an affair before they were married?'

Kate nodded and continued to pick at her nail. 'Yes. That's what we believe. He was always at the house. Apparently on mine business – his pits are on Penford land – but most people suspected there was more to it.'

'Most people? So, not such a secret then.'

Kate stopped picking. 'If you mean a secret worthy of blackmail, then no.'

Clara frowned. 'Blackmail? Why do you say that?'

Kate shrugged. 'The only thing my mother cares about – other than continuing the Penford name – is her reputation. And the only thing that would cause her to hire a detective to investigate an anonymous note is if it contained a threat to her reputation. So, it might not be blackmail – I'll admit that's a melodramatic scenario – but a threat to expose something about her. That would upset my mother – a lot.' She turned to Clara, her eyes shrewd. 'Am I close?'

Clara's knuckles tightened once more. 'I'm afraid I can't divulge that, Kate.'

'Hmm,' said Kate, thoughtfully. 'I think that's a yes, then.'

Before Clara could answer, the gates of Wallington Hall came into view. She wished she could turn the car around and continue her conversation with Kate Richner. But it was too late. A gatekeeper approached them and she was compelled to open her window and announce their arrival.

'Welcome Miss Vale – Lady Katherine – Sir Charles and Lady Molly are expecting you.'

Chapter 19

The grand hall of Wallington was very grand indeed. The central enclosed courtyard was surrounded by archways and pillars below a gallery, encircling the entire hall. The archways to the north and south were open, with corridors leading to the rest of the house, while the arches to the east and west were filled in with wall panels. But the most astounding thing that struck Clara was that every bit of wall, pillar and arch was painted with exquisite murals.

The murals depicted the history of Northumbria from the building of Hadrian's Wall during the Roman occupation, through the arrival of Christianity and the Viking raids right up to the industrial revolution in Victorian times. Lady Molly told her they were created in the middle of the last century by the famous pre-Raphaelite artist William Bell Scott, while the pillars were covered in botanical paintings by Lady Pauline Trevelyan and John Ruskin.

'What an utterly exquisite space! It must be the most exotic place I have ever taken fingerprints,' gushed Clara as she set up her kit on a table beside a grand piano.

'Well, it's the *only* place I've had my fingerprints taken,' said Lady Molly with a twinkle in her eye.

'Are you sure you don't mind?' asked Clara.

'Not at all. Sir Charles and I have nothing to hide and if it will help Inspector Hawkes find whoever killed that poor man then we're happy to oblige. Isn't that right, Charles?'

'Of course, my dear. And while I have had my fingerprints taken before I have never had it done by a lady detective. I believe it was fingerprinting that helped you solve the case of the picture house that burned down in Whitley Bay, Miss Vale.'

'That's correct, Sir Charles. That was my first case. Now, if you don't mind taking a seat there . . .'

Clara proceeded to ink and print the fingers of both the Trevelyans as well as the maid and valet who had accompanied them to Penford on Saturday night. When the job was complete, she asked if she might have a word with Sir Charles privately while Lady Molly and Kate withdrew to a drawing room to discuss their adult education curriculum.

Sir Charles led Clara to his study. When they were settled with him on one side of the desk and her on the other, he templed his fingers and leaned forward. 'How may I help you, Miss Vale? I must say I was intrigued when I received your telephone call this morning. Are you officially helping Inspector Hawkes with the case?'

Clara pursed her lips. 'Let's say semi-officially. I'm helping him with the fingerprints and I assisted Dr Malone at the autopsy. But I've not been formally contracted by the police if that's what you mean. However, if you'll oblige me, the real reason I'm here is because of my own case.'

'Ah, so it's true then. Rumours were swirling at Penford over the weekend that you were really there in your professional capacity.'

'Guilty as charged,' said Clara, wryly. 'But I'm still not at liberty to say what it is about.'

Sir Charles nodded. 'I understand. Client confidentiality.'

'That is correct. But . . .' she gave a rueful shrug '. . . I hope you will still be willing to answer a few questions even if I cannot tell you why I am asking them. And that you keep our conversation strictly to yourself – at least until my case is solved.' Clara held Sir Charles' gaze.

'I can do that,' said Sir Charles evenly. 'Go on.'

'Thank you.' Clara took out her notebook and pen. 'Well, firstly, do you know anything about regulations around coal production?'

Sir Charles raised an eyebrow. 'This is part of your investigation?'

'It is. What can you tell me?'

'Do you mind if I smoke?' asked Sir Charles.

'Not at all,' said Clara.

'Would you like one?'

'No thank you. But feel free to go ahead.'

Sir Charles nodded his thanks then lit up a cigarette, inhaling then exhaling a plume of smoke.

That suddenly reminded Clara of something. She reached into her bag and withdrew the photograph of the silver lighter that had been found in the wood – and had subsequently disappeared. 'Sorry,' she said, 'before we get on to my case, may I ask you something on behalf of Inspector Hawkes? He'll be showing people at Penford this photograph too. Do you recognise this lighter? Have you seen it before?'

Sir Charles leaned forward and examined the photograph. 'I can't say I do. No, sorry, I've never seen it before. Is it important?'

Clara nodded and put the photograph away. 'It might be. Thank you. Now, let's get back to coal production . . .'

Sir Charles nodded then leaned back in his chair, cigarette in hand. 'What you're asking about, Miss Vale, is the recent Coal Mines Act. It went through parliament earlier this year. It's quite complicated, but in short, what it does is control the production of coal at a national and regional level, so not too much or too little is produced. If too little, prices go up and the consumer suffers. If too much, prices go down and the industry suffers. The act also allows for the mine owners in a particular region to set quotas of how much each mine can produce to prevent unfair competition.'

'What kind of unfair competition?' asked Clara.

Sir Charles tapped his cigarette into an ash tray. 'Well, for instance, if one mine produced more coal and glutted the market so other mines in the area were not able to sell their coal. It's to do with making sure all mines have equal access to market. And, as a Labour member of parliament, this is my particular interest . . . that employment opportunities are spread equally around a region. It's to do with protecting as many jobs as possible. Of course, in the present economic climate with the turmoil in the stock markets, it's not possible to protect all jobs – far from it – but it's an attempt to shore up as many as we can.'

Clara nodded. 'I understand. And all the mines in an area have to agree to this?'

'They do. And they have. So far it's working well.'

'I see,' said Clara, tapping her pen against her notebook. 'Is it possible that one of the mines in this region could flout the new law and produce more coal than they should?'

Sir Charles shook his head. 'They could, but they wouldn't be able to sell it into the national market. The quota system wouldn't allow it and the other mine owners would prevent it.'

'Hmmm,' said Clara, mulling this over. 'Righto. So the domestic route would be monitored. What about internationally, could they sell extra coal on the international market?'

Sir Charles nodded. 'They can and they do. But again, there are quotas and it's monitored by the national Coal Board.'

'Officially monitored?'

'Of course.'

Clara raised an eyebrow. 'But what if they were to do it unofficially? To bypass the quotas?'

'Then that would be illegal and the mine in question could have its licence revoked.'

'I see,' said Clara. This was beginning to dovetail with the conversation Bella had overheard between Sir Bill and Baron von Schneider. 'So,' she continued, her pen tapping on the page, 'you're saying it's possible that exporting coal to a foreign country such as Germany *could* be against the law if it exceeded a certain threshold.'

'Germany?' asked Sir Charles, leaning forward. 'Oh, Miss Vale, Germany has a whole other level of complications! There are still restrictions in place from the war. Coal exports to Germany are even *more* tightly regulated – in order to restrict Germany's chance to re-arm again.'

'Do you think there's a chance that will happen? It's been twelve years since the war. Surely they won't do it a second time.'

Sir Charles sighed. 'I wish that were true, Miss Vale, I really do. But the signs are there that Germany might very well start re-arming again. And coal will be needed for that to happen.'

'Doesn't Germany have its own coal?'

Sir Charles nodded. 'It does. And the government of the Weimar Republic controls its production, import and export as much as we do, but . . . let's just say there are some vested interests in Germany – and in other countries – who will try to circumvent that in whatever way they can.' Sir Charles tapped out another tip of ash. 'Now, considering who was actually at Penford Manor this last weekend, your questions are raising many more questions. Is something going on with von Schneider and Fowler?'

Clara met his gaze. 'I honestly don't know.'

'But you suspect something.'

Clara nodded. 'I do. A suspicious conversation was overheard. But I need more evidence than that. Do you know anything about the baron's business interests?'

Sir Charles pursed his lips. 'Not intimately, but I believe his primary industry is steel. His family used to service the production of aircraft for the old German air force, but over the last decade, with restrictions on the building of military-grade aircraft, they have shifted to the domestic automobile market.'

'Hmmm,' said Clara, noting that this confirmed Bella's account. 'If I recall correctly, steel production requires an awful lot of coal. They use metallurgical coal – or coking coal – to heat the oxygen blast furnaces. And it takes around seventeen hundred pounds of coal to produce a single ton of steel.'

Sir Charles looked startled. 'That's correct, Miss Vale. I am most impressed.'

Clara wafted Sir Charles' praise – and errant smoke – away with her hand. 'Oh, no need to be. It's just basic chemistry. But let's bring this back to the baron and Sir Bill. Now, I'm just hypothesising here, but if Baron von Schneider intended to start producing steel for combat aviation again and was doing it – how does one put it – off the books, he would need a coal source that was off the books too.'

'That is an interesting hypothesis, Miss Vale. But that's all it is.'

Clara shrugged. 'Of course. There is no proof – as yet – other than an overheard conversation. But it's an intriguing theory, don't you think?'

'It certainly is,' said Sir Charles. 'I shall make enquiries. And if something comes of it, I'll let you know.' He stubbed out his cigarette. 'Is there anything else I can help you with, Miss Vale?'

'Actually there is,' said Clara. 'Do you by chance have the address of Harry Stanley? Seeing as he was a trade unionist.'

Sir Charles gave her a curious look. 'I do. Although not here. I'll have it on file at my Ashington office. But why can't you just ask Inspector Hawkes for that?'

Clara considered her next words carefully. 'Because,' she said eventually, 'this is to do with my case, not his.'

'The two are linked?' asked Sir Charles, startled.

'Possibly.' Clara leaned forward. 'But please, Sir Charles, I need you to keep this just between us. I have not yet established the link. Nor the link with Germany. But I promise you, when I do, I shall pass on any relevant information. Can you help me?'

Sir Charles appraised her frankly. 'Ordinarily I would say no. You are asking me to withhold information from the authorities and to allow you to possibly interfere in an official police investigation. But I've been following your career with interest, Miss Vale. What you did earlier this year in exposing that international smuggling ring caused a stir in the Foreign Office. It was most impressive. And that you are from my constituency has given me a great deal of pride.' His eyes twinkled. 'I assume I can count on your vote in the next election, Miss Vale.'

Clara smiled. 'Of course you can, Sir Charles.'

'Excellent!' He stood up. 'Then I shall get my car. You can follow me to Ashington.'

Chapter 20

Clara, after assuring herself that Kate would be able to get a lift back to Penford Manor without her, followed Sir Charles in his chauffeur-driven Bentley on the road to Ashington. She considered that it was an unusual look for a Labour politician, but she was aware that in recent years the socialist party had attracted a surprising amount of support from upper class circles.

Clara followed the Bentley over the Great North Road and past the turn-off to Penford Manor before continuing east for five miles towards the coast. Geologically she knew that the north-east coastal belt from north Yorkshire, into Durham then up through Newcastle into Northumberland, had produced bituminous coal since Roman times. But it was only in the last 150 years with the power-hungry furnaces and engines of the industrial revolution that the fields were mined on a mass scale. The rural landowners of the region gradually started licensing mineral rights until the once-idyllic countryside was now littered with mine-heads. Clara counted three on the road between Penford and Ashington. She knew that there was another one in Ashington itself and then another in the mile-long stretch between Ashington and Newbiggin-by-the-Sea.

Clara followed the Bentley down Ashington Main Street. Ashington was a relatively modern town, built in recent Victorian and Edwardian years to service the mining community of the area. The post office and police stations were probably the oldest buildings after the railway station, and the thoroughfare was lined with shops selling modern household goods and fashions to modern customers. They drove over the railway line, busy with freight trains hauling coal to the nearby ports of Blyth and Newcastle, then pulled up outside a complex of buildings that included a community hall and some offices. A sign on the wall declared they were at the Miners' Institute. Sir Charles gallantly opened her car door for her and then led her into the building.

'This area is actually in the Morpeth constituency and I'm the Newcastle Central MP, but my Labour colleague, Ebenezer Edwards, kindly allows me a small office here. I don't step on his toes, of course, but it's useful for me to keep a finger on the pulse of things in the greater region – if you'll excuse my mixing of bodily metaphors!' Sir Charles chuckled at his own joke.

Clara smiled indulgently. They walked down a corridor, passing a number of rooms with glass-paned doors. Through one she noticed a classroom.

'Is this where Lady Molly and Lady Kate teach the adult education classes?'

'It is.'

'Kate said she had met Harry Stanley here.'

Sir Charles nodded. 'Yes, she would have. Stanley was very committed to self-improvement. I would often see him in the library – reading newspapers and books.'

Clara remembered what Bella had told her about Sir Bill wondering how Stanley could have known about international law. 'Is that the library in there?' she asked, peering through one of the glass panes.

'It is. It services the miners and their families.'

There was a woman sitting at a desk. 'Do you mind if I pop in and speak to the librarian for a minute? I assume that's the librarian.'

Sir Charles looked through the glass and caught the librarian's eye. The woman smiled and waved. 'Yes, that's Miss Brown. Another Labour volunteer. I'll make introductions.'

A few minutes later, after Sir Charles shared the news of Harry Stanley's death with the librarian, Clara got to the point of her visit. 'Miss Brown, do you keep records of books the miners take out?'

'We do, Miss Vale.'

'And might you be able to tell me what books Harry Stanley has been reading over – say – the last two months?'

'Well, I think that might be private, Miss Vale.'

Clara glanced at Sir Charles. The MP understood. 'I think we can help Miss Vale with this, Miss Brown. She's supporting the police in their investigation into Harry's death.'

Miss Brown cleared her throat. 'Of course, Sir Charles. If you give me a few minutes I'll see what I can find.'

She indicated that Clara and Sir Charles take a seat in the small study area. But Sir Charles declined. 'I'll just pop to my office and get that address for you, Miss Vale. Back in a tick.'

Clara looked around as she waited. There were half a dozen desks, empty now as it was a work day, but she could imagine that in the evenings and weekends miners like Harry Stanley would be seated at them reading or writing or . . . she noticed the desk in the far corner of the room had a typewriter on it. She glanced up to see that Miss Brown was still consulting her records and so walked over to the typewriter. She peered at the hammers, trying to see if she could spot any anomaly with the letters. It was hard to tell. There was a pile of blank paper on the desk.

'Miss Brown!' she called. 'Do you mind if I type a few words?'

'Not at all! I won't be long though.'

'Righto. Neither will I.' Clara slotted a sheet into the machine and typed, e e e e, then she rolled the page up and checked. 'Yes!' she said to herself. 'Found it.'

Her heart raced as she pulled the page from the machine, noticing the chink on the bottom curve of the letter. So this was where the blackmail note had been typed.

'Miss Brown,' she said, heading back to her seat. 'Did you ever see Harry Stanley use that typewriter?'

Miss Brown sat down opposite her, holding a notepad.

'Yes, he used it. It's for public use. And I've also got that list of books you wanted. In the last eight weeks Harry took out three books or journals: *Bleak House* by Charles Dickens, the latest *Hansard* – that's where they list all the debates and laws in parliament – and *Coalmining International* – that's a journal of the industry.'

'Goodness me, that's quite an eclectic mix,' said Clara. 'Did he return them all?'

Miss Brown shook her head. 'No, he still had *Bleak House* but . . .' she tapped her finger to her mouth '. . . now that you mention that typewriter, I remember finding another book, one that isn't actually in the library, there last week – after Harry had used it. It must have been his own book. I kept it to give back to him next time I saw him.'

'Oh, what was it?' asked Clara, her interest piqued.

'It was a volume of poetry by R. W. Service called *The Rhymes of a Red Cross Man*. It's war poetry, published in 1916.'

'May I see it?'

'Of course.' Then she added sadly, 'I suppose I should give it back to Harry's family.'

Clara gave a sympathetic nod. 'I can do that. I'm going to see them now.'

Miss Brown brightened. 'Oh, are you? Then I'll get it for you.'

She went to her desk and returned a moment later with a red canvas-bound volume.

'Do you remember which day you found it?' asked Clara.

'Goodness,' said Miss Brown. 'Let me think . . . I only worked Monday and Thursday last week, so it must have been Monday.'

The day before the note was delivered to Lady Penford, thought Clara. She picked up the book, opened it and ran her finger down the contents list. There were around fifty poems. She wasn't sure what she was looking for, so she flicked through the pages until she came to a page marked by a dried cornflower. Clara gasped.

'What is it?' asked Miss Brown.

'I think it might be a clue.'

Miss Brown's eyes opened wide behind her tortoiseshell glasses. 'A clue to what happened to Harry?'

'Possibly, yes.' Clara scanned the page. It was a poem called 'Tri-Colour' which began:

Poppies, you try to tell me, glowing there in the wheat . . . then she read further until she came to the second stanza and her heart raced as she recognised words she'd read before:

Cornflowers, you say, just cornflowers, gemming the golden grain;
Ah no! You can't deceive me . . .

She placed the cornflower and the folded-up page from the typewriter into the book to mark her place. 'Thank you for this, Miss Brown.'

'I hope it will help.'

'I hope it will too. And can I have that list of other books Harry took out?'

Miss Brown passed it to her. Just then Sir Charles arrived. 'I have that address for you, Miss Vale, if you still need it.'

'Oh, yes please,' said Clara, clutching the book of poetry. 'Is it far from here?'

'Not at all. If you come out to the Bentley I'll show you on the map. Unfortunately, I can't accompany you as I have a meeting. And . . . what ho?' said Sir Charles, looking out the window. 'And here is my next appointment.'

Clara looked out the window to see Matt Fowler, the manager of Sir Bill's pits, getting out of a car.

Sir Charles and Clara met him on the doorstep.

'Good day, Fowler. If you'll hold on one moment, I just need to give Miss Vale some directions.'

'Not at all,' said Matt Fowler, tipping his bowler hat to Clara. 'How do you do, Miss Vale?'

Clara inclined her head in return. 'I am very well, thank you, Mr Fowler.'

Matt nodded to Clara's car. 'Well I'm glad to hear that. I heard about your run-in with Teddy's motorcycle yesterday. That could have been very nasty.'

'Indeed,' said Clara. 'Fortunately, neither of us were hurt and I was able to give him a lift back to the manor – despite the damage to my car. But the mechanic assures me it's only cosmetic. I'll get it to the panel beaters later this week.'

'Once this unpleasant business at the manor is over?'

'As soon as,' agreed Clara.

Matt nodded his understanding. 'It's been quite a shock for everyone. Are the police still raking over everything?'

'They are.'

Matt Fowler chuckled. 'I don't suppose my step-aunt is too pleased?'

'Lady Penford?'

'Yes, she will be put out with all the disruption to her extended social weekend.'

Clara gave a wry sigh. 'Murder can be quite inconvenient. But she's bearing up, as far as I can tell. Has Inspector Hawkes interviewed you yet about Harry Stanley? I believe he worked at your mine.'

Matt's demeanour saddened. 'He has indeed. Yesterday afternoon. But I'm afraid there was not much I could tell him. Harry was a good worker and even though he was outspoken on behalf of the men, it's not more than I would expect from a trade unionist. There was never any conflict and I'm not aware of any bad blood between him and any of the other miners.' He shrugged. 'And I also have no idea what he might have been doing at Penford Manor on Saturday night or Sunday morning.'

Clara nodded. 'Yes, that seems to be a mystery. Did you hear that he had been there earlier in the week too? To speak to Sir Bill about something?'

Matt looked startled. 'That is the very first I have heard of it! Do you know what he wanted to talk about? My uncle hasn't mentioned this at all!'

Clara shook her head. 'I don't know any details. Only that he was at the groundsman's cottage last Tuesday, asking to speak to Sir Bill.'

'Goodness me. I wonder what for.'

Clara gave a half-smile. 'I'm afraid Inspector Hawkes has not told me that.' She did not divulge that thanks to Bella overhearing Sir Bill and Baron von Schneider's conversation, she had more of an inkling than she was letting on. 'Perhaps you can ask Sir Bill next time you're at Penford. I expect that's exactly what Inspector Hawkes is doing now – if he hasn't already. But oh! That reminds me... Mr Fowler, as you're here, not there, I expect you haven't had your fingerprints taken.'

'Fingerprints?'

Clara explained the situation.

'Simply a matter of elimination, old chap,' offered Sir Charles.

'Of course,' said Matt. 'I shall head down to the local police station after work today.'

'Or I could do yours right now,' said Clara.

Sir Charles laughed. 'Miss Vale is a lady detective, don't forget, and she has her very own fingerprinting kit!'

Matt looked at his watch. 'I'm afraid I'm pushed for time, Miss Vale . . .'

'Oh, five minutes won't do any harm,' said Sir Charles.

Matt pursed his lips and shrugged. 'All right. What do you want me to do?'

Five minutes later and Clara had taken Matt Fowler's prints. She had also shown him the photograph of the lighter, which, like Sir Charles, he said he did not recognise. With her business there complete she then took directions from Sir Charles on how to get to Harry Stanley's house. She memorised them and put the map Sir Charles had drawn for her in her glove compartment. She waved goodbye to Sir Charles and Matt who proceeded to their meeting.

Just as she was about to start the engine, something under the passenger seat caught her eye. She leaned in to pick up the metal object – and gasped. It was the lighter.

What on earth is that doing here?

Chapter 21

In the three short days Bella had been pretending she was a lady's maid she had come to realise that to the upper classes, servants were almost invisible. Men and women clad in black slipped in and out of rooms, like wraiths moving among the shadows. Conversations were held between the gentry, airing thoughts and opinions without discretion, as if no one else were in the room. Bella watched and mimicked the other servants' deadpan faces and noted that one should not meet another one's eye nor give the slightest twitch that you had just overheard a juicy titbit. And heaven forbid you let on that you thought the speaker a right plonker! That, for Bella, was the most difficult thing of all. Oh, how tempted she was to roll her eyes and let it be known she didn't for one minute think Mister or Miss Almighty deserved an ounce of her respect, just because they talked posh. 'You're not fit to lick me shoes!' she wanted to say – but bit her tongue for the sake of Miss Vale.

Because Miss Vale was worthy of her respect. Miss Vale had earned it. She had earned it when they first met at the jiu-jitsu class and hadn't thought using the same changing room as the common lasses was below her. And she had earned it when she had seen that Bella was a better shop detective than she was – and wasn't too proud to say so neither. And she'd earned it when she'd chosen to give up the allowance from her rich daddy so she could work for a living like normal folk. Oh yes, thought Bella, she had earned it countless times in their joint investigations with her cleverness, her kindness, her bravery and her respect for Bella's talents and abilities. Miss Vale did not think she was better than Bella, but she did pay her wages, and for that she would always be Miss Vale and not Clara. And now

Miss Vale had asked her to keep an eye on proceedings while she was away from Penford Manor.

Bella had quickly noticed that a family member or guest would not ask why you were in this or that room as long as you carried a duster or tray. It was only the senior staff who challenged you, knowing who should really be where. So, Bella, armed with a feather duster, slipped in and out of the shadows from room to room, listening, watching and waiting for someone to slip up.

Inspector Hawkes and two fingerprint men – who had driven up from Newcastle – set themselves up in the library. Bella recognised one of the men from the case she and Miss Vale had worked on last Christmas, of the missing fairy godmother. Fingerprint evidence had proven crucial in that investigation – Bella hoped it would in this one too. She observed the servants, kept in order by the butler Mr Spencer, file into the room one by one to have their fingers inked. She had a list in her mind of which servants were supposed to have been here last Tuesday, the day the blackmail note was delivered, and she mentally ticked them off one by one. After the last one – Sir Bill's valet – was printed, Bella noted that only one was missing: Baron von Schneider's valet. The man who had chastised Gretchen last night. Perhaps, she thought, he is attending the baron and they are away from the house. But no, the baron soon presented himself for inking while his valet remained unaccounted for. She noticed that Inspector Hawkes had a list that he was ticking off. *Aye*, thought Bella, *he'll not let that slip.* And he didn't. He asked the baron where his man was. The baron shrugged and said he didn't know but would send him along as soon as he saw him.

Of the rest of the guests, she noted that Sir Charles and Lady Molly were missing – but she knew Miss Vale would be taking their prints. Also missing was Sir Bill's nephew, Matt Fowler, and Lady Kate. She made a note of that. Then it came to the rest of the family, led by Sir Bill and Lady Penford, who was making a show of expressing her disdain for the whole process, even though Bella knew she was in on Miss Vale's plan. *Good acting, Lady P.*, thought Bella. It was such a good performance that it prompted Lady Fitzgilbert to express her sympathies that Lady Penford had to endure such a humiliation – and subject her guests to it too. Finally, Teddy sat down to be printed. 'Where's Kate?' he asked.

'I have already met with Lady Katherine,' said Inspector Hawkes.

Bella noted that and ticked Kate off her mental list. Then she watched as Teddy had his prints taken. He didn't look in the least bit nervous. Bella knew that Teddy was one of Miss Vale's main suspects in the murder case, but they had not, as yet, any evidence to tie him to it. Bella wondered if his prints would link him to the blackmailing too. They'd have to wait and see.

It was eleven o'clock by the time the fingerprinting was finished and Lady Penford announced imperiously that there would be elevenses on the lawn and then croquet. If any of the guests were not up for it, they did not say. Everyone realised Lady Penford needed to be appeased.

Bella quickly exchanged her feather duster for a tray and made her way out to the lawn.

The servants had been preparing for this for the last two hours – in between getting their prints taken. Around the perimeter of the lawn set up for croquet, there were clusters of garden chairs and strategically placed awnings for shade. Six mallets were racked up and ready to be claimed.

'Let's have two teams! Teddy and Tony can be captains!' announced Miss Lily Fitzgilbert.

'Splendid idea!' said her sister, Elsie, while cousin Archie scowled. 'Oh, don't be like that, Archie,' said Elsie, linking her arm through her cousin's. 'Come, you be on my team with Teddy, and then Lily and Tony can be on the other team with . . .' She looked around. 'Oh, Kate's not here. Who should have the sixth mallet?'

Bella watched the Fitzgilbert girl scanning the rest of the party for another singleton. Eventually her eyes rested on Maggie Fowler, Sir Bill's niece.

Elsie sighed. 'I suppose it will have to be you, Miss Fowler. There's no one else.'

If Miss Fowler was affronted by the thinly veiled insult she hid it well. Bella watched the quiet, dark-haired woman dutifully take a mallet and join Tony and Lily on the blue team.

'Righto, Tony,' said Lily, sidling up to the handsome stockbroker, 'you're the captain.'

Bella thought he looked a little pained. *I bet he was hoping for Kate.* Miss Vale had already told her that her brother was on the hunt for a bride. But Lily Fitzgilbert, Bella had learned, was loaded. Far more than Kate. Lily and her sister were the recipients of a vast trust fund set up by the granddad they shared with their cousin Archie. Archie, of course, as the son of the eldest son, was the heir to the title and estate, but the money had been split evenly between the three of them. Tony Vale needed money. Lily Fitzgilbert needed a husband. It was a match made in . . . well, Bella couldn't yet tell if it would be heaven or hell. Her first impression of Lily when they met in Cairo had not been a good one. She was snobbish and rude. But perhaps Tony would overlook that in light of her bank balance.

And what about Maggie Fowler? The secretary was single and attractive. One of the 'surplus women' after the war. The ones always being told off for either not getting a husband from the diminished supply, or for taking jobs away from men through their selfishness. Bella wondered if Maggie Fowler actually wanted to get married. Or, like Miss Vale, would prefer to be single. However, today, she was having to play the game, and everyone knew the game wasn't *really* croquet. Although Bella doubted Maggie would be one of the lead players. As the niece of Sir Bill she must have some money. But the fact that she had to work for her keep suggested she wasn't drawing on a trust fund.

As the blues took the first turn – with Tony striking the ball through the hoop with the confidence of an opening batsman – Bella turned her attention to the red team. Elsie Fitzgilbert was the gigglier of the sisters, shrieking with glee at every quip or quibble made by Teddy Richner. Bella wondered how Lily and Elsie had decided who was to be matched with whom. On paper, Teddy Richner, Earl of Penford, was the better catch. He had titles – both here and in Germany – and a pedigree going back centuries. Tony Vale was a mere esquire, whose father had only been a knight for just over a year. Both men were handsome, there was little in that, so it really came down to which of their negative qualities were the least distasteful. Tony was part of the bright young crowd, who had charlestoned their way through the twenties, and whose exploits made it into every gossip column in the country. Not a good match for Lily Fitzgilbert, thought Bella, who, she suspected, was not in with the London 'in' crowd and, although physically not plain, was conservative and spinsterly in her dress.

But did she have it better than her sister? Tony might settle down. But Teddy . . . Bella appraised the young man wearing a pair of striped Oxford bags and a straw boater hat, leaning nonchalantly on his mallet and trying his best to look interested in what Elsie had to say. Everyone knew he had the shadow of insanity hanging over him, even though, it was widely acknowledged, he was much better these days. But Bella couldn't help wondering how long it would be before he was howling at the moon once more. There was a sadness about Teddy Richner despite all his wealth and privilege. Suspicions about his possible connection to the murder aside, Bella felt very sorry for him. Not so the other male member of the team: Archie Fitzgilbert. He too had made a bad impression in Cairo and Bella had very little respect for him. Although she did feel a tinge of sympathy as the woman he was supposed to be matched with – Kate Richner – had gone out of her way to avoid him the whole weekend. *Mind you*, thought Bella, *I'd do exactly the same in Kate's shoes.* She felt queasy thinking of Archie's sweaty palms and wet, fleshy lips.

It was now the red team's turn. But Bella, seeing Mr Spencer glowering at her from the other side of the lawn, decided to make herself scarce. She slipped behind a gazebo, out of sight of the busybody butler, but still in earshot of some of the guests.

Sir Bill, Baron Klaus von Schneider and Miss Vale's father, Sir Randolph Vale, were seated in deckchairs enjoying cigars.

'How's your lad doing these days, Randy?' asked Sir Bill. 'He took a drubbing on the markets I believe.'

Sir Randolph exhaled a plume of cigar smoke. 'He's rallying.'

'Not in need of any extra work then?' asked Sir Bill.

'What kind of work?'

'Well, I'm looking for an agent. *We* are looking for an agent,' said Sir Bill, nodding towards the baron.

'For what?' asked Sir Randolph, tapping out ash from his cigar.

'Can't say just yet, but we need someone who knows the international financial markets to handle some transactions for us. And perhaps it might be something you can help us with too.'

'Oh?' said Sir Randolph. 'In what capacity?'

'Klaus?' prompted Sir Bill.

The baron sipped at a glass of whisky then turned to the London banker. 'I believe your bank has a branch in Berlin, is that correct? Lenster's on Jägerstrasse?'

'That's correct. We have branches in most European capitals.'

'Good, good, that's what I thought. And it would prove most useful if our agent – if your boy were to agree to the position – had connections in both Berlin and London.'

Sir Randolph's eyes narrowed. 'What exactly are you asking, von Schneider? Nothing illegal, I hope?'

Sir Bill guffawed. 'Not at all, old man. Absolutely nothing untoward. But it is something we would like to be kept as quiet as possible. And if you were able to facilitate that then there may be a consultancy fee.'

Sir Randolph raised a shaggy brow. 'How much are you proposing?'

Sir Bill leaned towards Sir Randolph and whispered something in his ear. Bella could not hear how much was being offered but the look on Sir Randolph's face suggested he was surprised. Pleasantly surprised. He nodded, then indicated to a nearby footman that he would like another cigar. 'All right, I'll talk to Tony about it. I'm sure we could set something up.'

'Good man!' said Sir Bill, leaning back in his chair and chomping his jaws around the stub of his cigar.

The baron raised his glass. 'Bill said you are well connected in financial circles, Sir Randolph. That will be most useful. Most useful indeed. Chin chin.'

Sir Randolph raised his own whisky and the men chinked glasses.

Bella leaned in, hoping to hear more, but the conversation turned to the grouse shoot scheduled for the next day and the varying merits of different bird shot cartridges. She withdrew, carrying her tray.

'You there, girl! Get me a lemonade!'

Bella flicked her head to the left to see Lady Vanessa Vale hailing her.

'Yes, madam,' said Bella, having no idea where she would get said lemonade.

'Hold on,' said Lady Vale, peering at her. 'Aren't you my daughter's office cleaner?'

Bella tensed. 'I am your daughter's assistant at her enquiry agency. Me name's Bella Cuddy. Miss Bella Cuddy.'

'And what are you doing here?'

'Miss Vale needed a lady's maid for the weekend and asked if I would step in at short notice.'

Lady Vale gave an indelicate snort. 'My daughter has not had a lady's maid since she was eighteen!'

'Well, she has one now. I'll find out where to get that lemonade.' Bella turned on her heel.

'Hold on! Did I give you permission to leave?'

'I don't need your permission,' said Bella before she could catch herself.

Lady Vale's eyes narrowed. 'I see you have my daughter's impertinence.'

'I have your daughter's respect,' snapped Bella. 'And she has mine. Your daughter – Clara – is a grand woman. An admirable woman. Admirable enough for Lady Penford to engage her. You should be proud of her instead of always putting her down.'

'I beg your pardon?' fumed Lady Vale. 'The impudence! Lady Penford! This girl should not be allowed around guests!'

But before Lady Penford's attention was drawn, Mr Spencer, his face like thunder, made a beeline towards Bella and Lady Vale.

Bella thrust her tray at his chest. 'Don't worry,' she said, as he prepared to chastise her. 'I'm gannin.'

'I'll be having words with your mistress,' growled Spencer.

'Aye, you do that,' she said then stormed back to the house, muttering to herself: 'Not fit to lick me bleedin' shoes!'

Chapter 22

It was a short, five-minute drive to Newbiggin, past a mine-head and clusters of pit houses, until the vast expanse of the North Sea filled Clara's windscreen. She turned down the village main street, with its shops selling buckets, spades and windbreakers, and drove to the parking area outside St Bartholomew's church. The church, on the cliffy headland overlooking the harbour, had brooded there for over eight hundred years. Its graveyard, whipped by north-easters in winter, was the final resting place of farmers, fishermen and miners, and Clara wondered if that was where Harry Stanley would be laid to rest. Today the stones were warmed by the August sun, and only the gentlest of breezes ruffled Clara's summer skirt as she stepped out of her car.

Clara, following Sir Charles' directions, took the path down to the harbour. Seagulls squalled, squabbling like toddlers over scraps of food, stolen from beach-goers' picnics. It was the summer holidays and a few mams were treating their bairns to a day at the seaside. As it was a Monday there were no dads in sight. They'd be down the pit, if they were lucky enough to have kept their jobs in these difficult times. And if not, they'd be queuing at the dole office in Ashington.

The scene below her was a far cry from her well-to-do childhood holidays spent in Cornwall. There were no bathing boxes wheeled into the sea or badminton on the beach, or servants unpacking well-stocked picnic baskets. But there was a tired old donkey giving ha'penny rides. And young lads with their trousers rolled up paddling in the shallows. One lad and lass were building a sandcastle while their sibling was buried up to his lugs in the sand. A stray dog sniffed at him then cocked its leg, much to the hilarity of the children and screams of 'Hadaway ya mangey mutt!' from the mammy.

Clara chuckled to herself as she reached the bottom of the stone steps and turned along the beachside path. She passed a small café where fishermen sipped and smoked while waiting for their next shift, their boats pulled up onto the pebbles. Eventually she reached a concreted slipway where she turned right. At the top of the slipway was the lifeboat station, the oldest in the whole of England, dating back to the middle of the last century. Clara remembered stories from her childhood of the brave Grace Darling, who was stationed not far from here, up the coast in Bamburgh. The North Sea was almost pacific today, but Clara knew it would be wild and dangerous come the winter.

To the side of the station there were more boats. She walked up and around the back, and, as per the blackmail note, there were indeed lobster traps and pots behind the station. She looked to left and right, checking the coast was clear, then searched the traps and pots. After five minutes she conceded that there was no silver tea caddy. However, it was only Monday, and the note had said the money must be put in the caddy before midnight on Tuesday. There was still time for it to appear . . . She wondered if she and Bella should set up a stake-out, waiting to see who would put the tea caddy there and then collect the blackmail money – if anyone was still planning to do so, now that Harry Stanley was dead.

According to Sir Charles' information, Harry Stanley had lived in a terraced house behind the lifeboat station with his mother. Surely, that was no coincidence. Just as it was no coincidence that Harry possessed a copy of the poem that had been used in the blackmail note, and had been seen using the typewriter that had typed it.

She checked the house number and then knocked on the door. A dog barked enthusiastically. The door opened a moment later and Clara was greeted by a woman in her sixties holding a black and white Jack Russell terrier in her arms. Clara was relieved to see the dog looked curious but friendly.

'Aye, can I help you?'

'Mrs Stanley?

'Aye it is.'

'Ah, good. Then I'm at the right place. My name is Miss Vale and I am assisting the police.'

'Assisting with what?'

'I'm helping Inspector Hawkes from the Newcastle police investigate your son's death. I'm so very sorry for your loss, Mrs Stanley. What a terrible time for you.'

Mrs Stanley sighed and put the dog down. 'Aye, it is.' Then, nodding to the dog. 'Don't worry, he'll just sniff you.'

Clara waited while the terrier sniffed at her shoes. When she had apparently passed muster, the dog ran a circle round its mistress's legs. 'You'd best come in,' said Mrs Stanley, and stepped aside. The door closed behind them, and Clara followed Mrs Stanley into a small front room. The house was a two-up, two-down terrace, common in these parts. The other room, which Clara caught a glimpse of, was the kitchen, dominated by a black cast iron range. Upstairs she expected there'd be two bedrooms. The lavatory would be out back, next to the coal shed, and any bathing would be done in a tin tub in front of the range or a fireplace in the front room.

The front room was neatly kept with two armchairs in faded green velvet and a small dining table, covered with a lace tablecloth, in the window alcove. There were net curtains at the window and Clara could see the back of the lifeboat station about a minute's walk away. *Easy to keep an eye on who is delivering what*, thought Clara. She now knew almost without a doubt that Harry Stanley was Lady Penford's blackmailer. The questions now were: why? And who else was he working with? She very much doubted Harry himself had taken the tea caddy from the sideboard or slipped the note under Lady Penford's door.

The mantlepiece was shrouded in a black cloth with a bouquet of yellow irises in a vase next to a framed photograph of a younger Harry in a military uniform. Clara bit her lip at the sad irony of the flowers. She doubted Mrs Stanley knew about the iris petal found in her son's lungs.

Mrs Stanley indicated Clara should sit and the two women took their seats in front of the hearth, on opposite sides of the photograph. The dog settled down on a sheepskin rug between them.

'So the inspector's sent ya,' said Mrs Stanley, smoothing down the floral housecoat she wore over a black dress.

Clara caught her breath. She didn't want to lie, but nor did she want to be tossed out before she had a chance to ask her questions. 'We're working on the same case, yes.'

'I've never met a lady policewoman.'

'I'm a detective, not a policewoman,' said Clara, aware that omitting the word 'private' was a tad deceptive, and that Sandy Hawkes would not be happy.

But Mrs Stanley looked impressed. 'A detective, are ya? Well, what do you want to ask me, Detective Vale?'

I'm in, thought Clara, relieved. She reached into her bag. 'I have a few things to show you. Firstly, do you recognise this?' She passed the lighter – which she had already dusted for prints – to Mrs Stanley.

The woman took it and weighed it in her hand. 'I can't say I do, miss.'

'It isn't Harry's?'

Mrs Stanley shook her head. 'No. He smoked but he used matches. That's an expensive-looking lighter. Silver I'd think. Not something my Harry could afford on his pit wages. Why do you think it's his?'

'It was found near where Harry's body was discovered. But it could be completely unrelated.'

Mrs Stanley's eyes narrowed. 'Or it could be his killer's.'

'It's possible,' Clara conceded. 'Did Harry have any enemies that you're aware of? Anyone he's argued with?'

Mrs Stanley smoothed the fabric of her housecoat across her knees. 'No miss. I'll tell you what I told Inspector Hawkes. Harry was no fighter.'

'But he was a shop steward.'

'Aye, he was that. And he spoke out when he had to. But he was well respected at the mine. Even by the managers. Ask them. They'll tell ya.'

Clara smiled gently. 'Yes, I've already heard that from Mr Fowler, the mine manager. He spoke highly of Harry. Do you know why Harry might have been at Penford Manor the night he died?'

Mrs Stanley shook her head. 'I have no idea. He didn't come home that night. But he's a grown man. He sometimes stays out. I don't ask why or where.'

'I understand. But did he perhaps mention anything to you? About someone he might be meeting at the manor? Either on Saturday night or the previous Tuesday?'

'Why the Tuesday?'

'He was seen at the manor then too. He spoke to Sir Bill Fowler about something.'

Mrs Stanley clenched the fabric of her housecoat into a tight fist. 'That's the first I've heard of it. Did Sir Bill say what it was about?'

Clara shook her head. 'Not to me. But I expect Inspector Hawkes will be discussing it with him. If anything comes of it, I'm sure the inspector will let you know.'

Mrs Stanley nodded but her fist remained clenched. She looked to the photo of Harry on the mantlepiece and bit her lip. 'You know, he wasn't married. A man in his thirties, but not married. His younger brothers both are – and they've got bairns – but not him. He'd never shown much of an interest in the lasses. I thought he was a confirmed bachelor, as they say. But just recently – over the last year – I suspected there might be a lady friend. That that's where he might have been going on Saturday night. Because he'd been out quite a few nights lately. Only coming back the next morning.'

'And you think he was seeing a woman?'

'Aye, I do. Because when I washed his clothes there was a scent. A woman's scent.'

'You don't know who it belonged to?'

'No, Detective Vale, I don't. But if she was a decent lass he would have introduced us.'

Clara raised her eyebrows. 'Are you suggesting he might have been to see a prostitute?'

Mrs Stanley lowered her eyes. 'I don't know for sure. But I've been wondering. I didn't say nothing to the inspector – because of the shame – but maybe I should've. . .'

Clara nodded. 'Yes, I think you should have. Perhaps the woman can shed some light on what happened to him. And you don't have any idea who it might be?'

Mrs Stanley raised her eyes to Clara's. They were welling with tears. 'As I said, if she'd been decent, he would have had her round here. I thought a while back that there might have been a decent lass – I'd seen him walking with her along the beach front a few times – but it came to nowt. I asked him about her, when he was going to bring her to meet me, and he said it wasn't what I thought and that he didn't want to talk about it no more, and that their friendship was over.'

Clara leaned forward. 'Forgive the indelicacy, Mrs Stanley, but how do you know the woman you saw him with was not a prostitute?'

Mrs Stanley appraised Clara's dress and shoes. 'Because she was dressed decent, miss. Good quality clothes. Not a rich woman's clothes, but decent. I know, I used to work in a garment factory before I married Harry's father – God rest his soul. But also, me neighbour told me she'd seen the lass before. That she worked up at Penford Manor. That she was a lady's maid.'

Clara sat bolt upright. 'Can you describe this woman to me?'

Mrs Stanley raised her eyes to the ceiling, accessing her memories. 'Late twenties, maybe. Slim. Fair hair. She wore glasses.'

'Miss Wren!'

'Is that her name? Me neighbour didn't know.'

'Yes. Kitty Wren. She works at the manor as a lady's maid. When was this? That you saw your son with her?'

Mrs Stanley looked ceilingward again. 'About a month ago. But like I said, he told me there was nothing going on with them. If there ever was, I don't know. And I never saw her again after that.' She leaned towards Clara. 'Do you think it was her he was going to see at the manor?'

Clara shrugged. 'I honestly don't know. But I'll speak to the inspector about it. I was wondering, though, if Harry knew anyone else at the manor. Do you know if Harry had ever met Lord Penford, the young Teddy Richner?'

Mrs Stanley shrugged. 'I'm not sure of that. There are things at the mine that the Penford family sometimes come to. Sports events and awards ceremonies and the like. Sir Bill would be there. Not her ladyship though. She never came.'

'And the young Lord Penford?'

Mrs Stanley nodded. 'Aye. He'd sometimes come. Never looked happy about it, mind. Had a face like a slapped kipper he did. Not like his sister. Canny lass that. What with how she helps teach the bairns.'

'Yes,' said Clara. 'Lady Katherine is lovely. And she said that Harry had been in some of her classes. But you think it's possible that Harry might have met her brother too?'

'Aye,' said Mrs Stanley. 'It's very possible. Can't say for sure mind, but it's possible.'

'Thank you,' said Clara. 'Now, there's something else I need to ask you. Did Harry bring home a silver tea caddy? Either on or after last Tuesday. A beautiful one, embossed with blue flowers?'

Mrs Stanley thought for a moment and shook her head. 'No, I can't say that he did.'

'Might it be in his room?' asked Clara, looking towards the ceiling and hoping Harry's mother might let her search it.

Mrs Stanley shook her head vigorously this time. 'Definitely not. That Inspector Hawkes went through his room yesterday and showed me a few things he was taking away with him. There was no tea caddy. Then I gave the room a thorough clean afterwards. I would have seen it if it was there. Why do you ask about that?'

'It's just something that might be linked to the case,' said Clara, in what she hoped was a reassuring voice. 'Or it might not be. We're exploring all avenues at the moment. But there is one more thing I'd like to show you.' She reached into her bag and brought out the red leather book of poems. 'Do you recognise this?'

Mrs Stanley's eyes flashed in recognition. 'Aye, I do. Harry's been reading it. He was dead clever was my Harry. Always good at reading. Always wanting to better himself.'

Clara opened the book to where the dried cornflower was used as a bookmark. She picked up the flower between thumb and forefinger. 'Did Harry ever bring cornflowers home? Or did he ever mention them to you?'

Mrs Stanley frowned. 'No, nowt that I can remember. He wasn't much one for flowers. Which is why I was so surprised when he brought them for me.' She turned her head to the irises on the mantlepiece, caught her breath then whispered: 'Who'd've thought they'd live longer than him.'

Clara waited a moment for Mrs Stanley to compose herself. 'They're beautiful, Mrs Stanley. When did he give them to you?'

Mrs Stanley did not need to consult the ceiling this time. 'It was Tuesday, Detective Vale. He gave them to me last Tuesday.'

Chapter 23

Clara left Mrs Stanley with the promise to be in touch if she had more news. As she walked back along the sea-side path, where Harry had walked with Miss Wren, Clara did not need to check her watch to know that it was nearly lunchtime. With a grumbling tummy she dropped into the fisherman's café and bought a smoked kipper sandwich. She didn't feel comfortable sitting inside, aware that she was the focus of every man in the room, so she asked for it to be wrapped to go.

She carried her sandwich up the cliffside steps past the car park – now hosting half a dozen cars –and beyond the church. There was a grassy verge on the cliff on the far side the graveyard, overlooking the bay, where she could quietly sit and munch her sandwich. She found a nice sunny spot and settled down. She had lots to mull over, but first things first: she unwrapped her sandwich. A gull circled and swooped but wasn't quite brazen enough to make a grab for the food. Clara hoped she wouldn't be harassed any further, or she'd have to retreat to her car. But fortunately, no other gulls followed. Clara relaxed and chewed, turning her attention to the swaying sea, about forty feet below her, where a sleek black seal heaved itself up onto the rocks and napped in the sun. Clara smiled. A sun-soaked snooze would be lovely about now, but she had far too much to do.

So as she ate she considered what she had learned from Mrs Stanley. There was absolutely no way she could keep this information from Sandy Hawkes. She had promised that if she came across anything in her investigation that shed light on the murder, she would share it with him. The irises that Harry gave to his mother on Tuesday, the day he had visited Penford Manor to speak to

Sir Bill and the same day the blackmail note was delivered to Lady Penford, fell into that category. As did the revelation that Harry might have been stepping out with Miss Wren. Miss Wren, of course, was perfectly positioned to have taken the tea caddy and to have delivered the note on behalf of Harry. Clara wondered what the morning's fingerprinting at the manor would reveal. It was more than frustrating that Harry's fingerprints weren't on the note, but if Miss Wren's fingerprints were . . . well, the evidence would be stacked against her. And if Miss Wren was Harry's co-conspirator in the blackmail case, could she also be his murderer? Not on her own. Miss Wren was a slightly built woman and would not have been able to carry a body from the pond in the walled garden to the woods, even if she had been able to hold him under the water until he drowned. So, who could have helped her? Teddy Richner? Yes, it was certainly possible. But why? And why, for that matter, would Miss Wren? Mrs Stanley had thought their relationship – if there had indeed been one – was over. Was this simply a case of a lover scorned? Bella had told her that Miss Wren had been particularly upset by news of the discovery of the body – more than any of the other servants. Or was she just upset by her part in his death? That was something Sandy Hawkes would find out. Clara, who had witnessed the inspector interrogating a murder suspect before, knew he could be very persuasive.

However, Clara wondered if taking Miss Wren in for questioning too soon might alert her partner in crime and allow them time to flee. She would mention that to Hawkes as a possibility and hope that the inspector would be subtle in his approach. Clara, who had now finished her sandwich, reached into her bag and retrieved the lighter. She flicked it on and off with her thumb. Before leaving the Miners' Institute, Clara had dusted it for fingerprints – but there had been none. Who did it belong to?

Teddy was top of the list. He had been in her car just yesterday and she recalled him dropping the contents from his pocket when he had tried to pay her for the damage. Had he dropped the lighter then and, in the commotion, failed to notice? She had found it under the seat, so easily overlooked. If so, had Teddy been the one to retrieve the lighter from the woods? The only other person who had been in her car was Kate. But as far as Clara was aware, Kate didn't smoke. But Teddy did . . . She recalled seeing him last night searching for his lighter and not finding it. She flicked the lighter on and off again and then put it back in her satchel. That too would be handed over to the inspector.

Clara allowed her mind to consider Teddy's culpability. Could he have assisted Miss Wren in Harry Stanley's murder? Why would he do it? What was his motivation? And for that matter, what was Harry's motivation in the blackmail? Or Teddy's, if he were involved too. She took out the note and the volume of poetry.

Cornflowers, you say, just cornflowers,
gemming the golden grain;
Ah no! You can't deceive me.
£50 or your secret will be out.
Put in silver tea caddy (you know which one).
Find under lobster pot.
Newbiggin lifeboat hut.
By midnight 12th August.
Don't grouse about.

One by one the cryptic clues were giving up their meaning. She now knew that the cornflowers possibly referenced Lady Penford's relationship with her former husband. Teddy, of course, would know about that. Clara knew too about the tea caddy, which either Kitty or Teddy could have taken from the house. And that the lobster pots were in easy reach of Harry's house. And now – thanks to the volume of poetry she'd found at the library – she knew where the opening lines of the note came from.

She opened the book to the marked page.

TRI-COLOUR by Robert W. Service
Poppies, you try to tell me, glowing there in the wheat;
Poppies! Ah no! you mock me: it's blood, I tell you, it's blood.
It's gleaming wet in the grasses; it's glist'ning warm in the wheat . . .

Clara realised very quickly this was a poem about soldiers dying on the Western Front during the Great War. It was a moving poem – in the ilk of Wilfred Owen – using the imagery of flowers to depict the fragility of life and the tragic deaths of so many young men. The first stanza dealt with poppies, then cornflowers made their appearance in the second. She remembered what Ada von Schneider had told her about cornflowers having the same symbolic function as poppies when Germans remembered their dead.

The stanza opened with the familiar lines from the blackmail note and then continued.

Cornflowers, you say, just cornflowers, gemming the golden grain;
Ah no! You can't deceive me. Can't I believe my eyes?
Look! It's the dead, my comrades, stark on the dreadful plain,
All in their dark-blue blouses, staring up at the skies.

This is it, she thought. *This is the poem Harry used.* But why? she wondered. What was its significance to Lady Penford? She flicked through the book and came to the dedication page. The poet, Robert W. Service, had printed:

To the memory of
my brother
Lieutenant Albert Service
Canadian Infantry
Killed in action, France
August 1916

And then, in ink, on the adjacent blank page, someone had written by hand:

Dear Teddy, I send this to you in memory of our brother Mikey who died in August 1916 too. I am no poet, but the words in these poems by Mr Service express what I would say if I were. Have you heard the war will soon be over? So, I shall see you soon, God willing. But if not, then the Penford title is yours, dear boy. Do it proud.

It was signed: *Ru, 14th August 1918.*

Teddy! Teddy again! This is Teddy's book . . . had he given it to Harry? But why?

Clara considered what Harry's mother had said. She'd thought Harry was 'a confirmed bachelor, as they say' and that he had 'never been interested in women' – until she'd seen him with Kitty. Could Harry have been a homosexual? Could Teddy have been his lover? Was Kitty merely a smokescreen?

Clara considered this for a moment. Was this the secret that Lady Penford was keeping? It was certainly possible, but it was also pure speculation. For now she'd look at the evidence in front of her. The note was signed from 'Ru'. *That must be Rupert*, thought Clara, thinking back to what Kate had told her about her deceased brothers in the walled garden on Saturday. The eldest, Michael, had died during the war, in combat, and Rupert, the middle brother, had died after armistice when his troop carrier hit a German mine. Teddy had only been sixteen at the time but, as the only surviving male heir, then became the Earl of Penford. It was soon after that that their father, Baron von Richner, killed himself in Germany, and then Teddy inherited those titles too.

Why did Harry have this book in his possession? Was there a deeper secret than his possible relationship with Teddy? Was there something he knew about Lady Penford? Was that what 'You can't deceive me' referred to? What deception was she performing? Did it have something to do with the death of her sons? But what? And had Harry Stanley been murdered to keep it quiet? Or to remove him from Teddy's life? Or for both reasons? On the orders of Lady Penford . . .

Clara shook her head. No, that didn't make sense. If Lady Penford wanted the whole thing to be hushed up then why allow her, Clara, to continue with the investigation? If Lady Penford had already discovered the source of the blackmail and killed Harry, then what purpose did Clara play?

She was sick and tired of Lady Penford's obfuscation about all this. Clara decided that it was time to confront the lady with what she had found out. To show her the book of poetry and ask her its significance.

The bell of St Bartholomew's behind her struck one. It was time to go back to Penford Manor. Clara re-packed her bag, slung it diagonally across her chest, and stood on the edge of the cliff taking in the view one last time. And then she felt an almighty shove and stumbled forward. Her arms windmilled, trying to regain balance, but her shoes slipped on the shale, and she fell . . . over the cliff.

'Clara! Give me your hand! Reach up! Come on, you can do it! Don't give up!'

Clara was clutching a branch about five feet down the side of the cliff. The rocks of Newbiggin bay – thirty-five feet below – waited patiently for her fall. The seal had not even woken.

Sandy Hawkes' desperate face loomed above her. He lay on his belly, reaching down his arm. Clara wondered if she could hold onto the branch with one hand if she released the second to grasp Hawkes' hand. He was probably a foot too high.

'Take off your belt!' she instructed, surprised at how calm she sounded.

'Good idea!'

Hawkes pulled himself back up and a few moments later appeared with his belt in hand. He resumed his position and lowered the belt to her, with the strap threaded through the buckle creating a looped handhold.

Clara let go of the branch and slipped her hand into the loop. Then, when Hawkes had taken her weight, she braced her feet against the side of the cliff, let go of the branch, grabbed the belt and worked her way up the cliff. Eventually, with Hawkes' help, she heaved herself onto level ground. The two of them lay for a moment, side by side, to catch their breath, then pulled themselves up to sitting.

'Are you all right?' asked Hawkes, both hands on her shoulders and looking earnestly into her eyes.

'I am,' said Clara, then looked around. 'Did you see who pushed me?'

Hawkes shook his head and let go of her shoulders. 'No. I was walking up from the car park. I heard a scream. I saw a flash of someone running into the graveyard. But I had to choose between saving you or following them.' He looked her up and down. 'I made the right decision. Thank God you're all right, Clara.'

Clara was very pleased she was all right too. She expected she would have sore arms and shoulders tomorrow and no doubt some grazes on her knees and bruising on her hands, but other than that she was thankfully intact. She hadn't even dropped her satchel. But it could have been so different... so very different... Who had tried to kill her? 'Could you describe them at all?' she asked her rescuer.

Hawkes sighed. 'Unfortunately not. I couldn't say if it was a man or a woman. I just caught a fleeting glimpse of... something... someone...'

'Someone who tried to kill me.'

Hawkes' eyes were fraught with worry. Clara had never seen the usually unflappable police inspector this way before. But it didn't take long for the old Inspector Hawkes to return. He put his belt back on. 'What are you doing here, Miss Vale? I went to see Mrs Stanley – to ask her some more questions – and she said you had just been to see her, claiming you were there on behalf of the police.'

'I said no such thing!' Clara explained what she had told Mrs Stanley – that she was working alongside the police, and that she wasn't a police officer – and what she had learned in return.

Hawkes frowned. 'Well, you should have spoken to me first. You could jeopardise my investigation.'

Clara rolled her eyes. 'How would I do that? I was there conducting my *own* investigation. As we agreed, I could carry on with that, and if I came across anything pertinent to *your* investigation, I would tell you.'

Hawkes shook his head slowly from side to side. 'My dear Miss Vale. What am I going to do with you?' Then he stood up and reached down his hand to her. 'Let's get away from the cliff edge. I've got a flask of tea in my car. We'll have a cuppa then you can tell me everything.'

And so she did... most of it. As she told Bella later, there were a few things she needed to confirm first. She did not tell him about the German business angle – that was all still too speculative – nor did she mention the death of the Richner brothers and the book of poems. But she did tell him about the blackmail note, that she'd found the typewriter on which it had been typed, and all the reasons she believed Harry Stanley was the blackmailer. She told him too about Miss Wren. She also gave him the lighter.

'You found this in your car?'

'I did. Only two people have been in my car since the lighter went missing from the crime scene: Teddy and Kate Richner. I have a feeling it was Teddy who dropped it, but I have no proof.'

Hawkes took a sip of tea and pondered this a moment. 'What about the chauffeur-cum-mechanic? Didn't he have access to the car when he checked it over?'

Clara, disappointed that what she thought was a narrow suspect list might not be anything of the sort, conceded this point. And then gave a frustrated sigh. 'And who knows who else had access to it when it was in his care.'

'I'll find out,' said Hawkes. He looked at the lighter. 'You say it had been wiped clean of prints?'

'Yes. I wonder if it did just accidentally slip out of someone's pocket. Or if someone wanted me to find it. If that's the case, I wonder why?'

Hawkes flicked it on and off. 'To point the finger of blame at someone? Let us see if anyone at the manor can identify it. I've already shown the photograph around – and no one said they'd seen it – but perhaps the real object might spark some recognition.' He raised a brow in Clara's direction. 'And by "let us", I don't mean you, Miss Vale.'

Clara slammed down her tin flask cup on the dashboard. 'Oh for heaven's sake, Hawkes, I'm already involved. I've already helped you. And you have helped me. So let's – and by "let us", I do mean "us" – stop pussyfooting around. Have you got those fingerprints?'

Hawkes gave a low chuckle. To someone who didn't know him quite as well as Clara was beginning to, it might have been mistaken for a growl.

'I do.' He reached over to the back seat, his hand brushing Clara's shoulder as he did so. He did not apologise. She didn't mind that he didn't. In fact, despite her fleeting annoyance with him, she wouldn't have minded if his hand had lingered on her shoulder. However, the moment passed and he had a leather folder on his lap he opened to reveal a stack of fingerprint cards accompanied by a neatly written list of who had been printed. 'Did you manage to get the ones that weren't at the manor?'

'I did,' said Clara. 'I'll go through these when I get back to Penford. The photos of the prints I took from the sideboard are in my room.'

Hawkes pursed his lips. 'Hmmm, let's hope they're still there.'

'What do you mean?'

'Well, if someone tried to push you over a cliff, they might try to dispose of any evidence you have collected already. You and the satchel would have been in the North Sea if I hadn't been here. It wouldn't surprise me if your room has been searched too.'

Clara nodded. 'That's certainly a possibility. But it assumes that whoever pushed me today has access to the manor.'

'Well, you said yourself that you don't think Harry could have got into the manor himself. That he has an accomplice there. What about this Miss Wren?'

'She's certainly a suspect,' said Clara, although she struggled to envisage the slightly built Miss Wren shoving her over a cliff. But it certainly wasn't impossible. 'Will you question her?'

'I will. But I think you made a good point about doing it subtly, so as not to alert her that we're on to her – or any other accomplices. I share your suspicions of Teddy Richner, but there is, as yet, no hard evidence against him. And he willingly submitted to fingerprinting. But as for Miss Wren, having Mrs Stanley identify her as someone Harry stepped out with *is* enough to justify suspicion. I'll question a few of the servants together and let her believe it's just routine. I'll go to the manor now. Then we can arrange for someone to come and pick up your car.'

Clara shook her head. 'No, I'll drive it myself.'

'Are you sure? You've had quite a shock.'

'I'm absolutely fine,' said Clara and slipped the fingerprint folder into her satchel. Then she opened the car door and smiled back at Hawkes. 'I'll see you at Penford Manor.'

Chapter 24

Bella, as her mam would say, had the hump. She was sick and tired of kowtowing to these jacked-up gentry and their arse-licking lackies. After her run-in with Clara's mother and the butler she stomped her way back to the house with the intention of taking the rest of the day off until Miss Vale came home. There was nothing more she could do with the investigation for now. She had collected some juicy titbits of information by eavesdropping on Sir Bill, the baron and Clara's father, and looked forward to discussing its implications later. For now, she would go to the kitchen to see if she could scrape something to eat, then she'd have a little lie-down. God knew she deserved it.

Mrs Rogers was red-faced and flustered, directing the kitchen maid to slice more bread and to get another side of ham from the larder. When she saw Bella she thrust a tray of delicately cut sandwiches in her direction.

'Get that out there.'

Bella thrust it back. 'I'm not going back oot.'

Mrs Rogers' brow furrowed. 'Well, thanks for nothing.'

'Aye, you're welcome.' Then, remembering that the cook had been nothing but kind to her since she arrived, she softened her tone and added, 'Sorry, missus. But it's not me job. Me job is to help Miss Vale. And that's what I'm going to do.'

She was tempted to grab a handful of sandwiches but refrained and said: 'Mind if I help meself to something to eat from the larder?'

Mrs Rogers twisted her mouth. 'Go on. There's a pork pie in there. Have yourself a slice.'

'Ta, Mrs Rogers.'

Bella got her pie and a cup of tea and bid a hasty retreat.

But when Bella got to her bedroom there was no chance she could quietly eat her dinner then have a lie-down. Gretchen, the German maid, was sobbing on her bed.

Bella went in and put down her cup and plate on the table. She looked down at the sobbing Gretchen and touched her shoulder. 'Are you all right, pet?'

Gretchen rolled over and looked at Bella, her eyes red and swollen. She shook her head.

'Leave me alone, please. Sorry. But please leave me alone.'

'What's wrong?'

'It's . . . it's . . . oh, Miss Cuddy, I shouldn't have talked to you last night. I really shouldn't.'

'Are you in trouble with the baroness?'

Gretchen shook her head. 'No, not her. She's a good woman.'

'Then who? The baron?'

Gretchen's eyes widened in terror. 'I can't say. Please, leave me. It's best you leave me.'

'Aye, all right,' said Bella, picking up her plate and cup, 'but if you want to talk to me about anything you can. I hope you feel better soon.'

Bella harrumphed to herself as she left the room, unsure where she could go to eat her dinner now that the kitchen was a no-go and Gretchen was blubbing in their bedroom. Eventually she decided to go outside and sit on a bench in the stable yard.

But the yard wasn't as quiet as she'd hoped. It seemed all of the Penford Manor staff who weren't busy with the croquet and garden party were here, getting everything ready for tomorrow's grouse shoot. Miss Vale had told her that the 12th of August every year was the official opening of the grouse shooting season. It had been the law of the land for a hundred years that no one was allowed to shoot red grouse between 11th of December and 11th of August in order to allow the birds to breed and flourish. Bella was not sentimental and knew game had to be controlled and meat provided for the pot, but she did blanch at the relish with which the posh folk went about shooting anything with feather or fur while making a party of it.

Three men were oiling and tending a rack of rifles and shotguns while two lads were piling sacks that would be used by the beaters.

Half a dozen springer spaniels were milling about when suddenly a fight broke out between two of the dogs. The lads intervened and broke up the scrap. Then one of the dogs ran to where Bella was sitting and cowered behind her legs. Bella was worried she'd be caught up in the fight, but the lads locked the aggressor dog in a stable and waved to her that it was all right.

Bella reached down and patted the frightened dog. It eventually calmed down, helped by a crust from Bella's pork pie. It was wearing a collar and she noticed the tag: 'Sammy'.

'You're the groundsman's dog, aren't you?' And then Bella had an idea.

'Come on, lad, let's get you home.' She stood, and with the help of some food, encouraged the dog to go with her. Bella made her way behind the garages and towards the driveway that led to the front gate of the estate and the gatehouse that doubled as the groundsman's cottage. As she passed the last of the garages, she noticed the von Schneider valet getting out of a car. She'd heard Gretchen refer to him as Herr Meyer. She nodded as she passed him. He raised his hat in return.

'Good afternoon, Miss Cuddy.'

'Good afternoon, Mr Meyer.'

'Have you been at the croquet?'

'I was for a bit. But as Miss Vale is not here, I'm doing me own thing.'

He smiled. 'Forgive me for saying so, but you seem to do your own thing quite a bit.' He took a step towards her. 'I like that.'

Bella stood her ground. 'You didn't seem to like it last night. And you've got poor Miss Klopp in tears.'

Meyer's lips tightened. 'Miss Klopp should know better. She is not free to do as she wishes. Not like you . . .' Another step. This time his eyes ranged up and down her body.

Bella bristled. She was not in the least bit frightened. She knew, with her jiu-jitsu skills, she could defend herself if he laid a hand on her, but she was fuming that she would even have to.

She put her hands on her hips and squared up to him. 'You've got the wrong end of the stick, me lad. And if you don't want me to beat you with it, I suggest you back off. Now!'

Meyer laughed but her words – and body language – had the desired effect. He did not advance further. Instead, he raised his hat. 'Then I shall bid you good day, Miss Cuddy.'

'Nowt good about it,' she said, and turned on her heel. She could feel his eyes on her as she left and wondered if Inspector Hawkes had managed to get the valet's fingerprints yet. It looked like Meyer had been for a drive and just returned. The Inspector and the fingerprint men had left the estate well over an hour ago. And Miss Vale wasn't here to get his prints either. She would mention it to Miss Vale when she returned and perhaps they could get them later. But best they do it together. It didn't look like a woman on her own was safe to be around Meyer.

She wondered too if all this fingerprinting would turn anything up. If it didn't, she wasn't sure what she and Miss Vale would do. Perhaps the typewriter with the chipped 'e' might still be found. Or perhaps the overheard conversations about Sir Bill's and the baron's seemingly shady business dealings might amount to something. But she wasn't sure what. However, she knew that with both Miss Vale and Inspector Hawkes on the case, the blackmailer – and the killer – wouldn't remain hidden for long. And she would help any which way she could.

For now, she thought she might have a chinwag with the groundsman. Hawkes – as usual – had not been very forthcoming as to what was said when the man was taken in for questioning. He said some information had come to the fore. But what? Perhaps she could find out. By now the dog sensed it was going home and no longer needed to be bribed by food. It ran ahead of Bella towards the gatehouse.

The windows of the stone cottage were open in the August heat and as Bella approached she could hear voices: a man and a woman. The woman she recognised as Miss Parker, Lady Penford's maid. Bella stopped under the shade of a yew hedge to listen.

'Do you swear you haven't told anyone, Arthur?'

'I swear on me mother's grave. Not the polis, not no one. But he wasn't askin' about that – that inspector from Newcastle – he was wanting to know about the fella in the woods. How he got there. If I'd seen him before. And I told him I had.'

Miss Parker's voice rose. 'Why did you do that?'

'Because it's a murder, Sally, someone's been murdered. And I think for a bit they thought I'd done it. I needed to prove I hadn't.'

'What did you tell them?'

Arthur Foster sighed. 'I told them the truth. At least about that. That the fella – Stanley – had been here last Tuesday wanting to speak to the master.'

'Do you know what about?'

'I don't. Sir Bill told me to make meself scarce when he talked to the fella. So I went out back and chopped some wood.'

'But you didn't tell them the other thing. Our secret.'

'Of course not! I swore to you fourteen years ago I'd never tell and I haven't. Not even when you turned down me marriage proposal. I could have then, Sally, out of spite, but I didn't. I'm a man of me word, and if you'd married me we would have had a good life together.'

'Oh stop it, Arthur! What's done is done. I made a decision back then and there's no going back on it. But I should never have told you. I was a young and foolish girl. But if you haven't told the secret, someone else has. Because I think that's what was in the blackmail note to Lady Penford.'

'How do you know it's a blackmail note?'

'Because I overheard Lady Penford talking to that Vale woman.'

'Overheard or eavesdropped?'

Bella, who was doing exactly the same thing, leaned in to hear more.

'I will not apologise for doing what I think's best, Arthur. To protect this family – even if it's from themselves.'

'What do you mean by that, Sally?' Arthur's voice had a worried edge.

'I mean, Lady Penford is doing herself harm by bringing Miss Clara Vale in on this. I know the master isn't happy about it. He asked Miss Fowler to not put on the appointment in Newcastle. But that didn't work and they met up anyway. The mistress wants Miss Vale to find out who sent the blackmail note to her, to try to keep the secret secret, but all it's going to do is get that dreadful woman on the scent. And from what I've heard about her, she's like a bloodhound. It's going to backfire on the mistress, you mark my words.'

Bella bristled at Miss Vale being described as a 'dreadful woman' but agreed with the bloodhound bit. Miss Vale would not stop until she had found the blackmailer . . . and now also the murderer. Bella was certain the two were linked, but proof still had to be found.

It seemed that Arthur Foster was thinking along the same lines. 'Do you think they're linked? The secret and the murder? Can't be a coincidence that it's all happened at the same time, can it?'

'No, I don't think it's a coincidence, Arthur,' Miss Parker answered. 'I suspect that Harry Stanley found out Lady Penford's secret and was blackmailing her. And that someone found out it was him and killed him.'

Arthur gasped. 'Who do you think did it?'

'That I don't know,' said Miss Parker. 'But whoever it is it's someone who needs the secret to remain secret.'

'That means it's someone who knows the secret.'

'Obviously. So I need to find out who.'

'And how are you going to do that, Sally?'

Bella could hear a smirk in Miss Parker's voice. 'Oh, I have my ways, Arthur. And I also have ways to make sure that Vale woman doesn't find out before I do. She needs to be stopped. And the sooner the better.'

'Oh aye? What's your plan then?'

But before Bella could hear how Miss Parker planned to stop Miss Vale, two cars pulled into the driveway. The first driven by Inspector Hawkes, the second by the very woman being discussed. Clara spotted Bella and stopped the car.

Bella tried shooing Clara away, not wanting the people in the cottage to know she was there. But it was too late.

'Bella! What are you doing here? Jump in and I'll take you back to the manor.' Clara smiled at her and nodded to the passenger seat beside her.

Bella cleared her throat and walked to the car, unavoidably passing the cottage window as she did so. Miss Parker, framed like a portrait in a gallery, narrowed her eyes and pinned them on the now exposed eavesdropper. Bella could feel the woman's eyes boring into her back as she got into the car.

'What is it?' asked Clara, seeing her assistant's face.

'I'll tell you in a minute, Miss Vale. But best we get out of here. Right now!'

Chapter 25

Clara wished she could lie in the bathtub all day. After the adrenaline from her near-fatal fall had worn off, her body ached from head to toe. Her shoulders, back and neck hurt from hanging onto the branch and her knees and shins were scraped and bruised from scrambling back up the cliff.

'Pass the sponge, please, Bella.'

She'd asked Bella to join her in the bathroom so she could clean herself up while filling her assistant in on the latest developments of the case. This needed to be a quick bath so she could get back to her investigation.

Bella, who had already expressed her shock and outrage that someone had tried to kill her employer, handed Clara the sponge. 'So, miss, who do you think did it?'

'Well, Miss Wren is certainly a suspect, but you say that you saw her at the croquet party?'

'Aye, I did. I left there about a quarter to one and she was still there. What time was your accident?'

'About one o'clock. Not much time for her to get there.'

'No, there's not. And that's assuming she can drive. There was no time to wait for a bus. And it's too far to walk in that time. And—'

'And she's back here already,' finished Clara, who had left Inspector Hawkes to speak to Miss Wren and some of the other staff while she cleaned herself up. She'd check in with him later. 'So we're doubtful it's Miss Wren.'

'Aye. What about Harry's mam?'

'Mrs Stanley?'

'Well, she did know you were there. Maybe she wanted to stop you finding out more about her son's blackmailing efforts.'

Clara shook her head. 'I don't think so, Bella. I think she'd want me to find her son's killer. And I'm not convinced she knew much about Harry's more questionable activities. So, who else could it have been? What about Teddy Richner?'

Bella shook her head. 'Not likely. He was captaining one of the croquet teams and they were just finishing when we got back to the manor.'

Clara sighed. 'You're right. It couldn't have been him. Then who else?'

Bella's eyes narrowed. 'What about Mr Meyer?'

'Who's Mr Meyer?'

Bella went on to tell Clara about the von Schneider valet and how she'd seen him getting out of a car. 'It was around half past one. So that fits the time frame.'

'And he wasn't around this morning to have his fingerprints taken,' observed Clara as she finished rinsing the soap from her arms. 'I'll tell Sandy.'

'Sandy?' said Bella, with a teasing smile.

'Sorry, Inspector Hawkes. Don't get any wrong ideas, Bella.'

Bella chuckled. 'Oh, I'm not sure they're wrong.'

Clara scowled at her. 'Pass the towel.'

Clara got dressed then she and Bella laid out on the bedroom floor all the fingerprint evidence they had acquired so far, including the photographs of the prints from the cabinet, the letter and the individual prints taken over the last two days. To their immense disappointment there were no matches at all.

'Well, that's us back to square one. What a bloody waste of time!' Bella sat back on her heels.

'Not quite,' said Clara. 'Remember, we don't have Meyer's prints yet. And he was around last Tuesday when the letter was delivered.'

'Aye,' said Bella, relaxing a little. 'There's still him. Should we go see Hawkes?'

But Inspector Hawkes was not ready to see them. He was now interviewing Sir Bill and Lady Penford and, so Spencer, the butler, informed them, had asked not to be disturbed.

'What should we do now, miss?' asked Bella. 'Should we talk to Miss Wren?'

Clara shook her head. 'No. Not before I've heard what Hawkes found out from her first. I tell you what, why don't we go to see the groundsman, Foster? You didn't get to talk to him, did you?'

'No, I didn't have a chance.' Bella had already told Clara what she'd overheard between Arthur Foster and Miss Parker.

'Then let's go there now. Perhaps we can find out more about this secret that he's trying to protect. I want to find out as much as I can about it before I have my next powwow with Lady Penford.'

On the way to the cottage, at Clara's suggestion, they stopped off at the estate garages to speak to the chauffeur, Mr Rogers. 'Yes, Mr Meyer did borrow a car. Early this morning after breakfast.'

'Did he say what he needed it for?' asked Clara.

'He did not. Sir Bill had already told me Baron von Schneider might need to borrow a car while he was here. I assumed Mr Meyer was about the baron's business. And it was not my business to ask.'

'Of course not. Thank you very much.'

When they were out of earshot Clara asked Bella to point out which car it was. Bella indicated a black Model T Ford coupe.

Clara looked over her shoulder, checked no one was watching, then slipped over to the car. She checked the wheels and the bumper then, as Mr Rogers looked towards them, she quickly walked away with Bella matching her stride.

'There're traces of sand in the crevices,' she whispered. 'The car park at Newbiggin was very sandy. I've got some on my car too. More to tell Inspector Hawkes.'

'Aye,' said Bella, 'and we'd better keep our eyes peeled. If Meyer tried once, he could try again. Wish I knew where the toerag is now.'

Clara agreed. She wished she'd thought of packing her revolver for this trip. 'What could Meyer's motivation be?' she mused.

'I don't know,' said Bella. 'But what's the bet it's something to do with his boss's business arrangement with Sir Bill? And they're trying to get your dad and brother in on it too.'

'They're *what*?'

For the rest of the walk to the groundsman's cottage, Bella told Clara what she'd overheard at the croquet match.

'Hmmm,' said Clara. 'That does tie in with what Sir Charles Trevelyan told me this morning too. And Harry Stanley was reading a book about international mining law at the library. Is that the secret they're all trying to keep?'

'It could be,' agreed Bella, 'but then why was the blackmail note sent to Lady Penford instead of Sir Bill?'

'Good point. Yes, there does seem to be something more personal to this. Something more than a shady business deal. But that doesn't mean the two aren't connected.'

'Something else to ask Lady Penford?'

'I'll add it to the list.'

They reached the cottage a few moments later to find the dog, Sammy, whining and scratching at the door. He turned his dark eyes to Bella, imploring her to open it for him.

Clara sniffed. 'Do you smell that?'

'Aye, miss, gas.'

Clara tried the door. It was locked. 'And all the windows are shut.'

'They were open when I was last here.'

Clara ran to the window and peered through the glass. A man lay prostrate on the floor.

'Let's try the back.'

They ran around the back, but that door was locked too. Beside the door was a woodpile with an axe embedded in a stump. Bella grabbed it and swung at a window, smashing the glass with an almighty blow.

The smell of gas grew stronger.

Clara hitched up her skirt and covered her nose. 'Get that door open!' she ordered Bella.

Bella rained blows on the lock until it was smashed to smithereens. Clara rushed in, while Bella covered her own nose and followed.

Clara made her way through the small cottage to the front room to find Arthur Foster face down on the floor. She looked around and saw the source of the gas: a small Primus stove, exuding gas without a flame. Holding her breath, she switched it off. Then she rushed to the man on the floor. The dog, Sammy, was pawing at him.

Clara knelt beside him and checked his breathing. It was faint, but there.

'Take the dog out!' she said to Bella. 'And run to the manor. Get Hawkes. Don't take no for an answer. Tell him to bring his car. This man needs to get to a hospital.'

Bella grabbed the dog's collar and pulled it with her.

Clara turned her attention to Foster. She eased him onto his back and checked his vital signs again. His breathing was faint and his complexion an alarming shade of blue. Although the house was now ventilated there was still a strong smell of gas in the air. She grabbed the lapels of his jacket and heaved him out the back door onto the gravel. She checked his pulse again; it was slowing.

'Oh no! Oh no!' And then, to her horror, it stopped. She was not a qualified doctor or nurse but she had read enough scientific papers to know that external heart massage – by repetitively compressing the sternum – had reportedly jump-started hearts in dogs and was in the experimental phase in humans. It was worth a go. She pushed and pushed, and checked and checked, until she was at the point of exhaustion. But, just as she heard a car pull up at the front of the cottage, she detected a pulse again. Inspector Hawkes and Bella appeared a moment later.

'He's alive again,' said Clara, on the cusp of elation and despair. 'But I don't know for how much longer.'

Chapter 26

Clara did her best to stay awake on the drive back from Ashington. She was exhausted and the pain in her muscles was spreading, but there was just too much to talk about with Inspector Hawkes to give into it. Arthur Foster had not regained consciousness, but he was still alive and in the good care of the medical staff at Ashington Hospital who were used to treating miners who had accidentally inhaled noxious fumes. Hawkes, after seeing a welt on the back of Foster's head, had swiftly come to the conclusion that someone had tried to murder him. He'd arranged for the local constabulary to guard the patient until further notice.

'We can rule out attempted suicide, can't we?' asked Clara. 'Unless he got the bash on the head as he hit the floor.'

'On the back of his head? Probably not. And with someone already murdered on the estate and the attempt on your life earlier, there's good reason to suspect foul play. We'll know for certain when he wakes up.'

If he wakes up, thought Clara, but did not voice her pessimistic thoughts.

'So, Miss Cuddy,' continued Hawkes, speaking to Bella as she sat in the back seat of the car. 'You say you saw Miss Parker, Lady Penford's maid, at the cottage just an hour before you and Miss Vale found Foster in distress?'

'Aye, I did. She was very aggressive with him. And then she threatened Miss Vale.'

'What exactly did she say?'

'She called Miss Vale a dreadful woman and said she had to be stopped before she found out the secret. Then she said she had ways and means of stopping her.'

'What secret is that?' asked Hawkes as he turned the car towards Penford Manor.

'We don't know, do we, Miss Vale?' answered Bella, evasively.

'No, we don't,' Clara replied quickly, not adding that they were following some clues they hoped might unearth it. She waited for Hawkes to probe further, but he didn't.

'Well, whatever this "secret", she seems perturbed you might find out what it is. So, we will need to ascertain her whereabouts when you were in Newbiggin. I've arranged for a couple of bobbies from the Ashington station to head down there and question the locals. The folk in the fishermen's café, the vicar at the church, the crew at the lifeboat station, the families on the beach, Mrs Stanley's neighbours . . . Who did they see? Other than you and me. You never know, it might turn something up. I'd be doing it myself, but I need to get to Penford Manor.'

'Hopefully someone will have been spotted,' said Clara, stifling a yawn and repositioning her aching shoulders, 'but I don't think Parker could have got back from Newbiggin in time to talk to Foster and be overheard by Bella.'

'But Meyer did,' said Bella.

'What's that?' asked Hawkes.

With a nod of approval from Clara, Bella told the inspector their suspicions about the German valet.

Hawkes turned to Clara, frowning. 'I see there's a lot you have been keeping from me, Miss Vale.'

'With good reason,' snapped Clara, her mood not helped by her aching muscles.

Hawkes raised a surprised brow. 'And what good reason is that?'

'That you will shut down my investigation. I cannot afford to have two non-paying clients in a row. So as long as the two cases were not proven to be linked there was no need to pass on everything. But now . . .'

'But now it's obvious they are linked,' finished Hawkes.

'Yes,' said Clara, suddenly deflated. She didn't know what else to say. Hawkes was right. The cases *were* linked and she must turn the investigation over to the police. She would have to go back to the manor to tell Lady Penford she had no choice but to withdraw from the case, and then to pass on all her evidence to Hawkes. And that would be it. She and Bella would go back to Newcastle with an unfinished case and an unpaid bill. Again.

Hawkes drove on in silence, passing bucolic fields of grazing sheep. Clara hunched moodily in the passenger seat next to him. Bella slumped behind them.

Eventually Hawkes turned to Clara, his tone and demeanour conciliatory. 'Miss Vale, I must say, you and Miss Cuddy have been very helpful to me so far. You photographed the crime scene. You helped identify the likely place of death. You found the lighter which I still hope will be linked to either the killer or a witness to the killing. And as for Mr Foster, you've literally been a life-saver. The investigation's clearly far too big for me to handle on my own. I've asked the two bobbies to come to Penford Manor when they've finished in Newbiggin, but they can only spare one at such short notice. I'm afraid that will not be enough. I'll be calling in further reinforcements from Newcastle, but they won't get here before tomorrow. And that might be too late. I have a feeling that tonight might prove to be pivotal in this case. Things are coming to a head. And as such, I will be staying overnight at the manor. There has already been one attempt on your life, so I suggest Miss Cuddy sleep with you. And I shall request a room nearby.'

Clara bit her lip. She was irked that Hawkes was taking over. However, she *was* pleased to hear him say he still needed her help. She sighed, inwardly. She did *not* like playing second fiddle to anyone, but if this was the best she could hope for . . . *No!* What was she thinking? Why was she rolling over so easily? She gave herself a good internal shake. She would not be sidelined. She would not be hounded off this case. But she needed to tread very carefully.

'All right,' she said eventually, shifting her painful shoulders. 'You have a deal. I will share all the information I have with you as long as I am able to continue with my side of the investigation.'

He cocked his head. 'And which is *your* side?'

'The blackmailing case. That is what I was hired to investigate. That is the secret Parker was referring to. And when I find out what the secret is, it may be the key to both of our cases. I will of course confer with you as I go, but I need to be free to pursue this. Do you agree to those terms?'

Clara heard Bella chuckle.

Hawkes cleared his throat. 'You're pushing your luck, Miss Vale, but yes, I can agree to those terms. For now. When we get back to the manor, I intend to re-interview everyone in light of the attacks on you and Foster. And while I'm doing that, by all means do what you need to do. I shall let it be known that you have my blessing. Now, tell me *everything* you know. . .'

Hawkes, Clara and Bella pulled up to the estate garages to see a blazing row erupting between Sir Bill, Lady Penford and Teddy. On the sidelines were Ada von Schneider, the baron, and the valet Meyer. The chauffeur, Mr Rogers, stood nearby, looking embarrassed. He guarded two vehicles: the black Model T and the silver Rolls.

Hawkes parked the scuffed old black police car and got out, followed by Clara and Bella. They approached the warring party.

Teddy, with voice raised, pointed to the cars. 'I just want to borrow one of the motors. The bike's out of order so I want to use one of those. Is that such a crime?'

'You know there's a very important dinner tonight. Your mother expects you to be there. You need to be there for the announcement,' growled Sir Bill. 'We went over this the other day. Nothing has changed.'

'But I'll be back in time! For God's sake, can't you trust me?'

'Unfortunately we can't, darling.' Lady Penford's voice was sharp but not raised. 'You've proven yourself unreliable too many times. You know how important this is. You might get delayed. We can't take the risk.'

'Why do you treat him like a child, Justina?' This was from Ada von Schneider.

'I *do not* treat him like a child, Ada. And if you don't mind, this is none of your business.'

'But tonight's announcement *is* my business. Teddy is the heir to the von Richner estates too. And if what I think is going to happen does happen then it will very much *be* my business.'

The two women squared up to one another. Their respective husbands caught each other's eyes and agreement passed between them.

'Come now,' said Sir Bill. 'Let us not air our family business in front of the servants and guests.'

The baron said something to his wife in German which Clara assumed was along the same lines.

Then the baron said in English, 'This is why I offered for Meyer to take Teddy, Justina. To ensure he returns in time.'

'But what is so important that he needs to go *now*?' asked Lady Penford.

'I'm standing right here, Mother. Why don't you ask me?' Teddy was visibly agitated, his fingers twitching on his thigh.

'All right, what is so important?'

'I have business to attend to in Newcastle.'

'What kind of business?'

Ada von Schneider threw her hands into the air. 'He's not a child, Justina. He's a grown man. He does not have to tell you his business!'

Then, before Lady Penford could offer a retort, Inspector Hawkes stepped forward.

'If you don't mind, ladies and gentlemen, no one is going anywhere. And the only business that is going to be dealt with today is police business. No one is to leave this estate without my permission. And that is an official order. I will be placing a police sergeant on the gate. He has orders to not let anyone out and to inform me immediately if anyone arrives. Sir Bill, as your groundsman is indisposed, can you put someone in the gatehouse to back up the sergeant please?'

'I'll send my valet.'

'No, not him. Nor that man.' He pointed to Meyer. 'I need to speak to both of them. And to take *his* fingerprints.' Meyer was impassive. Then Hawkes turned to the chauffeur. 'You. Rogers, is it?'

'It is, sir.'

'You go.'

Rogers looked to Sir Bill who nodded his approval. Then Sir Bill turned to Hawkes. 'Foster. How is he?'

'He's alive. Thanks to Miss Vale. She saved his life.' Hawkes then went on to detail Clara's life-saving measures.

'Thank you, Miss Vale,' said Sir Bill. 'It's a terrible business. I would never have thought Foster would try to take his own life. What could have provoked him?'

'I'm afraid I do not believe it was a suicide attempt,' said Hawkes.

Clara watched carefully to see if anyone in the group did not look surprised at this revelation. But the shock appeared universal. Even Meyer.

Hawkes batted away the questions directed at him and said: 'There have now been two possible murder attempts and one murder in the space of two days.

'Two murder attempts?' asked Teddy. 'Who else?'

Clara braced herself. She had not told anyone, other than Bella, and Bella had not had time to mention it to anyone.

Hawkes looked to her. She nodded. Yes, he could tell them.

'It was Miss Vale. Someone tried to push her off a cliff in Newbiggin earlier today.'

'Good God! Clara, are you all right?' Teddy's concern appeared genuine.

'I am, thank you,' said Clara, not wanting to elaborate any further.

'Thankfully, I was there to save her,' said Hawkes, who was not averse to casting himself as the hero as he described her struggle to hang onto the branch and his valiant effort to haul her back up the cliff before she plunged to her death on the rocks below.

A collective gasp rippled through the group. Clara shuffled uncomfortably, waiting for the attention to turn back to her. But before it could, Hawkes continued with a voice of authority. 'So, in light of these new developments, I am now going to interview every single person on this estate – even if it takes all night. I'll need to set up shop in your library, Sir Bill, and I'll require the assistance of your butler to ensure everyone – and I mean *everyone* – speaks to me.

I'll start with you.' He pointed to Meyer. 'Oh,' he added, indicating the rack of guns being prepared for the grouse shoot, 'and I'll want that lot under lock and key until further notice. Bring me the key as soon as it's done.'

Lady Penford was affronted. 'But what about the Glorious Twelfth? We will need them tomorrow!'

Hawkes turned on his heel, incredulous. 'You do not seriously believe your hunt is going ahead, Lady Penford?'

'And why not?' She raised herself to her full height, her aristocratic chin jutting towards the police inspector.

Hawkes was not cowed. He too straightened his spine – he was a good six inches taller than the lady. 'Because, madam, there is a murderer on the loose. And this is an official police investigation. I have the authority to shut down whatever I deem necessary. And I deem *this* necessary. So, if you don't mind, Miss Vale has some questions to ask you – with my full support – and I expect you to *fully* cooperate.'

Lady Penford's ice-blue eyes sought and found Clara. 'Well, that's just as well. Because *I* have some questions for Miss Vale, too.'

Chapter 27

Clara wished she had time for a full rub-down with liniment oil, but the best she could muster was some aspirin powder in a glass of water. As Hawkes set up his interview room in the library, Clara arranged to meet Lady Penford in her private sitting room.

She knocked on the door and was surprised to see Lady Penford herself open it. The lady wasted no time. 'Sit down, Miss Vale. You owe me an explanation.'

Clara took a seat in front of the Japanese room divider. Lady Penford perched on a chair opposite, an occasional table between them.

'Is Parker not here?' asked Clara.

'She is not.'

And where is she? Clara wanted to ask, but she could tell that Lady Penford was on the verge of rage and did not want to provoke her.

'Well, I have a lot to tell you.'

Lady Penford tightened her lips like a drawstring bag. 'As you should. You have been most disappointing, Miss Vale. I expected results much sooner than this. I hired you to investigate this quietly, to keep a lid on everything and to expose the culprit with as little fuss and disruption as possible to my social plans. But it has been quite the opposite.'

'It is hardly my fault there has been a murder, Lady Penford. And there was no option but to call in the police. That would have happened whether I was here or not.'

'Oh would it? I'm not so sure. You see, I think it was your investigation – that you failed to keep secret – that brought all this on. If you had quietly gone about your business – as you were hired to do – none of this would have happened.'

Clara was astounded at how Lady Penford was twisting events to blame everything on her. But she forced herself to remain calm and to think clearly.

'I see,' she said. 'Well, I'm glad you also now think the death of Harry Stanley is linked to the blackmailing. I agree with that. And I now have evidence that it was very likely he who typed that note to you.'

Without waiting for Lady Penford's response she reached into her bag and withdrew the sheet of paper she'd typed at the library, along with the blackmail note. She laid the two side by side on the table and pointed out the chipped 'e' on each page. 'This proves that the blackmail note was typed at the Ashington miners' library. The librarian there confirms that Harry Stanley was using the typewriter last Monday, the day before the note was delivered here. Stanley was seen here on the Tuesday and Sir Bill spoke to him at Arthur Foster's cottage. So, he could very well have given it to someone to slip under your door then.'

Lady Penford leaned forward. 'Do you know who that "someone" was?'

Clara shook her head. 'Not yet. The fingerprints I took this morning are not a match for any that have been collected so far. The only person whose prints I don't have are Meyer's, the von Schneider valet. But I have loaned my fingerprinting kit to Inspector Hawkes, and he will rectify that as we speak.'

Lady Penford's eyes narrowed. 'So, Meyer is the accomplice?'

Clara shrugged. 'We don't have evidence of that yet, but we are considering it, yes.' Clara did not divulge the suspicion that Meyer – on the evidence of the sand on the borrowed car – might have been the person to push her over the cliff too.

'Why on earth would Klaus von Schneider's valet be working with a miner from Ashington to blackmail me? And how on earth do either of them know my secret?'

Clara raised her forefinger. 'Well, as to the first, hopefully Inspector Hawkes will get to the bottom of that. If he thinks there is enough to go on, he will arrest Meyer and take him in for interrogation. As to the second . . .' Clara reached into her bag and withdrew the poetry book. 'Have you seen this book before? *The Rhymes of a Red Cross Man* by the poet Robert Service.'

Lady Penford's eyes widened then suddenly narrowed. 'Where did you get that?' she hissed.

'Harry Stanley left it at the library.' Clara opened the book to the inscription page. 'It belonged to Teddy. Sent to him by your other son, Rupert.'

Lady Penford's hand flashed to her mouth as she stifled a gasp. 'Why did that man have Teddy's book?'

'That's what I'm hoping to find out,' said Clara. She went on to show Lady Penford the poem which had been quoted in the blackmail note.

'So you see,' she concluded, as the blood drained from Lady Penford's face, 'I believe the secret you are so desperate to keep has something to do with your two late sons and their death in the war. What is the secret, your ladyship? What is worthy of blackmail? Or murder. I can't help you any further if I don't have this most basic of information. If you don't tell me, I will have to ask Teddy – as this book is his.'

'No!' cried the lady as she snatched the book from Clara. 'Don't talk to Teddy! He's too fragile. He's . . .' Lady Penford's hands quivered as she held the book on her lap. She stroked the page on which her middle son had written to her youngest son in memory of her eldest.

'Teddy had his first breakdown when we heard that Rupert had died and then his father soon afterwards. This book, although sent before Rupert left France, only reached us after his death. I decided Teddy was too fragile to see it. So I confiscated it before it reached him.'

'What did you do with it?'

'I put it in a box in the attic.'

'You put it in there yourself? You went into the attic?'

Lady Penford shook her head. 'No. I asked Parker to put it there for me. Parker always understood Teddy's fragility – since he was a very young child – and helped me protect him.'

'Where is Parker now?'

'I don't know.'

'When did you last see her?'

Lady Penford thought a moment. 'At the croquet. She left early. She said she had a headache. I let her go.'

'And you haven't seen her since?'

'No.'

'You do know that Parker was seen at Arthur Foster's cottage just before the attempt was made on his life, don't you?'

Lady Penford nodded her assent. 'I do. Is the inspector going to speak to her about it?'

Clara nodded. 'Yes. When she turns up. For now, we are both following other lines of enquiry. Which brings me back to the book. So it went into the attic back in 1918. Could someone have found it?'

Lady Penford shook her head. 'Not easily. It was in a strong box locked with a key.'

'Who else had access to the key?'

'Only me and . . . Parker.'

Lady Penford got up and walked to a bureau. She opened it and retrieved a japanned box. She lifted the lid and retrieved a bunch of keys. She flicked through them and then turned to Clara, her face ashen. 'The key has gone.'

'All right,' said Clara, trying to sound calm and considered. 'That explains how this book emerged from the attic but not how it got into Harry's possession. We'll consider that in a moment. For now, I'd like to know if there was anything else in that box.'

Lady Penford's hands started quivering again. 'Yes. And if this has been taken from the box then . . . then . . .' she bit her lip '. . . that's how they found out my secret.' She slumped into the chair opposite Clara.

Clara leaned forward. '*What is* this secret, Lady Penford? It's not just that you kept a book from Teddy, is it? It's much more serious than that.'

'Of course it's more serious than that!' the lady snapped, steel returning to her eyes. She flicked through the poetry book and stopped at the dedication page to Robert Service's brother who died in 1916. She swallowed hard, composing herself. 'All right. I will tell you. Because Parker knows anyway. And when you – or that policeman – find her, she might tell you. So best it comes from me. I placed this book in the strong box along with some correspondence from the War Office and a letter from Ada von Schneider.'

'Does the baroness know this secret too?'

Lady Penford nodded. 'She does. My first husband – her cousin – told her about it. After Otto died Ada and I decided it best that no one knew – for the sake of both our families. That was the gist of the letter from her.'

'And the letter from the War Office?'

Lady Penford leaned back in her chair and sighed. 'Well, there was that and also a letter from one of my cousins. He was high up in the War Office at the time. I asked him to amend the report.'

'What report?'

'The report that concluded that my son, Michael, was shot trying to desert to the Germans in 1916.'

Clara was shocked but she would not allow Lady Penford to see it. 'I see. And may I ask what the report was amended to?'

'That he was on an intelligence sortie. Michael – like all my children – spoke German fluently. The report was amended to say he was planning to infiltrate the German ranks and act as a double agent. But then he was accidentally shot when one of his own men did not know the reason he was heading to the German trench.'

'I see.' Clara could understand why Lady Penford – whose family had been suspected of being collaborators during the war, and who had tried so hard to rehabilitate their reputation – would not want this information to come out. 'So, your cousin in the War Office knew what really happened?'

Lady Penford nodded. 'Yes, he and Ada were the only two who knew.'

'Where is your War Office cousin now?'

'He died a few years ago.'

'So it's only Ada who knows now.'

'Yes. And Parker. She always denied it, but I knew she'd sneaked a look at the correspondence.'

Clara tapped her finger to her chin. 'All right. But only Parker would have access to the key.'

'Yes. Do you think she is the one blackmailing me?'

Clara shrugged. 'I don't know. We'll only find out when we speak to her. But . . . there is still someone else involved. I took both Ada and Parker's fingerprints and they did *not* match the prints on the cabinet or the partial prints on the note. So, if they are in on this – either individually or together – then they used someone else to take the note from Harry Stanley and to steal the tea caddy.'

'And why on earth was Harry Stanley involved in this?' asked Lady Penford, bemusement writ large on her face.

'I don't know. Although there is a chance that he met your son Teddy at an event at the Miners' Institute. Now, I'm sorry if this is indelicate, but do you have any reason to believe that Teddy is romantically attracted to men?'

Lady Penford's jaw dropped. 'I beg your pardon?'

'I'm sorry,' said Clara. 'I know it's not something you would like to talk about, but is there any chance—'

Lady Penford's jaw closed and clenched. 'Absolutely not. In fact, quite the opposite. There have been times when Teddy's philandering with women below his station has been quite the embarrassment. So, you'd better scotch that line of thinking.'

Clara nodded. 'All right, thank you for clarifying that. But we still don't know who was working with Harry Stanley. Or how the book – and the contents of those War Office letters – were taken from the attic. We'll need to find Parker. She was the last person seen with Mr Foster before he was attacked, and she had access to your secret letters. It looks like she is now a suspect in both the blackmailing and the attempted murder – and possibly Harry Stanley's murder too. I'm afraid I'll have to tell Inspector Hawkes . . .'

'No!' Lady Penford stood up, knocking the occasional table over. 'You cannot tell him! You promised me, Miss Vale!'

Clara stood too. 'I must! It will come out anyway when Parker is found. Or whomever is the accomplice. Or if Foster wakes up. Or if Ada von Schneider decides to tell what she knows. I'm afraid it's just a matter of time, your ladyship, too many people know already. If I tell Hawkes myself, he will be able to use his police resources to find Parker and any other accomplices. He will not allow me to do much more investigating on my own. There is much that will be out of my hands. But I could still have a hand in this . . .'

Lady Penford walked to the window and looked out over the grounds of her ancestral home. After some time, she turned back to Clara. 'All right. You can tell him. But please, ask him to keep it quiet for as long as possible. I am absolutely devastated that Parker might have betrayed my secret. But there is a very important announcement to be made this evening at dinner. I do not want my guests – particularly your family and the Fitzgilberts – to hear about this before then. And when they do, I hope they will not blame Teddy for what his brother did.'

'It's been fourteen years since Michael died . . . the war is over. Emotions are not as high as they once were,' said Clara.

Lady Penford shook her head, sadly. 'For some the war will never be over, Miss Vale.'

Chapter 28

Clara left Lady Penford staring out of the window, deep in thought. As tempted as she was to go and have a lie-down, she needed to speak to Inspector Hawkes. On the way to the library, she passed the drawing room. Inside, four people were at a table playing cards: her brother Antony, Lily Fitzgilbert, Kate Richner and Matt Fowler. Antony said something and Lily leaned towards him and replied. Antony laughed and edged closer to her.

They're looking very chummy, thought Clara. Was Antony's mission to marry an heiress making progress? She was just about to move on to the library when Kate Richner spotted her.

'Clara!'

'Hello, Kate, I'll see you shortly. I must speak to the inspector.'

'Oh, please come here first. We've just heard what happened to you. Are you all right?'

Clara looked to the library where the door was still closed. Hawkes would still be there in a few minutes. She stepped into the drawing room. Kate jumped up and gave her a hug. 'Is it true? Did someone push you over a cliff?'

Clara nodded.

Kate paled and dropped back into her seat. 'Oh, it's just too awful. First poor Harry Stanley, then you.'

Matt patted his step-cousin's hand sympathetically.

'Don't worry, Kate, I'm all right,' said Clara.

'But you might not have been!' This was from Clara's brother, who tore himself away from the attentions of Lily to address his sister. 'Good God, old girl, who would do that to you?'

'We don't know yet. But Hawkes has some theories.'

'We were absolutely devastated when we heard, weren't we, Mattie?' said Kate, barely holding back her tears.

'We absolutely were.' Matt Fowler stood and offered Clara his seat. 'Do sit down, Miss Vale, you've been through quite an ordeal.'

Clara smiled at the mine manager. 'Thank you, Mr Fowler, but I really am all right. It was quite a shock, but I'm not seriously injured. By the way, I didn't know you were returning to the manor today.'

Matt remained standing. 'I was planning on coming this evening – Lady Penford has invited me to dinner – but I came early as Kate rang me at the office to ask for a lift.'

'I thought one of the Trevelyan staff was going to bring you over,' said Clara.

Kate nodded. 'I thought so too, but then Lady Molly needed to go somewhere and it was getting too complicated. So, I suggested I ask Matt instead. Seeing as he was heading this way after his meeting with Sir Charles.' Then her voice cracked as she shook her head in despair. 'And just as we arrived, we heard that poor Foster nearly died! Good Lord, Clara, what's going on?'

'These things always seem to happen around Miss Vale,' said Lily, sarcastically.

Clara glared at her. Antony laughed.

'Oh, come on, Clara, Lily is just jesting, aren't you, Lily?'

Lily batted her eyelids at him then gave Clara a disingenuous smile. 'Of course I am.'

Clara did not return the smile. 'Sorry, but I need to go. I shall see you all later at dinner.'

Antony caught her hand as she was leaving. 'By the way, Mother is looking for you, Clara. She's heard about your latest exploits. Best you soothe her.'

Clara sighed. 'I'll see her as soon as I can.'

A few moments later, Clara was knocking on the door of the library.

The door opened and Hawkes greeted her with: 'Miss Vale! This is not a good time . . .'

Clara looked past him to see Miss Klopp – the von Schneider maid – weeping in an armchair.

'Ah, I see,' said Clara. She lowered her voice to a whisper only he could hear. 'Sorry, but this is urgent. I've spoken to Lady Penford and there's something you need to hear. It should inform any further questioning you undertake.'

He nodded. 'I see. All right. I'll just finish up here. We're at a delicate point in our discussions but it shouldn't be too much longer. Where shall I meet you?'

'I think I need some fresh air. Will you come to the walled garden?'

Hawkes nodded again. 'I'll see you as soon as I can.'

Clara tried to find Bella but couldn't locate her, so she proceeded to the garden on her own. The day was still warm but dark clouds were brewing and the air was charged with the threat of an electric storm. Clara considered the elements needed for a thunderstorm: unrelenting heat, moisture, unstable air, and a nudge mechanism to push the heated air upwards. If the hot air continued to rise it would eventually reach the freezing upper atmosphere and when the heat and cold met, a thunderstorm would be unleashed.

That was exactly what was happening at Penford Manor. All the elements were brewing ready for an almighty clash. Clara's scientific mind spiralled onwards. The most dangerous part of a thunderstorm was the lightning. Lightning is a giant spark of electricity in the atmosphere. For a while, the air acts as an insulator between the positive and negative charges in a thundercloud. But when the difference in charge becomes too great, when the negative outweighs the positive, or the positive the negative, the insulating capacity breaks down and a bolt of lightning is produced – the consequences could be deadly.

The insulating capacity of Lady Penford's secrecy was breaking down. The negative was beginning to outweigh the positive. How long until lightning would strike? But it had already struck, Clara reminded herself: Harry Stanley and Arthur Foster. Not to mention a strike on her own person.

But what was the nudge mechanism that set it all in motion? If Lady Penford, Ada von Schneider and Parker had kept this secret for so long, why was it about to come out now? What had changed recently to upset the balance between positive and negative? Or what was about to change?

Clara considered the purpose of Lady Penford's gathering. Ostensibly it was to mark the beginning of the grouse shooting season. But Kate had told her that it was really to have a test run of opening the estate in future years to paying guests. However, from what Clara had seen, the real purpose was to try to match up the unmarried Kate and Teddy. Particularly Teddy. Isn't that what Kate had told her when they first walked to the walled garden? He was due to have his mental capacity reassessed. Both he and Lady Penford were hoping the trusteeship could be lifted and he would be able to take full control of his inheritance. And a stable marriage would be in his favour. So, that was what was about to change. Teddy would take control of all of this.

She looked around her and took in the vast grounds, the grand manor and the land beyond, including tenant farms and coalfields, all the way to the coast. The coalfields were owned by the Penford family, and the mine operators were granted a licence to exploit the mineral deposits – but they did not actually own the land they mined. Now, who would lose out if Teddy did not reissue the licence or changed the terms of it? Clara nodded to herself. Yes, it was obvious: Sir Bill Fowler. It would be in Sir Bill's interest to keep Teddy under his control. He was the court-appointed guardian as long as Teddy was considered mentally incompetent. But now that might change. And if it did, Sir Bill's shady business deal with Baron von Schneider, to circumvent restrictions and export coking coal to Germany, would be in jeopardy.

She still suspected the von Schneider valet had something to do with this. Was he acting on the instructions of the baron and Sir Bill? She would be interested to hear what Sandy Hawkes had found out about that in his most recent questioning. She remembered that the baron and Meyer were out and about on the morning when Harry Stanley was murdered. They were each other's alibi. Could they have killed Stanley? It was certainly possible. And Meyer had the capacity to have driven to Newbiggin, pushed her off the cliff, driven back, seen Bella then tried to kill Arthur Foster too. She would mention her theory to Hawkes.

But, she realised, her theory – her hypothesis, if you will – still had a lot of unproven parts. How, for instance, did any of this tie in to Lady Penford's secret about her eldest son deserting to the Germans during the war? What was the connection between Meyer and Parker? Were they working together? Had they both been in cahoots with Harry Stanley? And were they being controlled by someone else? Sir Bill and Baron von Schneider? It was certainly possible. And plausible. But what about Miss Wren? Why had she not mentioned that she knew Harry Stanley? And then there was Teddy and the lighter. If it hadn't fallen out of Teddy's pocket as she'd suspected – or perhaps, but less likely, Kate's – might someone else have slipped it into her car without her seeing, as she'd discussed with Hawkes.

Clara shook her head. The dots were still not connecting. Nor was the motive. How would the public exposure of Lady Penford's secret stop Teddy being declared mentally competent? Was it hoped that bringing up the memories of his brothers' and father's deaths, and telling him the shameful truth that Michael was a deserter, might push him back over the edge? In order to prevent that, would the next stage of the blackmail plot be to compel Lady Penford to keep her youngest son under trusteeship? Perhaps this first stage – pay fifty pounds or the secret would be out – was just to alert Lady Penford that someone knew about it. To put her on edge. To frighten her. And when she had taken the bait, showing she was prepared to keep the secret hidden by paying the money, then the next stage would be implemented. However, whoever was behind it – and behind Harry Stanley and Parker and Meyer – they had not expected Lady Penford to call in a detective. In fact, hadn't Sir Bill asked his secretary to try to stop his wife meeting with Clara?

Yes, that was it.

Lady Penford had been correct. It was Clara's presence that had been the destabilising nudge. And that's why someone had tried to kill her.

Clara had by now reached the old oak door that opened into the beautiful walled garden. But as she turned the iron ring to lift the latch, she heard a scuffling in the woodland behind her. She froze. Was someone following her? The scuffling stopped. Clara's breathing quickened. Was the killer from the cliff about to try again? She looked around her, wondering the best route to take. *Straight ahead*. She should get through the door and then brace it shut.

Something moved again in the wood, and it was moving very quickly. Clara wrenched the door open, flung herself inside and was just about to slam the door shut when something brown, white and furry slipped through the gap. Clara slammed the door, leaned against it with all her weight and looked down into the panting face of Sammy the springer spaniel.

'Was that you I heard?'

Sammy sat down, still panting, and raised his paw.

Clara's heart was still beating nine to the dozen, but she started to laugh. 'Oh, you did give me a fright! It was just you, you silly dog! Wasn't it?' She paused for a moment and put her ear to the door, still keeping her weight against it. But she could hear and feel nothing. She tentatively opened the door and looked to left and right, listening for the scuffling she had previously heard. All was silent.

Relieved, she patted the spaniel and headed down the gravel path towards the Greek temple folly with Sammy trotting at her heels.

The garden was bathed in that curious diffused light that comes when clouds darken but the sun is still shining. The cerise blooms of the hydrangea seemed richer and bolder and the blousy pink, purple and white delphiniums strained to outdo them. The wind was picking up, as though the coming storm was taking a few practice breaths, and the smooth surface of the lily pond – where Harry Stanley had lost his life – swirled in anticipation. Sammy stopped to drink from the pond, as the yellow irises, witnesses to the recent murder, started to sway. Then a wind chime picked up the rhythm, providing a discordant accompaniment to the dog's lapping.

Clara looked up to the swelling clouds: she was no meteorologist but she reckoned she had about a quarter of an hour before the rain started. She hoped Hawkes would get here before then – and bring an umbrella! If not, they could always find shelter in the Greek temple.

Clara made her way to the temple and seated herself on the bench so she had a good view of the path from the door. She would see Hawkes – or anyone else – as they arrived. As far as she was aware, the door was the only way in and out of the garden. Unless someone scaled the walls . . .

Clara, still unnerved by her brush with death earlier in the day, shot a glance left and right. Then chastised herself. If she was so concerned about being attacked again, why had she come here on her own? She would not be cowed. She could not wait for a chaperone to accompany her everywhere she went. But she would be vigilant. As long as she could see the area around her she felt confident she could defend herself from a physical attack. Or at least give herself time to escape. She had ensured she was wearing trousers and could run unencumbered by skirts and petticoats. But there was one place she couldn't see: the back of the temple. She did a quick circuit, checking she really was alone. And she was. But as she came back round the side, she noticed there was some carving on one of the pillars. She examined it more closely and discovered it was a carved heart.

It looked recent and did not bear the signs of any weathering. A carved heart was a sign of lovers. Had lovers met here, recently? Might Harry have lied to his mother when he said there was nothing going on between him and Kitty anymore? One of the questions that needed answering was why Harry Stanley was on the estate the night he died. And, specifically, here in the walled garden where he met his end in the lily pond. Clara had assumed it was to meet his fellow blackmailer. Up until now she was working on the assumption that the blackmailer would be exposed by their fingerprints. Only one set of prints was missing: Meyer's. But what if Meyer was not the only one Harry was meeting? What if he was meeting Kitty too? It seemed increasingly likely that there was a blackmailing team. Were Parker *and* Kitty part of the team from the house? The ball got rolling when Meyer arrived with the von Schneiders on Tuesday. The day the blackmail note was delivered. The note was typed in advance in Ashington – possibly on Monday – and would have needed to be passed on to someone at the estate. And that was why Harry was here on Tuesday. Not just to confront Sir Bill about his business affairs.

So, Meyer and Parker and . . . perhaps . . . Kitty. Clara had already concluded that due to timing Parker could not have pushed her off the cliff. Nor could it have been Kitty, as she had been seen at the croquet around the time it happened. But she could still be involved. She could still have been the go-between with Harry and then passed on the note to Meyer to deliver. He could have delivered the note and stolen the tea caddy while his employers were playing tennis on the day they arrived. There would have been time for that, but it would have had to have been planned in advance. Clara traced her finger over the heart. Harry and Kitty. Is this where the lovers met? Did they meet here the night he died? Did Kitty watch as someone killed him? Or did Kitty kill him? She would not have had the strength to hold him under the water if he was fighting back. But the autopsy had revealed a blow to the head. If unconscious, or even just subdued, Kitty could have held his head underwater. But she could not have carried him on her own to the woods. That would have required the help of at least one strong man . . . or woman.

But *why* would Kitty have killed him? Was it just the case of a spurned lover? Had he tried to break up with her that night? Here in the Greek temple? Or was it a falling-out among thieves? Had they – and the third or fourth person – disagreed on how to split the fifty pounds? Or how to conduct the blackmailing scheme? Or had Harry threatened to tell what he knew?

Suddenly there was a flash of lightning followed by a clap of thunder. The garden lit up and Clara saw the silhouette of a man walking down the path.

It started to rain.

Chapter 29

Clara was relieved to see Sandy Hawkes walking towards her. As the rain started, he picked up his pace. She waved to him and he soon joined her and the dog in the temple.

'I see you didn't bring an umbrella either,' he said as he joined her on the bench.

'No. But fortunately we've got some shelter.'

Hawkes fussed with the dog for a few moments. 'I hope someone's looking after this lad with his master in the hospital.'

'I'll take him to Mrs Rogers the cook,' said Clara. 'She looked after him when you had Foster in for questioning. Speaking of that, do you think that's why he was attacked? Because he spoke to you?'

Hawkes shook his head. 'No, it's because he didn't speak to me. He didn't tell me anything useful at all – even though I let it be known that he had. I was hoping to flush someone else out. But I think he *did* know something. And the killer knew he did and wanted to make sure he didn't change his mind and speak to me again. If he wakes up, hopefully he'll be willing to tell me then.'

Clara nodded. 'Yes, that makes sense. And I believe I know what it was that he didn't tell you. The thing that Parker was insisting he continue to keep quiet when Bella overheard them. You see, Lady Penford has finally told me her secret – the one she is being blackmailed about.'

Clara went on to tell him what she had learned from her interview with Lady Penford.

Hawkes took it all in. 'I see,' he said eventually. 'So, you think this is all about the eldest Penford boy being a turncoat during the war.'

'I think it's part of it, yes. It would ruin her, socially, and it would ruin the Penford name – which would have a knock-on effect on

Teddy and his inheritance. And also, I think she fears that bringing this all up will make Teddy ill again.'

Hawkes nodded. 'Yes, that would make sense. Those would be dire consequences, at least from her perspective. And now someone has murdered the blackmailer. I wonder if Lady Penford ordered the killing.'

'No. I don't think so.'

Hawkes shrugged. 'Motive, means and opportunity. She certainly had motive.'

'Did she though? If the only motive was to keep her secret secret, why did she eventually tell me? And don't forget, I'm not the only person who knows. The von Schneiders and Parker also know.'

'Well, Parker *is* missing . . .'

Clara was taken aback. 'Are you suggesting Lady Penford killed her?'

Hawkes shrugged. 'I have to keep an open mind about it. Harry knew, he's dead. It seems that Foster knew, he's nearly dead. You knew . . .'

'Yes, but that happened *before* I knew her secret.'

'That's true. But it was just a matter of time until you did find out.'

'But she brought me on to the case!'

'Perhaps she regretted doing so . . .'

Clara watched the rain fall into the lily pond. That was true, Lady Penford did seem to regret calling her. The investigation was now out of the lady's control. But it was inevitable that it would become so. The restrictions she put on it from the beginning would never have worked – murder or no murder. To do her job properly Clara *had* to push the boundaries. Lady Penford hadn't expected that. Had she really hoped Clara could find the blackmailer but not find out what the blackmail was about?

Clara decided – for a moment – to set aside her musings about Sir Bill and Baron von Schneider pulling Meyer and Parker's strings, and the blackmailing 'team' they had assembled. 'All right,' she said, eventually, 'in the spirit of keeping an open mind, let's say Lady Penford might be behind the killing – and attempted killings. Now that means the only people left who know the secret are the von

Schneiders. Which means they too could be in danger. From Lady Penford and whoever she got to do her dirty work.'

'Or they're involved too,' observed Hawkes.

Clara smiled to herself. So perhaps they were on the same page after all. 'Go on,' she prompted.

Hawkes took off his hat and laid it on the seat beside him. 'I had a word with the maid, Miss Klopp. She had some interesting things to tell me about the baron's whereabouts on the morning of the murder.'

'And the valet Meyer?'

'Him too,' said Hawkes. 'Unfortunately though, his prints do not match those on the cabinet or the blackmail note.'

'Oh no! I was *sure* they would. So that exonerates him.' Clara folded her arms and sat back in a huff.

Hawkes smiled. 'Not entirely, Miss Vale. There is certainly enough circumstantial evidence to put him in the vicinity of all three assaults. And that is enough to take him in for police questioning.'

'So where is he now?'

'I have formally arrested him and arranged for him to be held in a secure room until I can have him transferred to a police station.'

'You're taking him in this evening?'

Hawkes looked at his watch and shook his head. 'No. I will do it tomorrow. There are more people I need to interview. He'll be safe where he is for now. Besides, if Meyer was involved, he was not acting alone.'

'That I agree with,' said Clara, and stood up.

The dog jumped up, ready for action. Hawkes did not.

'Come with me, I've got something to show you,' said Clara.

'Out there?' asked Hawkes, sinking back onto the bench.

'Are you scared of a little rain, Inspector?'

Hawkes laughed. 'That's more than a little rain!'

The rain was now almost torrential. 'Hmmm,' said Clara. 'All right, I'll show you when it clears.' She sat down and went on to describe the heart and her theory about Harry and Kitty meeting here as lovers.

'My, my,' said Hawkes, leaning back on the bench and running his finger around the brim of his hat. 'So, you think Kitty Wren might be involved after all.'

'What did she say to you?' asked Clara.

'She confirmed Harry's mother's story that they were no longer stepping out together.'

'Could she have lied to you? Could she still have been seeing Harry?'

'That's certainly possible,' said Hawkes. 'Or perhaps she did tell the truth. The relationship was over, but that doesn't mean they couldn't still work together on the blackmail plot. However, she does have an alibi for both you and Arthur Foster. She was at the croquet match. Didn't Miss Cuddy say she was there?'

Clara nodded. 'Yes, she did. But if she and Meyer were working together too that doesn't matter. And she is perfectly placed. As a lady's maid she can go anywhere in the manor, saying it's on behalf of her mistress. Lady Penford said that the key to the box in the attic was gone from her drawer. Kitty could have accessed that. Or Parker could have accessed it for her. Parker had already been indiscreet and told Arthur Foster, perhaps she had been indiscreet and told someone else. Or Ada von Schneider might have. It seems like Lady Penford's bubble of secrecy was leaking like a sieve—' she smiled '—if you'll excuse the mixed metaphor.'

Hawkes nodded. 'Yes, and it is also quite plausible that Miss Wren went to the woods and retrieved the lighter before Dr Malone and I arrived. Her whereabouts at that time have not been verified.'

'Hmmm,' said Clara. 'But why would she need to retrieve the lighter? I don't believe she smokes so it wouldn't point to her.'

'No, she doesn't. But it's still my bet that it belongs to the male accomplice. The person who helped carry the body. And that's who she's trying to protect.'

'Have you shown it to everyone?'

'Yes. They all deny any knowledge of it. But I still think it could be pivotal to the case.'

'I agree,' said Clara. 'Which is why I don't understand why it would be placed in my car for me to find. Is someone trying to help us find the killer or to frame someone?'

'Yes, that's something I still need to follow up on,' answered Hawkes. 'I want to find out who had access to the car overnight. That's something I will ask Rogers. He's currently backing up Sergeant Wilcox at the cottage.'

'Good idea. So, what else are we going to do? What are our next steps?'

'*Our* next steps?' asked Hawkes, with a wry smile.

'Yes, *our*. Don't start that again. I thought we had agreed we were going to pool our resources on this.'

Hawkes raised both hands. 'All right, all right. Yes, we have. And you have very kindly agreed to accompany me to the Policemen's Ball on Saturday. I hope you haven't forgotten that.'

'I haven't.' Clara reached down to stroke one of the dog's ears. Hawkes did the same. The dog was delighted, his tail thumping the floor.

Clara chuckled. 'He might just swoon from all the attention.'

'I don't blame him,' said Hawkes, his voice falling to an intimate whisper. Then his forefinger reached across the dog's head and stroked Clara's hand. She caught her breath but did not withdraw.

No one moved.

The curtain of rain fell, separating them from the outside world of murder and responsibilities and consequences. Soon the rain would stop, and the moment would be over. So when Hawkes moved towards her on the bench, she moved towards him. He transferred his hand from the dog's head to her face, caressing her cheek and pushing her hair behind her ear.

No one spoke.

And as the rain continued to fall, she leaned in and pressed her lips to his. He responded, and with a mutual sigh they sank into one another's arms and kissed. And that might have been all that would have happened. Or perhaps something more. They would never know . . .

Three loud bangs startled the dog. Hawkes and Clara raised their heads.

'That's not thunder,' said Hawkes.

'No,' said Clara. 'It's gunfire.'

Chapter 30

Bella stood at the back of the servants' hall – the meeting room for the staff of Penford Manor – waiting for the butler, Spencer, to address them. Beside him stood the housekeeper, Mrs Barnes, looking pale and serious. After the dramatic showdown in the stable yard between Teddy, his parents and the von Schneiders, which she, Miss Vale and Inspector Hawkes had walked in on, shock waves had spread through the estate. Hawkes had established his authority and Sir Bill, begrudgingly, had complied. Even though on this estate he was lord, his authority did not trump that of a representative of the King's constabulary.

'Is it true that Mr Rogers has been sent to help the police?' asked Mrs Rogers, her mop cap at a jaunty angle on her head.

'Yes, Mrs Rogers, it is,' replied Spencer. 'There will be a policeman in the gatehouse to ensure no one leaves or arrives unmonitored. Your husband will be assisting him. I believe more police officers will be arriving in the morning.'

'Will the shoot be off?' enquired the master of the hunt.

'I believe so. Inspector Hawkes has requested the guns be locked up.'

'Aye, I'll see to that,' answered the huntsman.

More questions were shot from the floor, but Spencer raised his hands to silence them. 'This is what I know so far.' He went on to explain – punctuated by gasps from his audience – that there had been an attack on Mr Foster, how his life had been saved (leaving out Bella's role in it) and that there had been a prior attack on Miss Vale. This was on top of the murder of the miner, Harry Stanley, which they had all been questioned about already. 'So,' he concluded, 'the inspector wants to speak to everyone again. He is currently speaking to the German pair – Meyer and Klopp – but after that, he will speak to us in this order.' He read through a list and then pinned it to a noticeboard. 'The interviews will be in the library. As each person is questioned, I expect the next person on the list to be waiting outside. Do not miss your turn. I will be monitoring this. As soon as you have finished your interview, return immediately to your duties. Mrs Barnes will be supervising that. I know this is a great shock to everyone, but we at Penford Manor are up to the task. We are representing Sir William and Lady Penford. I expect you all to do your duty. The sooner this business is dealt with, the sooner we can get back to normality. Any questions?'

There was an eruption of questions and speculation. Spencer answered a few then brought the room to order.

'Now, that is all I have to say. Get back to your duties. I shall now go upstairs and supervise the interviews.'

But Bella had a question. She stuck up her hand.

Spencer frowned. 'What is it, Miss Cuddy?'

'Where is Miss Parker? She is on the list for questioning but I don't see her anywhere.'

'I'm sure she is with Lady Penford.'

'How do you know?'

Spencer's face darkened. 'Because Parker is a loyal maid. She will be doing her duty.'

'Has anyone seen her? Since the croquet this morning?'

Spencer pinned his cold eyes on her. 'I think you should leave the questioning to the professionals, my girl.'

Something in Bella snapped. She was not a *girl*. She was a 34-year-old woman. She had been married and worked for a living before and after her ne'er do well husband abandoned her. She was a trained shop detective, an expert in jiu-jitsu and now in the employ of a private detection agency. She *was* a professional. And she was sick and tired of licking the arses of the gentry and their grovelling servants.

She put her hands on her hips and squared up to the butler. 'If I'd left it to someone else,' said Bella, 'Arthur Foster would be dead now. Oh aye, that's right. Who do you think it was that smashed the door in? I used an axe and me own brute strength. And who was it who ran for help while Miss Vale tended to him? And who helped get him in the car when he was rushed to hospital in Ashington?' Bella glanced around her into the astounded faces of two dozen servants. 'Aye, that's right, it was me. I'm working with Miss Vale – who you all know now is not just here as a guest – and I'm assisting her and Inspector Hawkes in this investigation. Miss Vale and me are detectives. *Professional* detectives. So, you can tell me or you can tell the polis later why you didn't tell me when you had the chance. *Where – is – Miss – Parker?*'

A tentative hand went up. It was Miss Wren.

'Aye, spit it out.'

'I saw her. I saw Miss Parker. After she left the croquet – when she said she had a headache – I saw her in Lady Katherine's room.'

'Oh aye? I thought you were at the croquet the whole time, Miss Wren? That's what you told Hawkes.'

Miss Wren blushed. 'I was. Most of the time. But I remembered there were some repairs I needed to do for Lady Katherine. I thought I'd best get it done when she was away. So, I left a few minutes early. And that's when I saw Miss Parker.'

Bella's eyes narrowed. 'And what was she doing in Lady Katherine's room?'

'That's what I asked her. She was kneeling down, looking in the bottom drawer of my ladyship's chest of drawers. I asked her what she was doing. But she just pushed past me and didn't answer. She's senior to me. So I didn't make a fuss.'

'Did she have something in her hands? Had she taken something from the drawer?'

'Not that I could see, no.'

'And what time was this? How much longer after I left the croquet? You did see me leave, didn't you?'

Miss Wren blinked a few times behind her spectacles. 'Yes, I did. I saw you—' she flashed a worried look at the butler '—I saw you and Mr Spencer having words. I left a few minutes after you. So, it must have been no more than five minutes or so after that that I saw Miss Parker.'

Bella nodded, thinking through the timetable. She had left the croquet and gone to the kitchen to get something to eat. Then she'd tried to eat in her bedroom but had left due to the weeping Gretchen Klopp. Thereafter she'd gone outside to eat in the stable yard. It had taken her a while to get to Arthur Foster's cottage with the dog as she had been delayed further by her encounter with Meyer. So yes, there had certainly been time for Parker to get from the manor to the cottage before her.

'Thank you, Miss Wren,' she said and turned to leave.

'And where do you think you're going?' asked Spencer.

'Wherever I damn well please!' She slammed the door behind her.

Bella searched for Miss Vale. She was not in her room nor with Lady Penford. She checked every one of the communal rooms in the manor, asking everyone she met – including Sir Randolph and Lady Vale – but no one knew where she was. She then tried the library, hoping to speak to Inspector Hawkes, but was told by a sulky Mr Spencer that the inspector was taking a short break.

Bella thought she might as well take a break too. There was nowt much more she could do until she'd spoken to Miss Vale and Inspector Hawkes. Time for a cup of tea. As she descended the stairs to the kitchen, she caught up with Gretchen Klopp heading to their room. The German woman had stopped crying but was still red-eyed and distressed.

'Oh, Miss Cuddy. There you are.'

'Hello, Miss Klopp. Are you feeling any better?'

Gretchen sniffed. 'I am fine, thank you.'

Bella put her hand on the woman's shoulder. 'You don't look fine, if you don't mind me saying so. Are you sure you don't want to talk about it?'

Gretchen sniffed again, then let out a long sigh. 'Yes . . . yes, I would like to talk about it. But I have been warned not to.'

Bella frowned. 'Warned by who?'

'My . . . my . . . employers. But, I do not think they will be my employers for much longer.'

'And why is that?'

'Because I have spoken to the policeman. They will soon find out.'

'And what did you tell him?'

Gretchen shook her head. 'I cannot say.'

Bella gave her a sympathetic smile. 'That's all right. I will find out myself. You don't have to tell me.'

'But how will you find out?'

'I will ask Miss Vale. She is working with Inspector Hawkes and I am working with her.'

Gretchen looked startled.

'You do know we're both detectives, don't you?'

'I . . . well . . . I had heard that. But I thought they were just rumours.'

Bella chuckled. 'No, not just rumours. It's true.'

'So . . . you . . . you are a *detective*?'

'I am,' said Bella, not trying to keep the pride from her voice.

'And you will find out anyway?'

'Yes, I will. But—' she squeezed Gretchen's arm '—I would prefer to hear it from you. Will you tell me?'

Gretchen looked quickly up and down the hall. Then she lowered her voice. 'Yes, I will. But not here. Do you want to go for a walk?'

Bella took one look at the sky and insisted they go back for their raincoats. Suitably attired, they headed off to walk the grounds. It did not matter really where they went, the purpose of their perambulation was to talk. And talk Gretchen did.

'This morning when you walked in on me crying I had just been giving a warning that I could lose my job.'

'Because of what happened last night?' asked Bella. 'When Mr Meyer came in and saw you drinking with me?'

Gretchen nodded. 'That was some of it. But there is more.' She paused and her brow furrowed. She appeared to be struggling to decide whether to continue. To Bella's relief, she did.

'You see, Miss Cuddy—'

'Please, call me Bella.'

Gretchen gave a grateful smile. 'Bella. Thank you. You see, Bella, Herr Meyer is a jealous man. When I first joined the baroness's employ, he took a – how do you say in English – a *fancy*. He took a fancy to me. He can be a charming man. I believed for a while that he might propose marriage. And I would have been happy to marry him. I am now thirty-six years old. I was twenty when the war started, twenty-four when it ended. In Germany – and I believe it is similar here – many of our young men were killed or severely injured, and so young women of my age did not have so many opportunities to marry. Two million of our soldiers died in that war. Some were married and left widows and orphans at home. Some were unmarried. Most, I think, were unmarried. And so, we were left with nearly two million – how do you say – *extra* women.'

'Surplus women,' said Bella. 'That's what they call them here.'

Gretchen smiled sadly. 'You too are a surplus woman?'

Bella laughed. 'No. Not me. I thought me husband had died in the war, but turned out he just went off with another woman.'

'I'm sorry,' said Gretchen.

'Not as sorry as he was after I kicked him in the conkers!' The two women laughed. Then Bella brought the conversation back to Gretchen. 'So, Meyer proposed then, did he?'

Gretchen shook her head. 'No. I think he was going to. But I saw him carrying on with some of the young girls in the household. One of them, a kitchen maid, became – how you say – with child?'

'Pregnant.'

'Yes, pregnant. So, I did not want him after that. I said he must marry the girl. He did not. But he became angry with me and . . . and . . . he struck me. I told the baroness, and she told the baron, and they warned him to leave me alone. But since then he has found other ways to hurt me.'

'Such as?'

'He looks for ways to get me fired.'

'And that's what happened last night?'

'Yes. I think it will now happen. You see, the baroness can get another lady's maid. The baron cannot get another valet.'

'Why not?'

'Because,' said Gretchen, as they turned towards the wood, 'Herr Meyer knows things about the baron. He is a keeper of secrets. And if the baron doesn't want them to come out, he must keep Meyer happy.'

'I see,' said Bella. *So, he's got a track record in blackmail. Interesting. Very interesting.*

The wind was picking up and she stopped to button her raincoat. 'Do you know what these secrets are?'

Gretchen stopped and turned to her, waiting for Bella to finish the buttoning. 'I do. I too have ears. I hear the baron and baroness talking. I hear telephone calls and see letters left on tables. But unlike Herr Meyer I have never told the baroness that I know. I have never even thought of using the information . . . until now. Because now I need protection.'

'From Meyer?'

Gretchen nodded. 'Yes, and possibly from the baron and baroness too if what I know is told.'

Gretchen's blue eyes bored into Bella's own. Bella felt as though her soul were being searched.

'Will you protect me, Bella?'

'Why do you think I can protect you, Gretchen?'

Gretchen swallowed hard. Trying to contain her emotion. 'Because you are a detective. And your Miss Vale is a detective. And there is a policeman in the house.'

'Have you told Inspector Hawkes what you are about to tell me?'

Gretchen shrugged. 'I have told him some of it. Not all. He was only asking me questions about the movements of the baron and Meyer the night and morning that man died. And where Meyer was earlier today – when your Miss Vale was pushed from the cliff. And where he was when the man in the cottage was gassed.'

'And where was he?'

'Herr Meyer left early this morning. He borrowed one of Sir William's cars.'

'Do you know where he went?'

'Yes. I heard him talking to the baron. He was going to the ferry port – the Port of Tyne – to book an extra ticket for us to go home.'

'An extra ticket? Who for?'

'Another passenger. I will tell you who in a moment. But before I do, I will tell you about Meyer's movements, because that's what I told the policeman. I did not tell him about the passenger. Because when I do I will no longer have a job. And I need to know I have somewhere to go. Will you help me with that, Bella? Will you give me somewhere to stay – away from here – until I can get another job? Here in England?'

Bella remembered how she had given sanctuary to another young woman during the first case she had worked on with Miss Vale. 'I . . . well . . . I suppose I can. Aye. I can.'

Tears welled in Gretchen's eyes. 'Thank you. I knew I could trust you. You are different from the rest of the servants here. You are not afraid of the truth. So I will tell you the truth.'

Bella wished Gretchen would hurry up. Patience was not one of Bella's strong suits, but she knew she would have to go at Gretchen's pace, not her own. 'Go on, then . . . did Meyer try to kill Miss Vale and Mr Foster? Did he kill Harry Stanley?'

Gretchen shook her head. 'I'm afraid I can't say for sure. What I can say – and what I told the policeman – was that Meyer had time after coming back from the port to go to the place where Miss Vale was pushed. And I heard him say to the baron, when the baron asked him why he had taken so long to return, that he had been for a little drive up the coast and that he'd stopped off somewhere to look over the sea.'

Bella's eyes narrowed. 'Newbiggin-by-the-Sea?'

Gretchen shrugged. 'He didn't say. Just the sea. And he didn't say he had pushed Miss Vale. But he did say that the baron must not worry as he was going to make sure those who knew about the baron's business dealings didn't ever speak of it again.'

'Were those his exact words?'

Gretchen nodded. 'Yes. He said: "Do not worry, sir, they will never speak of it again."'

'Did the baron ask what he meant?'

'He did. And Meyer said, "It is best you don't know the details, sir. But just know they will be silenced."'

'And you told Inspector Hawkes all this?'

'I did.'

'But not who the extra passenger was.'

'No. He asked, but I said I didn't know. I lied about that. I was too frightened to tell until I knew I could be protected.'

Bella put her hand on Gretchen's shoulder. 'I will protect you. Tell me, Gretchen. I need to know everything if I'm to help you.'

Gretchen exhaled slowly. 'Yes, you need to know. The extra passenger is Lord Penford. Young master Teddy.'

Bella gasped. 'Teddy? Teddy is going to leave with the von Schneiders?'

Gretchen nodded. 'Yes, that's their plan. But they want to keep it secret. Because they think Lady Penford will try to stop it.'

There was a flash of lightning and a clap of thunder. Bella looked up as it finally started to rain. 'We should get some shelter.'

'I don't want to go back to the manor. Meyer is there. And the baron and baroness might now know what I've told the policeman. And they might think that I've told him about Teddy too.'

'All right,' said Bella as a large drop of rain hit the back of her neck. 'Then let's go to the groundsman's cottage. We can take shelter there until the rain passes. Let's cut through the wood.'

Gretchen pulled up the collar of her coat and followed Bella into the wood, which offered them some protection from the falling rain.

As they walked, Bella continued to question Gretchen. 'You said you knew about Meyer's whereabouts the morning Harry Stanley was found. Can you tell me more about that?'

Gretchen, keeping pace with Bella, nodded. 'Yes. I woke up just as you were leaving the room. I wasn't sure where you were going, but then I heard the men in the stable yard through the window saying that there was a dead body and they were waiting for the master. I wanted to catch you to ask you if you knew what was going on, but you were away and up the stairs before I could get dressed. So I decided to try to find out myself. The men in the yard were waiting for Sir William so I headed to the wood on my own. You hadn't got there yet.'

'No,' said Bella, wondering where Gretchen's story was going, 'I went upstairs to get Miss Vale. We followed Sir William and the groundsman and arrived at the woods after them.'

Gretchen nodded. 'Well, I got there before them. And I saw . . . I saw . . . Meyer and Baron von Schneider coming out of the wood. They were walking. Not running. They did not seem distressed.'

'Just like they were on a casual morning walk?'

'Yes, just like that. But they had come from the wood. The wood that the body was found in. I was frightened they would see me. And that they would know I had seen them. So, I ran back to the manor. I pretended I had not left and that the first I heard of any of it was when the other servants were told.'

There was another clap of thunder. The storm was getting closer and the rain heavier. Bella picked up her pace. 'But you do not know that Meyer and the baron saw the body – or had anything to do with the body – before Sir Bill and then Miss Vale got there?'

Gretchen shook her head. 'No. I can't say that. That's what I told the policeman. I can't say what the baron told him was not true. That they were just on a morning walk. But I did see them coming from the wood. And it's not a very big wood. It would be hard for them *not* to have come across the body, although not impossible.'

And as if to prove her point, the women emerged into the very clearing where Harry Stanley was found. There was still police rope marking off the area.

'Aye,' said Bella, 'that would be very hard. Tell me, Gretchen—'

But before she could continue with her question there was a bang, a whizzing sound and a thud as something hit a tree just to the left of her. Then there was another bang and another. It took her a few confused seconds before she realised the bangs were not thunder.

'Someone's shooting at us! Run!'

Chapter 31

Clara and Hawkes ran out of the walled garden, with the dog at their heels. The rain was still falling and it didn't take long for Clara to be soaked through her blouse to her skin. Thankfully she was wearing sturdy boots and splashing through the puddles was no bother. They reached the door and looked left and right.

'This way, I think,' said Clara. 'The shots sounded like they were coming from the wood.'

'Yes, I think you're right,' said Hawkes and they headed in that direction. 'Who the hell has got hold of a gun? I was assured they'd been locked up.'

'Those were the shotguns for the hunt. That didn't sound like a shotgun.'

'No, more like a rifle. Bolt action. Don't know how many rounds.'

Clara and Hawkes, their breathing laboured, ran as fast as they could. Just as they reached the edge of the wood they heard a further two shots. They stopped dead in their tracks and fell to their haunches.

'It's definitely coming from the wood,' said Hawkes. 'I don't suppose it would do much good to tell you to stay here while I went in.'

'No, it wouldn't.'

'I thought not. All right, but stay behind me. At least promise me that.'

Clara had no intention of promising anything, but she nodded her agreement to appease him.

Hawkes crept forward and took cover behind a tree trunk then waved for Clara to follow him.

Another shot went off. 'This way,' said Hawkes. 'He's over here.'

Or she, thought Clara, and followed him into the wood.

Bella grabbed the hand of the terrified Gretchen, pulled her to the ground then dragged the German woman behind a fallen tree trunk.

'Who is shooting at us?' Bella's voice quivered. She was confident she'd be able to defend herself – and Gretchen – against a physical assault, but not against a gun.

'Herr Meyer is a crack shot. He was a sniper in the army.'

'Do you think he'd actually try to kill us?'

'I think he would if he thought I was going to tell you what I know. And if he's already killed that miner and tried to kill Miss Vale . . .'

Bella felt a shiver of fear down her spine. But she would not go down without a fight. She grabbed a solid stick. 'You stay here and keep his attention. I'll sneak out and try to get behind him.'

'But you don't know where he is!'

That was true. 'We'll have to make him reveal himself.' Bella thought for a minute then shrugged out of her raincoat. She hung the hood of the coat over the stick and slowly raised it above the log. 'Keep your head down!' she whispered to Gretchen.

The ploy worked, drawing two shots from around twenty yards away. 'Got him,' whispered Bella; then, using trees and fallen debris for cover, she made her way towards the shooter.

But Gretchen didn't stay where she was either. And before Bella could reach the tree where she thought the shooter was hiding, another shot went off and to her horror she heard Gretchen scream and fall.

I just have a moment before his next shot . . . She ran towards the tree with her stick raised, but as she did her foot caught on a root and she stumbled to the ground, hitting her head on something hard. Dazed and winded, she scrambled to find her stick as a hooded figure in a green rain cape loomed above her, pointing a rifle. Her vision was impaired by rain and blood and she couldn't reach the stick. *Oh God, this is it* . . . She closed her eyes to meet her end.

'Stooooop, police!'

Then she heard someone running away. A moment later, Bella opened her eyes to see Miss Vale standing over her.

'Bella! My God! Are you all right?'

'He was going to kill me!'

'He's run off. Hawkes is after him!'

Clara fell to her knees. Bella shook her head from side to side. There was a bleeding wound on her forehead.

'Have you been shot?'

'No, I banged my head. But Gretchen! I think he got her. Over there!'

Bella clambered to her feet, aided by Clara.

Hawkes arrived, panting. 'I couldn't get him. He had too much of a head start. He's done a runner. Are you all right, Miss Cuddy?'

'I am,' gasped Bella, 'but I think Gretchen's been hit.'

Bella led them to where she'd last seen Gretchen. The German woman was lying in a foetal position, clasping her arm and whimpering.

'Gretchen! Are you all right?' Bella fell to her knees, followed by Clara.

Gretchen's terrified face turned to them. 'I've been shot.'

'Let me look.' Clara examined the quivering woman and with immense relief announced: 'Just one shot. In the fleshy part of the arm. I think you'll be all right. But we need to get you out of the rain.'

'To the cottage,' ordered Hawkes.

The rain was finally easing by the time the wet, bloodied and bedraggled foursome reached the cottage, with Sammy the dog not far behind. Hawkes banged on the front door calling for Sergeant Wilcox to open up. He did, and after expressing his shock, he ushered them all inside. As it was summer there was no fire on the go, but Rogers the chauffeur set about making one, after he had unearthed a basic first aid kit from Arthur Foster's kitchen. Towels were then found and the ladies retired to one of the cottage's two bedrooms to dry off and tend to their wounds, while Hawkes stayed in the front room to fill the sergeant in on what had just happened.

Bella and Clara helped Gretchen onto the bed, stripped off her wet clothes and made her comfortable. 'I'll check her out,' said Clara. 'You clean and dress the wound on your head, Bella. You're not feeling dizzy or anything, are you?'

'I'm not,' said Bella, and sat down in front of a dressing table mirror. After wiping away the blood she announced: 'It's not much more than a graze, Miss Vale, but I reckon I'll have a cracking headache for a while.'

'Sorry about that,' said Clara, with genuine sympathy. Her body was still aching after her escapade at the cliff. 'Let me check something.' She held up her finger and asked Bella to follow it, which she did without difficulty.

'I haven't been drinking,' said Bella, with a wry grin. 'Mind, I could do with one now.'

Clara patted her on the shoulder. 'I'll see what I can rustle up in a minute. But first, I need to see to Miss Klopp.'

Clara examined the bullet wound on Gretchen's arm. 'As I thought out in the wood, you've been lucky, Miss Klopp. The bullet just grazed your arm. It is not embedded in the wound, so we won't need to be rushing you to hospital.'

Gretchen nodded. 'I've never been shot before.'

Clara smiled and selected a bandage to dress the wound. 'Neither have I,' she said, 'and let's hope it stays that way for the rest of us. Bella told me on the way here you think it was Herr Meyer who did this.'

'I think it's possible. He is angry with me. He wants to silence me.' She went on to tell Clara what she had already told Bella about her history with Meyer, his – and the baron's – suspicious actions at the manor, and the von Schneiders' plans to whisk Teddy out of the country.

Clara nodded along encouragingly until Gretchen came to the end of her tale. 'That is all most interesting, Miss Klopp. I shall inform Inspector Hawkes of this shortly, although I know you have told him some of it already. But there is one thing that doesn't fit: are you aware that Inspector Hawkes arrested Meyer and currently has him under lock and key?'

'No! When?'

'After you spoke to the inspector. You gave him enough information to justify an arrest.'

'But I thought it was him shooting!'

'He could have escaped,' said Bella.

'I don't think so,' said Clara. 'He is being held in the other bedroom of this cottage.'

Bella and Gretchen gasped.

'So it must have been someone else who shot at you,' Clara continued. 'Did you get a good look at who it was, Bella?'

'Not really. Just a dark green rain cape and hood. I couldn't see properly what with the blood and the rain.'

Clara nodded. 'Yes, Inspector Hawkes said the same. The fellow fled before he could identify him – or her – just like at the cliff earlier today.'

'Her?' asked Bella. 'Do you think it could be a woman?'

Clara shrugged. 'We cannot discount it without evidence to the contrary. Was it definitely a man you saw?'

'I can't say for sure, no.'

'And you, Miss Klopp?'

'I did not see him – or her. I just know that Meyer is a good shot. But if he is here . . .' She looked to the bedroom wall and shivered.

'Who else could it have been?' asked Bella. 'Who would have access to a gun?'

'That is a very important question, Bella. And one I'm sure Inspector Hawkes will be asking too.'

Gretchen's eyes widened. 'No, no, it can't be.'

'What is it?' asked Clara.

'Baroness von Schneider. She too is a very good shot. She shoots in competitions. I believe she wanted to represent Germany at the Olympic Games in Paris, but they would not let women do that. So she played tennis there instead.'

Hmmm, thought Clara, the baroness was proving to be a person of interest in this case, in more ways than one. It certainly warranted another conversation with her. But first she must talk to Inspector Hawkes.

Clara walked to the wardrobe and opened it to reveal men's shirts and trousers. She took out four shirts and four pairs of trousers. 'They'll be big, but it's better than walking around in our wet underwear.' After pulling on a shirt and trousers, and using a necktie as a belt, she picked up the remaining set of men's clothes, which she draped over her shoulder, then all of the women's wet clothes. 'I'll see if I can get these dry in front of the fire. And I'll speak to Inspector Hawkes. Can you sit with Miss Klopp, Bella? I'll bring you some hot tea in a minute.' Then, with a wink, she added, 'And I'll see if there's a tot of something too.'

'Aye, miss, that would be grand.'

Hawkes was in his underpants and vest, drying himself at the fire, when Clara entered the sitting room.

'Sorry, Miss Vale,' he said and grabbed at a towel.

'Not to worry, Inspector, I've brought you some dry clothes.' She draped the shirt and trousers over the arm of a chair, then dropped the pile of wet clothes on the floor, before discreetly retreating to the kitchen while Hawkes got dressed. She'd sort the wet clothes out when he was decent again.

In the kitchen Clara noticed that the smashed-in door and window had been boarded up. Mr Rogers was busy putting the kettle on. 'Tea, Miss Vale?'

'Oh, yes please,' said Clara. 'And for the other ladies too.' She looked around. 'Where is Sergeant Wilcox?'

'He's checking on the prisoner,' said Rogers and nodded to the second bedroom.

'So, he's really in there?'

'Aye, miss. The inspector brought him here from the manor before going to meet you. Just before the rain started.'

He adopted a disapproving look. 'I knew it would be one of those foreigners causing all the trouble. Germans. Can't trust 'em.'

Clara didn't comment, knowing one of those 'foreigners' was a victim in this case. And she felt she could trust Gretchen Klopp. Bella did. When the tea was ready – with a tot of added brandy – Clara took the tray to Bella and Gretchen and then joined Sandy Hawkes in the sitting room.

Hawkes was now fully dressed in his borrowed clothes. And while the shirt and trousers were baggy on Clara, they were too small for him. Clara could not help but notice how his muscular chest strained against the fabric of the shirt. She filed the image away for future contemplation.

They sat on opposite sides of a small table with the tea between them. She had declined to put brandy in their brew as she knew they both needed to keep their wits about them. She proceeded to tell him everything Gretchen had told her.

'My, my,' said Hawkes, tapping his teaspoon on the edge of his saucer. 'That does put everything in a different light. I will have to speak to Meyer again. Would you care to join me?'

'I certainly would.'

Hawkes covered the short distance to the second bedroom and knocked on the door. It was opened a moment later by Sergeant Wilcox. 'Sergeant, Miss Vale and I would like to speak to the prisoner alone.'

'Aye, sir.'

Wilcox stepped aside and let Hawkes and Clara into the room. Seated on the bed, with one wrist handcuffed to the bedframe, was Herr Meyer. He had one hand free and was eating from a tray of food.

He appraised the newcomers, expressionless. He continued to eat.

Hawkes pulled up a chair for Clara and sat on the edge of the bed. He got straight down to business. 'What can you tell us about the baron and baroness's plans for leaving the country?'

Meyer continued chewing a slice of bread then reached for another slice.

Hawkes snatched the bread from his hand, tossed it on the tray and moved it out of reach of the prisoner. 'I asked you a question.'

Meyer pursed his lips, glanced at his uneaten food, then answered, 'Does the baron know you have taken me?'

'I am asking the questions. Now, this is your last chance. Answer me or I'll take you to a police cell – and it won't be anywhere near as comfortable as here.'

'You have no proof of anything against me.'

'Ah,' said Hawkes, 'but that is not the case. I have a witness who will make a sworn statement.'

'A statement about what?'

'Your involvement. But if you tell me what I want to know now, things will be easier for you. I understand that you are just a man acting on orders. If you are not acting alone then you should not take all of the blame. That just wouldn't be fair, would it? And if you were unable to disobey an order, a court will take that into consideration.'

Meyer weighed this up, then said: 'But that is assuming I did something unlawful on the order of someone.'

'That is indeed what I am assuming,' answered Hawkes. 'And I have enough evidence, putting you in the vicinity of three of the current crimes under investigation, to justify your arrest. You may be innocent, but that will be for a court to decide. And it could take a long time before this gets to court. So, if you have anything to tell me that exonerates you – or implicates someone else in your stead – then now would be a good time to tell me.'

Clara was impressed with Hawkes' strategy. She sat quietly, watching the master at work.

Meyer did not appear as impressed, but nonetheless he weighed up the implied offer he was being given and replied: 'All right, I'll tell you about the von Schneiders' plans for travel. But not while *she* is here.'

He gestured to Clara.

Hawkes shook his head. 'I'm afraid you don't get to dictate terms, Meyer.'

Meyer smirked. 'I'm afraid that is the only way I will comply.'

Hawkes gave a mirthless laugh. 'Oh, it's not the only way you'll comply. But for now, I'll go along with it. Miss Vale, would you mind? And perhaps when you are out there you could question Rogers about this.' Out of Meyer's sight he slipped something from his pocket and into Clara's hand.

Chapter 32

Clara joined Sergeant Wilcox and Rogers in the kitchen.

'Has he done much talking, miss?' asked Wilcox.

'Not with me there, but he's talking to the inspector now.'

'That's good. The inspector'll get to the bottom of this. It's a knotty case.'

'It is,' said Clara. 'Did you find anything out when you questioned people in Newbiggin?'

'I still have to hear that, miss. Two of my constables were doing that.' He looked at his watch. 'One of them will be along here shortly and we should get news. Of that and of Mr Foster's condition at the hospital. When he arrives then Mr Rogers can go, as I'll have someone else to help me.'

Rogers, who was sitting stroking Sammy the dog, looked relieved.

'Oh, Mr Rogers, would you mind coming with me to the sitting room?' asked Clara. 'I have a few questions for you.' Rogers' eyes widened.

Clara adopted a friendly demeanour. 'Oh, nothing to worry about. Just about my car.'

Rogers relaxed. He was in comfortable territory now. 'Aye, miss. Not a bother.'

Rogers, Clara and Sammy repaired to the sitting room. Clara was pleased to see that someone – either Rogers or Wilcox – had found a clothes horse and the wet clothes were drying in front of the fire. Sammy found a way through the clothes and settled on the hearth rug.

Rogers and Clara settled down too.

'Right,' said Clara. 'I would like to ask you about yesterday when I brought my car to you.'

'Aye, miss. Did she run all right today?'

'She did,' said Clara. 'Thank you. You did a sterling job. But I was wondering if anyone else helped you with the car or would have had access to it overnight.'

'Well, I have a lad who helps me. I'm training him up to learn mechanics.'

'What's the lad's name?'

'Joseph. Joseph Lamb. We call him Joey.'

Clara tried to visualise the list of people Hawkes fingerprinted. Yes, there was a Lamb on there. So young Joey was in the clear as far as the fingerprints went. 'Righto. Well, I will need to speak to Joey then. When the constable arrives to back up Sergeant Wilcox, could you find Joey so I can ask him some questions?'

'Aye, miss, I can. But he's a good lad, Joey. He'll have nowt to do with any of this.'

Clara nodded encouragingly. 'Oh, I don't doubt that. And I am sure you had nothing to do with anything either. As does Inspector Hawkes, or he wouldn't have asked you to help out. But . . .' She reached into her pocket and withdrew the lighter. 'I need to find out if either you or Joey saw this lighter in the car yesterday, or if either of you saw someone near the car, after I left it with you, who could have slipped it in. It was under the passenger seat.'

She passed the lighter to Rogers. He took it and shook his head. 'I'm sorry, miss, but I didn't see it. Joey might have, I'll ask him. But it's not likely if you say it was on the passenger side. Neither of us sat in the passenger seat. We took our turns in the driving seat as we tested the engine. And of course we were under the bonnet and opened the boot, but neither us had a need to be in the passenger seat – or the back seat. So if it was there, we'd not have seen it.'

Clara absorbed this information. 'All right, I understand. But did either of you see someone else near my car? Did anyone come and look at it while you were there?'

Rogers shook his head. 'No, miss, there was no one else. Everyone in the house was all hands on deck for the dinner last night, and the grounds and estate folk were all busy preparing for the grouse shoot. Not that that'll happen now . . .'

'All right, so just you and Joey. What about when you were finished with the car? When you left it in the garage? Could someone have sneaked in and put the lighter in the car then?'

Rogers eyes opened wide. 'Why would they do that, miss?'

Clara smiled. 'The why and the how are two different questions for now. Can you tell me if it was possible?'

Rogers pulled at the hairs of his moustache. 'Well anything's possible, miss, but not likely. I locked your car when I was finished with it. And I kept the key with me until I gave it to you the next morning. You see, young master Teddy has a habit of taking the cars for a ride at odd hours. I didn't want him taking yours, miss.'

Clara nodded. 'That was very sensible of you, Mr Rogers, thank you. So what you're saying is that no one could have put the lighter in the car overnight, but it could have been there, undetected, when I delivered the car to you?'

Rogers stopped pulling at his moustache hairs. 'Aye, miss. That's the sum of it. I will ask the lad too, but I don't think he'll say no different. If you found the lighter in the car this morning it's because it was already there when you brought it to me yesterday afternoon.'

And who was in the passenger seat yesterday afternoon? thought Clara. No one else but Teddy Richner.

So, Teddy was back on the ever-growing suspect list. Clara thought over what Gretchen had told her – and what Hawkes was currently trying to confirm with Meyer. Meyer had been sent to purchase an extra ticket for the von Schneiders' return journey to Germany. They would be travelling on the ferry to Amsterdam and then catching a train to Berlin. This was planned for Friday – after three days of grouse shooting. Gretchen had told her that she had overheard Baroness von Schneider talking with her husband. The baroness was upset at the way Teddy was treated by his English family. And she was angry that Teddy had not been allowed to return to Germany to take up his title as the new Baron von Richner, as was his due after his father's and brothers' deaths. So the von Richner estate was in limbo. She had taken legal advice and had been told that the trusteeship order under the British Lunacy Office could only be applied in Britain. It did not apply internationally. So, if Teddy were to leave England for Europe, he would not be subject to it. In other words, nothing stopped him from taking up his inheritance as Baron von Richner. Ada von Schneider was hoping to encourage Teddy to leave with them. Had Foster somehow found out about it and that's why there had been an attempt on his life? And perhaps Harry Stanley too. Which of the Penford Manor staff were in on it? Miss Wren? The missing Parker? And how did the whole blackmail plot fit into it? Was this going to be the next phase of the plan? Threatening to tell all about the turncoat eldest son unless Lady Penford let Teddy go?

Goodness me, thought Clara, *this is becoming more and more complicated!*

Suddenly there was a toot of a car horn. Clara went to the window and saw a police car at the gate. She called Sergeant Wilcox, who went out to open the gate and admit his colleague. As he did, Inspector Hawkes emerged from the bedroom. He looked frustrated.

'Excuse us a minute please, Mr Rogers, but I need to speak to Miss Vale alone.'

'Aye, sir. I'll just be in the kitchen then.'

Hawkes waited for the chauffeur to leave then turned to Clara. 'He's a tough nut, that German.'

'Hasn't he talked?' asked Clara.

Hawkes shrugged. 'Yes and no. He has confirmed that he went to the ferry port to book a ticket for Teddy Richner to accompany the von Schneiders to Germany on Friday, but he has flatly denied that he had anything to do with the Stanley murder, the attack on you or the gassing of poor old Foster. He seems well aware that the only evidence I have against him for those crimes is purely circumstantial in that he had the potential to be at all three crime scenes. And as he rightly pointed out to me – smugly – the potential to do something does not mean he did it. And he's right. I will need more evidence.'

'So you'll have to let him go?'

Hawkes shook his head. 'Oh no, I have enough to hold him for the next twenty-four hours, but I will need to find something else – something far more concrete – between now and then.'

'I wonder if this will help.' Clara went on to tell him what she'd learned from Rogers about the lighter. 'So, it suggests that the lighter had been there *before* I took the car to Rogers for repairs. And Teddy had been in the car. So it's quite possible that Teddy had the lighter in his pocket and it dropped out accidentally. Which means that Teddy was the one who went to the wood to remove the lighter from the crime scene on Sunday morning. Why would he do that unless he was involved in some way?'

Hawkes nodded. 'Yes, that is an interesting question. I'll need to speak to Teddy again about the lighter. I've gone easy on him so far – at the request of his mother, due to his fragile mind – but this new evidence demands further examination. What I'd like you to do, Clara, is follow up with Baroness von Schneider. Probe her for more information. Try to confirm, if you can, what Miss Klopp has told us. And also her whereabouts during the rainstorm when Miss Klopp was shot. I'll be questioning everyone else regarding their whereabouts, but if you can probe the lady specifically, I'd be grateful.'

'Of course,' said Clara. 'However . . .' Her voice trailed off as, like a skilled chess player, she considered the potential outcome of future moves.

'What?'

'Well,' said Clara. 'Two things. Firstly, what if we keep it quiet that Gretchen has been shot? No one knows but us here . . . and whoever shot her. If it comes out that there's been another attempted murder, there'll be hysteria at the manor. I think they're *just* about coping with what's happened so far. Hearing about this could tip them all over the edge.'

Hawkes nodded. 'Yes, I see where you're going with this. We should keep the recent shooting a secret for now to see what emerges while the waters are relatively calm – and see if anyone pokes their head above water.'

'Exactly that. But I expect the baroness will be wondering where her maid is. She would last have been seen walking into the grounds with Bella. So, I propose saying that Gretchen slipped and sprained her ankle. As they were near the gatehouse cottage at the time, they came here for help. Miss Klopp is now resting her ankle and won't be available for duty for at least tonight. And possibly tomorrow. And no, the baroness cannot visit her here as the police are using the cottage as their headquarters and Miss Klopp was only allowed in because of her injury.'

Hawkes smiled. 'A tenuous yet plausible explanation. It might work. And if it doesn't, we can always fall back on "because I said so". I do, after all, have authority here. For now . . . but unless we get results soon, that won't last.'

Clara agreed. 'Yes, time is running out. Do they know that Meyer has been arrested?'

'The butler knows, so I expect everyone will know now.'

'How are you going to handle that?'

Hawkes grinned. 'With my authority. However, if the baron insists on Meyer having a lawyer, I'll have to comply. But—' he looked at his watch '—it's now five o'clock. So I doubt he and Sir Bill will be able to arrange for anyone to come out here before tomorrow morning.'

'And if they can get someone this evening?'

'Then I'll let the lawyer see him. No one else.'

Clara nodded. 'Yes, that could still buy us some time. But if the von Schneiders are guilty of anything other than just wanting to help Teddy get away from his mother, they might try to flee if they think Meyer will spill the beans. Or Gretchen.'

Hawkes agreed. 'Yes, leaving the country with Teddy – a grown man – is not a crime. And that might be all they are involved in. But they are not yet clear of the blackmail and murder. So, when I get back to the manor I will use the telephone to alert the police at the Port of Tyne to look out for them. And of course, they cannot get out of here by car without going through this gate.'

At that moment, Sergeant Wilcox and a young constable came through the front door. 'This is Constable Markham.' He made introductions. 'Markham tells me Mr Foster has not regained consciousness yet, but the doctors say he's in a stable condition.'

'Oh that's a relief,' said Clara.

'Yes, it is,' said Hawkes. 'And what about the questioning at Newbiggin? What did you find out, Constable?'

Markham recounted that he'd questioned everyone who lived and worked between Mrs Stanley's house and the church, including Mrs Stanley and the café staff (who were all shocked to hear of Miss Vale's accident), the volunteers at the lifeboat station, fishermen and even the families that were still on the beach when he arrived. 'But it was only the vicar at St Bartholomew's who had anything useful to tell.'

'What did he say?' asked Hawkes.

'Apparently, he was up in the bell tower polishing the brass. He saw Miss Vale's dark red car arrive, then Miss Vale got out and walked towards the lifeboat station. After that a black Model T Ford arrived. The driver waited in his car. The vicar saw Miss Vale return from the direction of the lifeboat station and then past the church, without returning to her car. Then he saw a man get out of the Model T and walk the same way as Miss Vale.' Markham stopped.

'And then?' asked Hawkes.

Markham gave an apologetic shrug. 'And then the vicar said he went to the vicarage to have his dinner. He didn't see anything else. He didn't know what he'd seen was even suspicious until I asked him about it.'

'Hmmm,' said Hawkes. 'But at least he can identify the man and the car.'

Markham gave another shrug. 'Not really, sir. He said his eyesight's not the best. He could see the cars – but naturally didn't look at any licence plates – and all he could see was first a young lady then a man. He said the man seemed youngish – thirties maybe, but could be a fit forties – but couldn't tell me any more about him. He was wearing a hat and coat. But what kind of hat or coat the vicar couldn't say. Dark, he thought, but that's all.'

'But he knew it was a Model T?'

'Aye, he did, but only because he says the bishop has one, so he knows what it looks like.'

'And it's a very common car,' added Sergeant Wilcox. 'There's a lot of them about.'

There were indeed a lot of them about, thought Clara. So even though Meyer had borrowed the Penford Manor Model T, it was not distinctive enough to identify it definitively. Now if it had been the silver Rolls . . .

Hawkes tutted his annoyance. 'All right, thanks for that, Constable. It's better than nothing. When I arrived at the car park there were a few cars there. I remember a Model T Ford coupe but didn't think anything of it at the time. As you say, it's a common car. And I don't recall it being there when Miss Vale and I returned from the cliff top. But at least we now know it was a man – not a woman – who attacked Miss Vale. And that he was driving a black Model T. That still points the finger at Meyer. So, I can continue holding him for now. But we need more evidence. About the attack on Miss Vale and the one on Miss Klopp. Meyer might very well have been the one to push Miss Vale, but it wasn't him who shot at Miss Klopp. We need to find out who that was.' He reached into his pocket and brought out a bullet cartridge.

'I picked this up at the tree where the shooter was standing. Wilcox, I want you to go question the huntsman about what weapons are available on the estate and who has access to them. Try to get a match for this. It's from a rifle, we know that much. Find out which one, where it is now and, if the stars align, who used it last!'

'Aye, sir,' said Wilcox. 'I'll just show Markham the ropes here so he can take over from me, then I'll be off.'

'I might as well be off too,' said Clara. She felt her blouse and trousers on the clothes horse. They were dry enough. 'I'll see if Bella is ready to return with me.'

'All right,' said Hawkes, 'I'll walk you both back. But . . .' He reached into his pocket again and withdrew a revolver.

Clara gasped. 'I didn't know you had that! Why didn't you use it in the woods?'

'I didn't have it in the woods,' explained Hawkes. 'Sergeant Wilcox found it in a drawer here. It belongs to Arthur Foster.' He handed the gun to Clara.

'I was going to keep it for protection tonight, but I think you might need it more than I do.'

Sergeant Wilcox cleared his throat and looked concerned. 'Pardon me, miss, but do you know how to use that?'

'Of course she does,' snapped Hawkes.

Chapter 33

It was half past five by the time Clara, Bella and Hawkes arrived back at the manor. Even though their clothes were dry, they all looked bedraggled, and the Elastoplast on Bella's forehead was the finishing touch. Spencer opened the door for them and informed Hawkes that Sir William and Baron von Schneider wanted to see him immediately. They were waiting in the library.

'Excellent!' said Hawkes. 'I would like to see them too.'

Spencer hovered for a moment, not knowing whether to accompany the policeman who was striding towards the library, or to supervise Clara and Bella.

'Don't worry, Spencer, we're more than capable of finding the way to our rooms,' said Clara.

Spencer barely disguised a disapproving shudder, then followed Hawkes.

'Let's get cleaned up,' said Clara. 'Why don't you get your suitcase – as Hawkes suggested – and move in with me for tonight. Safety in numbers, eh?'

'Aye, that's a good idea,' said Bella. 'But I'll do it later. After supper. I want to do some more investigating downstairs, first.'

'Are you sure you're up to it?' asked Clara, eyeing her assistant's battle wounds.

Bella pursed her lips. 'With all due respect, Miss Vale, don't mollycoddle me. I know if I'm well enough or not. Having that accident in Cairo didn't stop me, did it? And that was a lot worse than a little scrape on the head.'

'Yes, it was,' said Clara, suitably put in her place. 'And I'm sorry. What do you plan to do downstairs?'

'What I always do, Miss Vale: watch and listen.'

Before Clara ascended the stairs, she decided to do a quick recce of the reception rooms downstairs to see who was about. The library door was closed, but she already knew Sir Bill and the baron were in there with Hawkes. She popped her head into the downstairs sitting room and saw the back of the blonde head of Lady Penford in conversation with Lady Fitzgilbert. Clara retreated immediately. She did want to speak to Lady Penford, but not now. Next to the sitting room was the drawing room, where earlier the youngsters had been playing cards. The room was still occupied. Kate Richner was at the piano playing a mournful tune, while Archie Fitzgilbert sat meekly nearby, listening. Through the open French doors, on the terrace, Matt Fowler and Teddy Richner were chatting and smoking. Maggie Fowler was in a corner, on her own, reading a book, while Lily Fitzgilbert was paging through a magazine and pointing something out to her sister, Elsie. Lily looked up and saw Clara. 'Ah, Miss Vale, Tony's looking for you. He said something about your parents wanting to talk to you both.'

Tony, thought Clara. *How familiar of her.* 'Thank you. I'll find him,' she said, with a strained smile.

She really needed to speak to the baroness – as she'd agreed with Hawkes – but she couldn't avoid her family for ever. No one had said tonight's dinner was off, and if it wasn't, it would be awkward to have her mother hankering for a word with her when she wanted to observe the other guests. No, best she get it over and done with now. Besides, after what Bella had overheard at the croquet, she should probably speak to her father too.

Clara knocked on the door of her parents' suite. Her mother's maid answered and ushered her in. Her mother, father and brother were gathered in the small sitting area, sipping sherry. The maid retreated to a corner and stood next to the valet.

'Hello, old girl,' said Antony. 'We thought we'd stay out of the way up here. Sir Bill and the baron are spitting nails, Lady Penford is doing an imitation of the queen in "Snow White", and that policeman friend of yours is intent on dragging everyone off to prison!'

'He's not dragging everyone off to prison, Antony, don't be so melodramatic. He has arrested one person – von Schneider's valet – because there is evidence to suggest the man was in the vicinity of all three attacks. He might be released in due course – if shown to be innocent.'

'Do you think there will be more arrests?' asked her father.

Clara needed to be careful about what information she divulged, but she was grateful that her father, for once, did not sound condescending and seemed genuinely interested in her opinion. She sat down and accepted a glass of sherry from the valet.

'I think it's possible, Father. Inspector Hawkes does not believe only one person committed all these crimes.' She did not mention that a fourth attack had just taken place and that it was impossible for the man in custody to have done it.

'And I believe you were one of the targets of this maniac, my dear.' Her father looked concerned.

'I was. But fortunately I suffered no serious injury. Inspector Hawkes pulled me back up the cliff before I could fall.'

Her mother shuddered and shook her head.

Sir Randolph nodded in sympathy. 'Well, I shall have to thank the inspector for saving you. We're very grateful, aren't we, dear?' He directed this to his wife.

'Yes, we are,' said Lady Vanessa. Her reply was terse. Clara expected it wouldn't be long before her mother would speak what was on her mind. For now though, she was grateful for at least her father's sympathy. And her brother's warmth.

'And I heard you saved a fellow's life! Started his heart again. Jolly good show, old girl,' said Antony, his eyes sincere.

'Thank you,' said Clara, surprised that a lump was forming in her throat. She was so used to doing battle with her family that this rapprochement was taking her by complete surprise. 'We've just got word from Ashington that Mr Foster is doing well, all things considered. It's a huge relief.'

'So he's awake?' asked Sir Randolph.

'No, not yet. But the doctors say he has stabilised and is no longer in danger.'

'And all thanks to you! My sister the life-saver!' Antony raised his glass to her. 'Chin-chin, old girl!'

Clara raised hers in return. And smiled. 'Chin-chin.'

Clara flashed a glance at her mother. She was still stewing about something. *Just spit it out*, she thought, and considered prompting her to do so. But then decided it would be wiser to take advantage of her father's goodwill while it lasted.

'Father,' she said, 'I believe you may be going into business with Sir Bill and Baron von Schneider. And that Antony might be involved too.'

'Where did you hear that?' asked Sir Randolph.

Clara smiled. 'Oh, there have been a lot of conversations about a lot of things these last few days. I can't recall where. But I did hear it. Is it true?'

Sir Randolph indicated to the valet that he'd like another glass of sherry. 'It is. Jepsons is a well-respected and well-connected bank. Sir Bill and the baron would like to do some business with us in Berlin.'

'And Antony . . .' prompted Clara.

'The details are still to be worked out,' her brother chipped in. 'But they want me to work for them on a specific project – as a financial consultant.' He pulled out his cigarette case. 'And as I'm currently between projects, I have agreed to help them.'

'I see,' said Clara, choosing her words carefully. 'No doubt your experience in the City, and with all the financiers you know, will prove useful.'

'That's what they seem to think too,' said Antony, and extracted a cigarette from the case. He flicked it and gave a pointed look in the direction of the valet who quickly produced a lighter from his pocket.

'Have they said what this specific project entails?' asked Clara.

'Not yet,' said Antony and grinned. 'Everyone's too busy proving they're not a murderer. It's just like one of those Agatha Christie novels.'

'Tawdry,' mumbled Lady Vanessa. 'All so very tawdry.'

Clara ignored her. She turned to her father. 'Well, the last thing I want to do is put a damper on your new business prospects, but I feel I must tell you something.' She went on to explain that she had it on good authority that Sir Bill and the baron were setting up an illegal or at least unethical trade relationship that the dead man knew all about, and that his murder might have had something to do with it. 'So you see, it's become part of the police investigation and Sir Charles Trevelyan is looking into it at a government level with the Coal Board. So, I think it would be in your best interests—' she looked from her brother to her father '—*both* of your best interests, not to commit to anything just yet. At least not until the police investigation is completed and everything – and everyone – is in the clear. As I said, I don't want to put a damper on anything, but—'

'But that's exactly what you've done!' Lady Vanessa exploded. 'It's what you *always* do. You put a damper on everything! Running around playing detective, embarrassing our hosts and fellow guests, cavorting with policemen, not keeping your uppity Geordie maid in check, failing to follow proper etiquette . . . you're an embarrassment to your class and you're an embarrassment to me! And now here you are, trying to ruin your brother's prospects, yet again! I told you, Antony, she would ruin your engagement, and here she is doing exactly that!'

Clara was utterly astounded. She knew her mother was preparing to give her a piece of her mind but she had not expected quite so much of it. She didn't know what to say. She knew her mother disapproved of her chosen life, so that did not come as much of a surprise, but there was something else that had taken her by complete surprise. She glared at her mother. 'Well, thank you for your kind and loving support.' Then she turned to Antony. 'What does she mean, your engagement? What engagement?'

Antony also glared at Lady Vanessa. 'You could have told her in a nicer way than that, Mother.'

'Told me what?'

Sir Randolph cleared his throat. He frowned at his wife then turned to his daughter. 'Your brother is about to be engaged. He wishes to propose and is now seeking permission to marry.'

'But to whom?' A cinemascope of images of the various women Antony had been associated with over the years ran through her mind: the flappers, the It girls, the socialites and heiresses . . .

'The lovely Miss Lily Fitzgilbert,' said Antony.

'Lily? Are you serious? I've noticed the two of you getting chummy. But I hadn't realised it had gone *that* far.'

'What do you mean, *that far*?' asked Antony.

'An engagement, Antony. An engagement! You've barely been here twenty-four hours!'

'I told you she would do this!' blustered Lady Vanessa.

'Oh do be quiet, Vanessa!' snapped Sir Randolph.

'I beg your pardon?' His incensed wife stared daggers in his direction.

'It is your daughter's pardon you ought to be begging. Now, calm down. Everyone. Clara,' he said, lowering his voice, 'thank you for the advice about Sir Bill's business. The last thing I want to do is bring the bank into disrepute. In fact I asked him and the baron that very thing when he proposed it. I told them I would not be involved in anything illegal. So, I shall not be signing anything until this is all cleared up. But I do not want it being put about that I am about to do anything illegal or unethical. Nor that I have been duped into anything. Is that clear?' His tone reminded Clara of when she was twelve and being given a dressing-down for having scuffed shoes.

'Yes, Father, that is clear. I expect you will do due diligence on this. I just thought it would be helpful of me to inform you that there are questions abroad.'

'And I thank you for that. Although no doubt I would have discovered that myself in due course.'

'No doubt,' said Clara, meekly, not wanting to inflame the situation further. She skirted a glance at her mother, but Lady Vanessa held her tongue. Relieved, Clara turned to her brother.

'So, you are proposing to Lily Fitzgilbert. Have you done it yet?'

Antony shook his head. 'Not yet. I thought I would run it past the pater and mater first. But I have spent much of the day with Lily and—' he grinned '—let's just say I don't think the lady will protest too much.'

'But you hardly know her!'

'That's not true. We have attended some mutual events in London. We have a few acquaintances in common. In fact, we were both in the Royal Enclosure at Ascot this year! I have admired her – from afar – for a number of years.'

Clara doubted that very much. But she knew that Antony was in grave financial difficulties and that Lily was desperate to get married . . . she sighed, inwardly. The thought of having the spiteful Lily Fitzgilbert as a sister-in-law was not a very pleasant one. But in reality she would not have to see much of her. She barely saw Antony these days. And there was a chance the mismatched pair would actually be happy together . . . or happy enough . . .

She produced the warmest smile she could muster under the circumstances and said: 'Well, I wish you all the best. Both of you.'

Tony smiled back, then raised his glass again. 'Thank you, old girl. To me and Elsie.'

'Lily.'

Antony laughed. 'Of course! I was just jesting. To me and Lily.'

Clara clinked her glass against his, then downed the sherry.

Chapter 34

It was six o'clock and, as the first dressing gong went for dinner, Clara rushed to her room to change. She had an hour before the guests were to gather for pre-dinner drinks at seven o'clock. *Just enough time to visit Baroness von Schneider*, thought Clara. But before she did, she slipped downstairs, wearing her Chanel-inspired teal gown, and located the downstairs cloakroom.

The cloakroom was lined with coats hanging from pegs, umbrellas drying out after the storm and a row of wellington boots. She eyed the coats, searching for the green rain cape she'd seen on the shooter. Like the Model T Ford car there was unfortunately nothing distinctive about it, and she soon located three candidates. Two of them were damp. She checked the pockets and found only a used handkerchief in one of them. Nothing as helpful as a stray bullet. Nonetheless, she slipped the handkerchief into her evening bag in case it could be linked to a suspect. So, she thought, two people who had been out in the rain were wearing these coats. Did either of them take a potshot at Bella and Gretchen? Whatever gunshot residue – or stray hairs – that might have clung to the fabric would have been washed away in the rain. Sadly, there would be no forensic investigation possible.

Who did they belong to? If she had thought about it earlier, she could have asked Gretchen if her mistress owned a green rain cape. Or perhaps she had just borrowed one. Anyone could have come in here and worn any coat without being questioned about it. There was, however, usually a maid in attendance . . . Clara exited the cloakroom and looked around. There was a maid refreshing the flowers on the centre table.

Clara questioned her and was relieved to discover that this was, in fact, the young woman who assisted in the cloakroom.

'Aye, miss. Two people today wore those green capes. The young master – that's Lord Penford, miss – and the German lady. The baroness.'

'Did they go out together or apart?'

'Together, miss. Just before the storm started. In fact, it was not long after you left. I saw you go and was going to call after you to give you a coat, but I didn't. I should have, miss. You must've got soaked.'

Clara smiled. 'Yes, I did. It was my own silly fault. But thank you for thinking of me. And thank you for telling me about these two capes.'

The maid suddenly looked worried. 'I'm not getting anyone into trouble or owt? Am I?'

Clara gave the girl a reassuring pat on the shoulder. 'Not at all. You're just doing your job.'

But the girl didn't look reassured. No doubt it would be around the servants' quarters in no time that the lady detective had been asking about rain capes. *Best I go up to see the baroness before the whole house of cards collapses*, thought Clara.

Clara knocked on the door of the von Schneider suite. With both her maid and her husband's valet out of service, Ada von Schneider answered the door herself. She was wearing a gold silk dressing gown.

'Oh, it's you, Miss Vale.'

'It is. I was hoping to have a word with you before dinner. Were you expecting someone else?'

'My maid, actually. Klopp. Have you seen her?'

'Actually, I have. And that's why I'm here. May I come in?'

Ada stepped aside and allowed Clara in. 'What can I do for you, Miss Vale? Where is Klopp?'

'Well, I'm sure Inspector Hawkes is telling your husband about it right now. But as no one seems to have told you, let me put your mind at rest. Miss Klopp is fine.'

'Then where is she?'

'She sprained her ankle while out walking with my assistant, Miss Cuddy. They got caught in that storm and so Miss Cuddy helped her to the nearest shelter, which turned out to be the groundsman's cottage, near the gate.'

'Why was she out in the storm with your maid?' asked Ada, her eyes narrowing.

'Why shouldn't she have been?'

'Because,' said the German woman, 'I gave her leave to be interviewed by that policeman, then I expected her to return. She did not return.'

Clara nodded her sympathy. 'That is very frustrating. And it looks like you've been waiting for her all afternoon. May we sit?' she asked, indicating two armchairs.

'Of course,' said Ada with a sigh. 'My apologies. And thank you for coming to tell me about Klopp. How is she?'

Clara smiled as the two women sat. Ada was clearly on edge but was at least trying to be gracious. Clara needed to keep her as calm and cooperative as possible.

'Oh, she's all right. Nothing's broken. Fortunately, the inspector and I were in the vicinity so I was able to help. I have strapped her ankle. She'll need a day or two of rest though. Could you ask Lady Penford for a temporary maid to help you?'

Ada raised her eyebrows and rolled her eyes. 'I doubt she has anyone to spare! I've heard her maid is also missing. Parker. I don't suppose you found her on your travels, too?'

Clara shook her head. 'I'm afraid not. Just Miss Klopp. Who was, as I say, with Miss Cuddy.'

Ada's eyes narrowed again. 'And why was she with your girl? Do you know?'

Clara nodded. 'Actually, I do. Which is why I wanted to talk to you. To clear a few things up.'

Ada crossed her legs and the silk dressing gown opened to reveal a long stretch of bare thigh. Clara noted she had magnificent legs for a woman in her fifties. An athlete's legs.

'Well, Ada – may I call you Ada?'

The baroness nodded her permission.

'I have learned a lot since we last spoke at dinner on Saturday night. It is now no secret that I am here working as a detective to discover the identity of Lady Penford's blackmailer. And since the discovery of the body on Sunday morning, I am also working with Inspector Hawkes to identify the killer.'

'Do you believe the two cases are linked?' asked Ada.

'I certainly do. And I'm afraid your husband's valet, Meyer, has been linked to both of them too.'

'Meyer! On what evidence?'

'I can't divulge that without the inspector's permission. He is busy talking to your husband about it now.'

Ada sighed. 'Yes, I'm aware of that. And to be frank, I'm not entirely surprised. Meyer has always been of questionable character. I have asked my husband on a number of occasions to get rid of him. But he won't.'

'And why is that?'

Ada shrugged. 'I have no idea.'

'Are you sure?' asked Clara, leaning forward. 'Because Miss Klopp has told me that she expects to lose her job because Meyer has influence over you and your husband. That he knows secrets that you do not want divulged.'

'What utter nonsense!' Ada pulled her dressing gown closed and uncrossed her legs.

'Is it nonsense? Because Lady Penford has told me the same thing. She has told me that you know her secret, the secret that she is being blackmailed over. About Michael . . .'

Ada's eyes widened in surprise. 'Justina told you about Michael?'

Clara nodded. 'Yes, I'm afraid she had to. She told me that she, her maid Parker and you knew about it. That you had kept it a secret for all these years. But now the secret is out. Is it possible that Meyer knew about it too?'

Ada shook her head. 'I can't see how . . .'

'But he knew about other secrets. Such as your husband's plan to circumvent international trade controls and to import furnace coke to power steel manufacturing to service German re-armament.'

'How on earth . . .' But then Ada raised her hand. 'No, I will not confirm that. It's simply a ghastly rumour.'

'Is it though? I have come across evidence to suggest that the dead man, Harry Stanley, knew about it too. And that your husband and

Meyer were seen leaving the wood a few minutes before Stanley's body was found.'

Ada got to her feet and pointed an accusing finger at Clara. 'How dare you! How dare you suggest my husband is a murderer!'

Clara stood too and faced the woman square on. 'Well, if he's not the murderer, you need to help me find out who is. Because, you see, there was another incident this afternoon that Meyer could not have been involved in because he was in custody. Who else could it be? Where was your husband this afternoon?'

Ada flushed with anger. 'He was with Sir Bill and your father discussing business. Your very own father can vouch for him, *Miss* Vale.'

Clara remained calm. 'Thank you. That is very helpful. I'm sure Inspector Hawkes will be hearing the same. So, if Meyer was in custody and your husband was in a business meeting with my father, that means someone else was trying to shoot Miss Klopp in the wood this afternoon.'

'Shoot? Good God! You said she had a sprained ankle.'

Clara shrugged. 'She doesn't. I just said that to explain her absence without raising any alarm. But I might as well tell you the truth now. Gretchen Klopp was shot in the arm. It is just a flesh wound, but I believe the shooter tried to kill her and my assistant Bella. Did you see anyone out during the storm?'

Ada shook her head, vigorously. 'I wasn't out in the storm. I was here.'

Clara's eyes narrowed. 'Are you sure?'

'Of course I'm sure!'

'You weren't out walking with your cousin Teddy?'

Ada took a step backwards. 'I . . . well—'

Clara sighed. 'Take a seat, Ada. I know you went for a walk with Teddy. A maid saw you leaving together and I believe this is your handkerchief.' She reached into her bag and took out the hanky. Ada took it from her without comment. Clara took this as an admission.

She waited a moment for Ada to compose herself and then asked: 'Where did you go? What did you talk about?'

Ada scrunched the handkerchief into a ball in her fist. 'What I talk about with my cousin has nothing to do with you.'

Clara shrugged. 'Inspector Hawkes will ask you the same questions. You will have to tell him. And we already know that Meyer was booking a ticket for Teddy to leave the country with you on Friday. Miss Klopp knew too. She feared she would lose her job if she told anyone. So, we know that you were going to take Teddy with you to Germany to inherit his titles there. And that you didn't want anyone to know about it so that Lady Penford couldn't stop it. Is that why you tried to kill Gretchen Klopp today? To keep her quiet?'

Ada leaped up and raised her hand to strike Clara. Clara put her hand into her evening bag. 'I wouldn't do that, Baroness, I have a revolver here. I will defend myself if necessary. So please answer the question: did you shoot at Miss Klopp and Miss Cuddy while you were out in the wood with Teddy today? Or was it Teddy? The shooter was seen wearing a green rain cape. Both you and Teddy were seen walking out in the rain in matching capes. So, which one of you was it?'

Ada lowered her arm. 'It wasn't me.'

'Can you prove that? You have represented Germany in shooting, I believe.'

'I have. But it wasn't me.'

'Was it Teddy?'

Ada sank back down onto her chair. 'I don't know. We left the manor together and had a little walk. But then he went off on his own.'

'What were you talking about?'

'Whether he would still come to Germany with us.'

'Why wouldn't he?'

Ada shrugged. 'I'm not sure. He is getting cold feet.'

'What was his demeanour when he left you?'

'Anxious. Angry.'

'Angry at what?'

'At me. He said I was putting too much pressure on him. That he didn't know what to think any more. He said he needed to talk to someone else about it.'

'Who did he need to talk to?'

Ada shook her head. ‘I don’t know. He didn’t say. He just left.’

‘Did he have a weapon with him? A rifle?’

‘No. I would have seen if he did.’

‘Would you have seen it if he had it under his cape?’

‘I suppose not.’

‘And did you have a weapon with you?’

‘Of course not!’ Ada straightened her back. ‘Now, Miss Vale, I think I’ve answered all the questions I am prepared to. If your policeman friend has evidence to tie me or my husband to these crimes let him arrest us. But I do not think he has. Frankly, I’ve had enough of all this. We shall be leaving the manor in the morning. Now, please leave.’

She stood and pointed to the door.

Clara had no authority to remain.

Chapter 35

Clara went back downstairs and saw the staff readying for pre-dinner drinks under the critical eye of Spencer. She was the first of the guests to arrive. She spotted the cloakroom maid and called her over. Loud enough for the other staff – and particularly the butler – to hear, she said: 'You, girl, I've left something in the cloakroom. Will you help me find it?'

The girl looked to Spencer who nodded his permission. When they were inside and out of earshot Clara said: 'There was something I didn't ask you before. You said Master Teddy and Baroness von Schneider left the manor together. Did they return together too?'

The girl looked terrified. 'Oh, miss, I don't want to get anyone into trouble . . .'

Clara smiled at her kindly. 'I told you before, you are not doing anything wrong. And I shall tell Mr Spencer, Lady Penford and Sir William that myself. Don't worry. But please, you need to tell me now. Did they return together?'

The girl shook her head.

'Who returned first?'

'The baroness.'

'And when did Master Teddy return? How much longer after her?'

The girl bit her lip, thinking. 'I'm not sure, miss. Half an hour? I can't say for sure.'

Clara nodded. 'All right. Can you tell me, though, whether it was still raining?'

The girl thought again. 'Well, it wasn't raining when they left. But it was when the baroness returned. It was raining very heavy. There was thunder and lightning too.'

'Yes, there was. It was quite frightful. So, the baroness returned when it was raining. Was it long after it started?'

'No,' said the girl. 'Not long at all. Enough for her to still get wet though.'

'Yes, I see. And Master Teddy?'

The girl shook her head. 'No, it had stopped by the time he got back. It hadn't stopped long, mind.' She looked at Clara like a puppy expecting its next instruction.

Clara smiled. 'Thank you. Emily, isn't it?'

'Yes, miss,' said Emily.

'That is very useful information. I shall make sure Mr Spencer knows that you have been a help. But for now, please, I need you to keep quiet about this. Until I tell you that you are free to speak. Is that understood?'

The girl bobbed a curtsy. 'Yes, miss.'

'Oh, and one more thing,' said Clara. 'Did anyone else go out? Soon before or during the rainstorm?'

The girl shook her head. 'Well, I can't say for sure that no one went out, miss, but I can say that no one else took coats from the cloakroom or returned them. Only Master Teddy and the baroness.'

Clara considered this a moment. 'Hmm, so it is possible that someone else went out and either didn't take a coat, like me, or wore one that they didn't get from the cloakroom?'

'That's correct, miss.'

'Who wouldn't leave their coats here?'

Emily lowered her eyes. 'I don't want to get anyone into trouble . . .'

Clara stifled her frustration and refrained from snapping. Instead, she took a breath and said: 'You won't get into trouble, Emily. But you need to tell me who else.'

'Well,' said Emily. 'Miss Fowler doesn't usually leave her coat here. She usually hangs it on the back of her office door. And Lady Penford usually insists Miss Parker takes her coat directly upstairs. She wears very expensive coats, does Lady Penford, and doesn't want just any Tom, Dick or Harry to borrow them. And sometimes Lady Kate doesn't get a coat from here. But then again, sometimes she does.'

'Did you see any of those three ladies go out?'

Emily shook her head. 'I didn't. But I don't watch the door all the time. They could have gone out without me seeing.'

Clara pursed her lips. 'Yes, I understand. Do any of those ladies have one of those green rain capes?'

'No,' said Emily. 'Not that I'm aware. They have their own coats. The green capes just hang here as extras for anyone who has forgotten a coat.'

Clara nodded. 'Thank you.' *There are too many cracks in these floorboards*, she thought. But still, she had managed to confirm Ada von Schneider's story that she and Teddy had parted ways. And the information about the rain hardly having started when Ada returned, but having stopped just before Teddy arrived home, was very useful too. That cleared the baroness. The shooting went on for quite a while during the rainstorm. But Teddy, it seemed, would have had time to shoot, dispose of his gun and then return to the manor. She wondered what Sergeant Wilcox had found out about the rifle. She reached into her evening bag, careful not to let the secreted revolver be seen, and found a small purse. She rewarded Emily with half a crown and a reminder to keep their conversation quiet.

Emily bobbed another curtsy and they left the cloakroom together.

As they emerged, Clara spotted Inspector Hawkes heading towards the front door, accompanied by Spencer. She hurried over to catch them.

'Oh, Inspector, might I have a few words with you?'

'Miss Vale! Yes indeed, I've been looking for you. You weren't in your room . . .'

'No,' she said. 'Shall we step outside?'

Spencer hovered.

'Thank you, Spencer, that will be all,' said Clara. 'I'll be back in a few minutes. I know where the door is.'

Spencer's eyes narrowed but he held his tongue. Hawkes, with a twinkle in his eye, offered his arm and led Clara down the front steps as she held the skirt of her gown in the other hand.

'You look utterly splendid in that dress,' he whispered.

'Why, thank you,' said Clara, surprised at how pleased she was to hear a compliment from him. Her hand felt the warmth of his arm and even when they separated at the bottom of the steps, she could still feel a connection between them. But she did not have time to dwell on romance.

'Are you going to dress for dinner?' she asked, noting he was still in his now-dry brown day suit.

He chuckled. 'No. I haven't been invited. Quite the opposite. I was pointedly told that I was not invited to the formal dinner, and that I could either join the servants in the kitchen or I could have a tray in my room.'

Clara rolled her eyes. 'Goodness me, the pettiness. I'm surprised I'm still invited.'

'Well, you are an official guest . . .'

'Not a very welcome one anymore, I fear. So, what will you do? Kitchen or room?'

He grinned. 'Neither. I'll go to the cottage and eat with my men.'

'Have you spoken to Wilcox yet? About the guns?'

He shook his head. 'No, I'll do that now. But before I go, what did you find out from the baroness?'

Clara recounted the conversation and the information she had gleaned from the cloakroom maid. 'So that seems to put both the von Schneiders in the clear for the shooting.'

He nodded. 'Yes, it does. And Sir Bill was with the baron and your father all afternoon.'

'What about Lady Penford?'

'She said she spent the first part of the afternoon sorting things out for this evening's dinner with the cook and the housekeeper. They have confirmed that. And thereafter she said that during the rainstorm she was talking to Lady Fitzgilbert.'

'Yes, I saw them talking together when I got back,' said Clara. 'She didn't look the slightest bedraggled. A woman like that takes a long time to do her hair and tend to her appearance, so I very much doubt she was out in the rain.'

'Did you see Teddy?'

'I did, actually, on the terrace having a cigarette with Matt Fowler. But from what the cloakroom maid said, he got back not long after the rain stopped. And it was a good hour after that that I returned. So I think he's very much still in the picture.'

'I agree.'

'Have you spoken to him yet?'

Hawkes exhaled his frustration. 'I have not. You know I was concerned about Sir Bill or the baron getting a lawyer for Meyer? Well, a solicitor will be arriving in the morning. But more than that, Sir Bill managed to track down one of his magistrate pals – who spoke to my superintendent – and told him how unhappy he is with my – and I quote – "unprofessional investigation". I spoke to my superintendent on the telephone, and he's ordered that I can't interview anyone further without their solicitors present. No one. That includes Teddy. So, I'm afraid that's all I'm able to do for this evening.'

'Golly,' said Clara, 'it's almost as if they've got something to hide.'

Hawkes chuckled. Then he turned serious. 'Please Miss Vale, be careful. Find out what you can this evening at dinner, but don't interview anyone else on their own. I shall be back here after dinner and I'll escort you to your room – I've arranged to sleep in the one next to yours.'

Clara bit her lip. She did not like being treated like a helpless victim. But it wouldn't do to annoy Hawkes. As Bella would say: *what he doesn't know, won't hurt him*. She fixed a smile on her face and said she'd see him after dinner. Then he escorted her back up the steps before heading off to the cottage.

The other guests had arrived for pre-dinner drinks while Clara and Hawkes were having their tête-à-tête. The gramophone was playing in the corner – a light jazz record that Clara thought one of the youngsters might have chosen – while groups of guests chatted, glasses in hand. From Lady Penford's perspective it would be business as usual, as if a murder investigation were not underway at all. Although some of the faces were more serious than usual. Sir Bill, Baron von Schneider and Clara's father were in earnest conversation, the weight of whatever business – or legal matters – they were discussing hanging heavily upon them. Lady Penford,

Lady Fitzgilbert and Clara's mother appeared to be discussing more pleasing affairs, and an air of self-congratulation swirled around them. Baroness von Schneider was nowhere to be seen. Clara wondered if she would even be coming to dinner. The lady had been very upset when Clara left her. Clara felt a smidgin of guilt for her part in that. As it turned out, the cloakroom maid had cleared the baroness of involvement in the shooting. But that didn't mean she was entirely innocent. There was still the case of the blackmailing. And Ada was one of the few people who had known about Michael Richner's attempted defection to the Germans.

Clara heard a screech of woman's laughter followed by a braying guffaw. She recognised both and was unsurprised to see Lily Fitzgilbert and her brother Antony in mutual fawning. In another, slightly more awkward-looking group, was Archie Fitzgilbert, his cousin Elsie and Teddy Richner. None of them looked happy to be there.

And then there was Kate Richner, Matt Fowler and his sister, Maggie. Sir Bill hailed Maggie – secretarial business, perhaps – and she left her brother and Kate. The two then visibly relaxed and started talking more freely. *Interesting*, thought Clara, *is there some tension between Maggie and these two? Maggie Fowler . . . Maggie Fowler . . . what was it the cloakroom maid had said . . .*

Clara stepped back into the shadows and made her way to Sir Bill's study with Maggie Fowler's office attached. She checked that the coast was clear and slipped in. Tempted as she was to have a good dig through Sir Bill's things, she knew she didn't have much time. So she went straight to Maggie's office and opened and closed the door. And there, hanging on pegs, were two coats: a woman's blue mackintosh and a generic green rain cape – identical to the ones in the cloakroom cupboard. *Well, well, well . . .*

Clara slipped out again and back into the hall, just in time to hear the dinner gong.

Chapter 36

Sir Bill and Lady Penford led the way into the dining room where Spencer seated each person in the position decided by Lady Penford. Clara found herself between Kate Richner and Matt Fowler. She didn't mind as she liked both of them; however, as far as opportunities for subtly continuing her investigation she would have preferred to be between Teddy and Maggie Fowler. Maggie was seated on the far side of her brother, so not entirely out of talking distance, but it would be awkward with Matt in the way. Teddy was seated directly opposite Clara, and while they were in easy talking distance they were not in whispering distance. To Teddy's right was Elsie Fitzgilbert who looked uncharacteristically anxious this evening. To Elsie's right was Antony, seated next to him was Lily and beside her, Clara's mother. Antony, Lily and Lady Vanessa all seemed to be delighted to be together. Clara wondered if Antony had proposed to Lily yet. And who would need to give permission. Lily and Elsie's parents were both dead and they had been wards of Lady Fitzgilbert and her late husband since they were children. But it would be Archie Fitzgilbert, as the male head of the family, who would be the one to ask. Archie and Antony were polar opposites and not likely to get on. Clara would be interested to see how that panned out . . . but she very much doubted anything would be announced tonight. Her mother would definitely want to be the queen bee when that happened. And here, the queen was without doubt Lady Justina Penford. And now that lady was looking pointedly at the empty chair between Sir Randolph Vale and Teddy Richner. When everyone was seated, it was revealed that that was where Baroness von Schneider was supposed to sit.

'Fifteen,' said Teddy, shaking his head. 'An unlucky number. Why can't we ever have the right number of people at this table? Where is she?' he asked Baron von Schneider.

'My wife is not feeling well,' announced the baron, and looked pointedly at Clara. 'She will be eating in her room.'

Clara felt very guilty. For goodness' sake, she had almost pulled a gun on the woman! But that had been before the baroness had been cleared as a shooting suspect by the cloakroom maid's information. And besides, she had been about to strike Clara! Still, Clara thought, she ought to have handled that entire interview more discreetly. She would apologise to the baroness as soon as she had a chance. For now, she just lowered her eyes when the baron frowned at her.

Looking equally morose was poor Archie Fitzgilbert whom, it had been suggested only a few days earlier, was there as a potential marriage prospect for Kate Richner. But Kate had ignored him since the first evening they had been seated together and now they were on opposite ends of the table. Had Kate insisted her mother seat them apart?

'Goodness me,' said Kate, turning to Clara, her eyes filled with concern, 'you've had quite the day, haven't you?'

Clara, whose entire body ached from head to toe, let out a long sigh. 'Oh, yes I have.'

'You should have stayed with me at Wallington,' said Kate, smiling sympathetically.

Clara chuckled gently. 'I'm afraid this is my job, Kate. It's not always quite this dangerous – no one has pushed me off a cliff before – but in the last year, I have been held at gunpoint, twice, nearly drowned, once, and had to fight off a very large man suspected of murdering his girlfriend.'

'And I thought teaching miners to read poetry had its challenges!'

'Oh, I'm sure it does,' said Clara. 'It takes a special sort of person to do the work you do, Kate.'

'Do you really think so?' she asked, her eyes lit with gratitude.

'Yes, I really do. And I believe you teach children and adults. That requires a lot of skill – and patience.'

Kate nodded. 'It does. I wish my mother and stepfather would see the value in what I do. And understand why I don't want to get married. If I were married, I would have to give up my work. At least with the children. Schools are not allowed to employ married female teachers.'

Clara frowned. She was well aware of the marriage bar in jobs such as teaching and nursing. How married women were thought not to need paying work as their husbands should look after them. Forcing women to either give up careers they loved or to carry on illicit affairs. Clara wondered if Kate had had an affair – or might still have one. Or would she remain a virgin all her life? Clara cast a glance down the table to the glum Archie Fitzgilbert, remembering how, in Egypt, he had made his sexual attraction towards her clear. She shivered. No wonder Kate was not interested in being palmed off on him.

Kate noted Clara's glance towards Archie. She raised a cynical brow. 'Yes, that is who my mother thought might be a match for me. Can you believe it?'

Clara shook her head. 'I'm so sorry. Has she given up on that idea now? I see she hasn't seated you together this evening.'

'Thankfully! Yes, I told her I would rather go and work in a coal mine than marry him. And I also threatened to—' She stopped suddenly and took a sip of wine.

Clara was intrigued. 'You threatened to . . . ?'

Kate put down her wine glass and smiled. 'Nothing. I just said I wasn't interested.'

Clara noted the change in tone. *Interesting, very interesting* . . . But she didn't press it. Instead, she asked: 'So, how did your planning with Lady Molly go today? Weren't you putting together a curriculum for the new term? Was that for the school?'

Kate shook her head. 'No, the school curriculum is set by the education board. This was for the adult classes Lady Molly and I teach. That's voluntary. And—' she smiled '—something I would be able to continue with if I marry. As Lady Molly has. But it's charity work, not a career.'

Clara nodded. 'You teach at the Miners' Institute in Ashington?'

'Yes. On Saturdays.'

'I was there today. Sir Charles and I visited. And I got to see the library. I learned that the dead man – Harry Stanley – spent a lot of time there. That he borrowed books and used the typewriter. You said you knew Mr Stanley a little.'

Kate took another sip of wine. 'He took some of my classes, yes.'

'Interesting,' said Clara. 'What kind of man was he?'

Kate shrugged. 'I'm not sure of his character outside of class, but he was a good student. Very diligent. He was particularly good at understanding poetry.'

'So I believe,' said Clara. And then a thought struck her. 'Did you, by chance, ever use the poems of Robert W. Service, the Canadian war poet?'

Kate pursed her lips, thinking. 'Yes, yes, I think I've used a few of his poems. Why do you ask?'

'Because,' said Clara, lowering her voice even further so Lady Penford and Teddy couldn't hear, 'Harry Stanley left a book of Service poems in the library. And in the front was a dedication to Teddy. Apparently, it was a gift to him from your other brother, Rupert. Do you know how it ended up in Harry's possession? Your mother didn't seem to know.'

Kate's eyes widened in surprise. 'Harry was reading Teddy's book?'

'He was. Do you know how he got it?'

Kate shook her head. 'I don't know, really. But a lot of books were donated from the library here at Penford Manor when the miners' library first opened. It could simply have been part of that donation.'

Clara shook her head too. 'No, that's not possible. The librarian said it wasn't a library book. It wasn't in their records. And your mother said she had not given that book to Teddy. That when it arrived it was after Rupert had died and Teddy was not very well. She kept it from him as she didn't want to upset him. She kept it – with some other papers – in a locked box in the attic. Do you know anything about that?'

'Absolutely nothing. This is the first I've heard of it – the book and the locked box.'

They stopped talking a moment as the hors d'oeuvres arrived: shaved salmon and asparagus purée, with a slice of lemon on the side.

As Clara squeezed the lemon onto her fish, she considered Kate's demeanour. She had been friendly and open all evening until she had, almost accidentally, mentioned that she had threatened her mother with something. Now she seemed very keen to deny any knowledge of the poetry book when she had already acknowledged that she had used poems by Service in her adult education lessons. The same lessons that Harry Stanley had attended. But when news of the identity of the body in the wood had first been revealed to everyone at breakfast on Sunday morning, Clara remembered that Kate had acted as if she didn't know him. But Clara also remembered that Kate had become emotionally overwrought and had left the breakfast room. On reflection, her behaviour seemed quite contradictory. Like that of a woman who knew the victim. Perhaps more than she had let on.

And then Clara remembered the carved heart she'd seen at the Greek temple. She had assumed it was for Harry and Kitty. But what if it had been Harry and Kate? It was a stunning thought, and one that was almost too shocking to pursue. But pursue it she must. Carefully, very carefully.

She scooped up a forkful of salmon and asparagus and chewed on it to give her time to gather her thoughts and consider her approach. After she swallowed she put down her fork and said: 'Kate, are you aware that your maid, Kitty Wren, was in love with Harry Stanley?'

Kate dropped her fork with a clatter. Everyone at the table looked up but then returned to their respective conversations. 'I . . . I had no idea. How do you know this?'

'Because I went to visit Harry's mother, Mrs Stanley, this morning. After I left the library. She told me that Kitty Wren had visited Harry in Newbiggin. That she thought they were stepping out together. But that Harry said the relationship had come to nothing. But his mother thought this wasn't quite true. She thought that there had been a relationship, but that it had come to an end. And then, when Inspector Hawkes asked Kitty about it earlier today, she admitted that there had been something. But she said it had ended too. But the inspector got the feeling that Kitty still held a torch for Harry. That she was still in love with him.'

Kate had gone as white as a sheet. Her hand, holding her fork, was shaking. She put the fork down and pushed back her chair. 'If you'll excuse me a moment, I need to powder my nose.'

And as the footman pulled out Kate's chair and she hurriedly left the room, followed closely by Maggie Fowler, Clara knew she had struck gold. Or was that silver . . . Kate had left breakfast in much the same way, followed then, too, by Maggie. That gave Kate – or perhaps Kate and Maggie – an opportunity to visit the crime scene and to retrieve the lighter. Perhaps it had not been Teddy who had left it in her car after all. Kate had been in the car too, just an hour or two before Clara found it. Clara had discounted the idea earlier, as Kate didn't smoke – and, truth be told, Clara had been hell-bent on pinning it on Teddy. But could the lighter have been Kate's? Or had it been a gift from Kate to Harry, despite his mother saying she had never seen it before? Could the lighter have something to do with their relationship? And what did Maggie have to do with it? Maggie with the suspicious rain cape hanging on her door? Was she Kate's accomplice?

But before Clara could ponder this further, Sir Bill stood and trilled his glass with a spoon. 'Ladies and gentlemen, before the next course is served, I have an announcement to make. I would wait for Lady Kate and Miss Fowler to return, but they might be a while. So, without further ado, Lady Penford, Lady Fitzgilbert and I are proud to tell you that Teddy, the honourable Lord Edward, Earl of Penford, and Miss Elsie Fitzgilbert are to be married. So, I ask you all to stand and toast the happiness of the bride- and groom-to-be.' He waited for everyone to take up their glasses as Elsie and Teddy remained seated. 'To Teddy and Elsie!'

'To Teddy and Elsie!'

'Hear! Hear!' said Antony. 'Jolly well done, old man.' He clapped Teddy across the shoulders.

Teddy lowered his head. Elsie at least tried to smile. Clara felt desperately sorry for them both.

As everyone took a seat she turned to Matt Fowler beside her. He was not looking pleased. 'Happy news, isn't it?' said Clara.

'It's happy for the estate,' said Matt, between gritted teeth. 'The Fitzgilberts can bring a healthy injection of capital.'

'And what of their happiness?' asked Clara, noting that Teddy still hadn't raised his head.

Matt cleared his throat. 'I suppose he'll come round. Kate tells me she told you that the marriage is considered necessary to convince the Lunacy Office that Teddy is living a normal life. So if he wants to step fully into his inheritance, he should cooperate.'

'But what if he doesn't want his inheritance? What if he wants something completely different from life?'

Matt's eyes narrowed. 'Has Teddy said anything to you, Miss Vale?'

'He hasn't, no. But just from my personal observations I wonder if he's cut out to run an estate.'

Matt nodded his agreement. 'I don't think he's cut out for it either. But it's his birthright, I suppose.'

'And if he doesn't want it? Could he renounce it?'

Matt let out a sigh. 'He could. In fact, he and I have spoken about that very thing today.'

'Oh really? When was that?'

Matt took a sip of wine. 'This afternoon. In fact, when you popped your head into the drawing room, that's what Teddy and I were talking about on the terrace.'

'He told you he was going to give up his birthright?'

Matt shrugged. 'Not in so many words. But it's certainly the direction he appeared to be moving in. He said something about having other options available to him.'

'Did he say what these were?' asked Clara, wondering if Teddy had mentioned the German titles.

'I'm not at liberty to divulge the details of our conversation,' said Matt. 'But I can tell you that he asked me if I thought he could turn his back on it all.'

'What did you say?'

Matt gave a sympathetic smile, and then tried to catch Teddy's eye. But Teddy, by now, was talking to his new fiancée.

'I told him he shouldn't let his mother force him into anything. That if he wanted to give it all up, he could. Because if he did, the next in line would be Kate.'

'Would Kate want it?' asked Clara. 'I thought she only wanted to teach.'

Matt shook his head. 'No. I don't believe that's the case. Kate – whom I have known since we were both children – wants to be useful. She wants to teach because it's something to do. But if that something to do was running an estate, then I think she would find that very stimulating.'

'More than teaching?'

Matt nodded. 'I believe if given the opportunity, she would. And she wouldn't have to give up the estate if she were married.'

'Ah, so she's told you about that too?'

'She has,' said Matt, quietly. 'Now, tell me, Miss Vale, what did you say to Kate to upset her? She rushed out very quickly.'

'I'm really not sure what provoked that, Mr Fowler.'

'No?' said Matt. 'Well, hopefully my sister will find out.'

And at that moment Kate and Maggie returned. Kate had recovered her composure but pointedly didn't return to the seat beside Clara. Instead, she and Maggie switched seats, and to Clara's surprise, Kate took a seat next to Archie Fitzgilbert. Archie perked up immediately and both Lady Penford and Lady Fitzgilbert looked immensely pleased.

'Goodness,' said Clara, to Matt. 'Perhaps she's had a change of heart.'

'Perhaps,' said Maggie, icily, 'you should keep your opinions to yourself.'

And for the rest of the meal Maggie pointedly ignored her, while Matt fell into conversation across the table with Clara's father on the evils of socialism and the failings of the current Labour government.

It was a very long meal.

Chapter 37

Bella wanted a bath. She did not care that Mrs Barnes had said that servants were not allowed to take baths in the early evening. She was not a servant. And if Mrs Barnes didn't want her using the servants' bathroom, she would find a bathroom somewhere else in the house. When the housekeeper considered the horror of Bella barging into one of the upstairs bathrooms, she recanted, but gave dire warnings about not using too much hot water or taking too long about it.

Bella took as long as she liked.

Back in her bedroom, Bella towel-dried her hair as she considered what to wear. The maid's uniform she had been given by Juju Levine was torn and dirty after her excursion in the wood. She was tempted to just put on her ordinary clothes – making a point that she was not really a maid – but she realised that wearing something nondescript would help her blend in. She still had some investigating to do, and it would be easier to slip in and out of rooms in a black dress than wearing her bright yellow summer frock. However, she only had *one* maid's uniform with her. *Hang on, what about*... She got down on her knees and pulled Gretchen's suitcase from under the bed. She did not feel comfortable going through the woman's private belongings, but needs must. She would apologise to Gretchen later.

She was relieved to find a clean black dress that looked like it would fit her and some black stockings. But as she pulled out the stockings she dislodged an envelope. She retrieved it from the floor, ready to return it, when she noticed the return address on the back of the envelope was one Miss M. Fowler, Penford Manor, Nr Ashington, Northumberland, England. Intrigued, she turned the envelope over and saw that it was addressed to Fr. G. Klopp with an address in Berlin, Germany.

What was Miss Fowler doing writing to Gretchen in Germany? She opened the envelope and slipped out a typewritten letter. To her disappointment, it was written in German. She skimmed the letter and picked out a few names: Teddy, Kate, Penford, Fowler, von Schneider and Parker. She had no idea what the letter was saying about them all, but from the date it was clear that Miss Fowler was corresponding with Gretchen some weeks ago. Why? And what on earth did Parker have to do with it? The missing Miss Parker . . . And why had Gretchen not mentioned this to them when she was confessing all at the cottage?

Miss Vale, Bella knew, could read a bit of German. She would show it to her after the big upstairs dinner. Bella got dressed and put the letter into her pocket, while considering her next steps. Inspector Hawkes had told Bella and Miss Vale not to do any further investigating until the solicitor arrived in the morning. But they all knew his order would be ignored. Miss Vale, at this very moment, would be upstairs doing her best to figure out who among the gentry had motive, means and opportunity to commit murder. Bella would do the same with the servants. And the first person she would talk to would be Miss Wren.

Bella found Miss Wren in her room, darning some stockings. The maid looked up as there was a knock at the door. Her eyes grew wide behind her round spectacles as she saw who was visiting her. 'M-Miss Cuddy. What can I do for you?' Her voice was fearful.

'Evening, Miss Wren. I need you to take me to Lady Kate's room.'

'Oh, I can't do that, Miss Cuddy.'

'Oh, but I think you can,' said Bella, and gripped Miss Wren firmly by the elbow and pulled her to her feet.

Clara was relieved when dinner was finally over. The gentlemen retired, as usual, to the smoking room for brandy and cigars. The ladies withdrew to the drawing room for sherry and to admire Elsie Fitzgilbert's engagement ring. Clara very much doubted Teddy had bought it himself. After a quick sherry and, under her mother's hawkish supervision, an effort to be pleasant to her potential future sister-in-law, Lily Fitzgilbert, Clara made her excuses. As everyone already knew she had had a near-death experience earlier in the day, no one objected when she said she needed to have an early night.

But Clara had absolutely no intention of having an early night. She had arranged to meet Inspector Hawkes after dinner and so she waited for him in the hall, seating herself quietly in a corner. So, when Teddy and Matt Fowler emerged from the smoking room, they did not realise she was in earshot.

'I just can't go through with it, Matt,' said Teddy, looking like the weight of the world was on his shoulders.

'Why did you agree to it, then?' asked Matt.

'I didn't think I had a choice.'

'But what about your cousin Ada? You said she had an alternative for you.'

Teddy sighed. 'She did. She does. But . . . but . . . I don't know if I'd cope in Germany any better than here. I've never lived in Germany. What if things go wrong there too, Matt? And if I stay here, what if my marriage is a disaster? I don't even *like* Elsie. And I don't think she likes me. But she'd rather marry me than remain a spinster all her life.' He laughed, mirthlessly. 'If I'm her best chance, God help her.' He started shaking his head from side to side while wringing his hands. 'Say, old chap, do you have any of that snuff?'

Matt looked around and lowered his voice. 'I do. But I thought you were off that now. After you ended up in hospital the last time.'

Teddy's shaking grew worse. 'Please. Let me have some. Just to take the edge off.'

Matt put his arm around Teddy. 'All right. But not here. Let's go upstairs.'

Clara watched them go. She knew that 'snuff' meant cocaine. Once used for medicinal purposes, it had been outlawed in the Dangerous Drugs Act of 1920. But people like Teddy, who had got addicted while it was still legal and could be bought over the counter at an apothecary, found it hard to shake the habit. And here was Matt Fowler, aiding and abetting him. She felt rage rise within her. Fowler should know better. She contemplated following them to intervene, but she doubted she'd be listened to.

At that moment the doorbell rang, and it was answered by a footman. Inspector Hawkes and Sergeant Wilcox entered. Clara emerged from her corner to greet them. Should she tell them about Teddy and the cocaine? No, she thought, that would have to wait. Far more important for now were her suspicions about Kate Richner, Harry Stanley and the lighter, as well as her discovery of the rain cape behind Maggie Fowler's door and how the cloakroom maid had exonerated Baroness von Schneider.

It was then Hawkes' turn to tell her that Wilcox had spoken to the huntsman who had admitted that one of the estate rifles was missing. 'So,' said Hawkes, gravely, 'someone is wandering around with a loaded gun. The superintendent said we couldn't interview anyone until tomorrow with a solicitor present, but that does not stop me from searching the premises for a dangerous weapon – room to room if I have to. And from what you've told me, I'll be starting with Maggie Fowler's office. But I'll have to let Sir Bill know. Have you seen him?'

Clara pointed to the smoking room. 'He's in there. And Maggie Fowler is still in the drawing room with Lady Kate if you need to speak to them too.'

Hawkes nodded. 'I'll start with Sir Bill and take it from there.'

'Do you need any help?'

'Not now. I think Sir Bill will respond better man to man. But I might need your help later with the ladies. Where will you be?'

'In my bedroom. Bella should be there too.'

'All right.' Hawkes nodded. 'I'll knock. Sergeant, come with me.'

The guests were still downstairs having their after-dinner brandy and sherry when Miss Wren and Bella entered Kate Richner's room.

'Show me where you saw Miss Parker after she left the croquet,' ordered Bella.

Miss Wren was quivering like a rabbit in headlights. 'She was on her knees in front of that chest of drawers.'

'Show me.'

Miss Wren got down on her knees and opened the drawer. On one side were cardigans and pullovers, on the other an assortment of bits and bobs, papers, a strong box and an object in a woollen sock.

'You said earlier that you didn't see Miss Parker put anything in the drawer or carry anything away,' said Bella.

'That's right. I didn't.'

'Is there anything in that drawer you don't recognise? That shouldn't be there?'

Miss Wren's voice was almost a whisper when she said: 'I can't say.'

'Can't say or won't say?'

Miss Wren fell to the floor, her head in her arms, sobbing. 'I can't! I can't!'

'Oh, for crying out loud!' Bella got down on her knees and started searching the drawer. She opened the strong box – which was unlocked – and found some letters. There was something from the War Office referring to the death of Michael Richner during the war and a letter from Ada von Schneider to Lady Penford. Bella didn't have time to read them, but from what Miss Vale had told her about her earlier conversation with Lady Penford, she knew they had something to do with the secret referred to by the blackmailer. So, when she picked up the object in the sock, and weighed the size and shape of it in her hand, she had an inkling of what it might be. She shook out the sock and was not surprised when a silver tea caddy, embossed with cornflowers, fell onto the pile of cardigans. 'Finally!' she said. She had learned enough from Miss Vale about fingerprints to know that she ought not to touch the caddy with her bare hands. So she put her hand in the sock and used it to open the caddy. There was nothing inside. Then she searched the rest of the drawer but could not find anything else incriminating. She'd been half expecting to find a rifle.

Not in the drawer, but perhaps somewhere else . . .

So as Miss Wren continued to sob, Bella stepped over her and searched the room: under the bed, in the wardrobe, on top of the wardrobe, in the dressing room and even under the mattress. No weapon was found. But the caddy and the documents in the strong box were incriminating enough.

She pulled Miss Wren up from the floor and deposited her in an armchair. Then she found a handkerchief and gave it to the maid. 'Righto, missy, you're now going to tell me everything you know.'

'I can't! I can't!'

'You bloody well can if you don't want to be arrested for murder!'

'Murder? I didn't do anything!'

'Then tell me who did. Tell me why Lady Kate has this tea caddy in her drawer. Did Parker put it there? Or was she looking for it when you walked in on her?'

Miss Wren blew her nose. 'I don't know, Miss Cuddy. I really don't. I haven't seen these things before.'

'All right,' said Bella. 'Then let me tell you what they are. That tea caddy was mentioned in the blackmail letter that Lady Penford received last week. The blackmail letter that caused her to hire me and Miss Vale to investigate. And we now have evidence that your fancy man, Harry Stanley, was involved in the blackmail. So why is the caddy in Lady Kate's drawer? Did you put it in there?'

'No!'

'Were you helping Harry to blackmail Lady Penford?'

'No!'

'Then who was? Parker?'

'I . . . I don't know. I don't know what she knew . . .'

Bella's eyes narrowed. 'Knew about what?'

Miss Wren lowered her eyes.

Bella leaned towards her and softened her voice. 'Tell me, Miss Wren – Kitty – tell me what Parker might have known.'

Kitty raised her tear-soaked eyes to meet Bella's and said: 'She might have known about Harry and Lady Kate.'

'What about them?'

Kitty swallowed and bit her lip. 'That they were lovers,' she said, eventually. 'They met when Lady Kate taught classes at the Miners' Institute in Ashington. They've been having an affair for well over a year.'

'Were you in love with him too?'

Kitty caught her breath. 'I was. But I never had a look-in. It was Lady Kate he loved, not me. But there'd be no future for them, I told him. Kate would never marry him. But I would. We could have had a life together, me and Harry. But he only had eyes for her.'

'So that's why you killed him?'

Kitty gasped. 'No! Never!'

Bella grabbed Kitty's wrists. 'Then who did? Who was Harry meeting the night he came here? Who did he meet at the lily pond in the walled garden?'

Kitty swallowed hard. 'I think it was Lady Kate.'

Bella eased the pressure on Kitty's wrists. 'You think or you know?'

Kitty swallowed again. 'I think. Because the next morning – before breakfast, before we were told about the body in the wood – I saw there was mud on Lady Kate's shoes. And I'd just cleaned them the night before. And she had mud and a hole in the knee of her stockings that wasn't there before. I told you the truth earlier, that I needed to sew up some stockings. That's why I came to this room to get them. That's when I saw Miss Parker on her knees in front of that drawer.'

Bella listened to the admission. It sounded plausible but everything would need to be checked and double-checked. She'd have to tell Miss Vale. And they still didn't know what had happened to Parker. What had the woman known? Had she been Kate's accomplice? Had she helped carry Harry's body to the wood? Two women could have done it together. Kate was fit enough. And Parker, although older, was strongly built. Parker could have gassed Arthur Foster too. She had been the last person seen with him. And Bella had heard them arguing about Lady Penford's secret. Perhaps Parker couldn't trust that Foster wouldn't talk, after all. Perhaps she'd tried to make sure of it. And then she disappeared . . . to flee the estate or to lurk around, trying to kill Gretchen Klopp who also seemed to know more than she was letting on, and perhaps had tried to frame Meyer . . .

Bella released Kitty's wrists. 'Thank you for telling me all this, Kitty. Do you think Miss Parker could have known about Lady Kate and Harry?'

Kitty shrugged. 'I honestly don't know, Miss Cuddy. I knew. But I hadn't told anyone else. I swear it. Lady Kate would have sacked me if I had.'

'All right. Well, for now, don't tell anyone else. We'll have to tell Inspector Hawkes in the morning, but for now this must remain our secret. If you promise not to tell anyone about our conversation, then I'll promise to do my best to protect you. Is that a deal?'

Kitty nodded as she pushed her spectacles back onto the bridge of her nose.

'All right,' said Bella, putting the tea caddy in the strong box and wrapping it all in one of Lady Kate's cardigans. 'I'll show these to Miss Vale. You can go back downstairs. But remember, not a word to anyone. Off you go.'

Kitty got up and scampered to the door. Bella shut the drawer, had one more look around the room and then exited. But as she closed the door behind her, she turned to see Spencer striding towards her.

'You! Girl! What are you doing in Lady Katherine's room?'

Bella's heart sank. The snooty butler was the last person she wanted to see right now. She turned to face him, holding the cardigan-wrapped box under one arm. 'I was just seeing if Lady Katherine was in. I wanted to talk to her. But she's not. So, I'll be on me way.'

'What's that under your arm?'

'None of your business.'

'It is my business if you've been stealing from Lady Katherine. Give that to me, missy!'

He reached for the cardigan. Bella took a step back.

Spencer took a further step and loomed over her. 'I said give it to me.'

Bella held her ground. 'And I said it's none of your business, matey. So, get out of me way and let me get on.'

Spencer's face turned an alarming shade of puce. 'I've had enough of your insolence! It's time someone put you in your place. If your mistress won't, then I will.' He raised his hand and prepared to slap her.

But in an instant Bella dropped the box, grabbed his arm, twisted around, doubled over and flung the butler over her shoulder. He landed with a thud and a groan. Before he could recover, she knelt on his back, pinning his arms behind him. Then she leaned down and hissed in his ear:

'*This* – is – my – place – Mister – Spencer.'

Chapter 38

Clara rounded the corner and was nearly bowled over by an irate butler. 'You'd better take that girl of yours in hand!' he blustered. 'I'll be reporting this to Sir William! I'll have you both out of here in the morning!'

'Bella? What's she done? What's wrong?'

But Spencer, too enraged to reply, stormed past her and down the stairs.

Clara hurried to her room. Inside she found Bella examining an array of objects laid out on the bed, including the fingerprint evidence Clara and Hawkes had collected earlier in the day.

Bella turned to greet her, her face alight with excitement.

'What on earth's wrong with Spencer? What happened?' asked Clara.

'Oh, don't worry about him, Miss Vale. I didn't hurt him. Just put him in his place, that's all. Now look here, you won't believe what I've found!'

She proceeded to tell Clara about her encounter with Kitty Wren and what she'd found in Kate Richner's drawer.

'Good grief!' exclaimed Clara as she examined the tea caddy. 'So, it was Kate who had it all along. How did we not pick that up in the fingerprint evidence?'

'Because,' said Bella, pointing to the list of people Hawkes had fingerprinted, 'we didn't get Kate's prints. She told you Hawkes had taken them, but he hadn't. And he thought you'd taken them, but you hadn't.'

Clara slapped her forehead. 'You're right! Kate has been playing us all along.' She went on to tell Bella her suspicions about Kate heading to the wood during breakfast to retrieve the lighter – which then fell out in her car. 'And now that all makes sense after what Kitty told you. Harry and Kate were lovers. It looks like Kate got wind of her mother's secret – perhaps Parker told her, or perhaps she overheard something – and she got her hands on the key and the strong box. She was the one who gave the poetry book to Harry. And then they concocted this blackmail plot. I'm still not entirely sure to what end, it's not as if Kate needed fifty pounds. But our theory about that just being a test shot to flush out her mother and see how she'd respond is still a sound one, I think.'

'But why did she kill Harry?' asked Bella.

Clara shrugged. 'I don't know. But when I suggested to her at dinner that Kitty was in love with Harry, she became very upset and left the table. Perhaps she believed Harry was cheating on her with Kitty. I don't know.'

'But she couldn't have done it alone,' said Bella. 'I think it was Miss Parker. And now Parker's done a runner.'

'Or it could have been Maggie Fowler,' said Clara. And went on to tell Bella about the rain cape and Maggie's attitude towards her at dinner. 'And let's not forget it was Maggie who tried to scupper Lady Penford's attempt to hire us in the first place. She blamed Sir Bill for that, but I never did follow that up with him.'

'Could it have been Maggie *and* Parker? Could there have been three of them in on it?' asked Bella.

Clara nodded. 'It certainly could've. Having three of them would help to explain how different people were in different places during the various key moments. Let's think about this a minute.' Clara cleared some space on the bed and sat down. 'So, starting with the theft of the tea caddy and the delivery of the blackmail note. Kate – as the only one who hasn't given us her fingerprints – is the likely culprit there. She had access to the sideboard and would have been able to slip a note under her mother's door without being detected. Then we have the night of Harry's murder. Kitty thinks Kate was meeting Harry that night. Her muddied shoes and stockings are the evidence. Not watertight, I admit. But add to that Kate's behaviour the next morning at breakfast – the way she got upset and rushed off – suggests she was heading out to retrieve the lighter. The question is why she didn't get it earlier when she, with help, dumped the body.'

'Perhaps she only remembered it at breakfast,' offered Bella.

'Perhaps. Perhaps she didn't expect the body to be found so soon.'

'Aye. That's possible. What about Parker, then? Where was she during the time of the murder and when the lighter was retrieved?'

'We don't know that,' said Clara.

'No, we don't,' agreed Bella. 'But we do know where she was just a short time before poor old Arthur Foster was gassed.'

'Do we know where Maggie Fowler was at that time?'

Bella nodded. 'I saw her at the croquet party.'

'Could she have left after you? And got to the cottage after you left? After I picked you up?'

'That is possible,' said Bella. 'Just as Miss Parker managed to get there ahead of me. I didn't go straight to the cottage. There was about a half-hour delay. Parker, though, was seen in Kate's room during the croquet party by Kitty. But there was still time for her to get to Foster before I arrived. Perhaps after seeing what was in Kate's drawer. Perhaps then she knew the secret was out and wanted to make sure Foster hadn't told anyone.'

'But who told Kate?' asked Clara. 'If it wasn't Parker?'

'Baroness von Schneider?' posited Bella.

'Yes, that's possible,' agreed Clara. 'But back to Kate. The third attack was on me. I left Kate at Wallington Hall speaking to Lady Molly, but I don't know at what time she left there. She said she asked Matt Fowler for a lift back here, and she was at the manor after we got back from the cottage. But she didn't say what time she got back here. Could it have been in time for her to gas Arthur Foster because of what he knew? And she didn't say whether Matt had picked her up from Wallington. She could have been dropped off in Newbiggin first . . .'

'But what about the man in the black car?' asked Bella.

'That could still have been Meyer,' said Clara, her mind whirring through the possibilities. 'It's possible that Meyer could still have been part of this whole conspiracy. He may have been cleared of the shooting, but he has still been acting suspiciously and he is still the most likely person to have pushed me over the cliff. The vicar saw a man driving a black Model T. And he saw that man follow me along the cliff. And I found sand in the estate's Model T that Meyer borrowed . . . No, Bella, I'd be reluctant to exonerate him just yet.'

Bella nodded. 'All right, so that means the suspects are Kate, Parker, Maggie and Meyer. How and why did they all start working together?' And then she gasped. 'Oh, Miss Vale! In all of the rigmarole, I'd forgotten I'd found this.' She reached into her pocket and retrieved the letter she'd found in Gretchen Klopp's suitcase. She briefly explained to Clara how she'd discovered it. 'You can read German, can't you, miss?'

Clara grimaced. 'A little. I studied it at school. Before the war. Give it here, I'll do my best.'

Bella handed Clara the letter. Bella had been correct. It had been written by Maggie Fowler to Gretchen Klopp, postmarked a month ago. After a few stops and starts Clara haltingly started to translate the letter . . .

'"Dear Miss Klopp,

I am writing to you . . . in light of the . . . the conversation we had the last time you were here with the von Schneiders. Since then there have been a number of . . . of . . . developments I think you should be aware of. And to tell you that the . . . financial . . . arrangement we discussed is still in place. In . . . in . . . addition to that, as what I am going to ask of you now might cause you some problems with your . . . your . . . employer, I will . . . erm . . . I'll . . . undertake to find you secure employment in England if you so wish. I recall you saying you would like to live and work here. I believe you could work as a . . . a . . ." Goodness me, what's this . . . "a . . . governess . . ." Yes, that's right. ". . . a governess, teaching German. Or as a teacher. If that arrangement is . . ." hmm, I think it's agreeable – yes . . . "agreeable to you, then this is what I would like you to do in return . . ."'

Before Clara could continue there was an urgent knock on the door. 'Hawkes,' said Clara.

Bella jumped up and opened the door. But instead of the police inspector, Bella was confronted by Kate Richner with a look of utter devastation on her face. 'May I come in? Is Miss Vale here?'

Bella took a step back and ushered her in. Then she closed – and locked – the door behind her.

Clara stood to meet her. 'What's wrong, Kate?'

Kate viewed the evidence on the bed and crumpled into a nearby armchair. 'So it's true. You know. Spencer told me he'd seen your girl in my room. That she'd stolen something from me. When I checked I saw what she'd taken.' She looked up at Clara, her eyes pools of despair. 'You know, then?'

Clara sat down opposite her.

'Yes, we know. But it's better if you tell us in your own words. It will be helpful if you confess everything to us now.'

Kate nodded. 'All right. I will. This whole thing has gone too far. And I don't want anyone else to be hurt.'

Clara nodded her encouragement. Bella stood behind Kate's chair, wary and watchful.

'Well, it all started last year. With Harry. I could tell he was particularly gifted. He was streets ahead of the other men. But I had to deliver lessons that they could all keep up with. But Harry was hungry for more. I offered to give him private lessons . . . and that's where it happened. Oh, Clara, I have never met such a man! If he had been of my social station, I would have married him in an instant! Even if it meant giving up teaching. I would not have done that for any other man. But Harry . . .' her eyes filled with tears '. . . Harry was special.'

'I see that,' said Clara, impatient to get to the meat of the confession. 'So how did the blackmail come into it?'

Kate leaned her head back on the chair and closed her eyes. 'I never should have done it. Never. It was a mad idea.'

'What?' said Clara, losing her patience. 'What did you do?'

Kate opened her eyes again, her shoulders sagging in defeat. 'The last time she visited, Cousin Ada told me about how Michael died. I wanted proof before I spoke to Mother about it. Ada said my mother had told her the evidence was in a box in the attic. I found the box but not the key. I searched my mother's room and found it. The evidence was indeed there—' she nodded to the strong box '—I don't know why she didn't just destroy it all. But there you go. She didn't. And now I had it. And when I saw the book of poetry too – the book she'd kept from Teddy – it made me angry. How had she kept this from us all these years? Didn't we deserve to know the truth? And I was angry because I knew she would go to any lengths for Teddy to inherit everything, forcing him to get married if needs be – so he could father a new male heir. But at the same time, I knew she would deny me her blessing if I married Harry. It just wasn't fair. I told Harry about all this. And it was he who suggested we use my mother's shame against her – for our own advantage.'

Clara leaned in. 'Go on . . .'

'Well, he wanted to test how willing she would be to keep her secret. So we came up with the fifty pounds in the tea caddy ploy. The caddy and the cornflowers were my idea as I knew my mother would realise it had something to do with my father, Michael and the war. The poem underlined all that. The plan was to see if my mother would cough up the fifty pounds. If she didn't, then we'd know she wasn't desperate enough to keep her secret. If she did . . . then we'd know she would be pliable.'

'Pliable to what?' asked Clara.

'To the deal I would offer her. She would grant her blessing for my marriage to Harry, without cutting me off from my allowance, and then just let me get on with my life. I'm not the Penford heir. I am surplus to requirement. But now we'll never know if she would pay or not. She brought you into it, Clara, and since you've been here . . . well . . .' she opened her hands '. . . all hell has broken loose, hasn't it? So now you know it all. What are you going to do about it?'

Clara shook her head, angrily. 'I don't know it all. You have completely omitted the most important thing. Why – and how – you killed Harry. And who helped you do it? Was it Parker? Maggie? Meyer?'

Kate gagged. 'I beg your pardon? You think I killed Harry?'

'Didn't you?' asked Bella, leaning ominously over her.

'Of course not! Why would I kill him? I love him!'

'Then who did?' asked Clara.

Kate threw her hands in the air. 'I have absolutely no idea!'

'But you went out to meet him in the early hours of Sunday . . .' prompted Clara.

'Yes, I did. We'd arranged to meet. And . . . well . . . it was a warm night. We could spend time together too. At the temple as we'd done before.'

'And he was there? Unharmed?'

Kate nodded. 'Yes. He was right as rain when I left him. We arranged that I'd meet him again on Monday at the Miners' Institute to give him the tea caddy – so he could put it under the lobster pot in time for the Tuesday deadline.'

Clara nodded. 'I see. But of course you didn't give him the caddy on Monday, because he was dead. You say he was fine when you left him.'

'He was. I swear.'

'So how did you get the hole in your stocking?' asked Bella.

'The hole in my stocking? How do you know about that?'

'Just answer the question,' said Clara, losing patience.

'Well, during our, you know . . . But I swear, I did not hurt Harry. I have no idea who did. And it was only the next morning, at breakfast, that I found out what happened to him.'

'So you rushed to the wood to see him?'

'I did. But Foster was there. Guarding the scene. So I waited. Eventually he became distracted when the police car arrived – with Hawkes and that doctor – he wandered to the edge of the wood to watch. His back was to the body – to Harry. I didn't have much time, so I sneaked in to see if it was really him. It was. I searched his wallet to find a photograph I'd given him of me. I took it out. Then I looked for the lighter in his pocket. I'd tried smoking for a while – I didn't enjoy it, so I gave up and gave the lighter to Harry. Still, I was convinced everyone would know it was mine. But when I searched the body it wasn't in his pocket. Had someone already taken it? Were they about to come looking for me too? I was petrified. But then . . . I found it a few yards away. What a relief! I just managed to get it before Foster returned with that police doctor. I got away without them seeing me. And I thought I'd managed to remove all the evidence pointing to me. But, then . . . well, can you believe it? It dropped out of my pocket in your car this morning. That blasted lighter! It's as if it was destined to incriminate me. I knew someone would eventually realise it was mine. And I've been waiting for it all to unravel ever since . . .'

Clara listened but didn't quite believe it. 'But you must have had something to do with his death. Or know who did. Come on, Kate, what are you not telling me? Who killed Harry if it wasn't you? Who tried to kill Foster and me? Who shot at Gretchen Klopp . . .'

'Klopp's been shot? What on earth are you talking about?'

'Show her the letter,' said Bella.

Clara nodded. 'Yes, let's finish reading this. Bella found this letter in the von Schneider maid's things. It's from Maggie Fowler. We were just reading it as you arrived.'

She gave it to Kate, who read it. She looked up, shocked. 'My God.'

'Read from there.' Clara pointed. 'In English. We haven't finished reading it yet. And don't try to deceive me, I know enough German to get by.'

Kate nodded. Her voice quivered as she translated, starting at the place Clara had stopped reading.

'"If that arrangement is agreeable to you, then this is what I would like you to do in return. I need you to find out as much as you can about the baroness' plans regarding Teddy – and to let me know what they are. The baroness has hinted that she would like Teddy to return with her to Germany. To undergo treatment with one of the excellent psychiatrists you have in your country. We don't know how serious she is about this or if she has made any formal arrangements. We would like to know what they are *before* Lady Penford finds out. Because we think it would be an excellent idea for Teddy to move to Germany. Teddy is not well and my brother and I are concerned for his wellbeing.

'"However, we know that Lady Penford will not want to let him go as she fears he will give up his English title to take on his German one. We do not think that will necessarily happen but believe it would be in everyone's best interest if it did. Teddy needs a clean start. And if Teddy renounces his title here, before he has fathered a child, the title – and the estates – will pass to his sister Kate. I know this because as secretary, I have access to both Sir William's and Lady Penford's legal papers. Now I must swear you to secrecy here, and you will be rewarded for your discretion. My brother intends to propose marriage to Lady Kate—'

Kate was suddenly interrupted by furious barking. Clara's window – the one that overlooked the stable yard and garages – was open. She glanced outside to see what was causing the commotion and saw Arthur Foster's dog barking and growling at Matt Fowler who was approaching his car, carrying a suitcase.

'Good God! That's it!' said Clara, pointing and gesturing for Bella and Kate to look. 'Matt drives a dark blue Model T! Why didn't I think of it before? The vicar's eyesight is poor. A dark blue car can look black! It was Matt! My God, it was Matt!'

And then everything fell into place. And she recalled the last time she'd seen Matt. With Teddy . . .

'Kate, go to your brother's room now! I think something might have happened to him.'

'What? When?'

'Now! Go now! And be prepared to call a doctor! Bella! Go find Hawkes and Wilcox. Get them to come to the stable yard.'

'Where are you going?' asked Bella.

'To catch a killer.'

Chapter 39

Clara kicked off her shoes, hitched up her skirt and ran downstairs as fast as she could, with her evening bag slung over her shoulder. By the time she got to the stable yard the stand-off between man and dog had escalated. Sammy was jumping up and clawing at the boot of the car. Matt, with his suitcase held in front of him for protection, was edging towards him. The dog stopped its clawing and snarled at Matt.

'Calm down, boy, calm down.'

Clara lowered her skirt and called out to Matt. 'What's going on?'

Matt looked over his shoulder. His eyes opened wide in surprise. 'Miss Vale! Sorry if the dog disturbed you. He's gone a bit mad. I'm not sure what's wrong with him.'

'Is that your car?' asked Clara.

'It is. I was just going to put my suitcase in the boot but the dog's gone doolally.'

'That's Arthur Foster's dog,' said Clara.

'Is it?' asked Matt. 'I've never seen it before.'

'Well, it seems to have seen you. And taken a dislike. What's in the suitcase?'

'Just my overnight clothes.'

'Oh,' said Clara, edging forward. She needed to delay Matt long enough for Hawkes to arrive. 'I thought you were staying the night.'

Matt shrugged. 'Change of plan. I have an early start at the mine tomorrow. I thought I'd head home now.'

'But the inspector said no one was to leave the estate. He has a police constable posted at the gate.'

'Does he? Oh, I'm sure he'll make allowances for me. I have a mine to run.'

'I'll be very surprised if he does,' said Clara. 'Perhaps you should wait and ask the inspector.'

The dog sniffed and clawed at the boot again, then began to whine.

'What's in there, Mr Fowler? Why is the dog so obsessed?'

Matt laughed. 'I have absolutely no idea.'

The dog suddenly spotted Clara and wagged its tail. It ran to her.

'Aha! That's done the trick. Thank you, Miss Vale, you seem to have calmed it down.' Matt opened the passenger door of his car and put his suitcase on the seat.

'Aren't you going to put it in the boot?'

'And get the dog worked up again? No, that's all right. Now I'll bid you good evening, Miss Vale. Toodle-oo.'

He was about to go. She had to stop him. And there was only one way to do so. She reached into her evening bag and withdrew the revolver.

Matt gasped. 'What the hell are you doing?'

'I am keeping you here until Inspector Hawkes arrives.'

'Well, that's a bit extreme. You could have just asked me.'

'Really?' said Clara, pointing the gun at him. 'And if I just asked you, would you open the boot to show me what the dog is so worked up about?'

'Happy to,' said Matt. 'Just hold the dog's collar, will you.'

Clara did so, while holding the gun steady.

'This is all very melodramatic, don't you think?' said Matt as he opened the boot. 'There,' he said, 'nothing to hide.'

Clara had to step around the side to see what he was referring to. And as she did, still trying to hold onto the dog, he bent into the boot and emerged a moment later with a rifle, trained on Clara.

He smiled. Chillingly. 'Well, well, Miss Vale, it looks like we're evenly matched now. I could shoot you, or you could shoot me. I wonder who's the better shot?'

'I think that would be me, Mr Fowler. You didn't manage to shoot anyone this afternoon, despite having a few goes. Quite pathetic, really.'

'I shot that German maid!'

'Did you now? Well, that's a confession if I ever heard one.' Inspector Hawkes had arrived with Bella. 'Put the gun down, Fowler,' he said.

Hawkes stood a few steps to the left of Clara.

Bella took hold of the dog's collar.

'I think there's something in the boot,' said Clara. 'The dog's been sniffing at it. And I don't think it would have smelled the gun. Bella, go have a look.'

Fowler scowled.

Hawkes took a step forward. 'I said, put the gun down, Fowler. Miss Vale is an excellent shot. She has the advantage. You know that. You'll have to choose who to shoot. Miss Cuddy, Miss Vale or me. You might get one of us, but that will be it. Miss Vale has only to shoot in one direction.'

Bella and the dog had edged around to see what was in the boot. Matt tracked her with his rifle but then quickly returned it to point at Clara.

'See what I mean?' said Hawkes.

'Bleedin' Norah! It's Parker!'

'Alive?' asked Clara.

'No. The poor woman's dead,' said Bella, shaking her head.

Clara swallowed hard. 'When did you put her in there?' she asked Matt. 'After you tried to kill Arthur Foster?'

Matt's eyes were flitting from side to side. 'It's not what you think. It was an accident.'

Clara tried to adopt a sympathetic air. 'I'm sure it was, Matt. I'm sure you didn't want any of this to happen.'

'I didn't,' he said, his voice and hands quivering, but he still held his rifle pointed at Clara.

'Tell us what happened, then. As Inspector Hawkes will confirm, the more you tell us the easier it will be on you.'

'Miss Vale's right,' said Hawkes, his tone conciliatory. 'Helping us understand why you did what you did can only make things easier for you. So come on, Fowler. What happened?'

Matt bit his lip. 'All right. But I'm not turning myself in. You understand?'

'Yes,' said Clara, 'we understand.' She held her gun steady, aware of Hawkes beside her. Sergeant Wilcox was nowhere to be seen. She wondered if he was skirting the area, planning on jumping Matt from behind. She needed to keep him talking. 'Go on,' she said. 'We already know that Kate and Harry Stanley were having an affair. She's told us that. She also told us that she met him on Saturday night and stayed with him at the Greek temple until the early hours of Sunday. She said he was alive and well when she left him. So, what happened after that?'

Matt looked near to tears. 'I just could not believe Kate – beautiful Kate – would be interested in that fellow. He was so far beneath her. But I'd been aware of their affair for a while. I almost walked in on them at the Miners' Institute, and overheard them planning to meet at the Greek temple after midnight on Saturday. I wanted to confront Harry, to let him know I knew, and then to threaten him with losing his job – and his mother losing her house – if he continued. But by the time I got there they were already . . . well, I don't want to go into too much detail, but they were having relations. I wanted to barge in and stop them, but I didn't want Kate to know that I knew. I wanted to get rid of Harry without her ever knowing about my part in it. Because she would not forgive me. And that would stop her from falling in love with me. With Harry out of the way, I knew I could woo her, but only if my role in it remained a secret.'

Clara, her hand still steady on the gun, interjected. 'Did you plan to get him out of the way permanently?'

'No! No! I didn't plan that. I wasn't going to hurt him. Just warn him off. Threaten his livelihood. In this economic climate he wouldn't easily get another job. He needed the work.'

'I see,' said Hawkes, his presence beside Clara strong and reassuring. 'But it obviously got out of hand. Tell us what happened, Fowler.'

Matt swallowed hard. His hands were shaking. Clara worried that he might accidentally squeeze the trigger. But he gathered himself and continued his confession.

'Well, it was after I heard them talking about this mad blackmail plot and their plans to get married. I expect you know by now, Miss Vale, that it was Harry and Kate who sent that letter to Lady Penford.'

'I do,' said Clara. 'But go on. What happened then? After Kate left.'

Matt's eyes narrowed as he remembered the events. He looked suddenly angry, thought Clara, as if he were being consumed again by jealousy and hate.

His voice matched his eyes. 'Well, I confronted him. I told him I knew all about the sordid business – his affair and the blackmail. I told him to leave Kate alone or I'd tell Lady Penford and Sir Bill. For blackmail he could go to prison. Then I also told him he'd lose his job, and I'd arrange for his mother to be turned out.'

'I assume that didn't persuade him,' said Hawkes.

'No,' said Matt, quietly, 'it didn't. And that's when he attacked me.'

'He attacked you?' asked Clara. 'I must say, Matt, I saw you on Sunday and you didn't have any visible bruises. Harry, on the other hand . . .'

'Well, he did,' he snapped. 'It was self-defence.'

Clara was incredulous. 'He was hit from behind and then held under the water until he drowned. How is that self-defence?'

Matt growled at her. 'I really don't care if you believe me, Miss Vale, but that is the truth.'

Hawkes gave Clara a warning look. She understood what it meant.

'All right,' she said, not wanting to antagonise Matt further. 'We'll take your word for that, won't we, Inspector Hawkes?'

'For now, yes,' said the inspector. 'But you need to tell us everything, Fowler. We can't help you – or Kate – unless you make a full confession.'

Matt thought about this a moment then nodded. 'All right, for Kate's sake. What else do you want to know?'

'Well,' said Hawkes. 'After you killed Harry – in self-defence – you carried the body to the wood and left it there. Why did you do that? Why didn't you put it in the car like you did with Miss Parker?'

Matt nodded. 'Yes, that would have been better. And it's what I planned to do. But I thought the sound of the engine would wake people at the manor. So, I moved the body to the wood until morning. I was going to retrieve it then – when the engine wouldn't sound unusual. But before I could, that bloody dog sniffed out the body. And then . . . well, you know what happened after that.'

Clara did, and the rest of Matt's explanation didn't surprise her.

With a murder investigation now underway, Matt realised he needed to cover his tracks before Clara and Hawkes found evidence to point to him – or to Kate. So, when Matt heard that Clara was going to speak to Harry's mother in Newbiggin, he worried she would find out about Kate's involvement. He needed Kate to be free to marry him when he eventually proposed – not in prison because of a foolish blackmail scheme. So, Matt drove to Newbiggin after his meeting with Sir Charles at the Miners' Institute and waited for Clara to return to her car. When she bypassed the car and walked along the cliff, he followed her.

'Did you intend to kill me, Matt?' Clara willed herself to sound calm.

'Of course not! I just thought you might be injured. Enough to slow you down.'

'You pushed her over a bleedin' cliff!' This was Bella, her face furious.

'I didn't realise it was so high,' snapped Matt.

'Likely bloody story.'

Clara stepped in quickly before Bella could antagonise him further. She kept her voice light. 'Well, lucky for me Inspector Hawkes was in the vicinity and was able to pull me up. So, after that you drove back to Ashington and met Kate at the Miners' Institute. Is that correct?'

'It is,' said Matt. 'She needed to pick some papers up from her office to prepare for the next term. So I gave her a lift back to Penford. But I can assure you, she knew nothing of what I'd done. Nothing. Kate is completely innocent of all this, Inspector, I swear.'

Hawkes nodded. 'All right, I can believe that. But you aren't completely innocent though. And we need to know the rest of it – to help clear Kate. What happened with Arthur Foster?'

Matt, his rifle still trained on Clara, explained the rest of the story. He'd got it into his head that Foster had seen him wandering around the morning of the murder, and worried that he might tell the police. As he approached the cottage, he saw Bella standing outside, so he hid. Then Clara arrived and picked Bella up.

With the two women gone, he finally went into the cottage to speak to Foster, without realising Miss Parker was there too. She, it turned out, suspected that it was Kate who was blackmailing Lady Penford. She had been to Kate's room and discovered the incriminating evidence. She said she was going to speak to Kate about it later, but first she wanted to check with the only person she'd told about Michael Richner: Arthur Foster.

So, Matt needed to silence them both. He fought with Foster and knocked him unconscious. But in the commotion Parker escaped. Matt chased her and caught up with her near the woodshed. He did not explain how he killed her, but again suggested that it was self-defence.

Clara doubted a judge would believe him, but for now, in order to keep him talking, she knew she had to at least pretend that she did.

'Yes, I see. It was just bad timing that she was there, wasn't it?'

Matt nodded, relaxing a little. 'Yes, it was. Very bad timing.'

'Bad bloody timing for Miss Parker!'

Clara raised her hand to silence Bella. Then with an encouraging nod from Hawkes, she continued questioning Matt. 'So what did you do with her body?'

'I put it in the woodshed until I could retrieve it later and dispose of it away from the estate. I was determined not to make the same mistake I had with Harry's body.'

He went on to explain that he then concocted a plan to buy himself time. He would make Foster's death appear to be a suicide. So he came up with the idea to release the gas. Afterwards, he went back to the manor, making sure he was seen playing cards, to give him an alibi.

In the meantime, Clara and Bella saved Foster, unaware that poor Parker was in the woodshed. With Foster, Hawkes, Clara and Bella away at the hospital in Ashington, Matt was able to get back to the cottage and retrieve Parker's body. Not knowing what else to do with it, he locked it in the boot.

But he wasn't finished yet. Gretchen Klopp also needed to be silenced. She could reveal his plan to try to get Teddy shipped off to Germany so Kate could inherit the title – and he could then marry an heiress.

So, when Matt saw Bella and Gretchen going for a walk later that afternoon, he donned a rain cape and took a rifle from the hunting store while it was unsupervised. He hoped to kill Gretchen under the cover of the storm. He admitted that unlike the other two deaths, this had not been in self-defence, but he still contended that he had no choice: Gretchen had to die. Fortunately for Gretchen, he was not a very good shot. He was, however, a good runner. He outpaced Hawkes, got back to the manor, hung the cape on the back of his sister's office door, dried off, and joined Teddy on the terrace of the drawing room before Clara returned.

'And that finally brings us to Teddy,' said Clara. 'I think I know what happened there. When Teddy backed out of the arrangement to go to Germany and agreed instead to marry Elsie, your plans were in shreds, Matt. I expect if Teddy had not asked for the cocaine, you would have given it to him anyway. If Teddy would not renounce his title and leave the estate to Kate, you felt you had only one choice: kill the last remaining Richner male so the inheritance would fall to her. Then you would propose to her. And you really believed she would say yes.'

'Of course she would say yes! I know Kate has feelings for me. It would just be a matter of time.'

'She'd have to do a lot of grieving first,' observed Clara. 'First Harry, then her brother . . .'

'I'm sorry about Teddy,' said Matt, quietly. 'I've always been fond of Teddy. But he would have ended up killing himself sometime anyway. Just like his father.'

'But Teddy's not dead,' said Hawkes, his voice calm and authoritative. 'We found him in time. Thanks to Miss Vale.'

'Teddy's still alive?'

'He is. And I know you'll be relieved to hear that.' Hawkes took a step forward. 'It's time to give up, Fowler.' He stretched out his hand. 'Give me the gun. There's a good man.'

'Never!' shouted Matt and turned the gun on Hawkes.

Clara pulled the trigger.

Chapter 40

Saturday 16th August 1930, Newcastle upon Tyne

The Assembly Rooms in Newcastle were ablaze with light. Policemen and their partners stepped out of cars and taxis, the men in their ceremonial uniforms and medals, while their partners wore taffeta, crêpe and silk.

Clara, as requested, wore the wine-coloured Charles Worth gown with gold embroidered gardenias running down the side. She tucked her hand into Hawkes' good arm. His other was in a sling, but it was only his hand that was bandaged. Fowler's wild shot had caught him in the fleshy part of the thumb, while Clara's shot hit where she had intended: Matt Fowler's shoulder. As she'd hoped, he dropped the rifle and Bella retrieved it. Then Clara stood over him, gun trained, until Sergeant Wilcox arrived to take control.

That was five days ago. And what a five days it had been. Fowler had been taken to hospital but was transferred into police custody after two days. Meanwhile, Teddy had been brought back from the brink of his overdose and Arthur Foster had regained consciousness and been reunited with his dog. Hawkes had allowed Clara to sit in on all the interviews and interrogations and she finally had a complete picture of what had happened at Penford Manor.

There were three intertwined mysteries: the von Schneider plan, the blackmailing plot and the murder. As revealed in the letter to Gretchen – and confirmed under interrogation – Matt and Maggie Fowler were hoping that Ada von Schneider would go through with the idea to take Teddy back to Germany. Matt and Maggie, meanwhile, tried their best to convince Teddy to go. However, their plan was sidelined when Matt discovered that Kate was having an affair with Harry Stanley and that the two of them had concocted a hare-brained plan to try to force Lady Penford to allow them to get married.

Kate, cleared of any involvement in Harry's murder, admitted her complicity in the blackmailing and begged her mother for forgiveness. Her mother, in turn, asked that no official charges against Kate should be laid, as she did not want any further embarrassment for the family. Clara did not know whether Kate and her mother would ever be reconciled, or whether Kate would be free to marry and work as she so desired. But thankfully, Lady Penford agreed that the bill for Clara and Bella's investigative work would be paid. The blackmailers had been revealed. The case was now closed.

Meanwhile, Sir Charles Trevelyan quietly warned Sir Bill that he would report him to the Coal Board if his business plan with Baron von Schneider went ahead. The deal was now off and the von Schneiders, and Meyer, were returning to Germany – without Gretchen Klopp. Gretchen had been cleared of any criminal charges and hoped to find work in England as a German teacher. Bella had agreed to help find her somewhere to live.

Miss Wren also resigned her position, and she too was seeking work elsewhere. Bella said she would put in a good word for her at Fenwick Department Store in Newcastle.

Meanwhile, Maggie Fowler's role in it all was still under investigation. It was not yet decided if there was sufficient evidence to charge her with aiding and abetting a murderer. A charge which she so far steadfastly denied.

And finally, Teddy. The last Clara heard, the engagement to Elsie was off and he was once again considering going to Germany. This time his mother agreed that it would be in his best interests to be treated by a psychiatrist there.

The only happy note in all of this was that while everyone else was distracted by murder, attempted murder and blackmail, her brother Antony had proposed to Lily and she'd accepted, with the permission of her aunt, Lady Gertrude, and cousin, Archie. Clara's parents were delighted, partly because their son seemed genuinely happy with his bride-to-be – even if he occasionally forgot her name – and secondly, because their financial woes might finally be over. Cleared of all involvement in the criminal goings-on at Penford Manor, the Vales and Fitzgilberts were free to go, with a morose Elsie in tow. Clara hoped she'd soon realise she'd dodged a bullet by having her engagement to Teddy called off – perhaps literally.

Clara drove her family to the station to catch their train to London. Her mother was in an uncharacteristically cheerful mood as she kissed Clara goodbye. 'Well, my girl, I'm relieved to see you got through your little investigation without getting yourself killed and ruining things for your brother. All's well that ends well. And now you can look forward to being a bridesmaid!'

Clara could think of nothing worse.

But for tonight she would not think of that. Tonight, as she'd promised, she was accompanying Sandy Hawkes to the Policemen's Ball. As the band struck up the first number, he took off his sling and reached out his good hand. 'May I have the honour of this dance, Miss Vale?'

She smiled and placed her hand in his. 'Only if you call me Clara.'

Historical Notes

Anyone who knows the north-east of England will know it was once renowned for its coal mining. Indeed, the phrase 'taking coals to Newcastle' originated here. Coal mining first started in this region – on a large scale – in the late eighteenth century and continued to expand through the industrial revolution and then the two world wars. One of my paternal great-grandfathers was a coal miner in the 1910s and my maternal grandfather went down the pit in the 1940s. The coal mines of this area, however, are now mostly shut, due to the mass downscaling of coal production in the UK during the 1980s. But pitheads still litter the landscape, and it was inevitable that one of the Miss Clara Vale stories would be set against the backdrop of coal mining.

But try as I might, I couldn't get started on a coal mining story for Clara. Then, on a wedding anniversary weekend at Eshott Hall, a country estate in Northumberland, only a short drive from the old coal mines of Ashington, I had the idea for a story set at the home of a wealthy aristocrat who owned mines in the area. There was precedent for this as the real-life Percy family of Northumberland (whose ancestral home is the world-famous Alnwick Castle) owned many of the coal mines in the region. Beyond the coal-mining connection, the Penfords of this story are not based on the Percys and are a completely made-up family. Penford Manor is also fictional. Although it is inspired a bit by Eshott Hall, I have allowed my imagination to freely wander to create a setting suitable for a murder mystery in 1930.

Sir Charles and Lady Molly Trevelyan, on the other hand, are real people. Their ancestral home, Wallington Hall, is very much as I describe it in the book and was donated by Sir Charles to the National Trust in 1942. It is well worth a visit, not least for its stunning murals and breathtaking walled garden (which inspired me in my creation of the walled garden at Penford). Sir Charles was indeed the Labour Member of Parliament for Central Newcastle (1929–1931) and was a famous aristocratic socialist. It is said that he painted a hammer and sickle on the gates of Wallington Hall just to annoy his Conservative neighbours. However, his involvement in a murder mystery concerning a coal miner is completely imaginary.

Robert W. Service, whose poem 'Tri-Colour' is quoted in this book, is a real person. Born in Lancashire, he lived in Scotland as a child then moved to Canada to join the 1890s Gold Rush. He was an adventurer and prolific poet, known as the Bard of the Yukon. In World War I, he was an ambulance driver with the Canadian army. I found a first edition copy of his 1916 collection *The Rhymes of a Red Cross Man* in a vintage bookshop in York – and that gave me the idea for Lady Penford's secret. His literary estate has very kindly given me permission to use an extract from the poem. You can learn more about this remarkable man and his poetry here: https://lanseeg.wixsite.com/shop.

The Lunacy Office was a real institution set up to protect the financial affairs of mentally ill people. It functioned in a similar way to how I describe it in the book, but the idea that a marriage might be considered a sign of improved mental wellbeing and stability is purely conjecture on my part.

Issues around the post-war 'surplus women' and the marriage bar in certain professions, such as teaching, are as I describe them in the book. However, readers who recall from *The Picture House Murders* that male preference primogeniture (the practice of males automatically inheriting ahead of females) was outlawed in England in 1925, might be confused by the obstacles to Kate Richner inheriting the Penford title and estate. This is because there were loopholes in the law covering inherited peerages. In fact, it is still an issue in the United Kingdom and as recently as 2022 was challenged in the House of Lords. It has still not been resolved.

And finally, a note on the use of the term art deco. The style we now know by that name, first seen in Paris in 1925, was only called that retrospectively from the 1960s onwards. In the 1920s and 30s it was loosely called 'modern style', not to be confused with the later Modernism which more specifically refers to an architectural and interior design movement from the 1930s to the 1960s. However, I have chosen to allow Clara to use the term in 1930 as it conjures up such a strong visual image that readers know immediately what she is referring to. I felt that the need for quick, visual worldbuilding trumped strict historical accuracy in this case. This is, after all, a fictional tale and not a history textbook.

Acknowledgements

My thanks go to Dr Claire Hilton, historian in residence at the Royal College of Psychiatry, for pointing me in the right direction for information on mental incapacity and financial affairs in the early twentieth century. I am also grateful to former CSI Paul Trembling for telling me about historic paper fingerprinting techniques, and to Rod Smith, who advised me about weaponry. Thanks too to Charlotte Service-Longepe from the literary estate of Robert W. Service for permission to use the poem 'Tri-Colour'.

I am grateful to the team at Embla Books for making this book the best it could be. Particular thanks to Martina Arzu and Emma Wilson, and also to Abi Fenton for her thoughtful editorial suggestions. I am, as ever, grateful to the support and encouragement of my agent Sara Keane – who is my first reader.

And finally: to Rod and Megan. Always.

About the Author

Fiona Veitch Smith is a lover of Golden Age mysteries and historical fiction and has been shortlisted for the CWA Historical Dagger. She has worked as a journalist, a university lecturer and a communications manager, and mentors new novelists. She grew up in Northumberland, then spent her teens and twenties in South Africa. She now lives in Newcastle upon Tyne.

Visit http://www.claravalemysteries.com/ for information about the world of Miss Clara Vale.

Visit http://www.poppydenby.com/ for more information about the author, and about the world of Poppy Denby.

About Embla Books

Embla Books is a digital-first publisher of standout commercial adult fiction. Passionate about storytelling, the team at Embla believe our lives are built on stories – and publish books that will make you 'laugh, love, look over your shoulder and lose sleep'. Launched by Bonnier Books UK in 2021, the imprint is named after the first woman from the creation myth in Norse mythology. Embla was carved by the gods from a tree trunk found on the seashore; an image of the kind of creative work and crafting that writers do, and a symbol of how stories shape our lives.

Find out about some of our other books and stay in touch:

X, Facebook, Instagram: @emblabooks
Newsletter: https://bit.ly/emblanewsletter